On the roof of the Daily Planet Building . . .

Lois Lane stood just outside the shadow of the big golden globe. After days of rain, the sky was finally clearing and the newspaper's star reporter had ascended to the rooftop. She often came up here with her husband. It was one of their favorite "secret places."

But despite the clearing skies, there was an unpleasantness this afternoon. The very air felt heavy, oppressive.

It had been days since she'd last seen Clark—or even heard from him—and now she paced nervously around the globe. *What were you expecting, a note in a bottle? Maybe a message written across the sky?*

Lois looked up at the thought—and glimpsed what appeared to be a shooting star streak down from the heavens.

It quickly burned out.

The weird timing made her jump, and Lois felt a sudden, almost painful shiver of foreboding. She closed her eyes tight and made a wish. "Come home, Clark. Come home safe."

Also available from Pocket Books

JUSTICE LEAGUE of AMERICA™
SUPERMAN®

The Never-Ending Battle

ROGER STERN

SUPERMAN CREATED BY
JERRY SIEGEL AND JOE SHUSTER

POCKET STAR BOOKS

NEW YORK   LONDON   TORONTO   SYDNEY

An *Original* Publication of POCKET BOOKS

A Pocket Star Book published by
POCKET BOOKS, a division of Simon & Schuster Inc.
1230 Avenue of the Americas, New York, NY 10020

Copyright © 2004 by DC Comics. All Rights Reserved.
Justice League of America, Superman, and all related titles, characters, and are trademarks of DC Comics.

Superman created by Jerry Siegel and Joe Shuster

Cover painting by Alex Ross
Series cover design by Georg Brewer

ISBN: 0-7434-1714-3

First Pocket Books printing

10 9 8 7 6 5 4 3 2 1

POCKET STAR BOOKS and colophon are registered trademarks of Simon & Schuster Inc.

www.dccomics.com

Manufactured in the United States of America

For information regarding special discounts for bulk purchases, please contact Simon & Schuster Special Sales at 1-800-456-6798 or business@simonandschuster.com.

In memory of Gardner Fox, Mike Sekowsky,
and especially Julius Schwartz

Acknowledgments

While writers do most of their work alone in front of a keyboard, very few of us work in a vacuum.

This story would not have been possible if not for Gardner Fox and Mike Sekowsky—the original writer and penciller, respectively, of the Justice League of America—and their editor Julius "Julie" Schwartz, who launched a new age of heroes with stories that continue to entertain and inspire.

Moreover, there has been a small army of writers and artists—some of them, alas, no longer with us—who brought Superman and his fellow members of the Justice League of America to life for a generation of readers. Murphy Anderson, Ross Andru, Wayne Boring, John Broome, Nick Cardy, Joe Certa, Dick Dillin, Mike Esposito, Bill Finger, Ramona Fradon, Frank Giacoia, Joe Giella, Sid Greene, Carmine Infantino, Gil Kane, Robert Kanigher, George Klein, Joe Kubert, Jack Miller, Sheldon Moldoff, George Roussos, Bernard Sachs, Joe Samachson, Jerry Siegel, Dick Sprang, Curt Swan, and a host of others helped shape the lives of the World's Greatest Super Heroes. Their good work has set an example for all of us who have followed.

A debt of gratitude is also owed to Steve Sherman, Martin Pasko, and the great Jack Kirby, who created one of the most dangerous men alive and thus provided an adversary truly worthy of the Justice League; and to Marv Wolfman and Erik Larsen, who created the wondrous madman of this story's Greek Connection.

A special thanks to the inspiration of Kent M. Keith, who in 1968 at the ripe old age of nineteen first wrote the "Paradoxical Commandments." You can learn more about them at www.paradoxicalcommandments.com. (Tell 'em Superman sent you.)

And thanks to Jari Kuosma and Robert Pecnik, who invented the BirdMan suits and are even now bringing us closer to the day when ordinary people will actually fly. (Yes, of course these things are real. Did you think we just make all this stuff up?)

In writing this book, I was also aided by a number of very talented people who took time from their own busy lives to give advice and support.

Thanks then to Kurt Busiek, Tom Galloway, and John Wells for a wealth of information; to Mark Fennessy and Bill Turner for helping me acquire some much-needed reference; and to Mike W. Barr and Mark Waid for their welcome insights and good humor.

Thanks to my friendly neighborhood oceanographic expert David Brown; and to the real-life Michael Watkins and Neo for sharing their K-9 expertise. Mike is an officer with the Ithaca Police Department, and his patrol dog Neo really is a big black and tan German shepherd.

Thanks to Marco Palmieri for his invaluable suggestions, and to all the other good folks behind the scenes at Pocket Books who worked to ready this book for production.

A very big thanks to my patient and understanding editor Charlie Kochman, who put in many long hours, burning the midnight oils to help make the story better—and who, after eleven years, still helps me keep a healthy point of view. *Molte grazie, Carlo.*

And, as always, the greatest thanks to my wonderful wife Carmela Merlo, who proofread my rough drafts, helping to spot problems and devise solutions. Throughout it all she was always there, reminding me of the truly important things, trying to keep me from sweating the small stuff, and laughing at my jokes.

—Roger Stern
June 2004

PROLOGUE

A Guy Walks into a Bar

"—In national news, members of the Justice League of America this afternoon apprehended the last remnants of the radical underground cell that called itself the Power Elite. The Elite, a group of super-powered right-wing terrorists, were holed up in a rural Utah retreat, and had begun a standoff with federal authorities, when Superman, Wonder Woman, and the Flash arrived on the scene. Correspondent Andrea Levy spoke with the Flash—"

At the far end of the bar, a man wearing an old tweed cap looked up from his glass and scowled at the TV mounted on the wall. "Will somebody turn that crap off?!"

A dozen bleary eyes turned his way, and Tweed Cap realized too late that he was shouting. He had been sitting in the little South Side Chicago tavern for well over an hour, quietly drowning his sorrows as the skies outside grew dark and cloudy. But now he felt suddenly, uncomfortably sober.

The bartender stopped polishing glasses and added his gaze to that of his regulars. "You got a problem, pal?"

Tweed Cap seemed to shrink into his collar. "No. No problem. I just—" He stopped, lifted his glass, and drained it. "I just meant, can't you change the channel? It's about time for the game, isn't it?"

Five stools to his left, two of the bleary eyes blinked and turned their attention to the Koul-Brau clock over the door. "Hey, he's right! Switch it over to Channel Nine."

"Yeah."

"Don' wanna miss the first pitch."

"Hope we don't get rained out."

The bartender shrugged and thumbed the remote. The image on the screen flickered, shifting from a close-up of a smiling young man in a crimson mask to a long shot of Wrigley Field. "Huh! Will ya look at that—there's blue skies and sunshine at the ballpark." He glanced back out through the diamond window of the tavern door. "Still got a rainy sky here, though."

"Guess that's Chicago for you." Tweed gave the bartender a weak smile. "I mean, Wrigley *is* clear across town. Gotta be lots of little—what do they call 'em?—microclimates." He nodded toward the television and hoisted his empty glass. "Thanks, man. I'll take another of these bad boys, when you get the chance."

"Make that two."

Tweed froze. The new voice seemed to come from out of nowhere. He hadn't heard anyone enter the seedy little tavern in nearly an hour, and he flinched as a hand reached out beside him and slapped two fifty-dollar bills down on the bar. It was a big hand with long fingers, the sort of hand that Tweed's mother would have called elegant.

"And a round for the house. On me."

A weak, boozy cheer trailed off as the bartender picked up the fifties and examined them closely. A smile inched its way across his face. The cheer started up again as he began filling glasses.

The stranger eased onto the stool alongside Tweed. He was a big man, well over six feet tall, with a shoulder span that a bodybuilder would kill for. Tweed stared at him, slackjawed. *How the hell drunk am I, that a guy the size of a house could walk up without me noticing? What is he, a freaking ninja?* The stranger's dark hair fell to his collar in waves, framing his face, just as his neatly trimmed mustache and beard framed a wide smile. Tweed was instantly, self-consciously aware of the three days' worth of stubble that stretched across his own lower jaw.

Weirdest of all were the stranger's eyes. Their irises were very dark, almost as black as the pupils. Even allowing for the dim light of the tavern, they were the darkest eyes Tweed had ever seen. *Talk about 'two black eyes'!*

"To your health!" The stranger smiled, raising a glass in a salute.

Tweed blinked and finally hitched up his jaw, suddenly aware of a fresh drink in his own hand. "Uh, yeah. And yours." He clinked glasses with the stranger. "Thanks, mister."

"Call me Adam. I am, after all, my father's first-born son." He laughed softly, as if at some private joke.

"Okay, Adam it is." The glasses clinked again. "And I'm Mark."

Adam nodded. "I know who you are, Mark. I've been looking for you."

Mark's glass paused halfway to his lips. "Is that so?" He took a slow sip of his drink and set it back down. "Sure you got the right man? It's a pretty common name." He let his right hand drop toward his knee.

But just below the surface of the bar, his wrist was suddenly caught in the stranger's hand. *Guy's got a grip like a vise!* Pain shot up Mark's arm as he tried to pull free.

Adam's voice dropped to a whisper. "That wouldn't be wise. I know all about the weapon that you keep strapped to your right leg under your trousers. It was foolish to reach for it. I had heard that you don't need to grasp it in order to draw on your power." The stranger stared right through him. "But then, with all the alcohol you've consumed this afternoon, controlling that power isn't so easy without direct contact, is it?" He relaxed his grasp, and Mark slowly drew his hand back to the top of the bar.

His right hand numbed and tingling, Mark grabbed his glass with his left hand and drained it with an audible gulp. "What do you want from me?"

"Just a little friendly conversation—on a proposal that stands to greatly benefit us both."

" 'Benefit,' huh? Yeah, right." Mark cradled his right hand in his left, trying to massage away that pins-and-needles feeling. He lowered his own voice. "Why should I talk to a guy who starts a 'friendly conversation' by trying to break my wrist?"

"Because you're not an idiot. Had I meant you any real harm, I would already have inflicted it. I could have killed you in any number of ways before you were even aware that I was here. But I didn't. Instead, I bought you a drink." Adam reached out and tapped the empty glass. "These last few days, you have been spending considerable time and effort dulling your intellect. But you still have a good native wit, and you must be feeling at least a twinge of curiosity."

Adam stood up, taking Mark by the elbow and urging him to his feet. He waved his own glass, indicating a booth at the rear of the tavern. "I think we'll have a little more privacy back there."

Mark let himself be pushed toward the shadowy booth. *Who is this guy? Doesn't act like a cop. Is he FBI? DEO?* That last thought nearly sent him running for the exit. He'd heard rumors of a crackdown by the Department of Extra-Normal Operations. *But why would they target a guy like me? I'm not a metahuman or an alien—I'm just a guy who lucked into a great little tool.* As Mark sat down, he caught a glimpse of his reflection in a bar mirror. A pair of bloodshot eyes stared back at him from around a crack in the glass, and he ran a hand over his stubbly chin. *Yeah, I'm just lucky as hell.*

Adam slid into the booth across from Mark. "There, that's better. To answer the question that's on your mind—I am neither a police officer nor an agent of the federal government." The stranger smiled. "No, I'm not a telepath, either. I don't need to read minds, Mark. I can read people."

"Uh-huh. So what do you read in me?"

"Potential, Mark. Vast, untapped, and unrealized potential." Adam set his glass—still full—on the table between them. "You have power. Great power! But it has never had the opportunity to flower. Society and its petty rules have held you back, made you an outlaw in your own land. Just look around us." His upper lip curled back in a sneer. "Should men of power be forced to hide away amid such filth? Should such slovenly places even exist in a truly enlightened society? No, they should not. This tavern, this city, this entire world has become hopelessly corrupted. And it falls on men such as us to set it right."

"Us? Set it right?" Mark felt confused, and he was reasonably certain it wasn't because of the booze.

"Yes, Mark." Adam leaned forward. "You are not alone. I, too, have been opposed and oppressed by a corrupt, unthinking world. I know how you feel. And there are others like us. We are many. Together, we can make a difference."

"Look, I'm not much interested in political movements—"

"Nor am I. Politics is not a solution, Mark, it is the

problem. It takes power from those who most deserve it, squanders the riches we should rightfully possess. Look around you. Is this the sort of life you want to lead, crawling from tavern to tavern?"

Mark's face flushed. "Why the hell do you care what kind of life I lead?"

"The more pertinent question is, do *you* care what kind of life you lead?"

Mark half rose from his seat, propelled by more anger than he'd felt for a long time. There was within him a rage to try something extremely stupid. *Buddy, if you were even an inch shorter—!*

But that was the problem. Adam was still as big as a damned house, and Mark's wrist still hurt like hell.

Mark hesitated, and his fury had time to turn into shame. He slumped back into the booth, muttering under his breath.

"What was that, Mark? I didn't hear you."

"I said, I don't know. I don't know if I care anymore."

"Mark, I told you before that you possess great potential. I still believe that. So I'll ask you once more— is this *really* the sort of life you want to lead?"

"No." Mark looked down at his hands. "No, it isn't."

"I didn't think so. Listen to me!" Adam's eyes again locked with Mark's. The stranger did not blink. "A time of great chaos is about to sweep the world. Those who are not prepared, those who are committed to the world as it is, will perish. Those who embrace the new will not just survive—they will reign supreme.

"I offer you a great opportunity. You can be part of a new world." Adam shoved his own glass—still full—across the table. "Or you can crawl deeper into the bottle and numb yourself to the destruction of the old." He broke eye contact and gestured to the glass. "The choice is yours."

Mark looked at his reflection in the amber liquid of the glass. He was about to say something—though what, he wasn't sure—when a whoop went up over at the bar.

"Cubs score! Cubs score!" One of the regulars lifted his arms in triumph and lurched drunkenly off the back of his stool. The old rummy hit the floor with a thud. He made one valiant attempt to raise his head. "Cubz . . . score . . ." And then he passed out, all to the laughter of those around him.

Mark looked on as two of the other regulars picked up the unconscious man and plopped him down in a booth near the door. The old rummy's eyes twitched, but he didn't wake up. Instead, he snorted and started to snore.

Mark lifted the glass, slowly swirling the drink, watching the last remnants of ice melt. Then he set it back down on the table and pushed it away.

"Okay, Adam, tell me more."

Outside, the clouds began to part.

CHAPTER 1

Ill Winds

He could see the bullet coming.

The big man in the windbreaker and ball cap had been leaning against a concrete security barrier in the heart of Metropolis's Federal Plaza, pretending to read the morning edition of the *Daily Planet*. But in the shadow of his cap, his eyes kept tracking from building to building, looking for trouble.

There wasn't much in the way of foot traffic in the grand plaza this morning. Twenty feet to the big man's left, a young woman in a business suit stood waiting at a bus stop. Fifty feet to his right, a tight crowd of men in dark suits moved down the marble steps of the Hamilton Courthouse to a line of black sedans idling at the curb. Across the street, a man with a pushcart was staking out a spot to peddle hot dogs to a lunch crowd yet to come.

And seven stories above, the barrel of a high-powered rifle suddenly jutted out from the cornice of an adjacent rooftop.

The rifle caught the big man's eye a split second before the shot was fired. And then, everyone and everything seemed to freeze in place around him.

Everything, except for the bullet. It flew on, spinning toward the center of that tight crowd of dark-suited men. The big man knew that the bullet was headed for a short, heavyset figure at the center of that crowd, a human target in a cheap overcoat who looked every bit as rumpled as the old fedora jammed tightly down on his head.

The big man sprang into action, leaping up in front of the crowd, his arms flung wide. The bullet ripped through the nylon of his windbreaker, the slug slamming into his broad chest, deforming slightly before ricocheting off at an oblique angle. His left arm shot out and he caught the slug in his bare hand. The big man stood suspended in midair, calling back over his shoulder to the crowd of dark suits: "Everyone okay?"

One of the suits shouted an affirmative. They had shoved the heavyset man down into a crouch at the sound of the shot, shielding him with their own bodies. Now, guns drawn, they were hustling him to cover behind another concrete barrier.

Up on the rooftop, the hitman was momentarily startled by the dark blur that had suddenly filled the telescopic sight of his rifle. He looked up, saw the huddle on the plaza below, and started to line up a second shot.

But now, all he could see through the crosshairs of the scope was a ripped-open windbreaker, framing a bold, red-and-yellow pentagon emblazoned with a stylized letter "S."

For a moment, the gunman froze. Then he turned and bolted away across the rooftop. He had carefully planned his escape route, but now his only hope was to move fast. The hitman prayed that the big man hadn't gotten a good look at his face.

At the far edge of the building he dropped his rifle and vaulted over a cornice, dropping six feet to another rooftop. As he pulled a small handgun from his waistband, the hitman spotted a stairwell housing fifteen feet away and headed for it at a dead run. He rounded the corner of the housing and ran smack into a tall form that had not been there a second before. The gunman fell back against the housing, slid down onto the rooftop, and sat staring wide-eyed at the figure he'd run into.

The big man was clad mainly in dark blue. Red trunks were secured at his waist by a yellow belt. The red of his trunks was matched by his boots and by the long cape that unfurled in the wind behind him. And there, once again, was the red-and-yellow pentagon, centered in the middle of the broadest chest the gunman had ever seen.

"S-Superman." The hitman still clutched the automatic in his hand. Though he recognized the man who towered over him, he reflexively leveled the handgun and squeezed the trigger.

This time, Superman didn't bother to catch the bullets that bounced off his chest.

Three slugs impacted harmlessly in the wall of the

stairwell housing. A fourth bounced almost straight back, striking just inches from the hitman's shoulder, and he stopped firing.

"New in town?" The Man of Steel reached down with one hand, grabbed the man by the front of his jacket, and effortlessly hauled him to his feet.

The cognitive part of the hitman's brain registered that Superman's voice was a deep baritone, good enough for TV or the stage. But his only physical reaction was instant and reflexive. He jammed the gun against Superman's gut.

"Better think twice before you pull that trigger." The Man of Steel looked him straight in the eye. "Unless you're dead set on saving the state the cost of a trial."

The gunman stared into Superman's face. He could see no fear there, only a look of what seemed to be disappointment.

"Yeah." He relaxed his trigger finger. "Guess you're right."

The next instant, the automatic was gone from his hand. He brought his empty palm up to eye level, staring at it stupidly for a moment before he noticed the gun in Superman's free hand.

"Time for us to take a little trip." Superman tightened his grip on his captive's jacket and leaped straight up into the air.

The hitman's breath caught in his throat as the Man of Steel carried him up and over the buildings. For a moment they seemed to hang motionless in midair— all of Metropolis spread out below them—and then they plunged down toward the plaza below, faster than an express elevator. Just as the hitman was about to scream, Superman slowed their descent and they touched down on the pavement as easily as if they'd hopped one step down off a ladder.

Instantly, they were surrounded. A dozen uniformed policemen had joined the dark-suited plainclothesmen, as had the woman in the business suit and the hot dog vendor. All had automatic pistols aimed at the hitman.

"He's all yours, gentlemen . . . and lady." Superman nodded to the undercover policewoman and let go of the hitman, who was grabbed and handcuffed by one of the plainclothesmen. The Man of Steel turned to an approaching figure. "He left his rifle on the roof of the Langley Building. I can retrieve it, if you'd like."

"You've done more'n enough for us, Superman. Forensics is already on their way up there."

The hitman looked up in surprise at the sound of the gruff voice. It was coming from his intended victim. As he stared in disbelief, the "little man" straightened up from a slouch, seeming to grow in the process. The human target now stood nearly four inches taller, his weight more evenly distributed over a broad, barrel-chested frame.

The heavyset man shucked out of the old overcoat and doffed the rumpled hat, revealing the balding head of Police Inspector Daniel Turpin. "Weren't expectin' to see my mug under here, were ya?" Turpin gave the gunman a wicked grin. "Buddy, you are under arrest!"

The hitman moved his mouth as if to protest, but no sound came out.

The inspector set a pair of wire-rimmed half-glasses across his broad nose and produced a tiny card from his pocket. He took his time, seeming to enjoy the discomfort he caused the gunman.

Superman had seen the inspector do this particular routine before, deliberately stretching things out to get under the perpetrator's skin. Later, he knew, an interrogator at the station house would "empathize" with the perp over Turpin's terrible behavior. "Yeah," they'd say, "he's always giving us grief, too." The routine worked almost every time.

"Awright, listen up now." Turpin cleared his throat. " 'You have the right to remain silent. Anything you say—' "

As if on cue, the hitman found his voice. "You mounted this whole operation just to trap *me?!*"

Turpin glared up at him over his glasses. "I'm not finished, Quick-Draw. I said, 'You have the right to remain silent.' And until I finish readin' you your other rights, you're damn well gonna *be* silent! Got that?"

The hitman started to protest, seemed to think better of it, and closed his mouth.

The inspector nodded brusquely. "I'll take that as a 'Yes.' Now, as I was sayin', 'Anything you say can and will be used against you in a court of law. You have the right to talk to an attorney before answering any questions. You have the right to have your attorney present during questioning. If you cannot afford an attorney, one will be appointed for you without cost, before or during questioning, if you desire. Do you understand these rights?' "

"Yeah, yeah, I understand already." The man shifted impatiently in the cuffs. "I don't *believe* this. What *is* it with you people?" He stared at Superman. "Why were you even here? I'm not a gang boss or . . . or some super-villain out to take over the world. I'm just an ordinary hitman! A working man! I'm like Joe Sixpack to you!"

Superman exchanged a look with Turpin, and the inspector folded his glasses in disgust. " 'Joe Sixpack,' he says. 'A working man,' he says. Like he services your car instead of plantin' you six feet under."

Superman turned to the hitman. "Sorry to spoil your day, but I don't limit myself to stopping criminal masterminds."

"Yeah." Turpin tucked his glasses back into a pocket. "Think of this as his contribution to crime prevention."

"And you—!" The hitman whirled to stare at the inspector. "You must be old enough to be my grandfather! What the hell are you doing, still playing cops and robbers?"

"Yer skatin' on thin ice, mister. *Real* thin." Turpin looked the hitman up and down. His nose wrinkled as if he smelled something foul. "O'Shaunessy!"

A uniformed cop snapped to attention. "Inspector?"

"Get 'im outta here." Turpin shook the old fedora. "An' will somebody get me my hat? My *real* hat!"

"Is this what you're looking for?"

Turpin turned to find Superman holding out a derby. "Yeah! Now *that's* a hat! I'll trade ya." He gleefully swapped headgear with the Man of Steel, polishing the derby with the back of his sleeve before setting it into place over his thinning hair. Turpin then pulled a cigar from his vest pocket and clenched it between his teeth.

A look of concern tempered Superman's smile. "You know, those things will kill you, Inspector."

"Aw, now don't *you* start in on me! My daughter Maisie's on my case all the time. I'm down to just one a month. An' I chew 'em more than smoke 'em anymore." The old detective took the half-chewed stogie from between his lips and stared at it forlornly. "See, I haven't even lit the blasted thing."

Superman nodded as he watched the hitman being loaded into a paddy wagon. "A good start, Inspector. You take enough risks as it is."

"Eh? An' what's that s'posed to mean?"

Superman swept his arm wide, gesturing to the plaza around them. "You put your life on the line here today, Inspector."

"All part of the job. The Feds were expectin' an attempt on the life of their star witness in the Intergang case. An' the Special Crimes Unit was eighty-five percent certain that a hit had been contracted with out-of-town talent. That's why I asked you to help out with my little decoy plan."

"You could've let *me* play the decoy."

"A big lug like you? Nuts! You never coulda made

yourself short enough to look like the Feds' star witness. Oh, maybe that Martian buddy of yours coulda tamped himself down enough to play the part. Or even that Plastic Man goof. But you? No way. I was the closest in body type to the witness, even though I'm better lookin'. 'Sides, this was my plan, my call. An' I'd never ask anyone to take a chance I wouldn't take myself."

Superman shook his head. "Too big a chance. If I hadn't spotted the sniper in time—!"

"But ya did. An' anyway," Turpin smacked a fist against his chest, "I was ready for 'im."

"If I'd been a second slower, that Kevlar vest wouldn't have done you much good." Superman poked a steely finger against the inspector's forehead, just below the brim of his derby. "The shot was aimed straight at your head."

"My head—?"

"Straight at it." Superman patted out the crown of the old fedora and smoothed the brim. "Given the angle of the bullet's trajectory and its velocity—there's no question."

Turpin swallowed hard, as if suddenly aware of a bad taste in his mouth. He looked again at the half-chewed cigar and then tossed it into a nearby trash can.

"Two points." Superman grinned and leaned back against a lamppost. He twirled the fedora in one hand and plopped it low over his brow.

"Yeah, pretty good." The inspector tilted his head slightly back and to one side, sizing Superman up.

"Ya know, you don't look half bad with that lid. You ever wear a hat?"

"Not in years, I'm afraid."

Turpin stared at the big man's profile. "Hey, you know who you look like?"

Superman kept his voice casual. "Who?"

"Dick Tracy!" The inspector clapped him on the shoulder. "Yeah, with that wide-brim hat—an' just look at that jaw line! All ya need is a yellow overcoat."

"You think so? That's a new one. I hadn't heard that particular comparison before. An artist I know once said I looked like Cap'n Easy."

"Yeah? Oh, yeah, I can see that." Turpin folded his arms. "But how does a young buck like you even know about Cap'n Easy? He hasn't been in the funny pages in years—not 'round here, at least. You must be a helluva lot older than you look!"

"Oh, I've always been a fan of the comics, Inspector." Superman thumbed the hat higher on his forehead. "Tracy, eh? Is my jaw really that square?" He rubbed his chin. "I've been told I resemble a lot of people, actually. Bond fans usually tell me that I look like Pierce Brosnan, or a young Timothy Dalton. My personal favorite was when a woman told me that I look like a young Gregory Peck."

"Nice. Very nice. I should be so lucky. Only actor I ever get compared to is Edgar Buchanan."

"Buchanan . . . Didn't he play . . . ?"

"Yeah, yeah—Uncle Joe on *Petticoat Junction*. Crazy show's *still* bein' rerun." Turpin took another look at Superman in profile. "Gregory Peck, huh? Sure, that works, too. 'Course, yer at least half a head taller than any of those guys—an' a whole lot broader in the shoulder." The inspector started chuckling. "I still remember the first time I heard a TV comic point out that you and Charlie Sheen had never been seen together—I just about busted a gut laughin'." He hooked his thumbs in his vest pockets. "That was years ago, but it's still funny. To me, anyway. Ya gotta wonder if those other guys think it's funny when they get compared to you. 'Cause ya know that happens. Betcha *every* tall, dark-haired Caucasian male gets told he looks like Superman. Ya know it's gotta cut both ways."

"Not too deeply, I hope." The Man of Steel smiled. "I just hope that the other men take the comparisons as a compliment."

Turpin snorted. "They'd be crazy not to."

"Well, thank you, Inspector." Superman doffed the hat and started to hand it over. "But I think you'd best return this to the police supply room. It's not a bad fit, but the style really doesn't go well with a cape."

"Heh!" Turpin reached out for the fedora, only to have a sudden gust of wind tear it from his hand. "Hey!"

Superman's hand shot out, caught the hat, and thrust it back into the inspector's grasp. "Better hold on a little tighter. Wind's picking up."

"No kiddin'." Turpin closed his eyes tight and clapped a hand to his derby as the men were suddenly caught up in a swirl of light debris. In seconds, the sky darkened and a gale was howling through the plaza. Superman's cape was sent flying straight out from his shoulders.

And then, just as suddenly as it had blown in, the wind died down to a pleasant breeze. The clouds broke up and—again, in less than a minute—the sun was shining brightly in a clear, blue sky.

"Dammit!" Turpin spit dust from between his lips. "As if last winter wasn't bad enough, now we gotta put up with this! Blasted weather's been screwy up and down the whole East Coast all month. It's gettin' so that when I wake up in the mornin', I don't know whether to put on sneakers or mukluks."

"Ah, 'the dazzling uncertainty of it.' "

" 'Scuse me?"

"That's how Mark Twain once described the weather in New England. I'd say it applies to Metropolis, as well."

"Yeah, too bad." Turpin brushed an errant cotton-wood seed from the band of his derby. "I don't suppose there's anything you can do about that?"

Superman stared off into the sky, as if he had suddenly become determined to see to the edge of space. He listened intently for a sound far beyond the range of human hearing.

"Superman?"

"Eh?" The Man of Steel looked back at Turpin. "I'm sorry. What was that?"

"I was askin' if there wasn't anything you could do about the weather."

Superman chuckled. "Sorry, Inspector. Holding

back the forces of nature is a bit more difficult than ap-
prehending a hired gun. But now, you'll have to excuse me." He took one step away from the detective.
"There are other matters that need my immediate attention." Another step, a leap, and the caped man shot
up into the sky, creating a small wind gust of his own.

Turpin waved his derby as he watched the Man of
Steel clear the tall buildings of the plaza. "Say what ya
want, Superman—but when it comes to battlin' nature, my money's still on you."

At that moment, halfway around the world, Mark
sat in a lotus position in a vast underground chamber,
his eyes closed. In the far corners of the room, purple
and gold silk tapestries flowed between massive marble columns. Beneath him, a soft woven mat stretched
out for several yards in every direction, cushioning
him from the smooth marble floor. In front of his outstretched hands lay a slender metal rod, half an inch
in diameter and a little over a foot long. It provided a
focus through which he channeled his energies.

At Adam's behest, Mark had spent more and more
time over the past few weeks focusing on the rod, becoming more in tune with his potential for power. He
was at the end of just such a session now.

Mark's respiration came in rapid breaths, as though
he were working out with free weights. Beads of sweat
collected on his brow and slowly trickled down the
bridge of his nose.

Soft pulsing lights illuminated his face, signaling
the end of the test session. In response, Mark opened

his eyes and his breathing began to slow. He gazed across the room to a display screen that monitored his vital signs via wireless sensors. His "working" pulse rate registered at sixty beats per minute, lower than his resting pulse used to be.

Mark rose to his feet, taking time to thoroughly stretch each muscle in turn, then bent and scooped up the metal rod. He crossed to the screen, checking his vitals one last time. Satisfied, he touched a finger to the corner of the screen.

"Show long-range results, Test Twenty-seven."

In answer to his voice command, his physical stats vanished from the screen, to be replaced by a series of swirling patterns superimposed over an outline of North America. Glowing amber circles on the display illuminated a series of locations stretching along the Atlantic coast from Maine to the Caribbean.

"Hah! Right on target every time." Mark brandished the rod in one hand as if it were a rapier and pretended to run through an imagined foe. *Adam was right. I am a man of vast potential.* He tapped the rod against his palm. "I think I deserve a little reward—don't you, Roddy-boy? Yes, I think a nice relaxing swim is in order. But first, let's put you away."

Mark again touched the display screen. "Code Twelve—'hide and seek.' " The screen swung away from the wall, revealing a secret compartment. "Better quarters for you, too, kid. Beats being shoved up a pant leg, huh?" He secured the rod to a set of clamps and closed the screen over it. "Now for that swim."

He padded in bare feet back across the woven mat

to a platform that looked out over the blue of a long elliptical pool. Mark dove in and swam several laps, luxuriating in the warmth of the waters.

Now this is living. I have won the freaking lottery! It had been over a month since he'd last had a drink, and he felt better than he had in years.

When Mark finally emerged from the pool, a small metal cylinder rose up out of the floor, dispensing a large, warmed towel. As he patted himself dry, a panel in the near wall slid open and a mechanical armature held out a silk robe for him. Mark smiled to himself. The first time he'd encountered these mechanisms, he'd reflexively blurted out a "thanks." Shaking his head at the memory, he slipped into the flowing garment, tying it around him.

A muted gong echoed, and Mark immediately snapped to attention as curtains parted along the far wall. Adam was entering the chamber. He strode deliberately around the pool, his ocher robes glistening as he walked. Mark had never asked, but he was sure that there were threads of gold filament woven throughout the fabric.

As his host approached, Mark brought his palms together in front of his face and bowed deeply from the waist. "Greetings, Sahib Adam." He held the position, looking up at the bearded man. "Is this right? Or should I have used your official title?"

"Please, rise. There is no need for formalities when we are not in the presence of the others." Adam smiled. "I trust that your accommodations continue to meet your expectations?"

Mark straightened up. "Are you kidding? Even at the top of my game, I never had a spread this lavish. I never imagined that anything could be so opulent and so exotic at the same time. Just look at this place! It's like Fred Astaire meets Bollywood, if you know what I mean."

"Yes, I have screened both *Top Hat* and *Flying Down to Rio*—and I am quite aware of the spectacles produced by India's film industry. Interesting diversions. But we must now clear our minds of all unnecessary distractions. The time for preliminary testing is over."

"You want to jump ahead to a full field operation?"

"Yes. A rare opportunity has arisen. We must ready ourselves to take advantage of it." Adam clapped his hands together sharply, and the mechanical armature again swung out of the wall panel.

This time the robotic arm produced a two-piece coverall and matching hood, both with an outer layer of tightly woven metallic mesh. At Adam's direction, Mark donned the garments; they had been tailored to fit him like a second skin. He caught his reflection in the burnished metal of the open wall panel and broke into a wide grin. "Nice. Green always was my best color."

"This is no time to indulge in base personal vanities." Adam's tone turned harsh. "It is both wasteful and unbecoming."

Mark bit off the smile and quickly bowed again. "Forgive me. What is our plan of attack?"

"Look here." Adam led Mark back to the display screen and pressed his palm to its surface. "Save and store test results. Show parameters for full field attack. New coordinates—Four-Alpha-Nine."

At Adam's command, the glowing amber circles winked out along the eastern seaboard, and a new circle—a much bigger circle, pulsing red—appeared far to the north and west.

Mark checked the new coordinates on display and let out a long, low whistle. "Wow! What this calls for is . . . big! Bigger than anything I've ever tried before. I'm not sure I'm ready for a workout like that."

"I am. Absolutely." Adam looked him straight in the eyes. "With every test, you have doubled and redoubled my original belief in you, Mark. This will be a true challenge to your new prowess, but I have every confidence that you can meet it."

"You do, huh?" Mark swelled with pride. No one had ever expressed such faith in him. "Well, you haven't been wrong yet." He looked again at the display, then stepped forward, released its secure locks, and retrieved the metal rod from the compartment behind the screen. "Okay. Okay, let's do it!"

"Excellent. Come with me, we must begin immediately. To do otherwise would be an affront to the gods themselves."

"I am ready, Sahib. *We* are ready." Mark took the rod in both hands and handed it to Adam in offering. "And we are at your service. Lead on."

CHAPTER 2

North to Alaska

Flying high above the city streets, Superman reached into the secret compartment of his belt buckle and retrieved a tiny transceiver that he slipped into his right ear.

"Superman here. I heard the emergency signal. Do you read me? What's the situation?"

For a moment Superman heard nothing but the soft hiss of background noise. And then a calm, even voice spoke in his ear.

"Loud and clear, Superman. This is Watchtower." Twenty-two thousand three hundred miles above the Earth, Dr. Raymond Palmer—the physicist better known as the Atom—sat in the communications bay of the Justice League's orbital headquarters, checking monitor readings. "The National Seismic Institute has confirmed a major earthquake, six-point-seven on the Richter. The epicenter's about five kilometers due southeast of Wasilla, Alaska. And we're getting reports of heavy damage in and around Anchorage. Sounds like a job for Superman, if not the whole League."

"I agree." Superman left downtown behind and flew low over the Hob's River to avoid the flight paths for Metropolis International Airport. "Who's on call, Atom?"

"Besides yourself, the monitor board is showing J'onn, Wonder Woman, and the Flash—all available." Palmer tapped a keypad. "The Batman is on a private mission in Bhutran. And Green Lantern is on vacation, apparently somewhere in the Caribbean. I haven't yet gotten a fix on his location."

"Understood. Have the first three meet me in Anchorage. And keep trying to find Lantern. I don't know that we'll need him, but—"

"—better to have him and not need him, than need him and not have him."

"Right. I'll report in as soon as I arrive on site. Superman out!" The Man of Steel continued on west over the mighty river, accelerating as he flew. He was no more than a red-and-blue streak by the time he shot past the nouveau riche suburbs of Park Ridge. As soon as he was a safe distance from the city, he took a deep breath and rocketed up to ten thousand feet—then twenty thousand—then thirty. Breaking the sound barrier, Superman left a series of gentle sonic booms in his wake as he continued his northwesterly ascent over the Allegheny Mountains. Within moments, the sky darkened, and all of the Great Lakes lay spread out beneath him.

Superman left the Earth's atmosphere behind as he passed over the great Canadian Shield. Miles above Saskatchewan's Reindeer Lake, he reached the apogee of his suborbital flight and began the ballistic dive that would carry him to Anchorage. Below and ahead of him, he could see the Gulf of Alaska and the Aleutian Islands reaching out toward the Bering Sea.

It was down there, in the middle of the Katmai National Park and Preserve, that Superman had first met the Justice League. *Hard to believe that was over a decade ago now.*

In a way, he had been the inspiration for them all.

Superman had been the first of a new generation of champions. His first public appearance in Metropolis seemed to trigger a new wave of costumed mystery men and women. Before a year had passed, a group of new young adventurers had joined together to form the Justice League of America.

But early on, their careers had very nearly been snuffed out.

Clark Kent had been at his desk at the *Daily Planet* when he first heard the bad news. Lois Lane was crossing the city room, when a strange item on the news wire caught her attention.

"I don't believe this!" Lois tore off the paper feed and headed for her desk. "But there it is."

As she hurried past, Kent looked up from his monitor screen. "There *what* is, Lois?"

"Just a few weeks ago, I would have said that the Justice League was a good idea." Lois started searching through her computer's phone list. "Flash. Green Lantern. Aquaman. Black Canary. Even that green-skinned Manhunter. They've saved the whole world a couple of times over already. They're getting almost as much media coverage as Superman."

"I doubt that Superman minds very much. In fact, I'd guess he thinks that's just fine."

"Well, he won't think it's fine that they're fighting one another."

"What?" Clark was instantly on his feet. "What are you talking about?"

"A bush pilot claims he caught a glimpse of them going at it." Lois grabbed her phone and started punching in a number. "Real knock-down, drag-out fight. Says he'd have stuck around to get some pictures, but he was low on fuel. Fortunately, he radioed it in. True or false, it's in the system now. It's news."

"Where—?" Clark reached for the printout, but Lois plucked it away.

"Alaska. Some place called the Valley of Ten Thousand Smokes." Cradling the phone with one hand, Lois clutched the copy to her chest. "And don't you even *think* about grabbing this story, Kent. It's all mine."

But Clark Kent was no longer there. The reporter was already out of the city room and five flights up the building's back stairway. Kent bolted up the stairs, four steps at a time, doffing his glasses and shucking off his street clothes as he ran. When he emerged on the rooftop, he was clothed in the brilliant primary colors of Superman.

He launched himself skyward, heading for Alaska, praying all the while that he would arrive in time.

As Superman neared the Aleutians, he spotted a strange series of flashing lights emanating from the Katmai preserve. Following the lights into the remote valley, he saw immediately that the bizarre report was true. The five founding members of the Justice League were fighting among themselves, without rhyme or reason.

The Flash was a crimson blur, darting in and out among the others, ducking under the Black Canary's kick, throwing a punch at Aquaman, trying to tackle Green Lantern to the ground. The Canary turned and bombarded the Manhunter with an ultrasonic cry that knocked him out of the air.

Each attack, every strike seemingly came at random, but more and more, the blows were hitting home. The five were rapidly wearing themselves down, and becoming more desperate in their actions. To Superman, it seemed as though they were determined to kill one another.

And then he spotted the robot.

"You saved us all that day."

Superman veered slightly to one side, momentarily startled by the "sound" of a voice in his head. "J'onn—? Is that you?"

"Yes. My apologies." A translucent form appeared alongside the Man of Steel, rapidly becoming more opaque. "I should have first announced my presence." In another instant, J'onn J'onzz—the Manhunter from

Mars—was fully visible, his blue cape rippling about his shoulders as he flew.

The Manhunter assumed his Justice League persona, a lightly humanized version of his true alien form. As such, he was a tall, green-skinned humanoid male. J'onn's scalp was completely bald. His body, in fact, was totally devoid of hair. His features were strong, his face rough-hewn, with a prominent brow that even an amateur caricaturist could easily capture.

He was not, generally, someone who was mistaken for Superman.

Which was humorous, because both men were extraterrestrials, and of all the members of the Justice League, it was the Manhunter whose powers and abilities came closest to rivaling those of the Man of Steel. Both were superhumanly strong and tough. Both could fly. And both possessed powers of vision and hearing that reached far beyond the normal human range.

Their differences were interesting as well. Working with a telepath, especially a telepath who could become invisible and otherwise alter his appearance, was never dull, to say the least.

The Martian tipped the Kryptonian a small salute. "I assure you, I did not mean to 'eavesdrop.' It was more that your surface thoughts were—ah—difficult to ignore. I meant no offense."

"None taken." Superman smiled to reassure his teammate. "I guess that, to someone with your talents, I was thinking out loud."

J'onn nodded. "In this part of the world, it would

be difficult to avoid thinking about that day. My own memories of that battle are as vivid as my recollections of the 1964 earthquake."

"You were here for that?"

"Yes, I aided in that rescue effort. Working undercover, of course, as I always did in those days." J'onn's normal monotone began to soften. "No one then ever saw me as I appear now, and I seldom imagined that anyone ever would. Your public debut changed everything. The JLA came together soon after, and in the League, I could be myself. The friendships we forged . . ." He bowed his head, his eyes nearly disappearing beneath the shadow of his brow ridge. "I still miss Barry and Hal."

"So do I."

Both Martian and Kryptonian slowed their flight as they neared the outskirts of the earthquake zone, scanning the terrain more closely. It was the Man of Steel who first picked up the subsonic rumble.

"I hope you're ready to put your earthquake experience to good use." Superman tapped his transceiver. "Atom? J'onn and I are about ten miles east of Anchorage, and we're about to get busy . . ."

Just a few hundred feet below, a three-mile-long stretch of highway suddenly split right up the middle. What had been a two-lane road was now nearly four lanes wide—but that new middle "lane" was a yawning chasm. At least a dozen cars and trucks skidded and slid about the broken asphalt surface.

Superman and the Manhunter dropped from the skies, flying fast and low over the ruined roadway.

They split up, darting back and forth from vehicle to vehicle, checking on drivers and passengers, looking for those most in need of immediate assistance.

The Man of Steel paused in midair and peered in at the driver of a rusty old sedan. "Are you all right, sir?"

"I-I think so." The driver looked up at him, perplexed. "Are you . . . Superman?"

"Yes, sir."

"Then I'm okay." The man grinned. "Yeah, I'm definitely okay."

Twenty feet away, the Manhunter reached out telepathically to calm the frazzled driver of a late-model pickup truck that had slammed into a guardrail. Then he carefully pried open the crumpled cab and helped her out from behind the vehicle's deflated airbag.

Most of the people along the road had merely been shaken by the suddenness of the event. Many were getting out of their cars and starting to help one another. For them, all that was needed was a word or two of reassurance.

For others, more immediate action was called for.

Superman found a gray-haired man slumped over the wheel of an SUV. The vehicle's frame sat on jagged pavement, its front tires sticking out over the chasm. The Man of Steel quickly reached under the SUV, lifting and pulling it back from the abyss.

For an instant, Superman was shaken. It wasn't just the pallor of the older man's face. Between the line of the driver's jaw and his wire-rimmed glasses, he bore a resemblance to Superman's own father. The Man of Steel gently tapped the older man on the shoulder.

"Sir! Sir, can you hear me? Are you okay?"

"Huhn?" The man stirred slightly. He lifted his head a bit, turning toward his rescuer and starting to open his eyes.

Very carefully, Superman eased the older man back into the car seat. His breathing improved immediately, and he opened his eyes wider, clearly trying to focus on the Man of Steel. "What happened?" He spoke slowly, but he spoke clearly, and Superman felt his own racing heartbeat slow down.

"There was an aftershock and I found you passed out. Do you have any medical conditions?"

"A spell of heart trouble now an' then. Nothin' too serious." The driver managed a rueful smile that made him look even more like Jonathan Kent. "They tell me I'm s'posed to avoid stress."

"Need any help?" A young woman was fast approaching with a medical kit. "I'm a nurse. And an EMT."

Superman made room for her, repeating his findings. She quickly set up a portable heart monitor, double-checked the man's vital signs and nodded in agreement. "Heart rhythms are okay. Looks like a major stress reaction. Just temporary, thank God." She patted the man's shoulder. "Sir, you've had a bad scare but you're going to be all right. Do you have your meds with you?"

As Superman stepped back to give the nurse more room, the driver of the crumpled pickup came trotting over, waving her cellphone overhead. "I called nine-one-one. They said that more help is already on the way."

"Good. We may need to medevac this man." Super-man turned to the Manhunter. "Any other injuries, J'onn?"

"A few bumps and bruises, but no broken bones."

"Then we got off lucky." The woman shifted nervously from foot to foot, glancing from the two caped men to the nurse and back again. "I can still remember the big one, back in '64. I was just little then, and it knocked me right off of my feet. Scared the bejeezus outta me. This one didn't seem so spooky, probably 'cause I was on the road. Just seemed like things got bumpier all of a—omigod! Here comes another one!"

The woman threw herself at Superman and held on for dear life as the pavement began to shake. The Manhunter leaped back to protect the nurse and her patient, stretching out an arm to steady the rocking SUV.

"It's all right . . . all right." Superman's even voice had a definite calming influence on the woman. "It was just an aftershock. There, see? It's already over."

"Help!"

About fifty yards away, the driver of a big gasoline tanker had just been stepping from the cab when this aftershock hit. The asphalt crumbled beneath his feet, and he grabbed hold of the door for support. Now he was hanging from that door as it swung out over the widening chasm. And he was losing his grip.

"HELP ME!"

Superman handed the nervous woman off to the Manhunter and streaked toward the tanker, even as the trucker fell screaming into the abyss.

The Man of Steel shot after the falling man, matching speeds with him and slowing his fall before flying him back up into the light of day.

"It's okay! I have you now."

The trucker relaxed for just a moment before stiffening in Superman's grasp. "No. NO!" The blood drained from his face as he looked back past his rescuer in horror.

The entire tanker, carrying thousands of gallons of fuel, was tumbling into the chasm.

CHAPTER 3

Victims of Circumstance

Superman dropped the trucker by the side of the road and streaked back down into the chasm. *The last thing we need is a massive gasoline explosion!*

But even as he reached out to stop the falling tanker, a slender glowing cord suddenly shot down from above, wrapping around the big rig and bringing it to a stop less than a foot from the Man of Steel's palms.

And then, the tanker slowly began to reverse its course.

Crouching by the side of the road, the trucker looked up and took a long, slow breath. "What . . . what was that?" His face showed a mix of awe and bewilderment. "What's going on?"

Smiling, Superman rose up from the chasm. "We both just got a helping hand from an angel."

As the Man of Steel landed beside him, the trucker gaped in amazement. A thin golden rope had pulled his tanker out of the chasm. In fact, the big rig now hung suspended several feet off the ground, its massive bulk perfectly balanced in cocoon-like loops of the lasso. The rest of the glistening cable stretched another twenty-five feet into the air, to where the early morning light shimmered off the wings of an exotic semi-transparent jet aircraft.

The plane hovered in the air, making not a sound. And astride one of the plane's wings, tightly gripping the other end of the lasso, stood a dark-haired woman of breathtaking beauty.

Crimson boots, trimmed in white, shod her feet. Her legs were bare, as were her arms and shoulders, but if she felt the chill of the morning air, it did not show. She was clad in blue trunks, spangled with white stars. A broad golden belt encircled her waist. She wore a crimson breastplate, boldly emblazoned with stylized golden wings. Gleaming silver bracelets encircled her wrists, reaching halfway up her powerful forearms. And across her forehead, framed by a cascade of raven hair, sat a golden tiara accented by a single crimson star.

"Did you say angel?" The trucker blinked. "That's no angel. She . . . she must be a goddess."

"She gets that a lot. And you're closer to the truth than you realize." Superman's smile broadened. "That's Diana of Themyscira, but most people call her Wonder Woman."

Overhead, the amazing robot plane slowly backed away from the chasm, carrying the tanker with it. The Man of Steel raised one arm in a wave to the Amazon

Princess. She smiled and removed one hand from her lasso, returning his gesture.

"I don't believe it." The trucker pulled off his cap and clutched it to his chest, as if in prayer. "That rig's carrying a full load. She's holdin' up ten thousand gallons of gas with one hand! That's not possible."

Superman shrugged. "It's not easy. But it can be done. Obviously."

"Uh-huh." The trucker replaced his cap, suddenly fully aware of just whom he was talking to. "Well, I guess you'd know better'n anybody." He stood and gaped as Wonder Woman lowered the big rig gently back down onto the side of the road. "An' okay, she's braced against that plane. But look at how she kept it balanced, and all with just that one rope! How is that possible?"

The Man of Tomorrow slowly shook his head. "I'd say it's magic—of a sort. Diana once told me that her rope was a gift of the gods, forged from the Golden Girdle of Gaea. And I don't think she'd make that up."

With a flip of the Amazon's wrist, the lasso disengaged itself from the truck and began rolling back up along its length, forming a compact coil in her hand. Fastening the coil to her belt, Wonder Woman leaped from the wing of her plane to join her colleagues on the ground.

"Th-thank you, ma'am." The trucker again doffed his cap and took a step back, trying hard not to stare. Up close, Wonder Woman was even more impressive, standing nearly as tall as Superman. "I still can't hardly believe it, but you saved my rig."

Wonder Woman smiled. "You're welcome. But Superman had already saved your life. He or the Manhunter could have caught the tanker easily."

"Yes, but your quick thinking insured that it would still be roadworthy, Diana." Superman turned to the trucker. "It should be safe to drive. Just take it easy."

"Sure thing." The trucker took Superman's hand and pumped it. "Thank you. Both of you." He tipped his cap to Wonder Woman one last time and sidled back toward the tanker's cab.

Other drivers clustered by the side of the road, some whispering into cell phones, but all keeping a respectful distance as the Manhunter joined Superman and Wonder Woman.

"Well done, Diana. A most timely assist."

"Thank you, J'onn. What's the situation here?"

"Under control in the immediate area. One mild cardiac case, stabilized. Everyone else is shaken and uneasy, but they are adjusting." The Martian glanced up at the shimmering craft hovering silently overhead. "That was good planning, bringing your plane."

"I was in Madagascar when I received the Atom's call. I may be blessed with the speed of Hermes, but the plane was my faster option. It enabled me to make a suborbital flight and arrive in time to do some good."

Superman grinned. "It certainly came in handy here. But speaking of the speed of Hermes, where in blazes is the Flash?"

"He's not with you?" The Amazon glanced around

them. "I would have thought that he'd be the first to arrive."

"And you'd be right, Wonder Woman."

The three turned to see a sleek figure in a scarlet bodysuit, crouching by the edge of the chasm.

The Flash got to his feet, shaking his head. "Man, when I passed through along this stretch earlier, it was still intact. I guess an aftershock did this?"

Superman nodded. "At least two. The initial quake obviously weakened the substrata beneath the roadbed. And when the aftershock hit—"

"Instant canyon. Gotcha. Anyway, I've been all over, around, and through Anchorage for about the last fifteen minutes, helping with rescue efforts as I found 'em. Heard about your arrival here thanks to a nine-one-one call." Flash tapped one of the winged earcups that flanked his mask. "If you tune your JLA transceivers to setting seven-one-A, you can monitor Anchorage Emergency Dispatch. We've got buildings down, land shifts of several feet up and down in places—but the locals tell me it could have been a lot worse. The quake hit just before six in the morning, local time, so most people were still at home." He gazed off into the bright blue skies. "Hard to believe it's still so early here."

"Land of the Midnight Sun, Flash." Superman slipped the tiny transceiver back into his ear.

For a moment, the assembled Justice League task force grew still, listening intently to a whole series of emergency calls.

The Man of Steel frowned. "Sounds as though there's plenty to keep us all busy."

"What I said. Could've been worse, but things still aren't great." Flash turned to Superman. "You're the current team leader, big guy. You want to divvy us up?"

The caped man nodded and set his transceiver to send. "Justice League Priority One. This is Superman, calling Anchorage Emergency Dispatch. The League is here and ready to help. . . ."

In moments, he'd made his decisions. "All right. Wonder Woman, you take the east side. J'onn, I think your talents are most needed along the northern perimeter. Flash, you're our foot patrol. And I'll head for the trouble spots near the port district. Everyone keep in touch."

"Of course."

"*Agreed.*"

"Will do."

As emergency vehicles began arriving on the scene, the Justice League task force headed out, dispersing across the municipality of Anchorage.

Within moments, the Flash was a scarlet blur streaking north along the Old Seward Highway, his yellow boots barely skimming the pavement.

As he ran, his transceiver crackled in his earcups. "Anchorage Emergency Dispatch to all cars—we have a nine-one-one call from inside a house collapsed at 1257 Hague Road, two miles west of the Old Seward Highway."

Hague Road? Didn't I pass a sign for that about eight

miles back? The speedster made an extreme U-turn and headed south. He found Hague Road and reached the house in seconds.

"Anchorage Dispatch, this is the Flash—JLA Priority Code Five. I'm on the scene, but 'collapsed' isn't exactly the right word for this place."

"Dispatch to Flash—explain, please."

"Well . . ." The Flash stood on a small knoll overlooking the property. "From the looks of things, this *used* to be a two-story house. But the ground at the center of the lot has dropped maybe twelve to fifteen feet. Both ends of the structure have risen up and sort of folded around the middle. Everything looks . . . crumpled. Are you sure that someone is still alive in there?"

"Roger that, Flash. A man and a woman are trapped in the interior. They're still on the line with one of our nine-one-one operators. She's trying to keep them calm. Do you require backup?"

"An EMT or two wouldn't hurt. Tell the folks inside that help has arrived." The Flash circled the lot, looking for an access into the broken dwelling. There were no longer signs of any doors. The glass in the few visible windows had all shattered, the frames flattened into long, narrow parallelograms. *This is more a job for the Atom than for me. Ray could shrink down to action-figure size and be inside in . . . a flash. And to think I used to razz him about having the power to "get small." Sure would be useful here.* On the back end of the wreckage, the Flash finally spotted a shattered skylight large enough for a normal-sized man to pass through.

"Dispatch, I've found an opening. I'm going in."

The Flash pulled himself onto the ruined structure, gingerly testing each footstep to make sure nothing shifted under him. *Careful. Easy does it now.* He got down on hands and knees, crawling the last few feet. The pace was maddening for a man used to moving at the speed of sound, but it couldn't be helped. *You don't want to bring this thing down on top of anyone.*

Reaching the skylight, the Flash dropped down into what had once been a second-floor bathroom. The toilet lay on its side, and water from a broken pipe was jetting out into a hallway. He reached down to shut off the water, and the valve broke loose in his hand.

"Of course. That would have been too convenient."

Leaving the bathroom behind, the Flash slid down warped and buckled surfaces that had once been walls as he picked his way through the darkened house.

"Hello?" It seemed that every floor in the place sloped or twisted away at some odd angle. *Make a nice fixer-upper—for M.C. Escher.* "Can anybody hear me?"

A muffled cry sounded about fifteen feet up and to his right.

"I hear you! Hang on, I'm coming!" Drumming his feet, the Flash quickly built up the momentum needed to scramble up the extreme angle of the tilted floor. At the top of the incline, he found an oddly angled doorframe.

The frame had held, though a jumble of fallen timbers and smashed furniture blocked it. Still, there was some light filtering out, and through the debris, the Flash could just make out a man and a woman. They sat huddled together on the now mostly horizontal wall of what looked to have been their bedroom, clutching a cell phone between them.

They were both dressed in flannel pajamas, and they were liberally powdered with plaster dust.

The Flash grabbed hold of the doorframe and pressed against the blockage. It didn't budge. *Have to do something about that.*

"Hello in there!"

"Yes!" The man looked up toward the sound of the Flash's voice. "Yes, we're in here!"

The woman held on to her husband, her voice breaking. "Get us out of here! Please!"

"Don't worry, I'm working on that. Are you able to move around in there?"

"Yes." The woman took a deep breath and composed herself. "It's not easy—ceiling's a little low—but we're not pinned down by anything."

As if to demonstrate, the man moved sideways a few feet. "Neither of us is hurt. We just can't get out. Took us forever just to find the phone."

"Okay. Listen carefully, I want you both to get as far back from this doorway as you can, and pull that mattress over on top of you. Can you do that?"

"Sure, but why?"

"Just do it. Things are going to get a little noisy in here."

As soon as he was certain the couple were safely behind the mattress, the Flash again became a soft blur. Turning his superhuman speed inward, he increased the vibratory rate of his body's molecules and reached out, slipping a hand *through* the atoms of the timbers blocking his path.

Then, the Flash dove through the solid matter of the debris. As he passed into the room, residual energy was transferred to the jumble, exciting the molecular vibrations of the wood.

The blockage exploded behind him in a brilliant flash of light.

The Flash maintained his increased internal vibrations until the dust and debris had settled. Then he slid across the room toward the bunched-up mattress.

"All clear! You can come out now."

Two heads poked out from behind the mattress. The couple stared at him, wide-eyed, in the dim light that filtered down through a fissure high up on the floor.

Flash sat back on his haunches and gave them his most reassuring grin. "Hi, folks. I'm from the Justice League, and I'm here to help. You can call me Flash."

The man reached out and shook the red gloved hand. "Al . . . Al McKinney. Real glad to see you, buddy. This is my wife Brenda. We woke up to everything shaking. Shook us right outta bed." Al looked around them. "And then one end of the room started sinking."

Brenda started shaking her head and couldn't seem to stop. "This morning has been like a nightmare. I fell into the closet and then the door slammed shut on me."

"Shh, it's okay." Al held her tight. "I gotcha out, didn't I?" He glanced up at the Flash. "Everything's so turned around."

Flash nodded. "It's going to be all right. Now that I know the way, I should have you out of here in two ticks."

"Take her first." Al braced himself and helped his wife up over the folded mattress to the Flash.

The next thing Brenda knew, she and the Flash were outside, and he was setting her down on level ground. "Wait here just a sec, Ms. McKinney."

"What—?" She blinked once and the Flash was gone. Before she could blink again, he'd returned with her husband.

"Babe!" Al threw his arms around his wife, and both began to cry.

"Uh, excuse me . . ."

The McKinneys turned to find the Flash standing just a few feet away, holding a bundle of blankets and clothing. He set the bundle down and handed them two bottles of water. "I found these in what was left of your kitchen. I'm afraid there wasn't much else of use in there."

Al turned back and got his first good look at the remains of their house. "Great God a'mighty. I can't believe we lived through that."

"Thank you, Mr. Flash. Thank you so much!" Brenda impulsively hugged the Flash while Al pumped his hand.

"You saved our hides, buddy. I don't know how we'll ever repay you."

"Hey, it's what I do. I'm not in this for the money. But the thanks are always appreciated." The Flash saw a rescue van pulling up, and waved to the paramedics. "Yo! Over here!" He turned back to the Mc-Kinneys. "I know you said you were both okay, but I'd still let these people check you over. It never hurts to get a professional opinion, and they'll help find you a place to stay."

The Flash stiffened, listening to another soft voice crackling in his ears. "But now you'll have to excuse me. More calls to answer!"

And then, he was gone.

From the cockpit of her translucent plane, Wonder Woman could clearly see a plume of black smoke rising from the industrial park far below. She sent the plane into a steep power dive, plunging to within a few hundred feet of the burning building.

And then, in response to the Amazon's thoughts, her plane braked to a gentle stop and hung motionless in midair.

Wonder Woman popped the canopy and flew free from her plane. Whispering a prayer of thanks for the powers given her by the gods, she dove toward a cluster of fire engines below.

As Diana descended, her shadow passed over a firefighter who pulled a bulky hose over the uneven ground. Glancing skyward, he stumbled and nearly lost his footing. The firefighter spun around and called out to his superior. "Cap'n! We got company. High-powered company."

Captain George Gleason looked up just in time to see the flying woman alight not ten feet from his command post. "Well, I'll be damned."

"For your sake, I hope not." Diana smiled. "You really wouldn't like Hades. Too many fires."

"Uh, yes, ma'am. No doubt. I'm Captain Gleason." He touched the brim of his helmet in salute and then covered his mouth as he cleared his throat. "Sorry for the language, Wonder Woman. Dispatch said you were on your way here, but you still took me by surprise."

"No apologies necessary, Captain. How may I help you?"

Gleason motioned her over to the command post and began pointing out sections of the building on a blueprint. "Here's what we've got. The quake severed gas lines and electric service in the rear of the building, setting off an explosion and fire that has spread through the south wing. The gas company's shut off that line, but now the fire is feeding on the plastics that were manufactured there, releasing some nasty toxics."

Wonder Woman pored over the captain's fire plan. "Was anyone inside when this started?"

"Three security guards. Two got out. I have a couple of men looking for the third now." Gleason turned to a man with a headset. "Michaels, where are Smith and Fullerton?"

The radio officer cupped a hand over his microphone. "They've worked their way up to the third floor, Captain. Still no sign of—"

Before he could finish, a loud pop came from the

building and a huge gout of flame blasted out through the glass of a third-story window.

Michaels leaned closer to the microphone and turned up the gain. "Say again! You're breaking up!" He turned to his captain. "Sir, they're cut off. Fire's engulfed the main stairs, and the other end's blocked." He flipped a switch back and forth on his console. "I'm losing them."

Wonder Woman pulled Michaels over to the blueprints. "Show me where they are."

He looked over the floor plan, stabbing a finger at one section. "There."

She straightened up. "I'll get them."

Gleason thrust a mask and air tank into her hands. "Take this."

"Right." Diana slung the tank over her shoulders and pulled the mask down over her face, tucking her hair up under its straps. Leaping into the air, she flew into the stream of one of the fire hoses, letting the cold water soak her down.

Then she dove through the blown-out window and into the heart of the burning building.

Flames licked their way across floors and up the walls. Thick black smoke poured out of several doorways. Wonder Woman drew her lasso from her belt, looped it, and set it to spinning overhead. The glowing coil began to disperse the smoke, even as it cast a soft light into the blackened corridors, and Diana saw signs of movement two rooms away.

A firefighter was down, half fallen through a section of flooring that had given way beneath him. The only thing keeping him from disappearing through the floor was his partner, who held on to him by the wrists and was desperately trying to haul him up.

"Don't let me fall, Smitty! The fire's underneath me! I can feel the heat through my boots! Don't let me fall!"

But as Smith struggled to pull Fullerton to safety, the floor creaked and groaned under his own feet.

Suddenly, a bare hand reached out through the smoke and seized the fallen firefighter by the collar.

Wonder Woman gave a single sharp tug, and Fullerton came flying up out of the hole. Grabbing both firefighters by an arm, she yanked them back as flame shot up through the hole and more of the floor gave way around it.

Both men looked amazed as the Amazon thrust a length of her glowing lasso into their hands. "Hold on to this, and follow me to safety."

Smith and Fullerton were too shocked to ask questions. Each man wrapped the lasso around his wrist and silently fell in behind her, following her glowing cord through the inky smoke.

Out in the corridor, the fire raged even more wildly than before. A fiery timber tumbled down from the floor above and Wonder Woman swung one arm out wide, knocking it away from them. Remembering what she'd seen of the blueprints, she turned down a small side hall.

"This way!"

"But that's a dead end," Smith protested. "We can't get out that way."

"Yes, we can. Come on."

Wonder Woman led them down the hall and into a small storage room. Smith pulled out his flashlight, playing its light across bare brick walls. There wasn't a single window to be seen. Diana ran a hand along the wall, giving it a couple of sharp raps with her fist. "About a foot thick."

"I told you. There's no exit!"

"There will be."

The Amazon took one step back from the wall, then spun around, leaping up and lashing out with a powerful kick.

Sunlight shone through a hole roughly sixteen inches in diameter and four feet off the floor.

Two more kicks and the hole widened enough for a large man to pass through easily. Wonder Woman stood in the threshold of the newly formed exit, waving the firefighters closer.

Smith's eyes went wide behind his Plexiglas mask. "Guess I was wrong." He stuck his head out the opening. "Still a pretty good drop. Do we do climb down your magic rope, or wait for a ladder?"

Diana shook her head. "I have a faster way." She grabbed hold of the two firefighters and leaped from the building. In the blink of an eye, she gently touched ground, handing Smith and Fullerton off to a team of paramedics.

Then Wonder Woman turned and disappeared back into the building.

Behind the line of firefighters Captain Gleason paced back and forth, shaking his head in dismay.

Now and again he stopped to stare at the burning building as his crews sprayed water and flame retardant foam into its interior. "Why'd she go back? It's a furnace in there. What was she thinking?"

A shout echoed from up the line. "Cap'n! There she is!"

Wonder Woman flew free of the fire. In her arms she cradled the missing security guard, her air mask now strapped to his face. A hush fell over the fire crews as she landed beside an ambulance and lowered the injured man gently onto a stretcher.

Diana waited pensively while paramedics worked on the guard. One of the med-techs finally looked up and smiled. "I'd say you found him just in time, ma'am."

As they started to lift the stretcher, the injured man reached out to Wonder Woman. She took his hand and walked alongside as the paramedics moved him to the ambulance. Just before they loaded him in the van, the guard raised his head, looked to those around him, and gave a shaky thumbs-up.

The cheer that went up could be heard even over the departing siren.

One hundred yards from the main runway of Elmendorf Air Force Base, a huge hangar had split in two. Half of the structure was still standing, virtually untouched, while the other half lay flattened on the ground.

Colonel Mark Hollister had been rousted out of bed by the quake and now found himself standing on the back of a large flatbed truck, directing base rescue and recovery.

"Colonel? Chief Master Sergeant Lopez reporting as ordered, sir!"

Hollister returned the salute of the young enlisted man who had just climbed aboard. "At ease, Sergeant. We've no time for ceremony this morning. What's the damage report?"

"Not as bad as it could have been, sir." The sergeant passed an electronic clipboard to his superior. "A number of fences are down—we have teams working on that now—but the perimeter is secured. Two taxiways have been shut down temporarily and will need extensive regrading and reconstruction. The runways all came through the big shake and the aftershocks virtually untouched." Lopez glanced back over his shoulder at the hangar. "Right there is our biggest loss."

"Too big." The colonel took a sip of tepid coffee as he scanned the clipboard. "We still have four people missing?"

"Yes, sir. Three airmen and a staff sergeant. It's believed that they—" Lopez paused, something catching in the back of his throat. "That they were in the hangar when it came down. We have a K-9 search-and-rescue team on the job, but . . . there's nothing so far, sir."

Hollister nodded. At the moment, there was no indication of whether the people trapped under the collapsed hangar were alive or dead. He wanted to believe that they were alive. He looked at the cranes and other heavy equipment that sat ready just a few yards away. *But until we know exactly where they are, trying to move the wreckage could only make matters worse. We have to find them—soon.*

A voice called down from overhead: "I share your concern, Colonel."

"Madre de Dios!" Sergeant Lopez drew his sidearm as the Manhunter's boots touched down on the truck bed.

"Put that away, Sergeant. I was expecting this man. He's with the Justice League."

"But, sir, he's . . . he's green!"

"That's right. And I'm black. And you're white Hispanic. Do you have a problem with any of that, Sergeant?"

"No, sir." Lopez shoved the weapon back into its holster and turned, shamefaced, to the green man. "I apologize for my reaction, sir. It was uncalled for."

The Martian bowed his head briefly. "Acknowledged and accepted, Sergeant."

Hollister extended his hand. "We could definitely use your help, Manhunter."

"That is why I am here, Colonel."

Sergeant Mike Watkins was peripherally aware that a couple of newcomers were arriving at the search-and-rescue site, but he paid them little attention. They were sensibly approaching from downwind and they weren't doing anything that might screw up the search. Everything else about them was irrelevant.

The sergeant's dog, a big black and tan German shepherd, was zigzagging across a broad swath of rubble, brisk and sure-footed. Neo never dawdled, but today he was searching even more energetically than usual. Watkins could see that the dog was picking up on his own nervous energy.

There was always that extra edge of intensity when the missing people were your own.

Neo's ears perked up and his tail started wagging furiously. He zigzagged more and more sharply, clearly zeroing in on something. The dog barked once, then abruptly sat and started scratching at a pile of debris.

"You find something, Neo?" Sergeant Watkins was instantly at his dog's side. "Good boy, Neo. That's a good boy!" He took hold of the shepherd's collar and turned to the others. "We're gonna need the heavy equipment—" The sergeant did a double take as he finally caught sight of the Manhunter. He blinked again, then broke into a broad grin. "Maybe we won't." He led Neo off the rubble. "Neo, hold. That's a good boy. We just got some major-league help."

Colonel Hollister trotted to keep up as the Manhunter, his right hand extended, strode over to Watkins. "J'onzz. I helped with the last Tokyo quake."

The sergeant shook the Martian's hand. "Watkins. I heard about Tokyo. You do good work." Watkins nodded at the site. "It's all yours."

Manhunter stared closely at the debris, slowly turning his head to the left, then tracked back and slowly turned to the right.

Watkins translated for his colonel. "Scents percolate out along gaps in the debris, and Neo homed in on the strongest source of the scent. Now, J'onzz is like Superman—he can see right through this stuff.

Starting from where Neo alerted, he's tracing those gaps back until he sees where—and how—our people are trapped."

Hollister relaxed enough to manage a half smile. " 'Where' and 'how,' Sergeant? You're not worried about 'if'?"

"No, sir. Neo is almost always right."

"And he is right again today." The Manhunter started to walk out onto the rubble. "I can see a woman and three men—alive. Two appear seriously injured. All are unconscious. They are trapped together within a small air space beneath a fallen beam." He took two more steps out onto the rubble, judging the strength of the concrete, and looked back. "Colonel, have your medical team stand by and wait for my signal."

"What do you intend to—?" To the Colonel's surprise, the color began to fade from J'onn's skin and clothing. "Manhunter?"

"—To do? The heavy lifting, of course." The now-translucent Martian turned away and began to sink into the rubble. Neo, who had been watching the Manhunter with professional interest, backed up a step and gave a short, rising howl. The dog stared at the disappearing figure, then looked up at his handler.

"Don't look at me, buddy. I have no idea how he does that." Sergeant Watkins crouched down to reassure his dog as the Martian vanished from sight. "But he's one of us . . . one of the good guys. That's all that matters."

* * *

Lowering his density, the Manhunter passed like a wraith through the rubble and down into the small air pocket where the enlisted personnel lay trapped. Carefully, he passed between the unconscious people. And then, crouching over them protectively, J'onn resolidified. The space was very tight, forcing him to stand hunched over. Making sure his feet were properly set, the Martian wedged his shoulders under the beam.

Then, he began to straighten.

A huge section of steel-reinforced concrete lifted up out of the rubble. Centered under the elevated slab, the Manhunter stood tall, his arms outstretched like the limbs of some mighty green tree.

For a moment, the waiting rescue team just stared at the Martian in utter astonishment. Then his voice rang in their heads—"*Here. Bring your stretchers this way.*"—and they scrambled over the rubble in answer to the mental summons.

"Careful with the airman to my right and the one directly in front of me. The first has a broken left shoulder and collarbone. The second has a shattered right knee."

As they knelt in the Manhunter's shadow, one of the Air Force medics looked up at him uncertainly.

"Not to worry, I will not let it drop. But please hurry. There could be further aftershocks."

J'onn could hear Watkins praising his dog as each person was pulled from the rubble: "Good boy, Neo. *Good boy!* We saved another one!"

Yes, thought the Martian, *very good.*

Scant minutes later, Colonel Hollister picked up a bullhorn. "Everyone is safe and clear, Manhunter. Hang in there! We're moving in a crane to lift the weight off you."

"Not necessary, Colonel."

The big concrete slab came crashing down.

The rescue team stood shocked, staring at the cloud of dust that billowed up from the rubble. The dog again began to bark.

Then, before their eyes, a ghost seemed to rise up out of the dust, changing from white to gray to green. As J'onn solidified, Hollister and Watkins burst into applause and Neo joined in with a volley of barks.

The Manhunter strode back to the waiting search-and-rescue team. "Sergeant, may I praise your dog, as well?"

"You *have* done this before! Sure, go ahead. Thanks for asking me first."

J'onn bowed his head. "He is a working dog. One should always ask." He crouched down and smiled at the shepherd. "Good boy, Neo! Good job! You did your job well, and all were saved." He held out a hand and Neo, grinning as only a dog can, slapped a forepaw to his palm.

A great clamor arose behind the Manhunter, and he stood to see a squad of airmen surging toward him. Every man and woman suddenly wanted to touch the green-skinned stranger, to shake his hand, to clap him on the back. Unaccustomed to such an outpouring, the Martian quietly acknowledged their thanks.

On the edge of the crowd, Colonel Hollister stood beaming. Catching the Manhunter's eye, he snapped off a smart salute. Watkins gave a thumbs-up as he led Neo away.

J'onn returned the salute and the thumbs-up. He reached out to shake yet another outstretched hand, and his smile widened. *This must be what it is like for Superman all the time.*

Superman was about twelve hundred feet over Northern Lights Boulevard when he spotted emergency flashers alongside an apartment building. The building looked even more lopsided than dispatch had indicated. *Must've been aftershocks here, too.*

The land under one end of the property had simply dropped away, forming a subsidence trough. Roughly a third of the apartment complex had sunk a full ten feet. Amazingly, though split in two, both sections of the building were still largely intact. It was only at the rooms along the break that there was noticeable structural collapse.

Police and volunteer workers were spread out around the collapse. They worked with levers, shovels, and in some cases their hands, digging out the rubble and carting it away.

The Man of Steel swooped down over the crowd. "Who's in charge here?"

"Superman! Thank God!" A policeman broke away from the group and waved his cap overhead. "Boy, can we use you!"

The caped man touched down beside the weary-looking cop, reading his name from the plastic tag on his uniform pocket. "Officer Jablonski? What do you need?"

"Just about everything. All the ground movement here was vertical, so the serious damage was mostly confined to the eight apartments at the split." Jablonski stopped to catch his breath. "We've already pulled a couple of people out of the rubble and got 'em off to the hospital, but there are still at least six we haven't been able to account for—kids, some of 'em."

"Then let's get to it."

Jablonski scrambled to keep up as Superman strode toward the work line. "Dispatch has promised us a search team and heavy equipment, but they haven't shown up yet. We've been trying to make do, but it's slow going."

"I'll do everything I can to speed up the process."

"Great!" Jablonski clapped his hands together for attention. "Listen up, people. Let's give Superman some space here! Whatever he says, goes!"

Superman nodded his thanks to Jablonski and turned his gaze on the collapsed apartments. He stared intently, tuning his vision through many wavelengths. Brick, wood, and sheet rock became transparent to his sight. Nails, wire, and pipes shimmered before his eyes and then faded from view as he peered through layer after layer. *No lead piping in these newer buildings. That makes this a lot easier.*

He saw the first signs of a human skeleton about six feet in and four feet down.

The crowd grew still.

Superman concentrated, adjusting the focus of his X-ray vision, and a body began to come into view around the bones. He saw a beating heart at the same instant as his ears picked up a muffled cry.

"I've found them. Tell dispatch they can reroute that backup." The Man of Steel ripped away a ten-foot section of crumbling brick facade. Then he grabbed the biggest shovel and dove into the rubble, scooping out huge mounds of it with each sweep. "I need supports!"

Men came on the run, hauling eight-foot jack posts from the back of a pickup truck. Superman grabbed the posts, two at a time, jamming them up to support the floor overhead, spot-welding them into place with his heat vision.

He never stopped moving.

A line of men and women with buckets and wheel-barrows stretched out behind him, carrying off the debris as he cleared it. Despite their best efforts, they kept falling behind, piles of buckets stacking up in his wake.

Within minutes a six-by-eight-foot space had been cleared into the collapsed area, and Superman slowed for just a moment, pacing out a small area. He bent down, running his index finger back and forth across the concrete floor, scoring out a new seam a half-inch deep. Then he thrust his fingers down into the slab and wrenched it up. A four-by-four-foot section of the floor flipped up and over as though it were hinged.

The Man of Steel jumped feet first down into the new opening. A squeal of delight echoed from below ground and a little voice cried out: "Daddy, it's Superman!"

Within moments the caped man arose from the hole with two small children in his arms. "They're all down here. They're all alive." He handed the youngsters to rescue workers and went back for more.

CHAPTER 4

The Gathering Storm

Six miles up over the coast of the Pacific Northwest, a bright green flare streaked down from the heavens like a verdant comet. At its center, surrounded by a protective energy field, the Green Lantern plunged earthward at three times the speed of sound. A lean, lanky figure dressed in black and green, the masked man had one thought on his mind as he skirted the West Coast: *I'm gonna be late. Real late!*

"Green Lantern?" The voice came from the glowing emerald ring on his right hand, but its true source originated thousands of miles away at the JLA Watchtower. "Where are you?"

The Lantern spoke into his ring. "G.L. here, Atom. I'm about thirty thousand feet above Coos Bay, Oregon, heading north by northwest. And, yeah, I know I undershot the trajectory a little. But I'll make up the time, I swear. I'll be in Alaska in minutes."

"Don't worry about that. You're actually just about

where I need you to be." The ring grew silent for just a moment before the Atom continued. "Yes, I'm tracking you now. Divert from your present course. Turn west twenty degrees and maintain your current speed."

"All right, if you say so. Just where am I supposed to be going?"

"Latitude, fifty degrees north—longitude, one hundred thirty degrees, forty minutes west."

"Okay, I can do that." As Green Lantern sped out over the ocean, he channeled his willpower through his power ring. Vivid green energy flowed from the band's gemstone, utilizing data transmitted from Global Positioning System satellites to create a navigational map that showed his current location, flight path, and destination. "Wait a minute! Are you kidding me? There's nothing in that spot but ocean."

"Let's hope so."

"What am I supposed to do out there?"

"Catch a wave, surfer boy." There was a hint of a smile in the Atom's voice. "You're going to catch a wave."

A hemisphere away, in another part of his underground hideaway, Adam stood before an entire wall of video images. There were no tapestries or marble columns in this room; it was lavish only in electronic equipment. The wall he faced held four rows of six large screens, and a control console at waist level showed six smaller displays. The images themselves were of varying quality, from the graininess of streaming webcam video to the sharp digital clarity of commercial network feeds. Across the top of the array were aerial views of the northern Pacific rim from various surveillance satellites. But at the moment, the screen that most held his attention was a cable news feed.

"Our top story this hour: Citizens in Anchorage, Alaska, continue to dig out—with help from the Justice League of America—after the major earthquake that hit that city in the early morning hours. For more on the story, we go to correspondent Michael Braun."

The screen cut from the news anchorwoman to an aerial shot of a city street. Large fissures were clearly visible in the pavement and cars were strewn about as though they were toys, dropped there by a careless child.

"Ellen, nearly a quarter million people in this region were literally shaken awake this morning. And no one here has gotten much sleep since."

The scene changed, showing a man with a hard hat helping a woman climb out through the sunroof of a car that had fallen into a hole in the pavement.

"The ranks of police, fire, emergency, and civil defense workers have been reinforced by scores of local volunteers . . ."

The screen cut to shaky footage—identified as coming from a viewer's camcorder—of Wonder Woman in flight. The Amazon carried a fire hose slung over her shoulder as she directed a stream of water into the smoldering fire of an industrial plant.

". . . and a special task force from the Justice League. Wonder Woman, Manhunter, the Flash—"

Another cut filled the screen with a much clearer

image—this one credited to Anchorage's GBS affili-
ate—of Superman. The Man of Steel emerged from
the portal he had dug in the side of a shattered building, his broad shoulders supporting a teenage boy
and a middle-aged woman.

"—and Superman have been credited with saving
dozens of lives and raising the spirits of local residents. Damages due to the quake are estimated to be
well over a billion dollars, and area hospitals are approaching their capacity to treat the injured. But thus
far there have been no reported fatalities—"

Adam muted the news feed, drumming his fingers
impatiently on the edge of the console. *The earthquake
attracted the League, just as I surmised. With their
strongest members in one area, this will provide the perfect
field test.* Once again, the Western Hemisphere's super
heroes were coming to the rescue, bringing hope to
those common mortals. *With their great powers, they
make it look so easy. It is no wonder that the rabble admire
them, even worship them.* Adam weighed the metal rod
in his hand, grasping it like a scepter. *But even the 'heroes' are not all-powerful. There is power that not even they
can overcome. Would that I could wield it myself!*

He turned away from the screens as two of his underlings approached. Both were dressed in the green
hooded coverall and amber sash of their order. Both
stopped at a respectful distance and bowed deeply
before him.

"A thousand pardons, Sahib."

"Well?" Adam's brow furrowed. "Report!"

The underlings dropped to their knees, their palms

pressed together in supplication. The one on the left spoke first.

"All is proceeding precisely as you ordered, Most Holy One. The initiate you call Brother Mark has been placed within the Power Chamber." The speaker touched his hands and forehead to the floor and the second underling continued.

"Energy feed lines have been attached and tested, as have the uplinks. All that remains is the initiate's linkage." The second one joined his fellow in embracing the floor.

"Good. I am pleased."

The first underling rose slightly. "Shall we complete the linkage then?"

"Did I bid you to speak further, worm?" Adam swung a foot out sharply, kicking the man in the side of the head, knocking him unconscious. The bearded man loomed over the second underling who cowered in silence. "Take him and bind his mouth. He is not to eat, drink, or speak for a full day. Is that clear?"

"Most clear, Sahib. Your will be done."

"Now be gone. I shall attend to the final linkage myself."

As the subordinate rushed to comply, Adam swept across the room. On the far side of the chamber sat a large cylindrical capsule—eight feet long and four feet in diameter—mounted to a frame that held it tilted up at a forty-five degree angle.

Adam waved his hand over the capsule and the top third of it swung back to reveal a quiescent figure. The encapsulated man reclined on a layer of foam molded to the contours of his back. His arms lay loosely at his sides. From the gentle rise and fall of his chest, he appeared to be sleeping.

"Mark, can you hear me?" In contrast to the harsh tones he had used with his underlings, Adam's voice was gentle, his manner solicitous.

"Yes. I hear you." The response was low and drawn out, as if spoken in slow motion.

Adam nodded. "You are now in Stage One, about to enter Stage Two." He reached in and pulled two sensor pads from within the sides of the capsule, placing them on his new recruit's temples. "We are almost there, Mark." Adam slipped the focusing rod into a special slot in the lid of the capsule and sealed it shut.

He took a step back, picked up a wireless headset from a shelf beside the capsule, and whispered into its microphone. "Can you still hear me?"

"Yes."

"Good." Adam returned to his control console. He adjusted the display, transferring an enhanced satellite image of Anchorage and the Cook Inlet to the center screen. The smaller screens on the console now displayed several views of the capsule's interior. With a glance, Adam confirmed that the satellite image was also being projected into the capsule. "You are now in Stage Two. I want you to concentrate on the image before you. Do you see it?"

Mark's eyelids fluttered, his eyes moving rapidly beneath them. "I see it."

"That's very good." Adam's voice flowed through the capsule like a soothing wave. "Clear your mind of all concerns. I want you to hold on to that image and build upon it. Concentrate. Concentrate . . . and visualize . . . a storm."

Across the chamber, the capsule began to glow.

Far out over the Pacific Ocean, Green Lantern spiraled down toward his target area.

"All right, I'm descending to five hundred feet. Explain to me again what I'm supposed to be doing out here."

His ring again spoke with the Atom's voice. "You're going to try to stop a tsunami. Based on the seismic data gathered from today's quake, our computers have calculated the force of the wave and its most likely path. The idea is to intercept it out at sea and wear it down before it can hit the coast of northern California."

"Okay, I've got that. But are you sure of your data? The ocean looks pretty calm to me. No sign of any waves that big."

"There wouldn't be. Tsunamis are open-ocean waves triggered when seismic activity—in this case, the Alaskan quake—generates large-scale motion along the ocean floor. They don't rise as waves until they run up against a coastline—or something like it."

The Lantern came to a dead stop in midair. "So what you're saying is, if I fake a coastline—"

"—you'll get a wave. A big wave! But you'll have to sink the barrier all the way to the ocean floor. Otherwise the tsunami will just roll right under it. Think you can handle that?"

"I'm willing to give it a shot."

"Then you'd better do it fast." There was a new urgency in the Atom's tone. "My calculations say the wave will pass through there in less than five minutes."

"I'm on it." The Lantern stared down into the ocean depths. "Let's see, we need something solid. Like a big reef. Or a barrier island. Yeah . . ."

Energy began streaming from the Lantern's power ring, breaking through the surface of the water, down to the bottom of the sea. Putting his imagination to work, he willed the energy to spread wide, forming an impenetrable field. Through the force of his will, the field grew, thrusting up into the air like green mountains.

In less than a minute, he built an entire island out of glowing green energy, complete with a pier, a beach, and swaying palm trees.

"Not bad." Green Lantern flew low over the "island," surveying his handiwork. "Get a load of this, Atom." He used his ring to create a flying video camera, beaming an image to the Watchtower. "Call the cruise lines, we're open for business."

"Very artful. But the important thing is that it stands up to the wave. And to do the job, it needs to be at least fifty-five feet above sea level."

"Don't worry, it is. Give me a little credit." Green Lantern landed on the highest peak of his creation, the camera following him. "Anyway, I'm still not convinced this tsunami of yours is really coming. Aside from my island, the ocean doesn't look any different."

"Be patient, G.L. If we've done this right, you should notice something in five . . . four . . . three . . ."

"Wait, I think I see—" Just a hundred feet north of the artificial island, the sea began to rise.

"Oh, man." A wall of water came rushing toward him, growing taller with each second. Before it had covered half the distance, it was twenty feet tall. Then thirty.

"Oh, *man!*" Green Lantern's ring blazed brighter, a glowing force-sphere forming around him.

The next instant, a forty-foot-high tsunami slammed into Green Lantern and his island at hundreds of miles per hour.

On the monitor screens in the Justice League's orbital headquarters, the ring-transmitted video image broke apart into thousands of pixels.

"Lantern!" The Atom boosted the power to his transmitter. "Kyle, do you read me?"

A signal came back. It sounded like a human voice, but it was very faint.

"Green Lantern? Repeat that."

"I said, 'I did it!' Woo-hoo!" The video transmission blinked back onto the Watchtower monitor: The waters were subsiding around the Lantern's construct as he leaped into the air, sending fireworks streaming from his power ring. "You should have seen it, Doc! It was great! Look, everything I made is still standing, even the palms!"

"So I see." The Atom let out a long breath. "Good work. I always knew—Eh? What's *this?*"

"What's what?"

"That's not right." The Atom stared at an adjacent monitor that showed a flashing red warning indicator.

"That's not right at all." Crimson-gloved hands flew across a keypad, calling up and correlating data with what he was getting on this screen. "These readings don't make any sense."

"Atom? You there? What's going on?"

"I'm not sure. But something new is definitely being added to the mix. And I think things just got a whole lot worse."

Superman crisscrossed the east side of Anchorage, shoring up buildings and rescuing people as quickly as dispatch could direct him. He had just finished handing off a grateful shopkeeper to the paramedics when the transceiver buzzed in his ear.

"Su-erman, -ome in."

"Atom? Is that you? I can hardly hear you over the static."

"Atmos-eric inter-ance. –ave a -mergency!"

"Yes, we're dealing with the emergencies. We've had pretty good luck so far, but—"

"No! We –re up –gainst a—*new* em—gency! -ig *storm!*"

"You're breaking up. What's that about a storm?"

One last unintelligible burst of static came over the transceiver. There was a moment of eerie silence, and then a gigantic bolt of lightning split the sky, followed by a deafening crack of thunder. Superman turned to see the blue skies rapidly turning dark. Giant thunderheads were forming overhead, seemingly boiling up from out of nowhere.

A ghastly howl arose, filling the air. Superman

stared at the sky in disbelief. He had grown up on the Great Plains of Kansas, and he thought that he'd seen it all when it came to storm fronts. But this was something new. *I didn't think it was possible for a storm to gather this fast!*

Gale-force winds blew in out of the southwest, churning up the waters of the Cook Inlet. In seconds, massive waves began slamming into the docks at the Port of Anchorage, threatening to smash them from their pilings.

Superman started for the waterfront, but as the clouds opened up and the rain hammered down, visibility quickly dropped to just a few yards. Between the driving rain and the chilling gale, even the infrared images of surrounding buildings began to blur before the Man of Tomorrow's eyes. *This is getting weirder by the second. These raindrops hit like hailstones, the wind is driving them so hard.*

As Superman neared the docks, the gale eased a fraction. He was just heaving a sigh of relief when the rain suddenly redoubled in ferocity and a powerful gust of wind, as sudden as a bolt of lightning, struck him sideways, unexpectedly, lifting him up and hurling him into the side of a building.

Superman wasn't hurt, but the impact briefly knocked the wind out of him, and that was startling enough. He grabbed hold of a building ledge and hung there a moment in shocked disbelief, catching his breath. This storm wasn't just big, it was massive.

Then, faintly, over the roar of the wind, he heard a voice echoing in his mind.

"Superman?"

The Man of Steel closed his eyes and concentrated on that voice. *I 'hear' you, J'onn. Where are you?*

"*I estimate less than a mile from your current location. Radio communication is down, so I took the liberty of playing 'switchboard.' *"

Good idea. How bad is it inland?

"*Not nearly as bad as where you are. Almost everyone has found safe shelter already, and we are helping those few who have not.*"

Good. Superman peered out through slitted eyes. If anything, the storm was worsening over the inlet. *I have to take care of something out in the harbor.*

Superman took a deep breath and kicked off from the building, launching himself back out into the storm. Flying low over the churning waves, he made his way to a breakwater weakened by the earthquake. Driven by the storm, water poured through a fissure, undermining the protective barrier.

Digging in with his feet, Superman stood tall against the churning waves, shouldering one huge boulder after another back into place in the breakwater. The boulders held, but the waves of the Cook Inlet beyond the barrier continued to build, surging over the rock wall, pounding hard against the Man of Steel.

Kicking off from the breakwater, Superman soared high above the punishing surf, surveying the rest of the harbor. He said a small prayer of thanks that no one was out on those waters. *At least the rain is finally slacking off some.*

The gale was another story. Just staying in place

against those gusts was a struggle, even now that he was prepared for them. Feeling humbled, he turned away from the wind. *J'onn, any luck?*

"*Some. Wonder Woman is with me, and the Flash has evacuated everyone from the port district. The city's Emergency Response Authority confirms that they have moved everyone back from the immediate vicinity to shelters farther inland.*"

Superman looked down and saw a red blur sweeping back and forth along the waterfront. *Yes, I can see Wally from here.*

The Flash seemed to be in constant motion—nailing up plywood over windows, snagging flying debris, and laying down a wall of sandbags just inside the docks.

Superman swooped low over the growing barrier, hauling another dozen sandbags with him. "Good work, Flash."

"Hey, thanks, big guy. Let's hope it— Look out!"

A massive lightning bolt arced down into Superman, striking him square in the back. His sandbags went flying and he himself dropped from the sky like a load of bricks.

"Superman!" Flash was under him in an instant, breaking his fall, easing him to the pavement. "Are you—?"

"I'll live." The Man of Steel sat up, rubbing the small of his back. "That bolt was . . . surprisingly strong."

"Yeah, and it was like it had your name on it." The Flash offered him a hand up. "I could see it coming, but I couldn't do anything about it. If you'd been on the ground, I could have pulled you out of the way, but—"

"It's all right, Wally." Superman scrambled to his feet. *J'onn, can you link us all together? We need you all on the waterfront, ASAP.*

"It is done."

Wonder Woman's voice sounded in the Man of Steel's head: *We're already en route.*

Okay . . . Superman turned to scoop up the sandbags he'd dropped. *We obviously face a whole new set of problems. Any ideas?*

"It is conceivable that I could expand to a size large enough to shelter the immediate area with my body. But in order to increase my density enough to do any good, I would have to draw so much mass from the surrounding terrain that I might well trigger more aftershocks. That would be too grave a risk."

For you as well as for Anchorage, J'onn. Superman started tossing bags onto the wall. *I can't imagine that kind of strain doing you much good.*

Expansion, huh? The Flash moved along the wall, reinforcing it on the run. *Hey, Wonder Woman, your plane can morph into all kinds of shapes. Could it—?*

No, Flash. If necessary, I would sacrifice the plane to save lives, but it cannot expand enough to shield an entire city. There are limits even to its exotic technology.

No one has to sacrifice anything, Diana. Superman stared up into sky and started to grin. *I believe the cavalry has just arrived.*

CHAPTER 5

United

In the stormy skies over Anchorage, Green Lantern willed himself forward against the wind, the emerald light of his ring shielding him from rain and lightning.

"G.L. calling the Justice League! Is anybody out there? Flash? Superman? Can you hear me?"

A telepathic voice answered: *"Superman and the Flash are holding back flood waters in the port district. Wonder Woman and I are working our way there."*

"Oh, uh—hi, J.J." Green Lantern turned west toward the harbor. "Yeah, I see them now." He stopped, reflexively throwing up an arm as a cluster of flying shingles splintered against his ring-aura. "Man! First an earthquake, and now this unreal storm. Talk about bad luck! Someone must really not like the people around here."

Superman's thoughts came across J'onn's telepathic relay: *Kyle, we need to shelter as much of the city as possible. How big a protective barrier can your ring create?*

The Lantern grinned. "Let's find out."

Gathering his will, Green Lantern faced into the storm and thrust out his right arm. The glowing ring on his second finger brightened in intensity, and a beam of emerald energy blasted from its gemstone. The energy stream widened, mushrooming against the force of the storm, until it had transformed into a gigantic umbrella, nearly a quarter of a mile across.

Superman, Wonder Woman, and the Manhunter flew up alongside Green Lantern, joining him just as his energy construct fully opened.

"Not bad, huh?" He willed the emerald umbrella to spin slowly.

Don't get cute! The Flash's thought shot across the mental relay. *This isn't* Singin' in the Rain, *and you're no Gene Kelly.* Far below the flying Leaguers, the Flash again became a scarlet blur, adding to and reinforcing his wall with another layer of sandbags, as even higher waves smashed against it. *And your big umbrella isn't helping* me *a whole lot.*

Superman looked at the Lantern. "Flash is right. We need something that can hold back the bay."

"No problem. If I can stand up to a tsunami, I ought to be able to handle this." Kyle's brow furrowed above his mask, and his energy construct began to expand and turn outward. At the direction of his will, the umbrella transformed into a great bulwark plunging down below the surface of the inlet. Its upper reaches curved back over the heart of the city, deflecting the force of the storm away from the areas most ravaged by the earthquake. In minutes, the barrier stretched for miles to either side of him.

Along the waterfront, the Flash skidded to a stop and stared up at the great green wall. *I see it, but I don't believe it. Where'd you ever find the juice to whip up something like this, Beavis?*

Overhead, Kyle answered his teammate's thought with a hoarse laugh through clenched teeth. *Never underestimate the will of a Green Lantern, Butt-head.*

Lightning played across the stormward side of the bulwark, throwing off dazzling bursts of white light where it hit.

Green Lantern grabbed his right forearm with his left hand, as if to steady it.

"Kyle? Are you all right?"

"Who, me, Princess? Like I said, no problem. I really did stop a tsunami in mid ocean, not half an hour ago. After something like that, what's a little wind and rain?" But despite his boast, the strain was already starting to show on the young Green Lantern's face.

"Kyle . . ."

"Okay, I'll be honest. This is no little storm." Sweat began running down around the edges of his mask. "In fact, keeping this shield up is starting to be a major pain."

Superman drew closer to the Emerald Warrior. "You're not in this alone, Lantern. How can we help?"

"Not sure." The muscles around Kyle's jaw were beginning to tighten. "Wish I could sit down."

"That's easily taken care of." With a thought, Wonder Woman brought her plane to her side. Its canopy slid open and the pilot's seat flew free of the cockpit and over to Green Lantern, morphing under him to form a contour fitting. "How's this?" An armrest extruded from the right side of the chair, giving additional support to his ring hand.

"Great fit. But what's holding it up?"

"Graviton propulsion."

"I'll take your word for it, Princess." Kyle settled back into the chair. "It does feel good." He allowed himself to relax for a moment.

Instantly, several ominous cracks began to form in the bulwark.

"Yow!" Kyle sat bolt upright in the chair. *Jeez, Rayner, keep it together. Think harder.* The cracks closed over. "That's better. Sorry, folks. My bad."

"Maintaining so huge a construct is clearly a strain. Perhaps if we added our wills to yours?"

"Nice idea, Eminem, but I don't think that'll do me any good. The ring's keyed to work for me and me only."

Superman looked out over the vast expanse of the bulwark. "What if we physically supported your wall? Would that help?"

Green Lantern thought for a moment. "It might. If you could diffuse the support somehow."

Superman shot a look at Wonder Woman. "Diana, could your plane—?"

"That, it can do." Diana gazed at her shimmering craft and it flew toward the bulwark, expanding and reshaping itself in response to her mental command.

In seconds, it morphed into a gleaming latticework that extended over nearly two-thirds of the green energy construct. "Come on, boys, let's do it."

Superman, Wonder Woman, and the Manhunter flew to the new support structure. The Man of Steel took up a position in the middle of the lattice, with Diana and J'onn flanking him, each of them about a half mile to either side.

As one, the three strongest members of the Justice League flew steadily against the latticework. Green Lantern could feel the weight of the storm begin to ease ever so slightly.

"Nuts! I'm not sitting this out." The Flash raced back and forth at the foot of the bulwark. His arms spun like windmills as he whipped up a wave of compressed air, adding his own support to Green Lantern's energy wall.

Five minutes ticked by.

Ten.

Fifteen.

Twenty.

Through it all, his teammates showed no visible signs of tiring, but Green Lantern was starting to see spots before his eyes. *That tsunami was tough, but at least it didn't last that long. This storm feels like it's never going to end!* He dearly wished that he'd gotten more than four hours of sleep the night before. *But I can't fail them now. Not after all this!*

And then, the skies began to lighten.

The relentless pounding of wind, rain, and wave against the emerald bulwark began to dissipate.

Guys? Green Lantern's thought sounded a hopeful note over the relay. *I think it may be over.*

The Flash urged caution: *Watch out, this could just be the eye of the hurricane.*

But the clouds continued to break apart. The sun shone through. And as suddenly as it had blown in, the storm was gone and all was calm again.

In his capsule, Mark awoke from a trance-like sleep. The first thing he noticed was a slight ache, like a pinched feeling at his temples. He blinked and looked around him, a bit disoriented by the golden light that seemed to ripple over the curved walls surrounding him. As the top of the capsule swung open, Mark raised his arms from his sides, stretching them up over his head. He brought his hands down in front of his face, staring at them as if seeing them for the first time.

"It worked." Mark looked up at Adam, who was leaning over him. "It worked, didn't it? I could feel the storm."

Adam nodded, removing the sensor pads from the other man's head. "Yes, Mark. It all went according to plan, just as I knew it would. But, tell me, how do you feel now?"

"Now?" Mark appeared slightly confused by the question. "You mean this very minute? Good. Great. No, incredible! Thank you, Adam! I never knew the power could feel like that. It was such a . . . such a total rush!" He tried to sit up, but fell back into the contoured foam.

"Whoa, sorry. Felt a little light-headed for a sec."

"I know." Adam lay a light, restraining hand on Mark's chest. "You'll want to take things a bit easy now. Wielding that much energy will take a lot out of you at first. But you'll find that it will get easier and easier with each mission."

"I'm sure it will." Mark shook his head slowly, awed. "I owe it all to you, Adam—you and your training. Made me see my full potential . . . for the first time. Training made it all happen." He ran a hand over the inner edge of the capsule. "Helped me get over my claustrophobia, too. I used to hate confinement. That's why I kept breaking out of jail—couldn't stand being locked up in those tiny cells. But now . . . I don't mind being sealed away in here at all. In fact . . . I kind of like it."

"Yes, yes." Adam's voice assumed a soothing, rhythmic tone. "It all becomes easier, doesn't it? Easier . . . as time . . . drifts by . . ."

"Yeah." Mark tried unsuccessfully to stifle a yawn. "There'll be a lot of missions. Won't there, Sahib?"

"Yes, Mark. Many, many missions. But now you must rest."

Mark nodded, and a hydraulic system in the supporting framework slowly raised the foot of his capsule. By the time it was fully horizontal, he was sound sleep.

Adam checked the sleeping man's vital signs, then closed the capsule around him. He crossed the room, activating a switch on the control console, and a wall slipped into place, sealing the capsule away. Then

Adam again turned his attention to the wall of video displays. A flickering webcam image now showed clear skies over the skyline of the Anchorage area, but none of the cable news stations had issued any updates.

One of the small displays on the console lit up. The signal briefly rolled and a green-hooded underling appeared on the screen.

Adam pressed a button under the screen. "Report."

The underling's head bowed obsequiously. "Most Holy One, preliminary readings indicate that the storm's duration was approximately forty-five minutes. At peak, its winds were in excess of one hundred and fifty miles per hour. Property damage from the storm itself remains to be determined. There were some injuries, but no apparent loss of life, thanks to the speedy intervention of the Justice League."

"Of course." Adam nodded. "I would have expected no less from them."

"Sahib?" The on-screen underling appeared confused by the tacit approval in his master's voice.

"Have our people in Anchorage continue to monitor the situation. They are to pay special attention to the activities of the Justice League."

"Your will be done."

The underling signed off, and Adam stood in silence before the muted screens. The League presented the most serious challenge to his plans. He had struck at them with the fury of the storm—and, united, they had withstood its power. But individually they could be worn down, weakened. Just as the mountain is eaten away by the wind and the rain. And even acting together, they could not be everywhere.

"Yes . . . there will be many, many missions."

Just after five o'clock local time, at the end of a very long day, Superman stood alone atop the Alaska Communications Systems Building in downtown Anchorage. Communications and city services were back up and running, and state and local authorities had things under control. The Man of Steel glanced down at the streets below, then looked out toward the horizon.

The distant mountains stood out in sharp relief in the clean, dry air. Seeing them now, it seemed hard to believe that visibility had been so low—even for him—just a few hours before.

Superman took a slow turn around the rooftop, looking out over the panorama of the sprawling city. As he walked, he kept one hand cupped around his transceiver.

"—And that's where things stand now, Atom. I'll file a more complete report later."

"Thanks, Superman." The Atom's signal once again came through crisp and clear. "Wish I could have given you all more warning, but that storm just appeared out of nowhere. Anything else I can do for you?"

"As a matter of fact, there is, Ray—thanks for asking. Can you patch me through to the Metropolis phone net over our secure line? I need to make a couple of private calls. . . ."

*   *   *

"Most Holy One, we have a possible situation." The hooded man, senior among Adam's followers, was already on his knees before his master.

"A situation? Explain."

"We have reason to believe that six containers of chemicals, shipped through secondary subcontractors in the Himalayas, have been tracked by the Batman."

Adam's response came not as a question but a statement. "The Batman." His voice grew cold. "Who allowed this to happen?"

"Sahib, none of the faithful betrayed your trust. Our operatives report that the Batman was in Bhutran on another matter, hunting down a party who supplied illicit drugs to criminal organizations in Gotham City." The underling cowered on the floor before him. "They now believe that during his investigation he discovered our containers as they sat waiting on a shipping dock. It was just an unfortunate happenstance."

"I do not believe in 'happenstance.' I believe in synchronicity. When did the Batman become involved?"

"Uncertain, Sahib. Perhaps as long as . . . as a week ago."

"A week?" He spat out the words as though they were a curse. "And this is just now being reported?"

"Forgive me, Most Holy One. Please understand that the Bhutran connection is but a hypothesis. The containers were shipped last week by air to our own facility in the Cape Verde Islands." Sweat poured out from under the man's hood. "By pure chance, a spot review of archived security camera footage turned up a single fleeting image. Computer enhancement and analysis indicates that the image is indeed that of the Batman. This was confirmed just seconds ago, Sahib."

"So. He made his way into the Cape Verde base—and back out?"

The subordinate's head bobbed nervously. "Yes, Sahib. The entire island has been locked down and scoured. He is no longer there."

Adam clasped his hands behind him, clenching his doubled fists until the knuckles whitened, seeking pain to counter his anger. *And if the Bhutran hypothesis is correct, then the detective followed six containers nearly a third of the way around the world.* "These containers? Where are they now?"

"On a freighter bound for the Antilles."

"I assume this freighter is one of ours?"

"Yes, Sahib. The ship's captain and crew are all believers. At our direction, they have searched their vessel most thoroughly. The Batman is not aboard."

"That does not matter. If the containers have drawn his notice, then he is even now tracking that ship. The Batman can be a most persistent foe." Adam grew silent, stroking his beard. "Chemicals, you say."

"Yes, Sahib. The containers and the rest of the freighter's cargo are all earmarked for Operation New Dawn."

"Earmarked, but not essential."

The underling swallowed hard. "No, Sahib. The freighter and its cargo are expendable."

"Then perhaps the Batman will soon be a problem no longer."

No sooner had Superman signed off than a gust of air shot up the side of the ACS Building. It was a crimson wind.

"There you are! We've been looking all over for you, big guy." The Flash circled the rooftop twice to slow down, calling over the edge of the building: "He's up here, checking out the sights." The speedster didn't brake to a complete halt until he was just three feet from the Man of Steel. "Say, I'm not interrupting anything, am I?"

"Not at the moment." Superman put his transceiver away. "I was just wrapping up some personal business."

"Sorry, Superman. I didn't realize . . ."

"It's all right, Wally. No harm done."

"Even so, I should've knocked or something."

"Hey, S-Man!" Green Lantern crested the roof, followed closely by Wonder Woman and the Manhunter. "You're missing another great feed. People just keep adding to the spread that the city laid out for the rescue workers." As they landed, he gently elbowed the Martian. "I thought we'd never pull Green-Genes here away from the desserts."

J'onn shrugged. "There were cookies. Chocolate."

Wonder Woman raised an eyebrow in the Lantern's direction. "I didn't see you passing up any seconds, Kyle." She handed a small brown bag over to Superman. "I brought you some sandwiches and coffee."

"Thanks, Diana." As he dug into the bag, his nostrils picked up a pleasant, if unexpected, scent. "Do I smell peppermint?"

"It's the shampoo." The Amazon shook out her thick, dark mane. "Even after all that rain, the chemical smell from the fire was still lingering in my hair. Hera bless the YWCA for allowing me the use of their showers."

Green Lantern exchanged a glance with the Flash. "Now there's an image—"

The speedster grinned and whispered back: "Keep those thoughts clean, Ringo!"

Kyle reddened. "I meant the image of the goddess Hera blessing the Young Women's Christian Association!"

"Sure you did."

Superman finished his first sandwich and took a long sip of coffee. "Well, I think we all did a great job today under battlefield conditions." He paused to swirl the liquid in his cup. "Does anyone have any opinions about the strangeness of today's events?"

"Just that I hope we never have to deal with two major emergencies like that again." The Flash leaned against an elevator housing, stretching out his hamstrings. "Not back-to-back, anyway. That was brutal!"

Wonder Woman nodded. "The sudden change in weather *was* strange, wasn't it? It was . . . capricious, like the act of a mad god."

"You would have more experience in such matters than we, Diana." The Manhunter then eyed the Man of Steel. "What are you suggesting, Superman? It is an unusual coincidence that one natural disaster should so quickly follow another . . ."

"But *was* it just a coincidence, J'onn? And was the storm truly natural?" Superman crumpled the sandwich wrappers and stuffed them back into the bag. "The earthquake showed all the normal seismic markers, and the tsunami was a natural after-effect. But I've never seen a storm like that before. And according to the Atom, neither have the weather services. Not only was it sudden and intense, it was more or less confined to this municipality. Outlying areas were virtually unaffected. It was as if the gales were directed right at us."

The Amazon raised an eyebrow. "You think there was a guiding hand behind it?"

"I don't know." Superman wadded the bag into a tiny ball. "Maybe."

"I don't believe this. You can't be serious!" Green Lantern stopped himself and shifted his feet. "Uh, what I mean is, that . . . that was a full-fledged hurricane. Or typhoon. Or whatever they call 'em in this part of the world. You can't just whip up something that powerful out of nothing. I can't, even with my power ring. I mean, I've never tried, but I don't think—"

"What G.L. is struggling to say"—the Flash moved in to back up his teammate—"is that he doubts there's anyone who *could* have caused that storm. Sure, I've fought guys who can make it snow indoors, but none of them have the power to generate a storm *that* big."

Superman drained his coffee and dropped the compacted bag into the paper cup. "I just think that we should consider the possibility."

The Martian nodded. "We certainly should not dismiss it out of hand. I propose that I return to the Watchtower. With the Atom's assistance, I can use our scanning systems to determine if there were any indications of weather manipulation."

"That is an excellent idea, J'onn. But in that case, I should go along and relieve the Atom from monitor duty." Wonder Woman swept an arm to the north, and her robot plane rose to roof height. "May I offer you a ride?"

The Manhunter inclined his head toward her, bowing slightly from the waist. "I would be honored to accept."

"If there's nothing else, we should be off." Diana lifted her hand, and the plane began flowing toward her and the Martian. In less than a minute, it had re-formed around them into a compact, transparent spacecraft. Just before it sealed shut, Diana smiled at her three remaining teammates and gave a little wave. "Later, boys!"

Then, the dartlike craft shot straight up into the sky. In seconds it was gone from human sight.

"There she goes, calling us 'boys' again."

"Doesn't bother me, Kyle." The Flash winked at the Man of Steel. "Does it bother you?"

"Never has." Superman wore his best poker face.

"There, you see, Kyle? Superman and I both feel secure in our manhood. You should really work on overcoming those feelings of inadequacy. I hear they sap the will."

Green Lantern shook his head. "I should know better by now than to give you any kind of straight line."

"Just another example of why I'm called the Fastest Man Alive. 'But I just wanna tell ya . . .'"

"Superman, help! Save me from the Fastest *Mouth* Alive."

"Sorry, Kyle. You're on your own."

"Yeah, relax, artist-boy. I only kid because I love. And because it's so easy." Flash threw an arm over the Lantern's shoulder. "Why so tense? Oh, I know! You're probably in a hurry to get back to your Caribbean getaway."

"Getaway? I wish!" Green Lantern threw up his hands. "I was down in San Maltese working on some promotional brochures for their tourist board. That whole trip was sold to me as a working vacation, but it turned out to be a lot more work than fun. The most I saw of the beach was from a window, and half the time it was raining! I had just finished up when I got the Atom's call." Kyle glanced off into the distance. "Right about now, I could use a *real* break. Something to . . . recharge the old batteries." He stopped and pointed off to the north. "Hey, isn't that Mount McKinley?"

Superman nodded. "Tallest peak in North America."

"Sweet. I've always loved mountains." He took a few steps back, looking again from a different angle. "Great vistas. Be nice to add it to my portfolio."

The Flash barked a laugh. "Listen to this. The great artist complains about one job, then tries to give himself more work."

"Hey, sketching isn't work. At least, it doesn't have to be. And I did make enough cash from that stupid brochure job to afford a little downtime. Yeah, I think I'll hang out around here for a while, take in some of the sights. Maybe help rebuild some roads."

"Suit yourself, slick." The Flash slapped his right hand into Green Lantern's. "Just stay in touch, you hear? Never know when we might need you and your magic ring."

"No problemo, man." Kyle's hand tightened around his teammate's.

"Wally's right, Kyle." Superman put a hand on the Lantern's shoulder. "We couldn't have done it here without you."

"Thanks, I . . ." Kyle's face reddened slightly around the edges of his mask. "I'm just sorry I was so late this afternoon. I mean, this morning. You ever need me, I'll be there!" A glowing green aura poured out of his ring and the Green Lantern lifted off. He paused fifteen feet over the rooftop and called back: "That's a promise!" Then, he turned away and headed north toward Mount Whitney.

"Take it easy!" The Flash waved after him. "What a character."

Superman looked thoughtful. "Wally, did I ever do anything to make Kyle . . . uneasy?"

"Uneasy?"

"Not during missions. In the heat of action, he's fine. But sometimes—like just now—he seems a little nervous around me."

"Well, sure. Kyle and I may be about the same age,

but I've been doing this since I was a kid. He hasn't had his power ring all that long. Once he's had a chance to really hang out with us, the problem should fix itself. But for now, as far as he's concerned, you're the pro and he's the rookie."

"You think I intimidate him?"

"Look, sometimes *I* intimidate him. And *you* are Superman, after all. You know—faster than a speeding bullet, more powerful than a locomotive? I've known you a lot longer than Kyle has, and you still intimidate *me* sometimes."

"I don't mean to."

"Oh, I know you don't *mean* to. You're not Batman, after all."

Superman looked askance for a moment, then slowly began to chuckle. "Thanks, Wally. I think."

"Hey, it's our problem, not yours. For what it's worth, I don't think you intimidate Diana or J'onn. And probably not Batman, but who knows for sure what the Bat thinks."

"I have a pretty good idea on that score. And I'm sorry we don't hang out more, but . . ."

"But you're Superman. I understand. You probably have the least free time of any of us." The Flash snapped his fingers. "Tell you what, big guy, if you want some hang time . . . It's a long road back to the Lower 48. What do you say we hit it together, just you and me?"

"You mean, run back?" Superman rubbed his chin. "Okay, why not? Be a nice change of pace. Are you ready to go?"

"More or less. You wouldn't mind a little detour along the way, would you?"

"I suppose not. What did you have in mind?"

The Flash glanced off toward the west. "I want to check out a little place called the Valley of Ten Thousand Smokes."

CHAPTER 6

Out on the Road Again

"Did you say the Valley of Ten Thousand Smokes?" The Man of Tomorrow stared at his teammate in surprise. "Why do you want to go there?"

"My Uncle Barry told me about the place, and I always wanted to see it. He said that was where he and the rest of the original Justice League first met you . . . back when *he* was the Flash, and I was just a punk kid." The Flash grew uncommonly solemn. "One of the League's earliest missions ended there. According to Barry, that probably would've been their *last* mission, if you hadn't come along."

"Well," Superman cleared his throat, "the valley *is* where we all first crossed paths. But the last part may be a bit of an exaggeration."

"I don't think so. I never knew Barry to stretch the truth." The Flash broke into a grin. "But I'm willing to hear your side of the story. How about it, big guy?"

"You may not believe this—"

"Try me."

"I was thinking of that day just this morning. On my way here. J'onn picked up on it, too."

"There, you see? Great minds still think alike. How could we not—?"

Superman stopped him. "You *do* realize that the valley is at least three hundred miles west of here?"

"Oh, yeah. And that's *so* out of our way." The Flash rolled his eyes. "Three hundred miles—we could cover that distance in the time it takes to argue about it."

"Do you know how to get there from here?"

"Uh, not really. I was hoping you remembered the way."

"All right. But the terrain in the valley is a little rugged, even for someone as surefooted as you are. Maybe I should give you a lift."

The Flash clicked his heels together and snapped off an exaggerated salute. "I'd be proud to fly with you, sir. Can I get a window seat?"

"Don't worry about that." Superman threw an arm around the Flash, gripping the speedster firmly just under his shoulders. "On Air Superman, they're *all* window seats!"

With a single bound, Superman rocketed into the sky and shot southwestward. In a matter of minutes, they had traversed the Cook Inlet and were over the mountains of the Katmai National Park. The Man of Tomorrow slowed, skirting a series of steaming, glacier-capped volcanoes, before dropping down into the valley.

The Flash craned his neck, looking all around as they slowly flew over gorges and canyons streaked with layers of vivid oranges and reds. "You know, Kyle is the real nut for sightseeing, but I have to admit, this place is amazing. Check out those colors!"

Superman nodded. "The whole area is a geological treasure trove. The biggest volcanic eruption of the twentieth century took place here, when the Novarupta volcano blew back in 1912."

"Novarupta? You're making that up."

"I'm serious. The eruption was at least ten times bigger than Mount Saint Helens—some say hundreds of times bigger. It darkened the skies over most of the Northern Hemisphere. This valley is the end result of that."

"Wow. And that's why they call it Ten Thousand Smokes?"

"No, that name came from the thousands of smoking fumaroles that dotted the valley."

"*Fumaroles?!* You've *gotta* be making that up."

"Steam vents. They've mostly cooled since then. But there are still over a half-dozen active volcanoes in the area."

Flash shifted around and caught his eye. "How do you *know* all this stuff?"

"I hiked the whole area once, when I was about nineteen. Got the story from a park ranger."

"You *hiked* it?"

"I saw a lot of the world that way in my younger days." Superman shot him a grin. "What, did you think I was born wearing this cape?"

"Actually, I'd never given it that much thought."

"Most people haven't." He came to a stop, his feet six inches off the ground, and took a step down onto the valley floor. "But here is the area you're most interested in."

They stood on a lonely plain in the middle of the vast valley. The Flash slowly paced around the area, taking his time for once. "So this is where it happened?"

"Your uncle was right about where you're now standing, when I first spotted the League . . . fighting one another. Not their fault, of course—they were being manipulated by Xotar. Barry told you about him, I suppose?"

"Xotar? Some self-styled weapons master from the future, wasn't he? Thought he was pretty hot stuff, traveling back in time to field-test his super-weapons against the League. Yeah, Barry said that he played with their heads."

"Which I figured out, once I saw his robot. It lurched out from behind that ridge." Superman pointed to a rocky outcropping. "It was a big one, roughly humanoid in configuration, and it glistened like gold. Would have been about twenty feet tall, standing erect, but it moved stooped over, like a big metal gorilla.

"I couldn't believe that none of the Leaguers saw the robot, it was so huge. But they paid no attention to it at all. They were so intent on attacking one another.

"Then I saw a faint ripple of energy, just beyond the visible light spectrum, coming from a turret mounted in the robot's midsection. So, I looked inside—"

"You looked—? Oh, right!" Flash smacked his forehead. "X-ray vision."

"And there, hidden away in the robot's chest, was this weird little man hunched over a control panel. I knew that he had to be behind the craziness."

"Right." The Flash grinned. "And that's when you came to the rescue. Just your entrance alone made the League stop fighting."

"My entrance?"

"Yeah, you . . . well . . . granted, I wasn't there, but Barry said it was really something. Don't forget, Xotar's ray cannon was beaming illusions directly into the Leaguers' brains. He made them think that this valley was on another planet, and made them see their teammates as hostile alien monsters. That's why they were clobbering one another. And when you came diving out of the sky, they saw you as this big honkin' eagle. The sight stopped them all in their tracks. Even Barry."

"That I didn't notice. I was focused on the cannon. I didn't know if it could affect me or not, but I wasn't taking any chances. I stayed out of range until my heat vision melted the turret. Then I was able to take more direct action."

" 'Direct'? Is that what you call it?" Wally hooted. "The way Barry told it, you slammed into Xotar's robot like a runaway locomotive, only more powerful. He said that you drove it into the ground, ripped through its metal hull, and gutted it with your bare hands—and in under a minute!"

Superman thought for a moment. "That's probably about right. I wasn't timing myself."

"Trust me. From the moment you slagged the cannon—and the illusions stopped—to your cornering Xotar in the wreck of his robot, it was no more than fifty-seven seconds, tops. Barry was always *very* good at estimating elapsed time."

"He was certainly good about explaining Xotar to me. I just about had my hands on that little warlord wannabe when he vanished on me." The Man of Steel's hands clenched into fists. "I didn't know what had happened. There was no sign of Xotar anywhere. I thought he'd escaped justice, until the Flash and Green Lantern—I mean, until Barry and Hal set me straight." Superman bit his tongue. "Sorry, Wally."

"Hey, it's okay. I still think of them as the Flash and Green Lantern, too." Wally bent down and scooped up a handful of dirt. "They were good men, Superman—great men. Barry . . . he was the best mentor a hyperactive kid like me could ever have hoped for. That's why I wanted to come here." He let the dirt trickle out from between his gloved fingers. "They once stood here—both of them. To me, this is hallowed ground."

"I understand."

For a full minute, Superman and the Flash stood side by side, heads bowed in silence, remembering. Barry Allen had been the Flash and Hal Jordan the Green Lantern when the League was founded. Both were gone now. Each had sacrificed himself in the line of duty. And each had left behind a great legacy.

After Barry's death, his nephew and protégé Wally

West had taken on the mantle of the Flash. Still later, young Kyle Rayner had been chosen by an ancient alien being to carry on the tradition of the Green Lantern.

Wally finally turned to Superman. "Thanks for bringing me here."

"Thanks for talking me into it." The Man of Tomorrow clapped his friend on the shoulder. "Was there anything else about that day you wanted to know?"

"Oh, I can think of a few hundred things, but what do you say we talk on the way home? I can run and talk at the same time. And I can listen, too—despite what Kyle might tell you. Really."

"Sure, let's go."

In less than a minute, they reached the rocky shores of the Shelikof Strait.

"Wally, when you talked about the long road home, I thought we'd be cutting across the Yukon and British Columbia."

"Nah, I saw northern Canada on the way here. Besides, it's more fun to run across water."

"For *you* maybe."

"Hey, you treated me to a free tour of the valley. It's only fair that I return the favor. C'mon, run with me along the bank and I'll show you a little trick."

Superman looked dubious but took up the challenge. After their third lap, Wally suddenly spun around and started running backward. "Okay, big guy, now gimme five!"

As Superman's hand made contact with the Flash's,

a crackle of energy erupted around the two men, and the Man of Steel felt a sudden surge of power.

"What—?"

"Don't ask. Just follow me!"

The Flash turned and shot out over the strait, moving so fast that his boots barely skimmed the surface of the water. And to his amazement, Superman found himself racing across the waves, keeping perfect pace with the Scarlet Speedster. The two teammates rounded Afognak Island and sped southeast across the Gulf of Alaska.

As they headed out into the North Pacific, Superman looked again at his hand, marveling at the miniature lightning display that rippled between his fingers. "I've never felt anything like this before. Is this . . .?"

"Just a little taste of the Speed Force." Wally grinned. "It's a sort of universal energy that all us Flashy-types tap into."

"I know, you've talked about it before, but how did you—?"

"Over the years, I've learned how to transfer a little bit of it to objects in motion. The effect is temporary, though, so don't get too used to it."

Hundreds of miles whizzed by as Superman settled into the rhythm. "Amazing. And you're not even breathing hard. You're nowhere near your top speed, are you, Wally?"

The Flash shook his head. "'Fraid not."

"And people think *I'm* fast!"

"You *are*, compared to them. I'm just faster. It's my

specialty. But listen, getting back to Barry and Hal, you said they set you straight about Xotar."

"Ah, yes. Hal used his power ring to trace him through a deviation in the quantum field. It turns out that Xotar really *was* from the future—the one hundred twentieth century, as a matter of fact. Evidently, he had some sort of fail-safe device that returned him to his point of origin—and directly into the hands of the police in his own time."

"Hah! That's great. I'm going to have to read the file reports on that. All I'd remembered about that part of the story was Barry saying that 'justice was done' or something."

"And he was right." Superman gazed off into the distance. "Look out, obstacle dead ahead."

"Huh? Where do you see—?"

About a mile ahead of them the ocean began to swell up. They easily avoided the swell, circling around it to watch as a thirty-foot humpback whale broke the surface. To the runners it was as though the giant cetacean erupted from the surf in slow motion. They continued to circle, watching until the whale rose completely up out of the water, before turning and streaking away.

"Nice call." Wally glanced back at the airborne whale. "Being able to see way below the surface must be one handy power."

"It is, but I *heard* Moby back there long before I saw him. Whale songs have an amazing range, but a lot of it is subsonic."

"Yeah? Aquaman has said much the same thing.

Couldn't prove it by me." With one last glance at the whale, the Flash turned back to his teammate. "So, what was it like for you, meeting the League for the first time?"

"It was great! They were all such very different people, but there they were, united, working together for the common good. It was inspiring. The JLA founders were an impressive bunch."

"I can imagine. You know, I was just in my teens when I became a Flash-in-training, and working with Barry was a dream. But every time I met one of his teammates, it just about blew me away. If more than two of them were around, I felt like a kid being allowed to party with the grown-ups. I wish I could have been there that day to see all of you together. That must have been legendary."

"It was also a little embarrassing. With Xotar's threat over and introductions made, the others gathered around me, as if they thought I could impart some great wisdom on how to be a 'super hero.' "

"Well . . .?"

"Well, what?"

"Did you?"

"Wally, I hadn't been on the job that much longer than the rest of them. Come to think of it, the Manhunter must have had more experience, working in secret all those years."

"Oh, sure, he had tons more experience . . . *working in secret!* J'onn spent entire decades in one disguise or another. That isn't being a public figure. And would he ever have gone public in anything near his true form if you hadn't set such a good example?" The Flash shook his head. "I don't think so. And before you object— yes, I know that J'onn still does a lot of undercover work. But now, it's mainly because he *wants* to, not because he feels he *has* to. He enjoys that whole cloak-and-dagger scene. Bottom line, you made the world safe for big strong guys from other planets."

"Hmm. J'onn said something to me just this morning, about how my public debut changed everything."

"And he was right. Face it, big guy—you da man! Superman sets the standard that we're all judged against."

"I know. But I've never liked that. We're all individuals. We should be judged by what we can accomplish with what we have."

"And you've accomplished more than any of us. You know, Barry always thought the world of you. I think you impressed him more than anyone he ever met."

"I hope I'll always be worthy of that confidence. Barry impressed me. He was a fine man, Wally—and far too modest about his own accomplishments."

"Hey, tell me about it. But you're just as bad. What *is* it with your generation?"

"My generation?!" Superman looked askance at the speedster. "I'm not *that* much older than you, tenderfoot."

"Whatever you say, pappy." The Flash shot him a grin before turning serious. "One thing I was never completely clear on . . . as I understand it, on the day you all met, Barry nominated you for membership in the League."

"Yes, he did."

"But you turned him down. What was up with that?"

"It seemed the wisest move at the time. As I said, I hadn't been Superman all that long, and I was still getting used to the idea of being a public figure myself. Just being Superman can be a full-time job. I wasn't sure I could do that, be a member of the League, and still have a private life. There are times when I still wonder."

"I think we all do," said Wally. "In a way, it's kind of reassuring to hear you say that. I always thought you could handle anything."

"A common misconception—seemingly held by all but my biggest enemies." Superman grinned wryly. "At any rate, the founding members of the League were pretty well organized. I let them know that they could count on me for help, if they were ever in a real bind. But I never thought they needed me around as a regular member."

"And yet—Whoops! The mainland's coming up fast." Just ahead of them, the rocky coast of northern California filled the horizon, rushing closer with each second. "Get ready, Superman—here's where I reclaim the lightning."

Their boots touched solid ground, and the Man of Tomorrow could feel the Speed Force drain away from him.

*   *   *

A continent away, a sleek eighty-foot catamaran sailed out into the waters of the Atlantic Ocean forty miles off the eastern coast of Trinidad. Three-hundred-horsepower diesel engines in each of the twin hulls hummed, propelling the craft swiftly through the waves.

Within the ship's vast cockpit, a tall, dark-haired man stood at the wheel. He was a handsome man. The movers and shakers of the financial world would have instantly recognized his blue eyes and strong features as those of Bruce Wayne.

Wayne was old money. Born to wealth, he remained the principle stockholder of the multinational conglomerate Wayne Enterprises. Some knew him as the founder of the philanthropic Wayne Foundation. More knew him only as a face on the society pages, yet another billionaire playboy who could be expected to crash and burn before he turned forty.

Few knew that he led a double life.

Tonight, Wayne's attention was riveted on two monitors before him. One showed a night-vision view of the open sea ahead of the craft. The other displayed a digital chart of the ocean, showing a telltale point of light.

At the rear of the cabin a distinguished, slightly acerbic voice echoed up from belowdecks. "I do wish you'd allowed me to stock the provisions for this excursion, sir." The voice was closely followed by a lean, balding figure. Between thumb and forefinger, he held a sealed packet. "The only thing in the galley besides fruit and bottled water is a large crate of these . . . MREs?"

"Meals Ready to Eat, Alfred."

The tips of Alfred Pennyworth's mustache drooped and he heaved a world-weary sigh. "Ready to Eat, perhaps. But Meals? I think not." He tossed the packet forward.

Wayne plucked the ration out of midair. "Sorry, but we had to move quickly. There wasn't time to gather anything but the basics. At any rate, I'm starting to believe that this won't be a long voyage."

"Let us hope not." The old family retainer joined his employer at the wheel. "What is the current location of our prey?"

"Take a look." Wayne pointed to the stationary light on the display monitor. "That's the global positioning signal from the freighter that set out from the Cape Verde Islands last week. They haven't moved in the past hour."

"They've stopped?"

"Dead in the water and right near the edge of the continental shelf. It's not too deep at their location. I think they've dropped anchor."

"Why do you suppose they've stopped out there?"

"I don't know. But something is up. Perhaps they're awaiting a rendezvous."

Alfred checked the display. "With whom? There are no other ships in the immediate area."

"No one with an active GPS transponder. But a ship without a transponder, or one running with it turned off as we currently are, or a submarine—the possibilities are endless."

"And I'm sure you've considered all of them."

"I try to." Wayne throttled down the engines. "I think this is close enough. I'd like to keep the horizon between this ship and the target." He hit a release switch, and the catamaran's anchor began its descent to the ocean floor. "Are my working clothes ready?"

"I have them laid out for you below."

Wayne clapped the older man on the back. "Then, let's get to work."

Alfred followed him belowdecks, waiting respectfully outside the door of the master stateroom while his employer changed. "If you don't mind my saying, sir, you've expended a great deal of time and energy tracking these containers across the globe. That's a lot of effort for what—a shipment of poisonous chemicals?"

"Components of a highly toxic compound, Alfred, derived from the venom of a particular elapid snake. But it's not so much what is in the containers as where they may be bound. After all, many such substances are used in legitimate scientific research."

"But you do not believe that is the case in this instance."

"No. I do not." Wayne stepped from his stateroom, dressed in a close-fitting dark gray bodysuit. Black boots reached from toe to mid-calf. Black trunks covered his lower torso, and a wide, pouched belt was cinched around his waist. Across his chest stretched the stylized silhouette of a bat. "The labeling on those containers linked them to an Asian company that is a front organization for the Order of Nulla Pambu, one of the deadliest cults I've ever faced."

Alfred repressed a shudder. "*That* lot? Mad as hatters, every one of them, and all under the sway of an absolute sociopath."

"Yes. I was sorely tempted to destroy those components, rather than let them fall into his hands. But that would have gotten the Order's attention too soon." Wayne pulled on a pair of black gloves. "And that fanatic has eluded me for too long. So, I let the poison pass unadulterated, risking that I could track him down and stop him before he gets a chance to use it."

"And what is one more risk in your life? You're so good at finding new ones to take."

"Life is all about taking risks, Alfred." The younger man pulled a black horned mask into place over his head, and suddenly Bruce Wayne was gone—replaced by the Batman. The dark figure stood differently, every muscle like coiled steel, ready to spring. Even his voice changed, becoming a harsh rasp. "I seem to recall you telling me that years ago."

"And of all the pieces of advice I've given over the years, *that* had to be the one you didn't ignore." The old gentleman's gentleman breathed a heavy sigh. "No cape tonight, sir?"

"No room, Alfred. It'll be tight quarters in my runabout." The Batman flipped a series of switches on the underside of a counter, and a section of decking slid aside, revealing a small one-man submersible.

As the Dark Knight popped the tiny craft's canopy, Alfred switched on a remote monitor and double-checked the GPS readings. "Still no movement from the freighter. I do wish you'd let me bring the catamaran in a little closer. They wouldn't see us running dark."

"Negative. If they're at all alert, they'd pick up the cat's engines on sonar, and I'd rather not announce my presence until I know more of what they're up to."

"But the submersible—"

"It's specially designed for silent running. If anything shows up on their scopes, it'll appear as nothing more than a school of fish."

Alfred drew himself up as tall as he could. "It also has just barely enough air in its tanks to get you there and back."

"I know." Batman clapped him on the shoulder. "That's why you're along. If something goes wrong, I'll whistle and you can come pick me up."

As Superman and the Flash raced up and over the rocky shoals north of Point Arena, California, the speedster obligingly cut his pace in half. In seconds, the two shot through the Redwood Empire and raced south into the San Joaquin Valley.

Five miles west of Modesto, the Flash picked up the conversation. "So as I was about to say—here you are today, a card-carrying member in good standing of the Justice League. Mind if I ask what made you reconsider?"

"Times changed. The League changed. The Manhunter is the only one of the founding members still active in the current team. The Black Canary left the active roster some time ago; Aquaman, more recently.

Think about it, Wally—how many different people have been part of the League at one time or another?"

"Beats me! There'd been a couple dozen by the time I joined. And I lost count after that. Now that I think of it, *I* joined before *you* did—as a regular member, I mean. What's wrong with that picture?"

"And how many deaths have there been among the membership?"

"Too many." Flash grew somber. "At least a half dozen."

The two Leaguers sprinted on through the passes of the Sierra Nevada mountains in silence, thinking of old friends and allies. A hundred miles passed before the Man of Steel again spoke.

"Maybe if I'd been a member of the League then, things would have turned out differently."

"Hey, you don't know that. I don't care if you *are* Superman, you can't take on the responsibilities of the whole world."

"The responsibility comes with the job, Wally—you know that. We're more than just super-powered individuals. Every time we put on these outfits, we become symbols of hope to everyone around us. But when we're in the Justice League, we're not alone— we're part of a community. I think that is why I joined the team. Because you're right. We . . . people like us . . . can't do it all."

The Flash nearly missed a step, but recovered instantly. '*People like us . . .*' He couldn't believe that Superman was putting them both on an equal footing. "No. No, we can't. But I want you to know—"

The Man of Steel put a finger to his lips. He seemed to be listening intently.

"What do you hear?

"Siren." Superman stared off into the darkness. "Looks like the beginnings of a high-speed chase about seven miles to the south."

The Flash grinned. "Shall we?"

"After you."

Twilight was giving way to night as a dinged and dented late-model pickup truck roared up Route 95, five miles north of Goldfield, Nevada. In the driver's seat, Orrin Skinner sat gripping the wheel, his foot jamming the gas pedal to the floor. On the passenger's seat beside him sat five cartons of cigarettes, several six-packs of beer, and a plastic bag holding one hundred forty-seven dollars in small bills and rolls of coins, all taken just fifteen minutes before from a twenty-four hour LexOil mini-mart at Scotty's Junction. Four cans from an open six-pack, drained and crumpled, rattled around on the floorboard.

Orrin tried to keep his eyes on the road as he nervously lit up a smoke, but he kept glancing back to his rearview mirror. When his truck cleared a rise, the mirror caught a glimmer of distant flashing red lights.

"Damn! Thought I'd lost 'im!"

"No. No, in fact, I think he's gaining on you."

Orrin coughed, spitting his cigarette up over the wheel and onto the dashboard. His head jerked to the left, and through the open window he saw a masked man, all in red, pull alongside his truck. On foot!

Orrin looked over at his speedometer. The indicator was just ticking past one hundred ten miles per hour.

"A hundred and ten? Tsk-tsk. You know, maintaining a speed like that isn't good for your engine. And I'd buckle that belt, if I were you. What if you had to stop suddenly?"

Orrin hit the brakes, and the man in red shot past him. His truck fishtailed as he fought to bring it under control. It veered off the side of the road and headed out across open country, slowing more as it bounced over the uneven ground.

"Now, you see, that's just bad for your suspension. Don't you agree, Superman?"

"Absolutely, Flash."

Orrin's head shot left and then right. Not only was the masked runner keeping pace with him again, but Superman—Superman!—now flew alongside his truck. That was too much for Orrin. He hit the brakes hard.

The pickup truck skidded to a halt, its wheels plowing a deep furrow in the dirt. Dust billowed around the cab as Orrin stumbled out, his hands raised high. "I give up! I give up! Please, don't hurt me!"

"Just keep those hands where we can see them, Chuckles." Flash gingerly pulled a small pistol from Skinner's right front pocket. "Now what have we here?"

"I-It ain't loaded. Honest!"

Superman stared intently at the gun, then nodded to the Flash. "No bullets."

"I wouldn't really shoot nobody. I swear!"

"No, you wouldn't shoot anyone—you just like to rob people." Superman pulled a long jack handle from behind the driver's seat. "Hands behind you now." The handle emitted a low, metallic moan as he bent it around Orrin's wrists. Superman then picked the man up by his belt and placed him in the truck bed. "Just sit tight, and I'll try not to drop you."

Orrin looked confused. *Try not to drop me? But he just set me down in the . . . !* "Omigod!"

Sheriff's Deputy Leroy Newman pulled off into the gravel that bordered Route 95, braking his patrol car to a halt. His high beams shined across skid marks and fresh tracks that led off the shoulder and into the darkness. "Dammit, he's gone off road."

Newman was just thumbing his radio to call the dispatcher when he saw a pair of headlights headed his way—about twenty feet off the ground. The startled deputy swung his searchlight up into the sky, and there he saw the Man of Steel carrying a pickup truck on his shoulders.

Superman landed just ten feet in front of the patrol car, setting the truck down along the side of the road. As Newman ran up to meet him, the caped man hoisted Orrin Skinner out of the back of the truck. "Deputy, I believe this is the man you were looking for."

The Flash hopped out of the truck cab, gesturing to the loot and the gun. "And this should be all the evidence you need to hold him."

Newman nodded. "Been looking for this particular bird for some time." He took Orrin by the arm. "All right, Skinner, you have the right to remain silent—"

"I know, I know! I did it, see? I robbed the mini-mart. Just take me away."

The Flash winked at Superman and dropped his voice an octave, "Well, Tonto, I believe our work here is done."

"Aye, *kemo sabe*."

And before the deputy could say another word, the costumed men vanished into the night.

Newman looked from the bag of loot to Skinner. "Did that just happen the way I think it happened?"

"It wasn't no pipe dream, if that's what you mean." Orrin half-turned in the deputy's grasp and showed Newman his wrists. A jack handle, twisted in a graceful figure eight, bound them tightly together.

The Flash started whistling the *William Tell Overture* as they raced across Utah and entered Colorado. It wasn't until Superman began reciting "A fiery horse with the speed of light—" that the speedster lost the tune and dissolved into laughter.

"Oh, man, was that great! After spending most of the day getting batted around by the elements, it felt so good to apprehend one simple criminal."

Superman smiled. "I know what you mean. There's a lot of satisfaction in stopping someone before they can hurt somebody else. Or themselves."

"Yeah, Chuckles was probably only half a beer and another five miles per hour from rolling that old truck."

Wally shook his head. "If only they could *all* be that easy."

"Yes. . . . Wally, back in Anchorage, you said that you'd fought opponents who could 'make it snow indoors.' "

"Sure have. Guys like Captain Cold and the Weather Wizard. Well, to be accurate, Cold is more of a walking ice machine with an attitude. But the Weather Wizard is the one who really lives up to his name. You name it, and the Wiz can produce it—rain, sleet, snow, or hail. Makes him sound like the Postal Service's arch-enemy, doesn't it? I've even seen him produce miniature tornadoes."

"But nothing like what we encountered today?"

"Oh, no way. The weather patterns that the Wiz can cook up usually cover a building or a few blocks. The biggest thing he ever hit, as far as I know, was a small town in Wyoming—and by small, I mean tiny! I've never run up against a rainmaker with the kind of power we faced today."

"I have—once." Superman frowned. "There was a man who called himself Stratos. But that was years ago. And he brought on his own death."

"Well, then unless his ghost is out and about, we should be able to cross him off the list. Hey, unless I'm mistaken, we've just crossed the Kansas state line."

Stands of corn and wheat whizzed by as Flash and Superman sprinted over the plains. With few obstacles on the flat, wide-open spaces, they shot across the thirty-fourth state in a matter of minutes. Soon the glow of Keystone City appeared on the horizon.

"Yeah!" The Flash pumped a fist into the air. "Almost home."

"Yes . . . almost home . . ."

"We made pretty good time. Say, do you want to stop in for a cup of coffee?"

"Thanks, Wally, but I'd better take a rain check on that. There are a few things I should be doing."

"I hear that. Never any rest for the weary, is there, Superman?" He skidded to a halt on a rolling prairie, and the Man of Steel did likewise. "You know, even with that storm on top of the earthquake and all, this was a good day. A long one, but a good one. Thanks for letting me bend your ear for the last three thousand miles."

"No problem, Wally. I really enjoyed that. And it's important to remember absent friends. We can't live in the past, but it's a bigger mistake to forget it. My father once said, 'You can't tell where you're going, if you don't know where you've been.' "

"Yeah? Your pop sounds all right."

"Yes, he is. I'm very lucky."

"I'll say. My father and I haven't gotten along since . . . well . . . ever, really. That's why Barry was so important to me."

"Wally, knowing your uncle as I did, I think he'd be very proud of you. He left some big boots to fill, but you've done well by him."

"You think?" Wally's cheeks reddened to nearly the shade of his mask. "You know, Wonder Woman said much the same thing to me just a couple of months ago. Coming from you—from both of you—that means a lot."

"I just call 'em as I see 'em, pal." The Man of Steel held out his hand and the Flash shook it.

"Thanks, Superman."

"Thank *you*, Flash."

And then, with a wave, the Flash streaked away toward the distant skyline of Keystone City.

For a moment, Superman stood alone on the prairie, staring after the departing speedster. The League *had* changed a lot over the years. *We were all so young when the team first got started. Except for J'onn, and it's hard to say how old he is.* He liked and respected the Manhunter, but the big Martian still remained something of an enigma.

Of the current membership, the Batman was the nearest to him in age, but in many ways the Dark Knight was even more remote than the Martian Manhunter. *And Diana came from such a different world. But Wally . . . I suppose it's because we both grew up out here on the plains, even though it was a decade later for him. His hometown isn't* that *much bigger than Smallville.*

Superman leaped high into the sky. When he reached an altitude of twelve thousand feet, he stopped and looked back over his shoulder. *All this talk about fathers . . .* He thought back to the unconscious man he'd rescued earlier that day along the road in Alaska—the one who had reminded him so much of his father.

The Man of Steel turned sharply back to the southwest and flew on until he came to a meandering tributary of the Elbow River. He descended to five thousand feet and followed the river toward the twinkling lights of Smallville, then skirted around the west side of town and flew south to Hickory Lane. Diving down beneath the canopy of a grove of trees, he circled around to alight in the shadow of a newly painted barn. A quick glance toward the house with his X-ray vision confirmed that no strangers were in sight. He slipped quickly from the shadows onto the back porch and eased open the screen door.

Superman cut through the big kitchen and passed down the hall to the parlor. He stopped for a moment by a row of bookcases that lined the wall. His parents were both avid readers and had passed their love of books along to him.

The Kent family library was an eclectic collection, holding everything from the collected works of Mark Twain and O. Henry to the latest bestsellers. One set of shelves housed his father's prized collection of Tom Swift books and science fiction pulps, while another held the Nancy Drew and Hardy Boys mysteries that his mother had inherited from a favorite aunt.

Atop one shelf was a framed copy of *The Paradoxical Commandments*. Superman smiled. He had been a young boy when Jonathan Kent had brought this copy home. He remembered helping his father make the frame. "Words to live by, Clark," Jonathan had said, as he'd ticked off the ten simple rules for facing life's adversity. "There will always be people who put you down, despite the good you do. Whenever that happens, just keep doing it anyway." *That's still good advice, Pa.*

The caped man walked on, running his fingers along the familiar shelves. *I must have read every one of these at least once. It's probably why I wound up writing for a living.* Near the end of the hall, something new caught his eye and he paused before six books that sat apart from the others, framed by bookends, as if in a place of honor. Each bore the author's name, Clark Kent, on the spine. *Ma's rearranged a few things since my last visit.*

He stuck his head into the parlor and rapped gently on the doorframe.

Jonathan Kent lowered his newspaper at the sound, and his wife Martha looked up from her laptop.

"Clark!"

"Hi, folks. Not interrupting anything, am I?"

"Not at all, dear! I was just checking my e-mail." Martha closed the little computer and got to her feet. "Jonathan, I told you I heard the back door open."

"You should listen to her, Pa. Her hearing's almost as good as mine."

"Better than mine, that's for certain. How are you, son?"

"Can't complain. Well, I could, but it wouldn't do any good."

"Oh, you! You're as bad as your father. But it's so good to see you."

"Yes, well, I was in the area, so I thought I'd drop by and see how my two favorite people in the whole world were doing."

"We're both in the pink, son. Got my cholesterol levels down to 150—and, of course, your ma gets prettier every day."

"Jonny Kent, if you think that your line of malarkey will get you an extra slice of pie—!"

"Pie?" Superman glanced from his father to his mother. "There's pie in the house?"

"Black raspberry, dear." Martha tilted her head at Superman and peered over her reading glasses at him. "Have you eaten at all today?"

"Oh, sure. The good people of Anchorage fed me quite well. But I'd never turn down a slice of black raspberry pie, especially tonight. I had a good all-terrain run this evening."

"I see. Well, we have plenty of cold roast beef in the fridge, too. If you'd like some of that, I'll heat it up for you."

"Now don't go to a lot of trouble, Ma. I know you two eat early."

"Nonsense, it's no trouble at all." Martha took her son by the elbow and steered him back down the hall toward the kitchen. "It'll take no more than a minute or two in the microwave."

Jonathan fell in close behind. "And I'll put a pot of coffee on."

Superman allowed his mother to lead him to the kitchen table, but when she pulled the roast from the refrigerator, he held up a hand. "You don't need to bother with the microwave, Ma." He tapped the side of his face near the corner of one eye. "Remember?"

"Oh. Yes, I guess that would be faster." Martha brought the roast over to the table, carved off two generous slices, and set them on a plate in front of him.

Superman stared intently at the plate. The air rippled a bit under his gaze as he projected beams of radiant heat from his eyes. In moments, the kitchen filled with the rich aroma of hot roast beef.

Jonathan finished filling the coffee maker and took a long, deep breath. "Ah, that sure does smell good." He looked at his wife a bit wistfully. "Martha . . . ?"

"Oh, all right. Another slice or two won't hurt your diet."

The three gathered around the kitchen table, Jonathan setting out plates, cups, and flatware, and Martha breaking out bread and condiments, while their son warmed the main dish. Soon they were all talking and laughing between bites.

"How is Lois, dear?"

"She's good, Ma. Busy, of course. She's been on the political beat lately."

"Well, I hope you're finding some time for yourselves." Martha leaned over and kissed her son on the cheek. "I thank the stars that you and Lois finally came to your senses and got married."

"Came to our senses . . . ?"

"Oh, as if you didn't know! You two used to get along like cats and dogs, even though you were both smitten with each other from the very day you met."

"It was Superman that Lois was 'smitten' with, Ma. She saw Clark Kent as nothing more than competition . . . at first. Fortunate, really. Otherwise, I'm sure she would have seen right through my disguise."

"The important thing is that you were in love with each other. She's all you ever talked about. And it seemed to take ages for you to get together."

"At least my double identity isn't coming between us anymore."

"Thank heavens for that." Martha smiled. "You two had the loveliest ceremony."

"Yeah, I'll second that, son. Most fun I ever had at a wedding that wasn't my own. Hey, do you and Lois have any plans for your anniversary? It's coming up fast!"

"Thanks for the reminder, Pa. I should try to surprise her with something special." Superman got up from the table. "More coffee, anyone?"

"Let me do that, dear."

"I can get it, Ma. You're not my waitress, you know." He shared a private wink with Jonathan.

"Well, we appreciate your stopping by after putting in such a busy day. Thank you, Clark, just half a cup." Martha added a little milk to her coffee, as Superman filled Jonathan's mug. "I saw on the cable news how you and your super friends were helping all those poor souls in Alaska after the earthquake—and that horrible storm!"

"Yep." Jonathan blew across the top of his cup and set it down to finish cooling. "That surely was a strange spell of weather. But then, this has been a year for odd weather. There was a late snow just a few weeks ago down in the Texas panhandle. Haven't seen such extremes in weather since back when you were born." He shook his head and took off his glasses to polish them with his handkerchief.

Superman sipped his coffee, thinking of the many times he'd seen his father perform that ritual, and of how Jonathan had changed over the years. *He's gotten older, but not old, thank God.* He thought again of the man in Alaska. *Hope he can bounce back as well as Pa did.*

The elder Kent had made a full recovery from a heart attack he had suffered a few years before, and was clearly taking better care of himself these days. *He's a good fifteen pounds thinner than he was before the attack. He may grouse about the dieting, but he's stayed with it.*

Jonathan slipped his glasses back on. "Eh? What are you grinning about now?"

"Nothing in particular. It's just so good to see the two of you." Superman turned to Martha. "Now, I believe you said something about pie?"

One hour and two large slabs of black raspberry pie (with a side of ice cream) later, Superman kissed his parents good-bye, gave them one final wave, and leaped away from the steps of their back porch. Rocketing straight up into the sky, he leveled out at about eight thousand feet and again turned eastward.

Superman soon left the plains of Kansas far behind him. But as he soared over the green hills of the Ozarks, his thoughts lingered on his family. *Pa looked good. Ma, too. They both look ten years younger than their actual ages. I hope they can stay healthy for a good long time. . . .*

As the Man of Tomorrow neared the Mississippi River, he focused all his senses on the mighty waterway, half expecting a hurricane or waterspout to emerge out of nowhere. All was quiet, but he still looked back over his shoulder as he crossed southern Illinois into Kentucky. He shook his head. *When I start feeling that paranoid, I* know *it's time to go home!*

CHAPTER 7

Home is the Sailor

It was just an hour after midnight when Superman returned to Metropolis. It was a moonless night, but unseasonably cool, and the lights of the great city illuminated an ethereal fog wafting in off the harbor, creating an ambient glow that could be seen for miles in any direction.

Superman picked up speed as he descended over downtown. Within moments, invisible to the human eye, he swooped low over a grand old apartment building at 1938 Sullivan Place, and silently dropped down an all-but-forgotten airshaft.

The shaft was the relic of an earlier, less air-conditioned era, and the windows that had once linked the building's apartments to it had been bricked over decades ago. But the Man of Steel had done a little work on the shaft since one particular newlywed couple had moved to the building. As he hovered in the cover of the shaft, one brick yielded to his touch and a secret passage swung open, admitting him to a darkened apartment on the upper floor.

Superman padded silently down the hall, his boots barely touching the fine old hardwood floors. Halfway down the corridor, he suddenly met another, equally silent figure. The second figure first circled the Man of Steel, then arched its back as it rubbed up against his boots, nudging its head against his shins. Superman paused, reaching down to scratch a furry head between its ears.

"Hi, Elroy. How's the mighty hunter tonight?" His whispered greeting was answered with a soft purr. Superman glanced through the adjacent walls into the kitchen. "I believe there's food in your bowl. Might even be tuna." Elroy's ears pricked up at the sound of "tuna," and he bounded away into the darkness.

Superman continued down the hall to where a pale light outlined the edges of a door left slightly ajar. He pushed the door inward to find Lois Lane propped up in bed by two huge overstuffed pillows. The late edition of the *Daily Planet* lay scattered on the floor where it had fallen from her side of the king-sized bed.

Lois was wearing an extra-extra-large *Daily Planet* T-shirt as a nightshirt and was dozing by the light of the television. On the screen, Humphrey Bogart was telling Ingrid Bergman that the problems of two little people didn't amount to a hill of beans. Superman stood stock-still for a minute, just watching Lois's breath rise and fall.

I am so lucky to have found you. He knelt down beside the bed and kissed her lightly on the forehead. Lois's eyes fluttered. "Mmm." She craned her head up and kissed him full on the lips. Her right hand came up, cupping his jaw, and he lay his hand gently atop hers. As they broke off the kiss, she let her hand trail down to his chest and began tracing over the bold S insignia with her index finger.

"Why, Superman!" A mischievous grin arched the corners of her mouth. "What would my husband say?" She glanced over at the empty spot on the bed beside her and made a game of looking under the pillows and covers. "Clark? Now where is that darned husband of mine, anyway? Don't tell me he's out working late again?"

Superman stood up and assumed a mien of mock solemnity. "I'll see if I can find him, Ms. Lane."

He crossed the room and entered a big, walk-in closet. Superman ran a finger along the underside of a shelf and the back wall slid to one side, revealing a smaller, hidden alcove.

Superman changed clothes literally in the blink of an eye. One instant he was standing there in his familiar blue and red costume, and the next he was in his bare feet, wearing nothing more than a simple pair of gray cotton gym shorts. He set his boots far in the back of the secret alcove and draped the cape and suit over special racks, tucking them away neatly before sealing the wall shut. Then he slid the hangered garments back into place and let his hands fall to his side.

The Man of Tomorrow stood with his head slightly bowed, just breathing deeply. Beginning with his neck and shoulders, he first deliberately tensed and then consciously relaxed each muscle group. From head to toe, he let his entire musculoskeletal system loosen up, settle in, and settle down as well.

In less than a minute, the commanding physical presence he projected as the Man of Steel eased into the milder, more comfortable body language of a man of flesh and bone. Even the contours of his face changed. He wasn't slouching by any means—his posture was still excellent (another of the many good habits his parents had instilled in him)—but he now stood several inches shorter and his shoulder span was narrower. *Inspector Turpin is a pretty good judge of height,* he thought suddenly. *Superman really is almost half a head taller than his lookalikes.*

Thinking of Turpin reminded him in turn of the contract killer they had caught. He recalled the outrage of the man who was so upset that a sting operation had been set up to trap someone who was "just" a hitman. It was only the first of several troubling images from the day's work that he deliberately conjured up, and then consciously let go.

After he released the grief and heartache, he happily recalled the day's positive images. He thought of the people that he'd helped, the lives that the Justice League had saved, the bonds he'd shared with friends and family. He remembered all the police and the firefighters; he thought about the ordinary citizens who were willing to dig with their bare hands if necessary, to help rescue total strangers. All those things, he fixed deep in his memory. For all the pain and suffering in the world, there were still a lot of good people out there, and he never wanted to forget that. Perhaps he'd write about it later in his private journal, if not in his newspaper column.

And finally, he thought once again of Lois, knowing that he would soon be with the woman he'd fallen in love with at first sight.

It had become a kind of ritual for him, to clear his head of troubling thoughts and worries. It was how he shed his Superman persona and again became the Kansas farm boy who had grown up and traveled the world as a respected writer and journalist.

He combed a hand back through his hair and squinted in the darkness, tensing certain optic muscles to slightly change the focus of his eyes. He slipped on his wedding band, and then, from long habit, Clark Kent put on his glasses.

"Uh, Lois?" The deep baritone of Superman's voice was gone now, replaced by a friendly, unassuming tenor.

"Well, *there* you are!" Lois stood alongside the bed, arms crossed, tapping one bare foot impatiently. "I haven't seen you all day. In fact, I haven't seen you in *two* whole days! Do you know what time it is?"

"Sorry I'm late, hon." Clark crossed the room, noting that she had used the intervening moments to switch off the television, gather up the scattered sections of the newspaper, and turn back the covers of the bed. "I was off chasing down a big story."

"Oh, I don't doubt that." Lois rested her hands on her hips and thrust her chin out at him. "Always trying to scoop me, aren't you, Kent?"

"Only like this—" He quickly slipped his arms between hers, grabbed her around the waist, and lifted her off the floor in a big bear hug.

"S-S-Stop that!" Lois's mock exasperation broke apart into a cascade of laughter.

"What's that, ma'am? Can't quite hear you for all the giggling." Clark kissed her lightly, first on the right cheek and then the left. "Was there something you wanted me to stop doing?"

"No." She lifted his glasses off the bridge of his nose and wrapped her arms around his shoulders. "Not anymore." Their lips met and held for several minutes.

He finally broke off the kiss, lowering Lois gently to the floor. "Missed you."

"Same here." She set his glasses down on the nightstand. "Let's go to bed, Smallville."

Clark glanced reluctantly toward the bathroom. "I should probably brush my teeth—"

Lois took his hand and pulled him toward her. "That can wait. . . ."

Out in the Atlantic, the tiny, one-man submersible silently drifted beneath a freighter at anchor. As it inched past the anchor chain, a claw-like device popped out from the side of the little craft, grabbing hold of one of the links. As soon as it locked onto the chain, the dark figure of the Batman emerged from the submersible, a slender air tank strapped to his chest.

The Dark Knight kicked off from his craft, following the chain up through the inky waters. He slipped under the keel of the freighter and moved along its hull just below the water level. Finding a cluster of barnacles stuck tightly to the hull, he loosened the straps of his air tank and slipped out of them. He then clamped the tank fast to the barnacles, took one last deep breath, and shut it off.

The Batman's head broke the surface, water sluicing off the horn-like ears of his cowl. He stretched up one hand, gaining purchase on the hull with a gripping pad covered with millions of microscale polyester hairs. Modeled after the feet of the gecko lizard, it held fast as the Dark Knight pulled himself up from the ocean. With similar "gecko pads" in his other hand and fastened to his boots, he quickly made his way up the side of the ship. In minutes, he swung his feet onto the deck of the freighter and disappeared into the shadows beneath an array of booms and cranes.

Two crewmen walked by, passing within inches of the Batman, never guessing he was there. They spoke softly in an obscure dialect of Hindi, and so rapidly that he could catch only every third word. But from that brief snatch of conversation, the Dark Knight could tell that they were nervous about the ship being placed on a high security alert.

Tying off a line, he dropped into the first of the forward cargo holds. Night-vision lenses within his mask clicked into place, and the chamber became as bright as day to him. He quickly surveyed the hold, missing nothing, and moved on.

In the third cargo hold, the Batman finally found

the containers he'd been tracking since Bhutran. He inspected them carefully, poring over every inch with a full-spectrum light from his utility belt until he was satisfied that they'd not been opened or otherwise tampered with since leaving Cape Verde. Then he checked out the rest of the hold's contents. Stowed alongside the venom containers were a series of crates full of clear plastic ovoids, each about the size of a small melon. They looked like toys, like children's playthings, and they looked so out of place that he snapped off a few pictures of the things with a miniature camera.

He had just resealed the crate when the lights came on.

The Batman was momentarily blinded, and caught out in the open as the crewmen flooded into the hold. There was nowhere for him to hide now, and there were six of them.

He leaped at them head-on.

The Batman's left fist dropped the first crewman before the man even had time to scream. The next two fell before his sweeping side kicks, but they bought the others time to pull daggers.

The blades did them no good.

The Dark Knight evaded the first knife-wielder, grabbing the man's wrist, disarming him, and swinging him around into the next one, hard enough to stun both. He then turned and threw the captured dagger hilt-first at the last man, knocking him out.

The Batman barred the door the six had come through and turned back to check on his prey. The man he'd disarmed had lurched to his feet; he stumbled forward directly into the detective's right fist and sank unconscious to the deck. But the other man pushed himself up with one hand, cried out an oath, and clenched his jaw tight before collapsing into convulsions. In an instant, the Batman was at his side, pulling an auto-injector from his utility belt and shooting its contents directly into the spasming man's neck.

His convulsions eased, the crewman looked up and scowled at the Dark Knight. "Your puny serums . . . will not long stay . . . my sacrifice, infidel. My master is ever . . . one step ahead of you. I will . . . tell you nothing. H-hail . . . Naja . . ." And with that, the man slumped to the deck.

For just a moment, the Batman's hands clenched tightly into fists and his lips mouthed a silent curse. Then he turned to the five remaining unconscious men and swiftly relieved them of their own poison pills. A quick search revealed that all of them bore a cryptic cobra-headed tattoo on their left shoulders. He bound and gagged them, then exited the hold.

There was no time to lose. Six men would soon be missed.

The Dark Knight swept through the ship, pausing only to shut down alarms and surveillance systems. One by one the lights winked out belowdecks. The crewmen in his path were rendered unconscious, and a series of gas grenades tossed into vent shafts insured that sleeping crewmen kept on sleeping.

Finally, there were only two left.

He found the captain in the freighter's radio room, angrily berating his first mate. "One hundred men on guard, and not one answers my call! Why? The Master is counting on us, Santosh. Where are they?"

Before the mate could open his mouth to speak, a thrown Batarang knocked him to the deck.

The Batman flung himself at the captain. He stunned the man with a sharp jab to the solar plexus, then gripped him by the throat. Long, powerful fingers reached into the captain's mouth and yanked out an artificial molar whose hollow held another suicide pill.

He shoved the captain into a chair. "You will not greet death so easily."

The captain rubbed his throat, staring up in disbelief at the dark-clad apparition that loomed over him. "You . . . you speak Paskosh-Hindi?"

"I speak many tongues. Now, you will tell me of your master's plans or—"

Behind him, the first mate pulled himself up to the radio console. Holding his breath, he reached for a switch, his hand trembling.

The Dark Knight's sharp ears picked up a soft rustle of movement. He spun on the ball of one foot and dropped the mate with a roundhouse kick.

But not before the man hit the switch.

The captain laughed bitterly. "Too late, 'Bat-man.' You have walked into our trap."

The Batman grabbed the man by the lapels and yanked him up off his feet, glaring at him nose to nose. "If this is a trap, you are caught in it as well.

Your 'master' cannot save you. Your crew cannot save you. Even if you had help waiting just beyond the horizon—and you do not—it would arrive far too late to do you any good." He dropped the man back into the chair. "Now, once again, what is your master planning?"

The captain spat at him. "Your death."

From outside the cabin there came an ominous rumble. The winds began to howl and the freighter's stern swung around. The captain flinched, startled by the abrupt change in conditions, his defiance shaken. The Batman was startled as well, but masked his reaction. He dragged the captain from the radio room and onto the outer deck. A cloudless night sky had given way to a violent storm. Lightning stabbed down into the sea all around them.

"We were told to prepare for the ultimate sacrifice, but I did not realize—!" There was stark terror in the captain's eyes as he struggled to break free of the Batman's hold. "Truly, this must be the work of the Most Holy! No one is beyond his reach, dark one. You can overcome mere men, but you cannot defeat nature!"

A huge wave surged over the deck, slamming into the Batman, tearing his captive from his grasp. The captain thrust out a hand, seizing a stair rail as a second wave smashed the Dark Knight hard against a bulkhead.

The Batman could feel a couple of his ribs crack.

Clutching a cable that hung from a free-swinging boom, he hauled himself painfully to his feet.

The captain scrambled to an upper deck and dropped

to his knees, raising his arms high as if in prayer. "Hail to thee, mighty Naja-Naja, our lord and master! We deliver unto you your enemy." Rain streaked his face as he stared, wide-eyed, into the fury of the storm. "Gladly we sacrifice ourselves to your greater glory. There shall be a New Dawn—!"

A bolt of lightning lanced down from the skies, striking the upper deck and silencing the captain's ravings. So bright was the strike that the Batman had to look away. But for an instant he swore that he could see the man's skeleton, standing black against the blinding light.

Two more massive bolts struck home, and the upper deck and the captain vanished in an awful release of explosive force. The lower decks heaved. In the engine room, gears went off track, grinding to a halt. Fuel lines ruptured.

Through a haze of pain, the Batman clenched the muscles of his jaw and a tiny microphone snaked out of the lining of his mask, stopping close in front of his lips.

"Mayday. Mayday."

He half staggered, half slid to the starboard side as the freighter pitched wildly. "This is a Code A emergency. Do you copy?"

Beneath his cowl was a transceiver that transmitted any reply directly into the mastoid bone, but all that came through was a staticky crackle.

"Repeat—Mayday! Does anyone copy?"

There was another sharp crackle from behind his ear, and snatches of what might have been a human voice, then nothing.

Too much interference from—

Before the Dark Knight could complete the thought, there came an ominous flash from belowdecks as the spilled fuel caught fire. *Time to bail.* Gritting his teeth, he leaped over the side.

The Batman hit the water hard, his broken ribs scraping together. Fighting the pain, he took a deep breath and dove down . . . down. There was no time to retrieve his tank from the hull now. He had to reach the submersible, reach the bigger tanks there.

Behind and above him the fire reached the ship's fuel tanks. There was one gigantic roar, and the freighter blew apart at the seams.

Sixty feet down, the shockwave slammed into the Batman, all but knocking the wind out of him.

And then all went dark, both above and below the waves.

Adam's monitors showed multiple views of a vast section of the Atlantic Ocean, ranging from the equator to the Tropic of Cancer and from mid-ocean to the Gulf of Mexico. But his main attention was on a screen showing a raging storm swirling on the edge of South America's continental shelf.

In the heart of that storm, a global positioning beacon had just shut down.

He cupped his hand around his headset's microphone. "Step back from Stage Two, Mark. Relax. Let the storm die out."

In minutes, the swirling patterns faded from the screen.

Adam punched up new views from two spy satellites and checked a dozen different readings, looking for any signs of the freighter. He could find none. The ship had vanished from the face of the earth.

Smiling, he again cupped the microphone: "Mark?"

Within the capsule, Mark's eyes fluttered. He could hear someone calling his name from far, far away.

"Mark, can you hear me?"

The buzz in his head was stronger this time. But it was too hard to open his eyes. It was so much easier to just drift.

"Mark . . . tell me where you are."

His head lolled slightly to one side. "Here . . . right here, Sahib. . . . I'm in the zone. . . ."

"That's good, Mark. You've done very well. Just stay where you are. We have one more mission today, and then you can rest."

"Whatever . . . you say. . . ."

Adam muted his mike and smiled. The freighter was lost at sea, and the Batman with it. Of that, he was now certain. *And with that accursed detective gone, we should have little trouble dealing with the rest of the Justice League. Yes, despite all their amazing powers, they will be no trouble at all.*

Shortly before dawn, Clark Kent awoke, and his eyes tracked to his left. There, Lois still lay snuggled up close to him, her head resting against his shoulder.

Holding his breath, Clark slowly slipped his shoulder out from under his sleeping wife, gingerly easing her head down onto the pillow. *I could spend the whole morning here, just watching you sleep.* He knew that all was not well with the world, but at moments like this, he felt as though it could be. Clark shifted over on his side, turning toward her, and Lois opened her eyes.

"Sorry, I didn't mean to wake you."

" 'S okay. . . .'Morning, good lookin.' "

"Good morning, beauty."

"Beauty? I wish." Lois pushed herself up into a sitting position and ran a hand through her hair. One stubborn strand kept falling across her face. "I know what I must look like. Classic bed hair, right?"

"You always look good to me."

She smiled. "And you always know the right thing to say."

"I try. I learned from the best, after all."

"Oh? And who would that be?"

"My father, of course. My folks both kept farmer's hours, but there were still a lot of mornings when Ma would be the first one on deck. Especially when she was taking a class at the community college. Pa would find her at the kitchen table, surrounded by books and papers, and he'd always say, 'Martha, how is it that you can get up even earlier than me, and still look so gorgeous?' "

Lois started giggling at Clark's impersonation of his father.

"And then she'd say something like, 'Gorgeous? Oh, please!' and explain how that wasn't possible as she'd barely had time to run a comb through her hair, or whatever. And Pa would tell her that it didn't matter, because she still looked gorgeous to him."

"Oh, that is such a romantic story. Your parents are so sweet. And such a good influence on you."

"Well, eventually. The first time I overheard them carrying on like that, I was mortified. I was just a kid, and I couldn't believe how mushy Pa sounded. I felt so embarrassed for them. And by them."

"Uh-huh. But then you wised up."

"I hope so. It's amazing how much smarter your parents get once you grow up. I mean, I always loved them dearly. But it wasn't until after high school that I realized just how well they worked together. It gave me hope that someday I'd be having the same kinds of conversations with my own wife. And here we are."

"Ooh, now that's even more romantic! I knew there was a reason I married you."

"Only one?"

"Among many." Lois glanced at the clock and frowned. "Do you have to go anywhere?"

"Not just now, no." Clark gently smoothed back her misbehaving hair. "Still, shouldn't you be catching some shut-eye? I can get by on two or three hours a night, but you need your sleep."

"I can rest later." Lois rubbed the last remnants of sleep from her eyes. "Besides, I'm more thirsty than sleepy."

"Shall I bring you a glass of water?"

"Would you? No, wait! How about some orange juice? A big glass would really hit the spot."

Clark momentarily vanished.

Lois blinked as her husband reappeared, handing her a tall tumbler full of the requested juice. She looked from the tumbler to Clark and smiled. "You know, we've been married almost two years, and I'm still not used to that. But I like it."

"I know." Clark slipped back under the covers.

Lois took a long sip. "Mmm, freshly squeezed!"

"Only the best for you."

She finished the juice and set the empty tumbler on her nightstand. "And you're sure you don't have to go?"

Clark paused a moment, listening intently. "Yep. Not so much as a single car alarm in earshot."

"That's good." Lois snuggled back up against her husband. "Because I never did get a chance to ask you how your day went."

"Probably not too much to tell that you don't already know from the wire services. Superman stopped a contract hit in Federal Plaza and apprehended the gunman. Then he flew up to Alaska to join the rest of the Justice League in assisting with emergency rescue from an earthquake." Clark frowned. "And we were just getting things under control when a typhoon—or something like one—blew in, and we had to deal with that." He shrugged. "Aside from stopping a holdup man and assisting some stranded motorists on the way home, that was it for Superman.

"Oh, and I dropped in to check on the folks. They both send their love."

"That's nice. Sounds like your day was busier than

mine." Lois looked at her husband thoughtfully. "Something bothering you?"

"I don't know." Clark's frown deepened. "There's been a lot of crazy weather lately. I know these things come in cycles, but there was something unnatural about how that typhoon struck. It was as if someone had engineered that storm. No one saw it coming—not the National Weather Service, not the Navy forecasters—no one."

"Meteorology isn't an exact science, Clark. They can't catch them all. The important thing is that you and the League were there to deal with it."

"I guess you're right." Clark ran his fingers through her hair. "So, how was your day? I believe you were going down to D.C.?"

"I was, and I did. Interviewed Senator Price about her new oceanic wildlife bill. Stopped by the Pentagon, where I was able to pump some old contacts about the Air Force's planned satellite recovery program. Caught the shuttle back in time to file my stories and catch a late dinner at Dooley's with Fran and Louise." Lois leaned closer, nibbling at his ear. "Then I came home to wait up for my sexy husband. Speaking of whom, how did the *Planet*'s ace reporter spend his day?"

"Who, *moi?*"

"I ask because when Perry White asks about the elusive Mr. Kent, I want to make sure I have my story straight."

"Good point." Clark grinned. "Yours truly managed to temporarily evade the wrath of his editors—I hope—

by leaving a couple of phone messages from the field. I assured all concerned that the new crime exposé was on track and that I'd have my copy in soon."

"And will you?"

"Pending any further catastrophes, I should. The first two installments are already composed up here." He tapped the side of his head, just behind the temple. "And I have rough notes on the rest. At this point, all I need to do is find a few spare minutes to spend at a keyboard."

"A few minutes? Well, thank you, speedy!" Lois playfully punched him in the arm. "When I think of all the thousands of hours I've spent sweating over keyboards—"

"And your writing is all the better for it. Of the two of us, who's received more awards for journalism?"

"All right, I have."

"Uh-huh, and who won an Edgar for her mystery novel?"

"I did."

"Look at it this way, Lois—it takes someone with super-powers just to keep up with you."

"You *always* know the right thing to say."

"Just one of my many gifts."

"Mm-hmm. And you're the gift that keeps on giving." She kissed him full on the lips. "How was I ever so lucky to find you?"

Clark laughed. "I was thinking the same thing about you just a few hours ago. Guess we're both lucky."

"I guess we are." Lois slid back on one elbow, tucking her legs behind her and looking her husband over, as if seeing him for the first time.

"What's wrong, Lois? Do I have something caught between my teeth?"

"No. Nothing. You simply fascinate me. That's all."

"I do?" Clark leaned back against the headboard, letting his pillow slide to the small of his back. He smiled shyly, almost taken aback. "Well, you do, too. Fascinate me, I mean. I love you."

"I love *you*. And I love that you're still so modest. I look at you sometimes and I just can't believe that you're real. And that you're here!" She slowly ran her index finger up the length of his arm. "Clark? What's it like . . . flying?"

"Come on, Lois, you've flown with me hundreds of times."

"That's just it, I've flown *with* you, but I can't fly on my own like you can. I know I've asked you before, but tell me again. What is it *like*, to be able to fly?"

"It's fun. It's the most incredible sensation. I have to confess, when I'm not flying to an emergency, I like to do aerobatics. I indulged in a few loops and barrel rolls on the way home last night. I love to fly over the Middle Atlantic states at just a few thousand feet. It really does look like a crazy quilt at that altitude—the woods and villages, farmland and cities, roads and rivers. I never get tired of it. It's an amazing sight."

"I'm sure it is. I'm so envious. But the act of flying itself . . . what does that feel like?"

"How do I explain?" Clark slowly stroked his chin.

"Well . . . it's kind of simple, really. First, you crouch down a bit—sometimes I'll take a couple of running steps—and you flex your muscles. The quadriceps and the hamstrings are important here. Then, you just leap into the air . . . and keep on going."

"Oh, you!" Lois caught him squarely in the face with her pillow.

"Hey, I thought I fascinated you!"

"Yes, you're a fascinating target!" Lois jumped on top of her husband, swinging the pillow again and again as he raised his arms to fend off her attack. It wasn't until her fourth swing of the pillow that she noticed that her feet were dangling off the bed.

"Clark?" The back of her head bumped lightly against the ceiling and she stopped swinging, her pillow falling to the floor below as she realized that they were suspended in midair over the bed. "Clark!"

"Well, you asked about flying. Sometimes, it's just a matter of thinking hard."

Lois felt herself slipping and drew in closer, grabbing hold of her floating husband. His arms went around her, holding her tight.

"Don't worry. I've got you."

She relaxed in his embrace, and as his feet swung back down to the floor, they kissed deeply.

But even locked in the kiss, Lois could feel the muscles in Clark's neck suddenly tense. Her heart sank a little as he pulled away. "Trouble?"

"Possibly. Coast Guard emergency Klaxon . . . priority code." He stared out through the south wall and beyond. "There's a cutter about six miles out and a

mile down the shore . . . and a lot of fog rolling in.
This might be nothing, but—"

"Nothing? On a priority code? Not likely. Sounds
more like a story in the making. Go—I'll catch up
with you later."

He nodded. There was a swirl of air and in the next
moment, Lois found herself in the embrace of Superman. "Maybe we can get together for lunch?"

"Yes—oh, no, darn!" Lois shook her head. "Today,
I'm supposed to cover the governors' conference at
the Civic Center."

"Dinner, then. If I'm not back at the city room before
five, I'll leave a message on your voice mail. Love you."

"Sure. I—" She felt his lips brush her cheek, and he
was gone. "—love you."

Lois ran to the window, throwing open the sash
and sticking her head out, just in time to see the soaring caped form heading out to sea. She stayed there
by the window until he was gone from sight.

To the east, the sky was already starting to lighten,
and there was a chill wind blowing down from the
north. Lois reluctantly turned away, pulling the
shades closed behind her, and setting the snooze
alarm. *He was right, I do need more sleep. I've run up a
big sleep debt and I have another full day ahead of me. We
both do. We always do.*

Lois picked her pillow up off the floor as she got
back into bed. There was a bit of movement by the
door, and a small orange-furred form nudged his way
into the room.

"Hello, Elroy. Come to keep me company?"

The cat scampered across the room, bounding onto the bed, where he plopped down across his mistress's lap.

"Oof!" Lois picked the cat up and set him back down beside her. "Getting a little heavy there, kid."

Elroy's only reply was to stretch and yawn.

"Yeah, I'm tired, too." She gently chucked the cat under the chin. "Tired and a little lonely. It's not always easy being married to a super hero. No, better make that *the* super hero."

Elroy yawned again and curled up into a ball.

"Well, thanks for listening, guy. Not boring you, am I?"

From off in the distance came a low rumble. A brilliant flash of light outlined the edges of the shades, followed almost immediately by a loud peal of thunder that rattled the windows. Even the cat looked up.

Oh, fine, more uncertain weather to contend with. Lois pulled the sheets close and sank deep under the covers. Reaching out for Clark's pillow, she hugged it to her. She could smell his scent on the pillowcase.

Clark always smelled good, even after a strenuous workout like the one he'd had yesterday. She knew it had something to do with the enhanced bio-electric aura that surrounded him. It was part of what made his body so invulnerable, but it also kept him from smelling sweaty. Bacteria just didn't seem to be able to grow on his skin. And given his lifestyle, that was a blessed side effect.

He's one of a kind. I just have to share him with the

world, that's all. He's like a doctor who's always on call. Or a cop. Or a soldier. Lois's mouth twisted into a wry grin. *I remember how Mom used to fret before Daddy retired from the Army. He was always getting called up, rushing off to some hot spot somewhere in the world. She never knew how long he'd be gone . . . or when she'd see him again. . . .*

Lois suddenly sat bolt upright, startling her cat. "Oh, my god! Am I becoming my mother?"

CHAPTER 8

And All the Ships at Sea

Alfred Pennyworth steered the catamaran in circles around the spot where the freighter had gone down. Pieces of flotsam, most of them frightfully small, bobbed amid the waves, the only indication that there had recently been a ship in the area.

From the catamaran's original position, the old butler had watched the storm suddenly boil up just over the horizon. He'd heard the thunder and seen the flashes, first of lightning and then of the explosion. When the freighter's GPS beacon disappeared from his monitor, Alfred had immediately fired up the engines and headed directly into the storm. With the ocean roiling around him, he'd broken radio silence and disregarded every other order he'd been given. Alfred had every confidence in the Batman's abilities, but the forces of nature trumped everything and—as far as he was concerned—voided all agreements.

By the time he'd reached the site, the skies were

again clear, and the sea calm. There was no longer any storm. No sign of the freighter. And no sign of the Batman.

Nor had the dawn brought any new revelations.

Alfred tuned up and down the maritime dial. There was some chatter from other vessels that had spotted the storm from far away, but none that had been in it. The tempest had struck suddenly and savagely, but in a very small area.

On channel after channel, Alfred broadcast a pre-arranged coded message. "Old Salt calling Young Salt, do you copy? Over." He had been trying it for hours.

There was no response.

By now the submersible's air supply would surely have been exhausted. But Alfred kept searching. He had served the Wayne family for decades, as had his father before him, and he refused to abandon their last son now.

Alfred Pennyworth had first come to work for Thomas and Martha Wayne shortly after the death of his father. Though his first love had been the theater, he had assumed his position as the Waynes' butler out of familial duty. And that sense of duty only deepened when the Waynes were murdered by a holdup man.

The death of the Waynes had changed Bruce forever. He became driven to learn and excel. Through long years of arduous study and exercise, he built himself into the epitome of mental and physical strength.

On the day that Bruce became the master of Wayne

Manor, he confided in Pennyworth his secret plan. He would use his skills and knowledge to wage war on the criminal element that had killed his parents. Unable to dissuade the young man, Alfred did the only thing he could do. He became an aide and confidant to the Batman.

But now, the old butler was running out of options. There were additional scuba tanks aboard, and he knew how to dive. He could search . . . but for what? And what if he encountered trouble below? The ocean stretched out in all directions around him, and he suddenly felt very alone. Perhaps he should call for assistance, but from whom? Superman? Or one of the Batman's other Justice League allies?

Alfred was switching radio frequencies when he noticed a strange rhythmic movement along the horizon to the east. He focused his binoculars on the area and saw a dolphin. No, dolphins. There were two of them, and behind them . . .

Alfred's heart leaped to his throat. The dolphins were towing the submersible! And balanced effortlessly on the tiny craft was a tall blond man dressed in green and gold.

"My word—Aquaman!"

Alfred spun the wheel, turning the catamaran in the direction of the approaching dolphins, and let out the throttle, rapidly closing the distance between them. He brought the ship's stern about and killed the engine as the dolphins swam up between the twin hulls.

The Sea King raised an arm in greeting, "Ahoy, the ship! Are you the 'Old Salt'?"

"Yes, I am." The Plexiglas of the submersible was cracked and scored, making it difficult to see within. "Is he . . . ?"

"Alive. And while not in the bloom of health, I'd say that he's at least still capable of recovery." Aquaman popped open the canopy and, with a strength capable of moving easily through the deepest subsea trenches, wrenched it free. He then stepped down into the craft and gently picked up the dark-clad form within. Aquaman carefully slid the Batman onto the canopy, and lifted it onto the back deck of the catamaran. "Be careful with him. At the very least, he has a couple of cracked ribs."

Alfred was already breaking out an emergency medical kit when the Batman raised a hand. "No painkillers. I need to stay alert."

"Far be it from me, sir, to interfere with your more masochistic tendencies." The butler produced a pair of scissors, cutting away the Dark Knight's jersey and easing off the Kevlar vest beneath. "Hmmph. A fine new set of bruises. Shall I photograph these for your memory book?"

"Just tape me up."

"Let me check for breaks first." Alfred gently felt his way along the Batman's rib cage, noting when the Dark Knight flinched. "Not as bad as it first looked. You do lead a charmed life, don't you?"

"Lucky me."

"I should say so." Aquaman crouched down to lend a hand. "In case you haven't noticed, it's a big ocean out here. If I hadn't been in the region—or if I'd been a mile farther away—I might not have noticed the storm. It caught my attention, and I swam in to check it out. Otherwise, I probably wouldn't have been close enough to pick up your distress call."

"Distress call?" Alfred momentarily paused in his ministrations.

"I'm not as much of a masochist as you think." The Batman grinned through gritted teeth.

"But, sir . . . I heard nothing."

"I didn't use our frequency, Alfred. I didn't want you drawn into that storm. I used my Justice League transceiver, but I couldn't raise the Watchtower."

Aquaman shrugged. "Not too surprising. That freak storm probably caused a lot of interference."

"Yes, no doubt that was by design."

Alfred stiffened. "I beg your pardon?"

"There was nothing natural about that storm." The Batman put a hand on Aquaman's shoulder and painfully pulled himself up into a seated position. "It blew up out of a clear sky and reached full fury just minutes after the freighter's radio operator sent a message that I was 'trapped.' That storm was artificially generated—and aimed right at me."

"You cannot be serious!" Alfred looked the Batman in the eye. What he saw there made him sit back on his heels. "You are. But . . . how?"

"And by whom?" asked the Sea King.

"The whom I already know. He's one of the most dangerous men alive." He canted his head at Aquaman. "We've both been on the receiving end of his schemes, Arthur. Remember Portugal?"

Aquaman's face darkened. "The Naja-Naja."

"None other. How he did this, I haven't a clue. But I intend to find out."

"If you need any help stopping him, I'm here for you."

"Thank you, Arthur." The Batman gripped Aquaman's hand as Alfred pulled the tape tight over his injured ribs. "I'm sure we'll be needing you before this is over. But for now, I'd appreciate your help in keeping this incident quiet."

"If you say so. But why?"

The Batman looked out at the debris that drifted past the catamaran. "The Naja-Naja brewed up a storm, destroying a freighter and everyone aboard. He sacrificed a ship full of his own men in an attempt to kill me. For now, let's let him think he succeeded. Maybe he'll get sloppy."

Dawn was inexplicably turning from pink to gray as Superman flew out over the ocean. Within seconds, he was enshrouded in a thick fog bank. So dense was the fog that it seemed as though the night was returning to the mid-Atlantic. Only the honking of the Klaxon and the heat signature of the Coast Guard cutter—visible to the Man of Tomorrow's extraordinary eyes—enabled him to find the ship.

Two Coast Guardsmen were feeling their way along the deck like blind men when Superman landed on the cutter. He led them belowdecks and made his way to the bridge.

The cutter's commander was pacing the control

cabin when the Man of Steel entered. "Superman! Good to see you!"

The caped man shook his hand. "How can I be of help?

The commander waved the Man of Steel over to a green-lit display. "We have half a dozen small to medium-sized craft caught out in this mess, and at least one full-sized ocean liner. Visibility is virtually zero. I'm a career man, and I have never seen a fog this thick. Never!

"Thanks to our instruments—radar, sonar, radio triangulation—we have a good idea of where the ships are, but we're having a hard time rendering any aid. We tried firing flares, but that's done no good. The fog swallowed up their light almost immediately. And there's a danger of collision even if we try an instrument approach."

"Skipper! We already *have* a collision." The radioman looked up from his headphones. "A tanker has just reported hitting a small cabin cruiser—about two kilometers due north. No damage to the tanker, but the cruiser is taking on water."

"Sounds as though that's the most urgent case, Commander. I'll do everything I can, but warn all ships to hold their positions."

"Will do, Superman."

Getting a fix on the location of the collision, Superman headed back out into the fog, reaching the site in moments. The tanker had a searchlight pointed down at the cabin cruiser and was trying to drop it a line, but the smaller craft was already listing badly to one side.

The Man of Steel flew low over the damaged ship. In the gloom of the fog, only the vaguest of shapes were visible, but his eyes could see the infrared silhouettes of three people hanging on to the wheel for dear life.

"Ahoy, there."

"Who is it? Who's there?"

"I'm Superman."

"Superman?" A hand reached out and clutched at his cape. "It is! It *is* Superman!"

"Don't worry. Everything's going to be okay. Radio the Coast Guard that I've arrived and that we'll soon be under way."

Superman dove underwater, putting his back to the keel of the ship. Rising up, he broke free of the ocean with the small craft carefully balanced on his back. Getting his bearings, he turned about and flew west.

As he neared the city, the air began to lighten around them. Suddenly, they broke out into clear sky, the port of Metropolis just a few miles ahead. A minute later, Superman lowered the boat into a repair berth at the local Coast Guard station.

As Coast Guard medics rushed to help the people from their boat, the Man of Steel came up from beneath the craft.

"Tow lines! I need at least six—as thick and heavy as you can give me."

Guardsmen jumped to comply, and in moments Superman rocketed back out to sea, the heavy lines slung over his shoulders.

* * *

"Good morning and welcome to *AM Metropolis* for Friday, June eighteenth! I'm Kelly Johansen—"

"And I'm Rick Raymond."

All across the city, people looked up from their morning coffee to see a smartly dressed young couple greeting them from their television screens.

"This morning we'll be speaking with writer Norman Brawler, author of *Beyond the Silver Screen*, and hearing the latest celebrity news from *The Scene*'s Vicki Vale."

"Should be a good one, Kelly. Plus, Chef Sheila will show us how to get the most out of rhubarb, and Doctor Dave will tell us what sort of weather we can expect for the weekend. But first, let's check in with Nora Cheung at the WGBS news desk. Nora?"

The two-shot of Kelly and Rick glided electronically to the left-hand side of the screen, making room for an elegant dark-haired woman whose image filled the right.

"Thank you, Rick. And good morning. Here are the stories we're working on for you this AM . . ." Kelly and Rick disappeared completely as Nora continued. "In Qurac, insurgent forces have issued a new list of demands to that nation's ruling council. In Washington, the President is scheduled to meet with the Markovian ambassador this afternoon to announce plans for a new trade agreement. And closer to home, a grand jury is expected to issue new indictments in the Intergang racketeering case. We'll have more on those stories later, but first—a daring rescue at sea is currently under way in the Atlantic, just outside of Metropolis Harbor. And correspondent Steven Benjamin is on the scene in the GBS news chopper. Let's go to him now, live. Steven?"

Nora vanished from the screen, replaced immediately by a soft gray expanse. A deep voice struggled to make itself heard over the sound of churning rotor blades.

"Thank you, Nora. I'd first like to assure our viewers that there is nothing wrong with their sets. What you are seeing is a fog bank that stretches for miles up and down the coast and out to sea. It formed here quite unexpectedly in the predawn hours, and it has caused a major navigational emergency for ships at sea in the region. The Coast Guard is reporting at least two near-collisions, but— Wait! I think I can see— Yes!"

From out of the fog emerged a bold figure clothed in red and blue.

"Yes, it's Superman! As I was about to say, the Coast Guard also reported that the Man of Steel had responded to the emergency and joined with them in an operation to guide— What on Earth?"

As the image of Superman sharpened, it was clear that he had a thick cable slung over his shoulder. Behind him, the cable stretched taut back into the fog, ending in a dark amorphous shape. As Superman flew on, the shape grew more distinct, turning into the massive bow of an ocean liner.

"Nora, this is absolutely amazing! I believe that's . . . yes, that's the *Queen Mary 2*. The . . . uh . . . the *QM2* was due into Metropolis this morning after the last leg of a special cruise that began in Hong Kong, and—Wow!

"Excuse me, but this is a first for me—I've never seen anything like this. Superman is actually towing a full-sized ocean liner! Harry, are you getting all this?"

The image bobbled a bit as Benjamin's cameraman nodded and then pulled back for a wider shot. On-screen, Superman began to resemble a small, red-winged bird pulling an object nearly two hundred times his length.

Nora Cheung's voice broke in over the image. "Steven, can you hear me? Are there any other vessels in sight? Because we're getting word from the Coast Guard that there may be as many as—"

"Yes!" There was elation in the correspondent's voice. "Sorry, Nora, but—Wow! Just look at that!"

On the twentieth floor of the Daily Planet Building, early risers were starting to filter into the offices of Metropolis's leading newspaper. The big double doors of the *Planet*'s city room swung open as a freckle-faced man shouldered his way through.

He looked almost young enough to still be delivering papers in the suburbs, but a press pass hung from a lanyard around his neck. The young man strode across the room, doffing his baseball cap to release an unruly shock of red hair. He shoved the cap into a pocket in the camera case that hung from a strap over his shoulder, and stopped to fill a cup at the water cooler, calling out to an older man across the room.

"What's up, Chief?"

Perry White glanced down from the wall-mounted television monitor that held his attention and waved the young man over. "Come see for yourself, Olsen."

Jimmy Olsen joined his editor in front of the monitor. "Checking out the competition? Hey, Superman— cool! What's he pulling?"

White thumbed a remote, and the monitor's volume went up.

"—continuing coverage of this live GBS exclusive: 'Rescue at Sea!' I'm Steven Benjamin. For those of you just joining us: We are miles outside of Metropolis Harbor where, at this hour, Superman is single-handedly towing a line of ships that became lost this morning in a gigantic fog bank that now stretches along a third of the Atlantic seaboard."

The camera panned past Superman, along the cable to the big ocean liner, and continued on. Another cable stretched from the stern of the liner to the bow of an oceangoing tanker, and a third line stretched from the tanker off into the fog.

"The Coast Guard now reports that the *Queen Mary 2* briefly powered up, which means that Superman did not start with the vessel absolutely dead in the water. But even so, this is a stupendously amazing sight. According to the Guard, the Man of Steel is towing at least half a dozen ships bound for the Port of Metropolis."

"Whoa! Six?" Jimmy started running numbers in his head. "That's a lot of tonnage. Hey, Chief, you want me to get down to the harbor? We should get some photos of this."

"Oh, do you really think so, Olsen?"

"Well, I just—!"

"Yes, yes, of course. Get down there on the double! Can't beat the damned boob tube for immediacy, but if we hustle, we can add some depth to the story in time for the afternoon edition."

The editor-in-chief muted the monitor's sound and called out to the reporters around him. "Come on, people, let's get on the story. Whit, I want the specifics on every one of those ships, everything from tonnage to ports of call. Fran, Danny—head down to the docks and interview the passengers and crew from that liner. Sal, get me some quotes from the Coast Guard." Perry checked his watch and looked around the city room. "Where in blazes is Clark Kent?"

"Out working on the Intergang story, remember?" A short, round-faced young woman handed White a short stack of papers. "He called twice yesterday. The top two messages are from him. And he's promised to have copy in by this afternoon."

"Oh. Yes. Thank you, Allie." He flipped through the stack of "While You Were Outs." "All right, that explains what Kent is up to, but where the devil is Lois?"

Allie handed him a phone. "Line one."

Just a few blocks away, Lois stood at a street corner, one hand clutching the early edition of the *Planet* and a large coffee, the other holding her cell phone to one ear.

"Yes, I know all about it, Perry. The coffee shop had

AM Metropolis on when I stopped in. Just a minute."
She thumbed the mute button and thrust her phone
hand high in the air. "TAXI!"

As a bright yellow cab glided to the curb, Lois hid
a yawn with the back of her hand. *Okay. Tonight, without fail, I absolutely* must *get more sleep.* She took a long
sip from her Gotcher Coffee Double-Caf Mocha Grande
and slid into the back of the cab.

"Ah, Ms. Lane." A pair of dark eyes smiled back at
her through the Plexiglas panel that sealed off the driver's compartment. "I thought that was you."

Lois glanced at the cabbie's license. "Bali, right?
You've picked me up—what?—three times in the past
month, and at all hours of the day or night. Don't you
ever sleep either?"

"Ah, my lovely wife Matrika and I are expecting
our first child. We need to feather the nest, and I have
found that the fares in this neighborhood are most
generous." He grinned. "Where can I be taking you
this morning?"

"Pier Seven." She showed him a grin of her own
and returned to the phone. "Okay, I'm back. What?
Yes, I know the captain of the *QM2*. Relax, Perry, I'm
headed for the docks now. Fran and Danny? Sure, I'll
keep an eye out for them."

A huge raindrop smacked against the windshield
of the cab, splattering to the size of a quarter. Several
more, as large or larger, followed in rapid succession.

"Uh, Chief? Better warn 'em to pack umbrellas.
We're in for more precip today. Later."

Lois clipped the phone into a special pocket in her

shoulder bag and felt around the interior. *Mini-recorder, press pass, PDA, breath mints—ah, there's my collapsible umbrella.* A loud clap of thunder echoed overhead, and the rain poured down. *I hope it'll be enough.*

Bali switched on his headlights and wipers as the rain sluiced over the cab. The cabbie lightly tapped his antilock brakes, hydroplaning only slightly as he made a right onto Twenty-seventh Street, and an ancient curse erupted from his lips. He choked off the last few profane syllables, looking a bit embarrassed. "A thousand pardons, Ms. Lane. But this rain is something which we surely did not need."

"It's all right, Bali. I didn't understand the vocabulary, but I agree with the sentiment." She stared ahead through the spotless Plexiglas at the windshield beyond, watching the rain distort the morning traffic after each pass of the wipers. "I think those are the biggest raindrops I've ever seen. Lovely weather if you have gills. I've lived in Metropolis half my life, but I've never gotten used to how changeable the climate can be here."

"You can certainly say that again. It is just one crazy thing after another."

Crazy. Lois pulled the collapsible umbrella from her bag and started playing with its closing snap. *The weather has been crazy lately—wind gusts, giant fog banks, storms. But surely Clark was exaggerating, calling it unnatural. It may not be normal, but . . . engineered?*

As Bali inched the cab forward, Lois watched the driving rain send pedestrians running for the cover of awnings and doorways.

Who in their right mind would ever add to this magnificent chaos?

On the northern edge of Metropolis's central borough, in a second-floor apartment just a few blocks from the Hob's Bay waterfront district, a big, heavyset man lay on his side, diagonally across his bed. One pillow cushioned his head, while another partially covered it, shielding his eyes from the dim light that crept around the shade of the half-open window. A bent and battered nose—the product of many a fight—protruded from under the edge of the upper pillow, and the air passed through his nostrils, making a raspy whistle.

This morning, the wind began blowing the shade open, wider and wider, and the rain peppered down on the sleeping figure. As the cool, wet breeze washed across him, the big man began to shiver. He reflexively pulled the covers up over him.

In his dreams, the man was back out on the docks, unloading cargo in the rain. He heard someone shout a warning—"Bibbo, look out!"—and looked up to see a huge net come loose from a crane and drop right toward him. Caught up in the net, he lost his footing and fell backward into the harbor.

"Bibbo" Bibbowski suddenly sat bolt upright, clawing at the cold, sodden cloth that clung to his upper body. Pillows went flying as he rolled off the bed, landing hard on the floor.

"Huh? Where'm I?" Still half asleep, Bibbo reached out, feeling the bed to his left and the underside of the windowsill to his right. "Wha's goin' on?" With that, the window shade overhead swung wide in the wind and a rush of water pelted down on him.

Bibbo came fully awake, lurching to his feet and slamming the window shut. He ran a hand over his closely cropped gray hair and stood glowering at the window as the rain washed over the glass. "What's wit' this? It wasn't s'posed to rain today!"

He glanced over at the illuminated face of his alarm clock. "Seven-thirty? I ain't been up at seven-thirty since I was in trainin'." Muttering to himself, Bibbo stomped into his bathroom, dragging the bed-clothes with him. He pushed the shower curtain to one side and slung the damp linen over the rod. His T-shirt followed. "Oh, well . . . coulda been worse. Coulda been snow I started dreamin' about."

Ambling back out into the bedroom, Bibbo looked from the now bare mattress to the clock. Its hands clicked to seven-thirty-five.

"Nuts. Might as well stay up now." He flipped on the lights and considered a mound of clothing on the floor beside a scarred and pitted old bureau. Plucking a shirt from the top of the pile, he sniffed it, made a face, and let it drop. "Okay, I gotta do laundry today." Bibbo rummaged through the drawers of the bureau for a few minutes, finally settling on a pair of old khakis. And from the top drawer, he pulled a navy blue sweatshirt. Emblazoned across the chest of the shirt, a bold stylized letter "S" filled a red and yellow pentagonal shield. Bibbo held his official Superman sweatshirt out at arm's length and smiled. This shirt was clean. He had six of them, in fact, and he made sure that they were always spotless.

Bibbo pulled on the pants and sweatshirt, then snatched up a battered old leather cap from the top of the bureau and plopped it on his head. He stepped into a pair of canvas shoes and looked himself over in a full-length mirror mounted on the back of the bathroom door. Bibbo sucked in his gut and raised two huge fists, as if he was about to box with his own image. "'Ey, old man, you think yer tough?" He gave the mirror a toothy grin. "Yeah, yer tough, all right—even this early in the mornin'!"

He turned, shooting punches into the air and bouncing from one foot to the other as he crossed the room. Opening the door, Bibbo paused for a moment on the threshold and looked back at his reflection. "Yeah, yer a lucky old cuss!" Then he pulled the door shut and headed down the back stairs to the tavern below.

Bibbo had drifted into Metropolis long ago, though no one was quite sure when or from where. In his youth, it was said, he had once been a heavyweight contender of some promise. But success in the ring had eluded Bibbo, and he had become a fixture on the Metropolis waterfront, drifting from job to job. During the flush years, he had earned good money working as a longshoreman. But even during lean times, Bibbo had always found a spot to rest his head, and had only rarely bedded down on an empty stomach.

Over the years, he had earned a reputation as a

carouser and a hell-raiser. It was certainly true that Bibbo loved a good fight. He had taken part in many a barroom brawl, usually coming out on top. But he also had a deep sentimental streak, often buying a meal for a friend who was down on his luck.

Bibbo was unquestionably tough—many claimed that he had the hardest head in Metropolis—and he had every right to consider himself a "lucky old cuss." Just a few years ago, he had found a lottery ticket that had netted him a fourteen-million-dollar jackpot. Some of his oldest cronies had advised him to take the money and leave the waterfront behind.

"Nothin' but moochers and lowlifes 'round here, Bibbo," warned one old rummy. "If I was you, I'd go buy me an island somewheres."

Instead, Bibbo had used the first year's installment of his winnings to buy his favorite tavern, the Ace o' Clubs, and the building that housed it. Holding court at the bar, he used his new fortune to help many of the neighborhood's hard luck cases.

This morning, as Bibbo strolled into the bar and put on a pot of coffee, he heard the soft snore of one of those cases. Highpockets Hannigan was asleep in his favorite chair just past the bar, his head resting on the table with a television remote control for his pillow.

Silently, Bibbo crept around the bar and bent down beside the slumbering man. He cupped both hands around his mouth and let out a bellow:

"Hannigan!!"

"Wha—?!" Highpockets jerked awake, his cap tumbling off his head as his shoulders hit the back of the chair. "Bibbo? Jeez, you almos' gave me a heart attack."

"Yeah, an' I oughtta give ya a kick in yer skinny butt. Whaddya think yer doing here?"

"M-My TV set was broke. A-An' you said that me an' Lamarr could stay an' watch the Bowery Boys movie on the bar's TV. Don't ya remember?"

"Yeah, I remember." He stared for a moment at Hannigan's face; the remote control had left an impression of reversed numbers on the man's cheek. "But I didn't expect youse to spend the whole night here."

"Sorry. I musta fell asleep." Highpockets scratched the top of his head, discovered that it was bare, and started looking around. "Hey, ya seen my cap anywheres?"

Bibbo scooped the cap off the floor and plopped it on his head. "So where's Lamarr?"

"Right here, Bib!" Lamarr Powell sauntered out of the men's room, zipping up his pants. "Heck of a storm coming down out there. It must be rainin' buckets!"

Bibbo shook his head. "Well, as long as we're all up, we might as well have us some breakfast." He went behind the bar, pulled a carton from the refrigerator, and started cracking eggs into a bowl. "'Ey, Lamarr turn on the TV. See if ya can find out where this storm blew in from."

Lamarr scooped up the remote and pointed it at the TV over the bar. "Hey, look, Bibbo—Superman's on *AM Metropolis*."

"Sooperman? My fav'rit?! Lemme see!" Bibbo thrust the bowl into Lamarr's hands and joined him on the other side of the bar. He pulled up a stool and parked himself in front of the tube just in time to see the camera pan in closer on the flying man. "Haw! Lookit 'im go! Ain't 'e somethin'?" Bibbo grabbed the remote and turned up the sound.

"—now have confirmation from the Coast Guard on the names of the ships that Superman is towing. The tanker in line behind the *Queen Mary 2* is the Lex-Oil *Sea Breeze*. That's followed by a tall ship out of California, the *Lady Joanne*, and by three smaller craft, the *Arabesque*, the *Limerick Rake*, and . . . *On Call*? Is that right? Yes, I'm being told that the name of the last boat really is *On Call*. Must belong to a doctor, Nora."

Rain streaks began to warp the shot, and the image on-screen began to break up. "Steven, can you hear me?" The screen cut back to Nora Cheung at the news desk. "We seem to be experiencing technical difficulties."

"Aw, nuts!" Bibbo tossed the remote down on the bar.

"Hey, too bad, Bib. But at least you got to see a little bit."

"Yeah, yer right, Lamarr. I guess it was a lucky thing that rain woke me up when it did. I woulda missed seein' my fav'rit! Didja see 'im towin' all them boats? Ain't nobody else in the world could do that."

"Jeez, I don't know about that, Bibbo."

"Huh?" Bibbowski's lips curled back from his teeth. "What's the matter wit' you, Hannigan? You sayin' Sooperman ain't the toughest there is?"

"No, no, Bibbo. I'm just sayin' there's other guys what could tow boats like that. Like that Martian Manhunter feller."

"The Manhunter? Gimme a break! 'E's like a *kid* compared to Sooperman!"

"Shh, both of ya!" Lamarr pointed up at the television. "I think the lady just said somethin' about the weather."

"—fog was as unexpected as the thunderstorms now blanketing the area. For more on that, let's look to the Weather Deck and check in with Doctor Dave McDonald. What sort of weather can we expect this weekend, Doctor Dave?"

The picture cut from the brightly lit studio to a wet, windswept outdoor set tucked away in a small plaza behind the GBS Building. Doctor Dave stood bravely in the middle of the "Weather Deck." Wearing a bright yellow slicker and tightly gripping an over-sized umbrella with both hands, he looked anything but happy to be there.

"Doctor Dave?"

"Yes, I . . . I hear you, Nora." Doctor Dave forced his mouth into a smile. "Our forecast is—or *was*—for clear skies and sunshine for the next three days. But as you can see, it's not exactly very sunny at the moment." In point of fact, the outdoor set grew darker even as the meteorologist spoke. "As things stand now, I'm about ready to give up on the forecast and go consult tea leaves or something." Doctor Dave flinched at a rumble of thunder that seemed to come from directly over his head. "Really, at this point it's anybody's guess what's gonna happen next."

The wind suddenly picked up, threatening to pull the big umbrella from the weatherman's grasp. As he struggled to hold on, a gust turned the umbrella inside out. And then the rain picked up, washing over the hapless Doctor Dave in sheets. His feet went out from under him. A technician ran over to help, only to go sliding off camera himself.

Doctor Dave got up on one knee. "Time to build an ark, friends!" Then, with a slightly crazed look on his face, he threw his arms wide and started chanting: "Rain, rain go away!"

The screen abruptly cut to a slide of the GBS logo and the words, "Please Stand By!"

In the Ace o' Clubs, Bibbo began laughing uproariously. Highpockets scratched his head. "Jeez, I think Doctor Dave is startin' to lose it." At that, Bibbo pounded the bar with one big fist, laughing so hard that tears came to his eyes.

"Hey, Bib, you okay?"

"Heh! You kiddin me', Lamarr? I feel great. That Doctor Dave usually makes me wanna smash my set, him an' his bum forecasts! But that . . . that's about the best thing I ever seen on TV!" He pulled out a big red handkerchief and wiped his eyes. "Now gimme back that bowl. I'm gonna fix us the best scrambled eggs either o' you have ever ate!"

By 11:45 A.M. the worst of the storm front seemed to have passed. But after four hours of dealing with ships, flooding, and resultant power outages, Superman was still a long way from calling it a morning. Flying over downtown Metropolis, he shot past the ninety-six-story LexCorp Tower and climbed high into the concealment of a passing cloud bank. Then he turned and dove—faster than the eye could follow— toward the great golden globe that topped the Daily Planet Building.

Entering via an access port on the underside of the sphere, Superman dropped rapidly down a back stairwell. After a decade of working for the paper, he knew every nook and cranny of the great building. Using his speed and super-senses to evade detection, he zipped into the locker room of the small health club on the fifteenth floor that the *Daily Planet*'s owners maintained for staff and management. He caught a quick shower, changed into his street clothes, and reclaimed a laptop computer from his locker, slipping out unnoticed before the regulars started arriving for their noontime aerobics class.

Back up the stairs, Clark Kent entered the city room by a rear door, checking for an empty office. As he'd hoped, Mary Powers had already left for lunch. Clark ducked into the feature editor's office, locking the door and closing the blinds behind him. He sat down in a side chair, booted up his laptop, and started typing.

Minutes later, Clark exited the features office, leaving behind no visible sign that he'd been there. He strolled across the city room, stashing his laptop in a desk drawer before sticking his head in through an open door.

"Dining in again, Chief?"

Perry White swiveled around in his chair, kaiser roll in hand. "Kent! About time you showed up." He dropped the half-eaten turkey sandwich back onto its waxed paper wrapper and reached for a napkin. "What do you have for me?"

"My first two in-depths on the Intergang case and an outline of the remainder, just so you'll know where it's going. It's all e-mailed to your computer. I should have the rest finished over the weekend." Over in the corner of the editor-in-chief's office, a printer motor started humming. "Oh, and since I know you like to have a hard copy to read over, there's one printing out now."

White wheeled across the room and skimmed the first few pages as they came out of his office printer. "Hmm, good opening. Nice hook. I don't know how you do it sometimes, Kent."

"Thanks, Perry. I had a good teacher." Clark pointed to the Pulitzer award certificates framed on his editor's wall. "You were getting the great stories and scooping the competition when I was still learning to conjugate verbs."

"Maybe so, but even on my best days I was never as quick at turning out the copy as you are. I've been in the newspaper business for forty years, and you have to be the fastest typist I have ever known." White glanced over the hard copy. "And never a single typo!"

Clark shrugged. "Spell-checkers do make that easier these days."

"Spell-checkers?! Those things are just smart enough to get you in trouble. I've yet to see one that could replace a good proofreader. The latest upgrade that's been foisted upon us has been *adding* typos! If you ask me—!" A ringing phone derailed the editor's rant. "Just a minute, Kent. Hello, White speaking. What? Son of a—! Yes, hang on!" White put the caller on hold and punched in another line. "Copy desk? I have Saulnier on line two. She's out in North Bakerline and— Listen, dammit, I don't care if it *is* your lunch break, this is big! The storm's weakened the locks on the barge canal, and they're about to give way. You can eat later—get ready to take her feed. And get a photog out there. If you can't find Olsen, send Levin or Jawarski."

White shoved the phone back in its cradle, shaking his head. "What a day. One damned thing after another, eh, Kent? Kent?"

The reporter could hear his editor's voice calling after him from blocks away. Clark Kent had already left the Daily Planet Building far behind.

And Superman was already halfway to North Bakerline.

CHAPTER 9

Blowing in the Wind

The Man of Steel swooped low over Metropolis Harbor, picking up speed as he shot past the sprawling warehouse district of the northern borough. But he was still over a mile from the Carter River Industrial Canal when the lower gates of Lock Number One collapsed.

Over a building chorus of sirens he heard the sharp crack of the lock gate tearing free, followed by an awful roar. Staring through a light drizzle, he saw a wall of water pour from the sundered lock, hurling a waiting coal barge backward as though it were a child's toy.

The hundred-ton barge slammed into a massive concrete pier and spun about, one side tipping high up into the air as the other slid beneath the churning waters. Screaming, two men tumbled from the barge's pilothouse, rolling down the tilted craft toward the rushing torrent.

But before they could hit the water, a strong arm

wrapped around each man and a caped figure pulled them up into the sky.

"S-Superman?!"

"Yes. You're going to be all right." The Man of Steel set them down on an adjacent service road. "Was anyone else aboard the barge?"

"N-No, sir." The larger of the two men sat on the pavement, shaking. "A-A larger crew isn't r-required on the canal. It's s-supposed to be a simple p-piloting job . . ."

"It's almost gone." The smaller man stared back down at the channel. "I wouldn't have thought it was possible for a barge to sink that fast. Omigod . . ." All the color drained from his face. "The pier!"

Superman followed the man's gaze. The concrete pillar that their barge had struck formed the eastern support of the old Coastline Railway Bridge. But now, great cracks opened in that pillar and it pitched nearly ten degrees to the west.

The Man of Steel whirled about even as he launched himself back into the air. "Stay here—help should arrive soon."

From off in the mists a loud, blaring horn sounded.

The Metro Superliner! Superman saw the bullet train fast approaching, knew that even if the engineer hit the brakes at that very moment, it would be too late. Momentum would carry the train onto a structure that could no longer support its weight.

He dove under the bridge. There was a growing gap between the sagging pillar and the steel beams that had rested upon it just seconds before. Superman threw himself into that gap, bracing the underside of the roadbed with his own back and shoulders. Beneath him, the concrete pier shuddered and dropped another inch. The pillar was sinking more and more. Superman could feel the strain building in the steel beams at his back. He pushed up to ease that strain and the pillar shifted yet again.

Then came the crushing pressure as the multiton engine reached the bridge.

Can't let this fall. Green Lantern, he knew, could create a new temporary support with a thought. The Manhunter could draw mass from the Earth itself and *become* a new pillar. But neither of them was there.

Superman would have to defy gravity to support the groaning framework of beams and trusses. *What did I tell Lois about flying? 'Just a matter of thinking hard'?* He gritted his teeth. *Got to . . . think . . . harder!*

Above him, he could feel the high-speed locomotive clear the bridge, then the next car and the next. Superman knew the schedule of the bullet train, knew that it would be full of people—some heading out of town on business, others perhaps setting out early for a long weekend—knew that all of those lives were literally riding on his shoulders.

Fifteen cars roared by before the pressure finally let up.

The Man of Steel then cautiously shifted the weight to one shoulder and started to reach for his transceiver when he heard:

"Superman? Is that you down there?"

"Yes!" He peered up between the overhead trusses

to see a railroad maintenance worker shining a light down at him.

"Couple of transit cops found the canal jockeys you rescued. They said— Holy jeez! Are you holdin' the bridge up by yourself?"

"One end of it. But I'd rather not make a career of this."

The worker thumbed his radio. "Affirmative on that pier impact. We need a crane and reinforcement beams down here on the double!" He looked back down between the rails. "Superman, can you hang in there another ten, fifteen minutes?"

"That would be a short enough career. Can you guarantee there won't be any more trains along in that time?"

"Yes, sir. All traffic's been diverted to alternate tracks."

"Then I can easily hang in here."

Rain continued intermittently along the entire Eastern Seaboard for the rest of the day, but only Metropolis was truly hammered by the storm. There, the downpour lasted until long past midnight. The deluge finally stopped by the time a special edition of the *Daily Planet* started rolling off the presses. The storm clouds began to thin shortly after the last bulk delivery of Saturday's *Planet*, and there were actually hints of sunshine by the time that home subscribers picked up their papers. People kept glancing outdoors, astonished that they could read the paper by natural daylight.

And there was plenty to read. The report on the

collapse of Lock Number One shared space on page one of the Saturday edition with news and features on the harbor rescues. In a special feature by Lois Lane, ships' captains and crews gave readers a glimpse of how they coped, minute by minute, with the suffocating fog.

By mid-morning Saturday, the hills and higher ground in Metropolis were bone-dry. The sky stayed only partly sunny at best, and clouds occasionally threatened more rain, but no further precipitation fell. In low-lying areas, residents and merchants assessed the flood damage and began the cleanup.

The next morning brought Metropolis a true *Sun*-day, with clear blue skies and glorious sunshine that lasted all day long. Even in the areas hardest hit by the storm, little block parties spontaneously broke out as people took time from shoveling mud and bailing out their basements. Sunday's *Daily Planet* featured updates on the storm's aftermath, as well as suggestions for how ordinary citizens could help.

On Monday's edition of *AM Metropolis*, Rick and Kelly had dozens of weather-related human-interest stories for their audience, including their own interview with the captain of the *QM2*. They also announced that Galaxy Broadcasting's Doctor Dave would be taking a little well-earned time off to recuperate from some injuries (just minor ones, they hastened to point out) incurred in last week's fall.

By mid-afternoon on Monday, under the second

day in a row of clear, sunny skies, Metropolis started
returning to something approaching normal. "See?"
people told one another. "It was bound to clear up
sooner or later." There was a feeling that a corner had
been turned.

So people went back to work, and helped their
friends and neighbors, and told themselves that everything was going to be all right. For most of the city, the
"Great Storm" was already becoming the stuff of instant books, news archives, and insurance claims.

And across the globe, after two days of rest, Mark
went back to work, as well.

Tuesday morning, Wonder Woman brought her
plane to a halt forty thousand feet above the eastern
outskirts of Gateway City, California. Giving the craft
a silent command to stay out of the local airlanes, she
popped the canopy and dove down toward the
sprawling West Coast metroplex.

It had been well over a year since the Amazon warrior had lived in the area. Then, Diana had worked as
a special advisor and visiting lecturer on Greco-
Roman mythology, working closely with Helena
Sandsmark, the curator of the city's Museum of Cul-
tural Antiquities. But in recent months she had been
named her native land's ambassador to the United
Nations, necessitating a move to Themyscira's New
York embassy. Now, a special U.N.-sponsored symposium on preserving the world's ancient artifacts was
bringing her back to the museum once more.

What goes around comes around, she thought. *It will*

*be good to see Helena and the rest of the museum staff
again. I wonder how much will have changed?*

On the east steps of the museum, a gathering of
dignitaries awaited her arrival, their numbers dwarfed
by the media and a huge crowd of the curious. Television cameras picked up her approach from the east,
and the crowd began to chant: "Won-der Wo-man.
Won-der Wo-man! WON-DER WO-MAN!"

But as the Amazon descended over the park across
from the museum grounds, she could see the black
clouds build and thicken in the west. She could feel
an unseasonably cold wind roaring in off the Pacific.

And then, the heavens seemed to shatter and fall.

Staccato crashes echoed down as fist-sized hail
slammed into the glass facades of the high-rise office
buildings just north of the museum.

"Get back!" Wonder Woman swooped low, shouting out to the assembled crowd. "Get inside—get under
cover! Now! Hurry!"

Police on the scene started herding people under
the building's east portico as broken glass and more
hail began hitting the pavement nearby.

Wonder Woman soared up into the heart of the
storm, reflexively raising her arms to a combat position.
Hailstones shattered on impact with her silver wrist-
bands, even as she realized that playing "bullets and
bracelets" with this storm would be futile. A shadow
fell over Diana, and she dove to one side. A hailstone
the size of a regulation softball hurtled past. She took
refuge beneath a rooftop water tower as chunks of ice,
wood, and metal showered down around her.

Under the shelter of the water tower, Diana closed her eyes and turned her head skyward. In seconds, her robot plane swooped over Gateway City. At Wonder Woman's mental command, the plane flattened out, morphing into a giant flying shield that hovered protectively over the urban center, hail shattering against its nearly transparent surface.

Diana flew up under her shield, directing it into the heart of the hailstorm. The Amazon warrior didn't know how long this onslaught would last, but she was determined to protect as much of the city—and as many of its people—as she could.

But as Wonder Woman steered her flying shield north to ward off the barrage of hail, the storm struck a mile to the south. A powerful bolt of lighting arced down from the heavens to strike one of the city's tallest skyscrapers, stabbing through the base of the twenty-foot-tall communications tower that stood atop it. The direct hit instantly overwhelmed the building's rooftop lightning arrestors. There was a concussive boom, followed by the wrenching shriek of metal twisting and separating.

The Amazon looked back just in time to see the tower topple over the side of the building.

"No!"

Diana spun around and shot across the sky, leaving the shield to follow the hail. By the time she reached the building, the tower was a deadly missile, already a third of the way to the street below, where dozens of cars sat stuck in traffic.

Wonder Woman dove under the plummeting

tower, matched speeds with it, and grabbed hold midway along its length. Her fingers sank deep into the metal tower as she strained to stop its fall without snapping it in two. And she began to silently pray.

Demeter, give me strength . . .

The tower's momentum carried them both down another fifteen stories.

. . . Hermes, speed my flight . . .

But after another ten, they were dropping half as rapidly. That speed was cut again by half with the next ten stories, and the next.

Twelve feet above the city streets, Wonder Woman brought the tower to a halt.

Slowly, the Amazon turned, delicately balancing the tower overhead. She flew around the corner of the skyscraper to a plaza.

"Please, give me room!"

The handful of pedestrians and sidewalk vendors who had ventured back out as the hailstorm moved north, now rushed to get out of her way. Not until she was certain that everyone was safely clear of the area did Wonder Woman land on the plaza. Diana lowered the tower to the pavement and leaned against its surface for a moment to catch her breath.

And then, the wind began to die down and the skies above lightened.

A cheer went up as people emerged from nearby cars and buildings. Wonder Woman numbly accepted the crowd's accolades. *The way they're acting, you'd think I stopped the storm. All I did was stand up to it and survive.* Her eyes narrowed. *This was too much like the Alaska incident. Superman was right. There was nothing natural about this storm.*

One time zone to the east, in Lakewood, Colorado, a tall man in a black suit and dark glasses stood beneath the shadow of an awning, the first in a line of people patiently waiting for a soft-serve ice cream stand to open. The sun burned hot and bright in a cloudless sky, and he loosened his tie a quarter-inch. Three spaces behind him, two small children giggled and whispered to each other that the tall figure at the head of the line dressed just like the "Men in Black." The tall man heard their whispers as clearly as if they were shouts, and held back a smile.

Finally, signs flickered on behind the glass front of the stand, and a short heavyset man slid open the serving window. A blast of cool air flowed out through the window, to the accompaniment of a Beach Boys oldie from a radio on the counter.

"Morning, Mr. Jones. How's my best customer? The detective business keepin' you busy?"

Jones tipped his head forward. "Let's just say it's keeping the bills paid, Arnie."

"Nothing you can talk about—I gotcha. What'll it be?"

"The usual."

"Comin' right up."

Jones watched closely as Arnie carefully constructed a large sundae, and let out a murmur of anticipation as the finished masterpiece arrived at the window.

"Here you go, one Cookies-n-Cream Double Delight—with extra cookies. That'll be three-fifty."

Jones handed over correct change and retired with his sundae to the tables and chairs that huddled under a series of big umbrellas along one side of Arnie's establishment. Settling in at his favorite spot, Jones stirred the chocolate cookie bits through the big mound of soft-serve. When he was satisfied that they were uniformly distributed, he scooped up a big plastic spoonful. Behind his dark glasses, the detective's eyes closed, and his poker face softened into a wide boyish grin.

After the first line of customers had been served, Jones wandered back to the window. During the temporary lull in business, Arnie grinned as he watched his best customer methodically scrape the wax cup clean. "You want a second one by any chance?"

"Don't tempt me, Arnie." Jones heaved a deep sigh. "This is like ambrosia. We didn't have anything like it back . . . where I grew up."

"So you've said. Gotta tell ya, I was surprised. I'd always figured you for a local. You sure sound like one."

"Thank you. I've lived here a long while now, but I was born and raised a good distance away."

"Was the weather anywhere near this roastin' hot where you grew up?"

"No . . . not at all. Far from it, in fact."

"Jeez, you must be dyin' in this heat. According to the forecast, this is supposed to be the fourth day in a row of temperatures in the hundreds. And summer's just gettin' started! What's it gonna be like in July?"

"I'd rather not think about that."

"Me neither. Glad I have an air-conditioned job and don't have to wear a suit and tie. Don't know how you can stand it."

The detective's shoulders moved slightly beneath his suit jacket. "You learn to cope."

"Yeah, your line of work, I guess you have to be ready to cope with anything." Arnie leaned his forearms on the counter. "If you don't mind my askin', what *is* your background? Were your folks in the foreign service? Or maybe the military? Yeah, I bet you're a whole lot like them."

Startled, Jones drew back, and the ice cream man held up both hands in a conciliatory gesture. "Sorry! None of my business, I know. But when you've been in my line of work as many years as I have, you take an interest in your regulars. I meant no offense."

The detective relaxed. "None taken, Arnie. It's just that . . . you're remarkably close to the truth."

Arnie smiled modestly. "Like I said, I've been years in the business and I've gotten to know a lot of people. Now, you told me there was no cookies-'n'-cream around when you were a kid—to me that says you must've grown up overseas, probably in a pretty rugged place."

"'Rugged' would be a fair description."

"Okay, so you became a private investigator—a fairly successful one, by the way you dress. You're obviously a tough guy, but from what I've seen you're no roughneck. So if you take after your folks, I figure that they were in the service or the diplomatic corps, posted to some trouble spot, dealin' with emergencies. Of course, maybe you ended up dressin' like Joe Friday because you're the rebel of the family. Then maybe your mom and pop were T-shirt-an'-jeans Peace Corps volunteers who brought you up in some desert or jungle somewhere. No, wait, you said it wasn't hot where you grew up. Okay, the mountains, maybe." The ice cream man leaned forward again. "But I'm seein' foreign service more than Peace Corps. So am I anywhere close to right?"

"Close enough, Arnie. I *did* grow up outside the States. And as far as I know, neither one of my parents ever wore a pair of jeans. But they did indeed have positions of responsibility. And I've always tried to carry on their legacy."

"So your folks are . . .?"

"They passed away some years ago."

"Damned shame. My folks died young, too. Heavy smokers, both of 'em." Arnie shook his head. "Any other family?"

"No, I'm afraid not. I'm the last of my line."

"Aw, jeez, I'm sorry. And here I was, babblin' on—!"

"It's all right, Arnie. This is home now." Jones gestured around him with the empty sundae cup. "My friends and acquaintances are my new family. And life goes on."

"Amen, brother. You sure got that right."

On the radio, the Southern California harmonies faded out and were replaced by a rhythmic fanfare and an urgent voice. "From the Twelve-Sixty Newsroom, this is Charles P. Irwin. Select areas of the Rocky

Mountains continue to swelter in the midst of a record-setting heat wave and dry spell that has state smoke-eaters jumpy. And University of Colorado meteorologists are describing as 'bizarre' the localized effects of—"

" 'Bizarre,' huh? That's not 'news.' I could've told them that." Arnie reached for the radio to change stations.

"No, wait." Jones's ears pricked up, and he reached through the window to stop the counterman. "I want to hear this."

"—raising further questions about their possible connection to, quote, 'clusters of anomalous weather events of increasing intensity,' unquote, currently being studied. Closer to home, one of our Twelve-Sixty Weather Watchers has phoned in with a report, as yet unconfirmed, of a series of lightning strikes in the mountains west of Eldorado Springs. And this just handed me—"

There was an audible gasp from the newsman.

"This is an official notice of the Emergency Alert System. This is not—I repeat—this *not* a test! The Colorado State Patrol reports a series of wildfires now raging along a line stretching from a mile south of Boulder to State Route 72. Routes 128, 93, and 72, west of U.S. 36 are being closed to all but emergency vehicular traffic. And an evacuation has been ordered for . . . Eldorado Springs."

"Oh, no! That whole area's been a tinderbox lately. I hope they can contain it." Arnie pulled out a cell phone and punched a preset number. "My niece

Shirley lives out that way. You'll have to excuse me . . ."

"Of course. I hope she's all right." Jones stepped away and Arnie slid the window closed. The detective crushed his sundae cup and tossed it in a nearby trash can. *Fire . . . there* would *have to be a fire.*

He blanched a little and his stomach knotted up, just at the thought of fire. *Come on, Jones, this is no time to weaken. If it is as bad as it sounds, there are people out there who could use your help. Remember what you told Arnie . . . carry on the legacy.*

Jones straightened up, cinching his tie, and sprinted behind the soft-serve stand. And there, the private detective faded from sight. Hidden beneath an aura of invisibility, he began to transform. He grew taller, his hair melted into his scalp, his brow bulged. Even his clothing began to change, the dark suit flowing into cape, trunks, and boots.

In seconds, the guise of detective John Jones was gone. In his place stood the Martian Manhunter, J'onn J'onzz.

The Manhunter launched himself into the sky, heading northwest toward Eldorado Springs. He flew invisibly through the western skies, up into the higher elevations, where a vast line of fire and smoke rose heavenward.

The Martian swallowed hard, fighting off a wave of nausea. Fire was his Achilles heel, a psychological vulnerability that fed a physiological one. If he let the fear get to him, he would weaken and burn.

Still, he was a Manhunter, sworn to act as a

guardian of his people. Mars was a dead world, his
people long since perished. He had lived on this good
Earth, in this area and among these people, for many
years. This was his home now, and these were his
people. He felt a responsibility toward them. And so,
he forced himself onward, past the caravans of evac-
uees, past the homes scattered among the trees.

Past the fear.

Onward he flew, into the fire zone itself. He hurled
himself bodily at a stand of trees, uprooting a score of
the driest ones in a matter of minutes. J'onn split one
huge, bone-dry tree trunk down the middle with his
bare hands and then flew on, holding it out before
him like the blade of a plow, scraping the forest floor
bare.

As fire crews moved into the area, they found a
wide firebreak already carved between the threatened
homes and the conflagration. The crew chief looked
around in astonishment. "Looks like someone beat us
to this section."

"My apologies." The Manhunter made himself visible just a few feet away. "When I arrived, I thought it
best to remove a fuel source from the path of the fire."

"You—you're—"

"I am the Manhunter."

The chief finally managed to get control of his
tongue. "Well, we're glad you're here. This . . . this is
perfect. It would've taken us hours to clear a break
like this."

"Is there anything more that I can do?"

"Just keep on doing what you've been doing,

brother. You take out the big stuff, and we'll follow behind to clear the underbrush. This is a bad fire now, but it doesn't have to stay that way."

The Manhunter nodded and threw himself back into his work. In minutes the firebreak was longer by a mile.

If he kept his distance from the fire, he knew he could continue to aid in fighting it. All he had to do was refuse to weaken.

Six hundred miles east of the wildfire, Wally West sat perched on the third stool at the lunch counter in Hayden's Drug Store, polishing off his second chili dog with cheese and onions.

"Here's your Cherry Soder, Wally." The counter lady set a tall glass down in front of him. "Finished with those dogs already? You shouldn't eat so fast, you'll get indigestion."

"From *your* food, Rosie? Never!" Wally stuck a straw into the glass and drew the lightly fizzing liquid into his mouth. He swiveled around on the stool to check out the magazines and newspapers on the long wooden shelves behind him. Down at the far end of the counter, two wire spinner racks squeaked merrily as old Pops Hayden loaded them with the newest comics and paperbacks. Wally smiled. As far as he was concerned, this was heaven.

From the stories his grandfather Ira used to tell, once upon a time all of the old area drugstores had featured lunch counters or soda fountains. Drugstores were mainly mom-and-pop operations when

Ira West was a boy, the sort of places where you could enjoy a soda or malted and buy a magazine to read while you waited to pick up your prescriptions. A lot of them had become unofficial hangouts, a friendly place where kids could safely congregate after school while they tried to decide which pack of trading cards to buy.

And old drugstores always had that great smell—a rich mix of cola syrup, aspirin, and newsprint, combined with whatever was the day's special.

Wally took a deep, appreciative breath. *Must have been sweet, growing up around places like this*. The drugstores he had grown up with were over-lit glass-and-steel clones run by some manager du jour for a remote corporation. They all smelled of plastic and cosmetics, and the soda they sold came in twenty-ounce bottles—plastic, of course—from behind a big glass-doored self-service cooler at the back of the store.

Yeah, they don't make 'em like this anymore. Hayden's was the last independently owned drugstore in all of Keystone City. When Pops retired, the soda fountain would go with him.

Wally looked around. The only other person at the counter was an older gentleman, two stools over, lingering over a bowl of bean soup while he read a science fiction magazine. "Not much of the usual lunch crowd in today."

Rosie shrugged. "A new Big Belly Burger just opened over on North Elias. I expect a lot of them are checking it out. I'm surprised you're not there."

"Eh, those places are everywhere. And you can't get a decent chili dog at a burger joint." Wally plucked the latest edition of the *Picture News* from the shelf and laid it on the counter. "Put this on my tab, too, Rosie. What do I owe you?"

"Including the paper, that comes to . . ." Rosie's pencil darted across her pad. "Six-fifty, hon."

"Cheap at twice the price." Wally grinned and reached for his wallet.

"Oh, go on with you!"

"I mean it. Your food should be considered haute cuisine. Don't ever let anyone tell you differently." But as Wally pulled cash from his wallet, he suddenly stiffened. "Do you hear that?"

"Hear what? I don't— Oh! Are those sirens?"

"Keepthechange, Rosie!" He dropped a ten-dollar bill on the counter and bolted from his seat, leaving the little bell over the drugstore's door dinging in his wake. By the time the waitress could turn around, Wally West was fifteen blocks away, weaving between the cars on South Tenth Street as though they were standing still. A miniature lightning storm seemed to crackle over his body, the Speed Force forming his sleek scarlet and gold uniform around him as he ran.

The Flash shot down a ramp onto the Hibbard Expressway and headed west out of downtown, nearly outrunning the wail of the sirens. These were no ordinary police, fire, or emergency vehicle sirens. He had already recognized the low, warbling howl as belonging to a special class of civil defense sirens. Wally's grandfather once told him how they were installed during World War II to warn of enemy air raids. Ever since the war's end, they had been used to warn of a different kind of aerial attack.

Five miles beyond the municipality's westernmost industrial park, a tornado roared along the expressway, closing fast on Keystone City.

Racing past the city's suburbs, the Flash dashed to meet the twister. *Whoa! This is a big one!*

The funnel was a thousand feet across at its base, and it reached up into the sky for miles. It was shot through with shutters, doors, and sections of shingled roofs. The twisted wreckage of cars and trucks, all apparently abandoned, bobbed about in the cyclonic winds. The air was brown all around the funnel cloud, day turning into night.

The Flash circled the tornado's base, quickening his pace, moving in closer and closer, until he was caught up by the winds and drawn bodily up into the tornado's funnel.

Then, in defiance of the power of the cyclone, he spun himself around and seized control of his course. Legs pumping madly, he spiraled up along the inside of the funnel. So fast did he move that he was able to run across the airborne debris as though it were frozen in midair.

And still he continued to accelerate, becoming a crackling streak of crimson in the tornado's upper reaches. In his wake, he generated a powerful downdraft, counter to the twister's updraft. The tornado began to slow, to shudder. And then, with one ground-flattening whoosh of air, it was blown out.

Debris rained down on the countryside. And the Flash found himself in free fall, a mile and a half above the ground.

He never panicked, not even for a moment. Instead, he started drumming his feet—faster, ever faster—compressing a column of air beneath him to slow and cushion his fall.

As the Flash touched down, he kicked up a huge cloud of dust and shot across the prairie, traveling a quarter of a mile before he could brake to a stop.

Debris continued to fall all around him for another three minutes, and he vibrated the molecules of his body, allowing the ruined fragments to pass harmlessly through him.

For a single blessed moment, all was calm. The Flash rose up from a crouch, took a deep breath, and let it out slowly.

That's when he heard an awful sound building behind him—the terrible noise that people always described as being like the roar of a runaway locomotive. Wally turned to see a second tornado, as big as the first, bearing down fast.

"Oh, man! Looks like this is gonna be one of *those* days!"

Kyle Rayner sat down at a table by the window of an Anchorage coffee shop and opened his sketch pad, flipping past the landscapes he'd sketched earlier that morning. As Green Lantern, he had spent the weekend in Alaska helping people dig out and rebuild after the earthquake and storm. But today, Kyle had switched from mask and uniform to a pair of well-worn jeans and a brand-new Iditarod Trail sweatshirt. He had willed his power ring to invisibility and set out to see the local sights, committing many of them to paper. He was finally on vacation and enjoying the break very much.

"Good morning. Welcome to Gotcher Coffee, 'We Gotcher Coffee—' "

" '—Right Here!' " Kyle favored the waitress with his best morning smile. "Sorry, I know the slogan and the jingle by heart. Can't forget 'em. I worked on that campaign."

She smiled back. "Oh, you're in advertising?"

"Sometimes. I'm a freelance artist." He stuck out a hand. "Kyle Rayner."

"Hi, I'm Shelli Ritter. That's Shelli with an 'i.' "

"Really? Ya know, I created a character who spells her name that way."

"A character?"

"Yeah, I also write and draw the City Dwellers comic strip." Kyle saw the blank look on her face. "For Feast magazine?"

The real-life Shelli still looked confused. "I don't think I've ever heard of Feast. Is it about food?"

"Uh, not really. It's more about music and fashion and urban lifestyles."

"I see." (But Kyle could tell that she didn't really.) "Well, ah, what kind of 'Gotcher' can I 'getcha'?"

"I'll have a Bananarama Cappuccino Grande."

"Sure. Coming right up."

As the waitress started to walk away, the air around the second finger of Kyle's right hand began to flicker with a green light. "Uh-oh." Quickly, he closed the sketch pad over his hand and willed the light into the infrared part of the spectrum.

"Yes?" Shelli turned back. "Is there something else?"

"Uh, no, but you'd better make that 'to go.' "

Minutes later, Kyle dashed up the stairs to his motel room, tossed the sketch pad on the bed, and dumped the empty coffee container into the trash. He clenched his right hand into a fist, willed his power ring to become visible, and spoke into the emerald gemstone: "Atom? Is that you?"

The ring glowed brightly again, generating a tiny holographic image of the Atom's head. "Yes, Kyle, I—"

"Jeez, Doc. Give me a little warning next time, okay? *Your* identity may be public knowledge, but some of us still wear masks for a reason."

"Sorry, but—"

"Aw, it's not your fault." Kyle took a deep breath. "That's the caffeine talking. My bad—I should have set the ring to vibrate for incoming calls. What's up?"

"It's these aberrant weather patterns—"

"Aberrant weather patterns?"

The hologram frowned. "You haven't been watching the news?"

"No, sorry. I've sort of been kicking back. Don't tell me there've been more typhoons."

"No, just impenetrable fog, flooding, killer hail, lightning, snowstorms, wildfires, and tornadoes—the last three still ongoing."

"Yow! So, do you need me to tackle the fires? The tornadoes?"

"Neither. J'onn and Wally are dealing with them. I need your help with a situation that's hit my own hometown. A blizzard swept into the Finger Lakes yesterday afternoon—dropped at least a foot of snow throughout the county, with even more in the city of Ivytown."

"Whoa, wait! A blizzard—in the middle of *June?* Even for Upstate New York, isn't that a little . . . extreme?"

"*Very* extreme, Kyle. I grew up in Ivytown, and we've never had snow past Memorial Day. The outlying areas have sometimes had a flurry or two in very early June, but not the city or the campus—and never a blizzard!" The holographic Atom shook his head. "The storm was so bad that the sheriff's department ordered the roads closed to all but emergency vehicles. That kept accidents down to a minimum.

"But today, just as everyone was starting to dig out, the winds picked up and another storm hit. From what readings I've been able to take, it's still in progress. And this time, it seems to be centered right over Ivy University."

"Bizarre."

"I know, Kyle, but it's true. I've had confirmation. A friend of mine, a fellow physicist, had snowshoed to the physics building this morning, after the first storm, to check on a special experiment and the grad students who were running it. And now I'm afraid that they may all be trapped in there."

" 'May'?"

"I'm not sure, Kyle. I have a private lab in that building with a satellite uplink. Doctor Negrini was using that equipment to brief me on the weather when the link went down. And I haven't been able to re-establish contact." The Atom's concern was evident from the look on his face. "My alma mater is getting plastered, my friend might be stuck in a building with very little heat, and fighting the weather is a little beyond the scope of my power. Can you help us?"

"Sure. Just give me a minute." *Blizzards in June! I'd better make sure my ring's carrying a full charge for this one.* Kyle swept the beam of his power ring across the top of a bureau, and the illusion of a table lamp dissolved away, revealing his power battery.

The emerald battery resembled a stylized lantern, and was both the inspiration for his name and the source of his incredible power. It was a creation of the Guardians of Oa, an ancient race nearly as old as the universe itself. Over the millennia, the Guardians had bequeathed such batteries to select individuals whom they had deemed worthy.

Kyle approached the power battery with reverence. Touching his ring to its surface, he could feel the awesome energy flow. And as he stood charging his ring, he began to recite a solemn oath—an oath that had become legendary long before his time.

> *"In brightest day . . . in blackest night,*
> *No evil shall escape my sight.*
> *Let those who worship evil's might*
> *Beware my power—Green Lantern's light!"*

Now fully charged, the power ring enabled the young man to perform virtual miracles, limited only by the force of his will and the scope of his imagination. Kyle turned the light of the ring back on himself, and in a burst of energy, his clothing was transformed into the proud uniform of the Green Lantern.

Gathering his will, Green Lantern rose up from the floor, passing through the ceiling and rooftop above like some great green apparition. He streaked up and away from the Alaskan city, faster than any missile. In seconds, he was on the edge of space. Shielded from the vacuum by the power of his ring, Green Lantern tapped into the Global Positioning System and rocketed east across North America. He re-established communications with the Watchtower as he crossed into New York State.

"Atom, do you read me? I'm currently about eight miles high over Lake Ontario, crossing over the southern shore and continuing my descent. I think . . . yes, I can see Rochester just off to my right."

"Roger that, Lantern. I have you on my screens. Ivytown is about eighty miles due south of your position. Can you see it from there?"

A pair of glowing emerald binoculars took form before Kyle's eyes. "Negative, Atom. I can see the lake—Anderson Lake, right?—and a couple of outlying villages, but the city is totally socked in. Looks like there's a big swirling cloud sitting on top of it."

"I was afraid of that. The last word I was able to get through the ground relays before they went down as well, was that Fox County Airport had closed."

"Well, at least I won't have to worry about air traffic. Here goes nothing. . . ." Green Lantern dove into the cloudbank. Instantly, he was surrounded by driving, blinding snow. Seconds later, his GPS link cut out. Kyle attuned his ring to act as radar and continued his descent into the bowl-like valley.

"Lan-ern? -re y- th-re?"

"Atom? You're breaking up. Hold on." Green Lantern came to a stop amid the swirling storm. So punishing were the winds that he was forced to shoot an energy anchor down to the ground to keep from being blown away. He fired a thin, coherent beam of energy up through the cloud cover. "Can you hear me now?"

"Loud and clear, G.L. I tried to warn you, this storm is kicking up a lot of electromagnetic interference. It makes communications difficult at best."

"Well, we won't have that problem any longer. I've set up my own personal laser link to the Watchtower."

"Good thinking. What's the situation like on the ground?"

"Well below freezing. My ring's telling me it's minus two. This is a full-tilt blizzard if ever there was one. I'd send a video signal up the link, but between the snow and the wind, there's not much to show. I literally can't see more than a few feet in front of—!"

From out of a white vastness came an awful cracking sound and a huge tree came crashing down, driving the Green Lantern to the ground.

"What was that, Lantern? Lantern? Hello?"

Shaken, Green Lantern suddenly found himself face down in the snow. Only the aura cast around him by his power ring kept him from getting a mouthful. It also saved him from serious injury.

"Kyle, are you there? Answer me."

"Yeah . . . I'm here. Give me a sec to collect my wits." The ring flared to life again, creating an oversized automobile jack that lifted the weight off his back. "There, that's better. Whew! It's like February down here. Snow's up to my knees. And a tree just fell on me!"

"You okay?"

"Yeah. I am now." Kyle shook his head. "Unreal."

"With a snow that heavy, that won't be the only tree down today. There are a lot of old silver maples in the area."

"Maples, huh? This looks more like a sycamore to me."

"A lot of those, too. Where exactly are you now?"

"Let me check." Green Lantern expanded his aura, pushing back the snow while leaving everything else around him undisturbed. Under the green glow, a sidewalk, curb and roadbed stood out in sharp relief. "Looks like I'm on a street heading up the east hill." He walked up the incline several paces, the aura pushing on ahead of him. "Yeah, here's a street sign. I'm at the intersection of Turner Street and Anbinder Avenue."

"Good. You're almost at Ivy University. If you turn north onto Anbinder, University Drive is three blocks ahead on your right, just past the Mr. Bagel."

"Sounds like a plan. Let me clear a path." The ring glowed brighter, and energy lifted Green Lantern several feet up off the ground, flowing around him to form a massive snowplow. "Yeah, make way for the King of the Road! Yee-hah!" Green Lantern sounded a horn and the plow moved swiftly up the middle of the avenue, scooping up the fallen, drifting snow and dumping it into the back of the truck bed. The rear bed filled up immediately. *Time to customize this sucker!* At Kyle's will the truck bed elongated, and as the bed continued to fill, its sides pushed inward, compacting the snow into cylinders. "Fire one! Fire two!" The cylinders were then shot high into the air on a trajectory calculated by Kyle's ring to bring them down safely in the middle of the nearby lake.

"What was that?" came the voice from his ring.

"Just getting rid of a little snow, Doc. You know, there aren't a lot of cars at curbside, not even buried ones. I expected to see more as I got closer to your campus."

"Not this time of year, Kyle. Graduation was over a week ago, and summer session classes haven't started yet. There shouldn't be many people on campus at the moment."

"Gotcha." Kyle gave the steering wheel a sharp tug to the right. "Okay, Atom, I'm turning onto University. Winds are a lot worse here . . . visibility's dropping. I'm extending a power field ahead of me to screen out new snow. . . . Okay, I see the gates of Ivy U. now."

"Good, good. Newhall Library should soon be coming up on your left. Just past that is East Campus Drive."

"Yeah, I see the library building. Man, the campus has been hit way harder than the lower valley. These drifts must be six feet deep. Whoops, there's Campus Drive—almost didn't see it."

"Turn left there. About a hundred yards ahead on the right is a service drive that will take you to Terkel Hall. That's where my friend, Doctor Negrini, called from."

"On my way." Halfway up the service road, the plow started to get hung up. With a quick thought from Kyle, the vehicle's wheels turned into tank treads, and it forged ahead. "Holy—! This is totally unreal. When did you last hear from your friend?"

"What is it? What's wrong?"

"Your Terkel Hall is covered in the white stuff— and I mean *covered!* The whole thing looks . . . frosted. Wind's whipping around the building like a mini-cyclone, and snowdrifts reach up to the second floor. And some of the windows are broken."

"Kyle, you have to get in there!"

"Relax, Doctor Palmer. G.L.'s Snow Removal is on the case. Nothing to worry about."

But as Green Lantern started to climb down from the cab of his plow, a wind gust caught the door, yanking it open and pulling him out into the blizzard. He went tumbling into the drifts, his protective aura flaring back to life, but not before several cubic inches of wet snow went down his collar. "Whoa! Cold! Cold!" Kyle reflexively turned up the heat on his aura, and a cloud of warm vapor rose up around him.

"What was that, Kyle?"

"Nothing to worry about, Doc. Just getting my footing." *'Nothing to worry about'—right! It's a good thing I'm not transmitting video. Wally'd never let me hear the end of this.*

From overhead came the sound of breaking glass. Kyle looked up to see a huge tree limb protruding from a shattered third-floor window. Then another big limb flew through the sky, slamming into the side of Terkel Hall. Branches and debris, driven by gale winds, began raining down on the snowbound building, shattering more windows, leaving cracks in the stone facade.

Now I know how the windows got broken. Time to get really serious. Green Lantern quickly deconstructed the plow, using the green energy to cast a protective hemisphere over the immediate area. The sound of splintering wood arose as more tree limbs smashed against the dome. Kyle pushed the snow away from him. *Got to get those people out, but I'd better not use heat around a science building. I know. . . .*

Kyle concentrated, his eyes narrowing to slits behind his mask. Energy again erupted from his power ring, this time taking on the form of a gigantic snow shovel. The shovel flew up under the dome, floated briefly alongside the building, and then came down hard into the story-and-a half-high drift. A long crack inched its way across the frigid surface as the emerald shovel drove several yards into the ice-encrusted snow.

"G.L.? What's happening?"

"We're almost there, Doc!" Green Lantern had to shout to make himself heard over the pounding of the storm against the dome. "I just have to reseat the blade. . . ." He channeled his will through the power ring, backing the shovel off a few feet before driving it hard into the opening it had made in the drift. There was a low, creaking moan as it drove closer to the building, and then the facing snow fell away from one side of Terkel Hall, collapsing in sheets before the side door.

"Yeah! I'm through!" The giant shovel suddenly divided into two, scooping the crusty snow away from the entrance. Green Lantern pulled the door open and shined his light into the darkened complex. "Hello, in there! Can anybody hear me?"

"Over here!" A rich contralto echoed from down a hall.

Kyle turned his light, and four figures came into view. In the lead was a statuesque brunette, followed closely by a shorter black woman and two red-haired young men. All were wearing jackets over lab coats in a vain attempt to ward off the chill.

"Doctor Negrini?"

"Yes, I am Enrica Negrini." The taller woman waved a dying flashlight. "These are my laboratory assistants—Shawna Waller, and Duane and Dennis Trigger."

"Hi, I'm Green Lantern." He shook hands and turned back to Enrica. Her hair was pulled back and she, like the others, looked rumpled and tired. But the artist in Kyle immediately saw past the surface details. *She has amazing cheekbones. And those eyes—gorgeous! This is the Atom's 'old friend'? She is one* serious *babe!* He smiled. "Doc Palmer sent me. Here, let me make you all a little more comfortable." His ring flared, and suddenly little green space heaters encircled the four with warmth.

"*Grazie*, Green Lantern. Thank you." Enrica pulled her parka tight around her, still shivering. "The heat had been shut off for the summer. When the building lost power and the windows started breaking, it was hard to keep warm." She looked around. "Is Ray— Doctor Palmer—with you?"

"In spirit, sort of." Kyle held up his ring, opening up a two-way video-screen linkage to the Watchtower.

"Ricki!" On screen, the Atom looked markedly relieved. "Are you all right?"

"We are now, Raymond—thanks to your friend."

"Listen!" Shawna Waller looked out the doorway, to beyond the protective dome. "The noise stopped."

Green Lantern led the party outside. It was true. Since he'd entered the building, the blizzard winds had noticeably decreased. The barrage of shattered trees had ended and the snow was diminishing to little more than a few errant flakes. Through the pale green of the dome, they could see the clouds begin to break. In minutes the sun was shining down, and Kyle tentatively opened the dome. Though the snow still lay piled in huge, dazzling white drifts, there was a new, warm breeze that spoke of summer.

"Cross your fingers, Doc, but I think the worst is over."

"Is it, Lantern?" On screen, the Atom looked uncer-

tain. "That's what I thought after Anchorage. Now . . .
I'm not so sure."

On the South Side of Chicago, a chill wind blew
through the open door of a tavern. A tall, dark-haired
man stood for a moment on the threshold, waiting for
the tint of his photosensitive aviator glasses to adjust
to the change in light.

"Hey, close that door!"

"Sorry, pal." The newcomer took a step inside and
pulled the door shut behind him. "Talk about bein' the
Windy City, huh?" He sidled up to the bar, showing a
lot of teeth under his mustache. "Gimme a Koul Brau
Dark, will ya?" He leaned an elbow against the bar
and nodded to the row of men already there. "Cold-
er'n a brass monkey out there. Great to be back in
Chicago, though. My name's Malone. . . ." He held out
his hand as if to offer a shake, but then, with a quick
flip of his wrist, produced a kitchen match out of
midair. "My friends all call me Matches." Drawing a
few appreciative chuckles, he stuck the wooden end
between his incisors.

"Cute trick." The bartender set a foamy pint down
in front of him.

"Thanks, buddy." Malone picked up the beer and
slapped a twenty down on the bar. "Ya got a nice
place here, a real nice place. Hey, I hear that my ol'
buddy Mark blew through town a few weeks back.
You wouldn't have seen him, would you?"

"We get a lotta guys through here."

"Ah, you'd probably remember Mark if you saw

him: pale blue eyes, dark hair—darker than mine, even. Stands about six-one. A lanky guy."

"Sorry. Don't ring a bell with me." The bartender set the newcomer's change down in front of him.

"You sure?" Malone put a hand over the money and eased it back across the bar. "I'd really like to hook up with him. I owe him fifty bucks, and if I know Mark, he could use it, huh? Hey, wait a minute." He reached into his wallet and pulled out a tattered snapshot. "Here, see? This is me and Mark in South Philly just a few years back."

The bartender palmed the cash and looked hard at the photo. "Yeah, there is something familiar about that face, but I can't quite place him. Hey, Jackie, you got a pretty good memory—you ever see this guy around?"

The portly man at Malone's elbow looked up from his pint and peered over at the photo. "Sure, I seen him. He was in here about a month ago. Left with that big guy, the one who looked like Jesus, only he had shoulders out to here. Remember, Lou? He bought a round for the house."

The match bobbed between Malone's teeth. "Mark bought a round? That doesn't sound like him at all."

"Naw, not the guy in the photo—the Jesus guy!"

"Oh, yeah. The guy with the beard." Lou the bartender scowled. "And the tan. Looked like he'd been out in the sun a lot. Him, I'll never forget." He tilted his head toward Malone. "Your buddy Mark ever wear a tweed cap?"

"Sometimes."

"Okay, I remember him now. He was here, all right. The middle of last month, I think it was. But he left with Mr. Jesus-of-Malibu, and I ain't seen him since."

"That's Mark for you." Malone slipped the snapshot back into his wallet. "Always making friends, wherever he goes."

"Friends like that one, he can keep to himself."

"Aw, c'mon, Lou," Jackie stifled a belch. "The guy bought us a round. His money was good. You said so."

"His money was good, yeah, but the creep had an attitude." Lou leaned closer to Malone. "He tried to come across like a big spender, but he had a way of moving—all high and mighty, like he thought he was too good for the room. Y'know what I mean?"

"Yeah." Malone chewed thoughtfully on the match. "Yeah, I think I do. You wouldn't happen to know where they went?"

"Sorry, Malone. I wish I could help you, but I don't have a clue."

"They was goin' to the airport." This time Jackie couldn't hold back the belch.

"The airport? You sure of that?"

"Well, pretty sure. See, the Cubs had just scored a home run. So when the commercial came on afterward, I went to the can, and I passed right by that booth in the back where they was sittin'. As I was walkin' by, I heard 'Jesus' say somethin' about how they had a world to cross. And I don't think he was plannin' to walk it." Jackie paused and chugged down the last of his drink. "Anyway, when I came outta the gents, they was gone."

Malone grinned broadly and threw an arm around the little man's shoulders. "Pal, let me buy you a drink. In fact, what the heck, drinks for the house! Let's all hoist one to ol' Mark."

The regulars gathered around, eagerly toasting Mark, then Matches, and finally the Cubs. Malone graciously accepted their thanks and filtered among the others, casually asking them what they could remember about Mark and his new friend. By the time Matches took his leave, spirits in the tavern were so high that no one noticed he had hardly touched his beer.

Malone left the bar, pulling his collar up against the gale. He walked no more than two blocks down the street when the wind began to die down. He stopped at a corner, plucked the match from between his teeth and snapped his thumbnail against the head, lighting it with one hand.

As if in response, a dark sedan with tinted windows pulled up to the curb. It was impossible to see inside, but the right rear door powered open and Matches hopped in.

From behind the wheel, Alfred Pennyworth looked over his shoulder at the man in the rear seat. "Will you be dressing up or down for the next gin mill, 'Mister Malone'?"

"Neither, Alfie. I finally hit pay dirt in that last dive."

"Splendid. Am I correct in assuming that the doctored photo did the trick?"

"I'll say it did. They bought it completely. Even I

was starting to believe that I'd been in Philadelphia with Mardon. Get us outta here."

"Certainly. Where to?"

"O'Hare. Go north to Ninety-fifth Street, then west to the Tri-State." The car pulled away, and Malone settled back into the seat. He doffed his aviator glasses and peeled away his mustache. From his nostrils, he pulled a pair of flexible appliances that had broadened his nose. But it was not until he had removed the wig that Bruce Wayne dropped the high, reedy voice of Matches Malone.

As Wayne used a treated cloth to remove the last vestiges of his assumed identity, Alfred steered the sedan through the Chicago traffic. "Your quarry departed by air, then?"

"That's the best guess, Alfred. Mardon left in the company of a large, powerfully built man. Most of that tavern's patrons described him as tanned, but one said he looked 'mixed.' All of them agreed that he had a beard."

"You don't think . . . ?"

"It wouldn't be the first time my old enemy has done some of his own field work. At any rate, I want to check through the airport security files." Wayne reached down and pulled a laptop computer from a compartment under the front seat. As he started to boot up the computer, he straightened too quickly and a sharp pain shot up his side.

"Ribs still smarting, sir?"

Wayne grimaced as he shifted in his seat. "That mirror is for keeping an eye on traffic, not on me."

"I quite understand your desire to keep your wits about you, but you could take *something* for the pain. Ibuprofen, at the very least."

"I'll take that under advisement, 'Doctor.' "

"A visit to a physician would not hurt in the least. I have Doctor Thompkins on speed dial."

"No. Leslie would just want me to take it easy."

"What *was* I thinking? Oh, yes, that you should spend some time in actual recuperation. And it wouldn't hurt you to get some sun and fresh air. You could lounge beside the pool, as young playboys are supposed to do."

Wayne's ears pricked up. "Alfred, did you say 'sun'?"

"Yes, it's apparently been quite pleasant at home these past few days. According to the papers."

Bruce Wayne sent his fingers clicking over the keyboard. In response, a new window opened on the computer screen, showing a webcam view of a park in downtown Gotham City. The sun beamed down brightly from a clear, blue sky. A flag flew proudly in a light breeze. Two more keystrokes gave him the temperature. "Seventy-seven degrees Fahrenheit. Light to moderate winds. Interesting. The weather is just about perfect."

"Well, it was bound to happen sooner or later, sir. Gotham can't be dark and dank all the time."

"And yet, the weather is wretched over much of the country. Droughts, flooding, severe storms, and unseasonable temperatures from coast to coast. There's even a report of a blizzard today in Upstate New York."

"Part of your adversary's master plan?"

"Perhaps. But why spare Gotham unless . . . of course. The worst of the weather has hit regions associated with members of the Justice League. And he's assuming that he already dealt with me. No need to pick on the old hometown if the person you most want to bedevil isn't there."

"Sir? Are you smiling?"

"I've fooled him, Alfred. The would-be overlord can be tricked. Which means he can be brought down. All we have to do is find him."

CHAPTER 10

The Greek Connection

Twenty-five thousand feet over the island of Crete, Superman turned north and shot toward the Aegean Sea at twice the speed of sound. Within minutes he was over the Cyclades Islands, beginning a rapid descent toward one particular isle.

It was barely a mile across, a rocky crag of an island whose cliffs rose steeply from the sea. A series of lavish buildings, patterned after the temples of the ancient Greeks, had been built at great expense atop its peaks by an eccentric billionaire who called himself Constantine Stratos.

Superman peered down at the alabaster buildings. *It's been years since I was last here, but things have hardly changed, at least from the outside. I told the Flash that Stratos brought about his own death, but I never did find the man's body. Could Doctor Stratos have somehow survived?*

Stratos remained very much a mystery to the Man

of Steel. Their one meeting had lasted just a few minutes, and much of what he knew about the man he had learned after the fact.

Constantine Stratos had been a foundling, abandoned as an infant at the foot of Greece's Mount Olympus. As he reached adulthood, he had become delusional, convinced that he was a child of the gods and that he, too, would one day rise to join their ranks.

Impatient for power, Stratos exploited a talent for particle physics and computer design to amass a sizable fortune. He then exhausted much of that fortune building his island retreat and funding research aimed at giving him control over the world's weather. Former research associates testified that he thought he was descended from Zeus, that he worked and schemed for the day when he, too, would be able to hurl thunderbolts down from on high.

With that as his goal, Doctor Stratos had designed a satellite that he launched into Earth orbit. Once his satellite was operational, he began bombarding the atmosphere with bursts of focused particle beams, causing radical shifts in weather patterns across the entire globe.

There was no way of telling how much damage he might have caused if his ego hadn't trumped his intelligence. The doctor had called the White House and taken full credit for his handiwork. He informed the President that he would make his full list of demands upon the world when they next spoke.

But they never spoke again. Superman had dealt with Doctor Stratos.

It had not been an easy mission for the Man of To-morrow. He'd encountered a gauntlet of hurricane winds, driving ice storms, and punishing lightning strikes. The memory kept Superman on his guard. *It was a lot like the recent weird weather, telescoped into a few hours.* He swooped low over the island, circling war-ily before he landed. It appeared completely deserted. Its buildings still bore the locks and seals he had placed on them so long ago. *What was it that the ser-vants said he called the main complex? Oh, yes . . . Castle Chaos. The perfect name for the home of such an unstable mind.*

Doctor Stratos had programmed a death trap, a devastating particle beam barrage, aimed at the Man of Steel. The particle beam had driven Superman to his knees, but then the trap backfired on its planner in horrific fashion. Stratos himself had been caught by the edge of the deadly blast, and Superman was un-able to save him. When it was all over, the Man of Steel dismantled both Stratos's command center and his satellite.

Now, after all these years, Superman again strode through the grounds. He searched the estate inch by inch, but he could find no sign either of Stratos or of anything connected with his satellite program.

After hours of thorough inspection, Superman stood on an outcropping, staring out to sea. *All right, no one has tried to rebuild here, at least. I didn't really ex-pect to find anything, but after all that's happened, I had to be certain. . . .*

From below came the labored wheeze of an engine,

and a small fishing boat chugged into view. A whiskery old man looked up from the wheel and, catching sight of the caped man, gave a greeting blast on the ship's horn.

Superman chuckled and waved back.

"Hola!" The old man shouted to make himself heard over the sound of his ship's engine. He stared up at the outcropping in wonder. "Are you . . . Superman?"

The Man of Steel stepped off into space and dropped like a stone toward the sea below. But as he fell, his fall began to slow. He came to a smooth stop and stood in midair just off the deck of the small vessel. "Yes, I am."

The old man blinked, then slapped the side of the wheel housing and gave a laugh that sounded as though it must have started somewhere deep in his belly. He killed the engine and raised his cap in salute. "Welcome! Welcome! Please, come aboard. I am Markos—Markos Papadiamadis. I apologize, my English is not so good."

Superman took a half step down onto the deck. "No apologies necessary, Mr. Papadiamadis. Your English certainly sounds much better than my Greek."

"Please, Superman—Markos! Everybody calls me Markos."

"Then so shall I, Markos." He looked around the ship. "You work these waters?"

"A little." Markos leaned back against the wheel. "The fishing here anymore is not so good. Not like when I was a boy—and even then it was not great. But my father did this, and his father, and his! So I fish a little, and I take tourists out to see the sights." He gestured up at the rocky peak. "What brings you to this cursed place?"

Cursed? "Just satisfying my curiosity, Markos. Some years ago I had a nasty encounter with the owner of that estate. A gentleman named Stratos."

"Gentleman?!" Markos turned his head and spit off the side of the ship. "Better you should call him a madman. I have heard stories, my friend—how he brought fire down from the skies. But he still could not kill you, eh?"

"No, he could not, Markos. But it wasn't for lack of trying. And he slowed me down so much that I couldn't save him from the fire. He fell, burning, into the sea." Superman gestured out to where the water lapped against a rocky shore. "It's always bothered me that I was never able to find his body down there."

"Ha, you looked in the wrong place. Stratos washed ashore on Kithnos, three miles west of here."

"What?" Superman stiffened. "When was this?"

Markos scratched his chin, trying to dredge up the memory. "Three, maybe four days after he brought down the fire."

"You're sure of that?"

"Sure." Markos slapped his chest proudly. "Was my own cousin Kostas who found him. Such burns Kostas had never seen. He said Stratos was raving mad—like he was not before, eh?"

"He was still alive?" Superman couldn't believe what he was hearing. "After three days in the sea?"

"Three, maybe four." Markos shrugged. "It is a mystery how he survived. But Kostas said that night there was a blinding light in the heavens. And the sea churned just before he found the madman. And Kostas, he is not one for tall tales."

"Did your cousin say how long he lived after that?"

"Stratos? For all I know, he lives still. Kostas told me how the doctors took him away to a big hospital in Kallithea. Near Athens."

"Markos, this may be very important. Can you tell me the name of the hospital?"

"But of course, it is very famous. It is named for Hippocrates!"

"Thank you, Markos!" Superman clapped the old fisherman on the shoulder. "You have been a great help to me. But now, you must excuse me."

"Of course, I—" Even as the words passed Markos's lips, the Man of Steel was already fifty feet up in the air and climbing rapidly into the western sky.

Markos waved his cap and gave a final blast on the horn. "It was an honor, Superman. The greatest honor!"

In Kallithea, Doctor Marina Papagos looked up from her paperwork as a tall, broad-shouldered figure dressed in blue and red was ushered into her office. He crossed the room and offered his hand as she rose to greet him.

"Thank you for agreeing to see me on such short notice, Doctor Papagos. I apologize for the imposition."

"It is no imposition at all, Superman." She shook his right hand, smiling broadly, and gestured to a chair in front of her desk. "Please, make yourself comfortable."

"Thank you, Doctor." The Man of Steel settled into the offered seat.

"My assistant said that you wished to inquire about one of our residents?"

"Yes, Constantine Stratos."

"Ah, Constantinos. I had not yet become director of the Hippocrates Institute when he was brought here, but I know his case well. He is a strange, sad one."

"What can you tell me about him?"

"Well, you must understand that his medical records are closed, as a matter of privacy."

"Of course, but you do realize that Stratos was once implicated in an act of international terrorism? I find it curious that there's no record of either the U.S. or the Greek government ever taking any action against him."

"That would be a pointless exercise, Superman. Doctor Stratos suffered severe burns that left him not only disfigured but also partially paralyzed. He has limited mobility and, to be blunt, he is mentally unbalanced. His own mind and body are more of a prison than steel bars could ever be. A gentleman from the American embassy came to question him some years ago, and left satisfied on that score."

"I see. Well, would there be any objection to my speaking with him?"

"That can be arranged." Marina pressed a button on her desktop. "I must warn you, he is quite delusional."

"I'm sure he is, Doctor." Superman glanced down at his clothing. "Even so, I doubt that he'll be happy to see me—at least dressed like this. Could I trouble you for something a little less . . . identifiable?"

Moments later, an orderly admitted the Man of Steel—now wearing plain green hospital scrubs over his garb—to a small, dimly lit room. The large hospital bed that dominated the space lay empty. Its occupant sat slumped in a wheelchair a few feet to one side. He was dressed in white from head to foot.

The first thing Superman noticed about Stratos was that his nose was gone. The fire had taken it, leaving a partially bisected hole in its place.

The man's hair had similarly been burned away, never to return, and a snug-fitting beret now protected his scalp. The cap was pulled down low, ending just above the two unnaturally smooth nubs that had once been ears.

The skin that showed between his collar and the beret was a blotchy pink and pulled very tight across his face. There was a shiny quality to it, as if the man had been sealed in plastic.

"Doctor Stratos?"

The eyes, which had been staring off into space, suddenly swiveled around in their sockets and focused on the disguised Superman. Teeth flashed behind the tight lips and the man spat out his words.

"Who dares speak unbidden to your god, the Lord Stratos?"

Delusional is right. Okay, if that's the way this has to be played. . . . The Man of Tomorrow made a subservient bow and lowered his voice. "I beg your forgiveness, my lord. I am but a humble sinner who has come from far away in search of that which only you can provide."

Stratos considered that for a moment before nodding stiffly. "Very well, mortal. Sit here beside your lord. What do you wish of Stratos? Speak!"

Superman pulled a wooden chair up beside the pale figure and spoke softly into his ruined ear. "I seek knowledge, Lord Stratos. It is written that before you achieved godhood, you walked among us as a man and employed great machines to command the weather."

"This is so. Go on, mortal."

"It is also said that you fought an epic battle against a Man of Steel, and were cast into the fire. Do you recall that?"

"Man of Steel." The words were like a growl from the back of Stratos's throat. "Yes, I remember him. The mortals called him a 'Super Man.' He survived our first encounter, but he shall not survive the next."

"Whatever you say, Lord Stratos. According to the stories I have been told, after the fire, you fell into the sea. They say you were as a dead man for three days, or perhaps four."

"No."

"No?"

"As I fell I was surrounded with a holy light, and drawn up into the heavens." Stratos's eyes took on a distant stare. "There I was tempted by a false god."

"A false god?"

"He treated the mortal wounds and banished the pain of my earthly form. But he gave only false succor. He sought . . ." Stratos raised one hand, stiff and misshapen under its protective cotton glove, to a small circular depression at his right temple. He softly stroked the spot with his claw-like hand, as if trying to prod a long-lost memory.

"Who was this false god? What did he seek?

"Chaos."

"Chaos? You mean, he sought your Castle Chaos?"

"Yes. No. I . . ." Stratos squinted his eyelids shut, wincing from the pain as the skin around them puckered. "He claimed to be a god in the service of Chaos. But all he really sought were the designs of my satellite. He wanted to know how it worked, how it made the energy flow. He coveted my secrets for controlling the weather." His eyes opened wide. "That's when I knew he was a pretender. Don't you see? What need has a god of a satellite?"

"You . . . confuse me, my lord. Didn't you build and use that satellite?"

"That was before." Stratos thrust out a hand and clutched at his visitor's scrubs. "I needed the machines only in the beginning. Once I was elevated to the pantheon of Olympus, I no longer needed such devices."

"I see." Superman gently patted the clutching hand. "Then, you didn't tell him what he wanted to know?"

"I told him it would do him no good. The power was no longer in the machines. It was in me! It had become part of my godhead." Stratos released his grip and sank back into the wheelchair, breathing rapidly.

"Stratos?" The Man of Steel leaned forward, feeling for a pulse. The one he found was strong and steady. *Despite the hell he's been through, his heart is still strong. His lungs are largely untouched. He could live here like this for years, decades.* "Listen to me. You are hyperventilating. Try to breathe more slowly. . . ."

The burned man's head lolled toward Superman. "He wouldn't listen, you know. The pretender would not believe the word of a true god. He tried to take advantage of me."

"How could he have done that, my lord? Didn't you just say that the power was already in you?"

"Yes, yes, of course. But I was still in a transitional state. And that snake was determined to rob me of my glory. He kept probing . . . probing . . ."

Superman's gaze went back to the odd depression at Stratos's right temple. There was, he now realized, a similar one on the left. They were the only parts of his head that seemed even remotely symmetrical. The Man of Tomorrow concentrated, looking beneath the layers of scar tissue, and located two tiny indentations, long healed, on either side of the man's skull.

"My God!"

"Yes, my son?"

"Someone actually probed your brain, didn't they? They probed your brain and then threw you back into the sea."

"Which was just what I wanted! Poseidon bore me back into the arms of Gaea, as I knew he would. And now, here I sit, lord of all about me."

"Haven't you told anyone else of this?"

"Phah! I speak but they do not listen. The god Stratos now shares nothing with non-believers! I speak only to the faithful."

Yes, why should they believe anything you say? "Lord Stratos, do you know who did that to you?"

"I already told you. It was a pretender."

"But who was the pretender? What did he call himself?"

"It is of no matter. He can do nothing more to me, now that I have achieved full godhood."

"If he learned how your satellite worked, he could do a great deal."

"That is not possible. It would no longer work for him. I am the power now." His brow puckered. "Do you doubt me? Do you doubt the power of Stratos?"

"Of course not, my lord. But perhaps, if you could show me some small sign of your power, I would have something with which to instill faith in those friends of mine who do not yet believe."

"You seek to deceive me."

"I wish only to—"

"Silence! Those who associate with disbelievers are *themselves* disbelievers." His burned, ruined face flushed red. "You wish a sign? Very well—may fire rain down from the heavens and slay you, betrayer! No . . . no, let the waters of the sea rise up to drown you. Yes!" A thin line of saliva trickled from the corner of Stratos's mouth as he raved. "And now, let the Earth herself open up and swallow you whole!"

Superman pushed back his chair and got to his feet. Stratos never noticed. To him, the visitor was already gone from his sight. The burned man slumped back in his wheelchair, lost in a world of his own.

The Man of Steel left the room to find Doctor Papagos waiting for him in the corridor. "Were you able to appease the great god Stratos, or did he consign you to Hades?"

"More the latter than the former, I'm afraid. But for a moment or two, I'd swear he was almost lucid."

"You should be honored then, Superman. Such moments are rare."

"Doctor, there doesn't appear to have been any attempt at reconstructive surgery. Why is that? I would think that giving him a nose, if nothing else, would be therapeutic."

"I agree. In fact, several staff members have suggested that. But Constantinos has no family to authorize such a procedure. And whenever the subject has been broached with him, he has rejected it out of hand. You see, part of the delusion is that he has already achieved his most perfect form."

Superman looked back through the door at the twisted man. "Doctor . . . was Stratos ever subjected to shock therapy? Or perhaps had his brain physically probed as part of any treatment?"

"What?" Marina Papagos looked shocked. "Absolutely not. There have been some CAT scans, but that is all. Anything else would be barbaric."

"I didn't mean to suggest that the institute would be party to any such thing. I meant before his arrival here."

"No. Did he make such a claim?" She shook her head. "More delusions."

"Yes." The Man of Tomorrow nodded. "No doubt." But still, he wondered. Were Stratos's claims nothing more than insane ramblings, or did they hold a kernel of truth? He had seen the marks on the man's skull with his own eyes. *And if there is any truth to what he said, who was the mysterious false god?*

From *Newstime* magazine, volume 71, number 26:

Fog, Floods, and Weather Most Foul

Last summer Europe sweltered under a blistering heat wave, while tropical storms battered American coastlines. Drought-stricken western states coughed up dust while vast stretches of the Midwest had more water than they could handle. With that freakish weather still fresh in mind, we all hoped that this year would be better.

Well, don't get your hopes up.

Even before the summer solstice passed, another season of weird weather was already upon us. Consider:

- Following a sudden storm that resulted in an estimated 160 million dollars in property damage, a ten-inch diameter hailstone was recovered in Gateway City. The stone topped the record seven-incher that fell on Aurora, Nebraska, almost exactly a year earlier.

- Repair work on Star City's landmark Capstone Bridge was halted when high winds and driving sleet threatened to send workers and scaffolding into Cazeneuve Bay.
- One hundred and forty-three (yes, 143) tornadoes struck northeastern Kansas in a 12-hour period.
- Over 200,000 homes and businesses in St. Roche, Louisiana, were without power for four days after a sudden storm brewed up over the Mississippi River Delta, flooding sections of the parish and hammering the area with 70-mph winds.
- And, even as this issue of NEWSTIME was being composed, a sudden fog formed along Metropolis's I-995 beltway near the busy Bessolo Interchange, resulting in a thirty-seven-vehicle pileup.

In the latter incident, motorists experienced a bit of good luck for a change. A van full of emergency medical technicians en route to a training symposium was one of the first vehicles to safely come upon the scene. The EMTs were able to stabilize the accident victims until further help arrived in the form of Superman. The fog prevented rescue helicopters from taking off, but the Man of Steel was able to fly crash survivors, medics, and entire ambulances to regional trauma centers.

In fact, if there has been any silver lining to the

recent storm clouds, it is that active and reserve members of the Justice League of America have been nearby to help when foul weather struck.

But even super heroes can't be everywhere. And the National Climatic Data Center says that current weather patterns are quite unlike anything anyone has seen since records were first kept. Whether this is a result of global warming remains unknown. But if the past few days are any indication, we may all be in for an uncertain summer.

A word of advice: Keep that umbrella handy.

—LOWELL MOSBAUGH

On the tenth floor of the Galaxy Communications Building, Charlie Maxwell sat hunched forward in the director's seat, running over his checklist as the clock ticked down the final seconds to six o'clock. "Fifteen seconds to air, people. Ready the opening and prepare to roll in five—four—three—two—one. Roll opening!"

Across the speakers and headsets in master control came a soaring fanfare of brass and strings. Simultaneously, the network feed monitors showed the image of a rotating Earth growing larger amid a dazzling starscape. Just before the globe could fill the screen, a stylized letter "G" suddenly came flying around the curve of the planet. It settled in the lower left-hand corner of the screen, and more letters flowed out of it, forming a bold logo. The fanfare's volume dropped as the voice of the network's booth announcer boomed across the airwaves:

"Direct from the Galaxy NewsCenter in Metropolis, this is the *GBS Evening News* with David Rowlands . . . for Friday, June twenty-fifth."

And in Studio A, camera one panned in to a medium close-up of Rowlands at his news desk.

"Good evening. We begin tonight with the weather. As most of you are aware, we have had quite a week of it—all across the world, really—but particularly on this continent. It seems as though there have been few sections of North America that have not experienced some form of extreme weather. We have seen every condition imaginable and some that border on the bizarre."

As Rowlands turned to his left, the director cut to camera two, and viewers instantly saw a long shot of the NewsCenter set. The anchor desk occupied the left-hand side of the screen, and to the right an earnest middle-aged man stood before a large weather map.

"And so, we've asked GBS science correspondent Doctor Gregory Linden to look into the matter and try to make some sense of it all. Greg?"

"After a week like this one, that's a tall order, David." The screen cut to a video montage of recent weather conditions. "From a blistering heat wave in the Rockies to the strangest blizzard ever recorded in New York's Finger Lakes region, it has felt as if the U.S. was under assault from its own weather."

Doctor Linden returned to the screen, and the map behind him came to life with computer-animated images of wind flow.

"Of course, uncertain weather is nothing new to

many people. In recent decades there have been numerous fluctuations in the world's climate patterns. We've all become attuned to phenomena such as El Niño and La Niña, and the shifts they have caused in climate patterns.

"But the past few days have seen a series of radical weather events, striking hard and seemingly at random in relatively small areas—a city or a township, for instance—and often for a very brief time. The duration of these events has been for as little as thirty minutes and as long as four hours. And, in many cases, they have not significantly been felt in the regions directly surrounding them. That now appears to be changing, however, as these radical events have been so numerous that they have also begun to alter the jet stream.

"Experts at the National Weather Service now believe that this most recent siege actually began last month with a series of smaller weather anomalies along the East Coast. At the time, they were considered nothing more than minor fluctuations—just typical seasonal annoyances. But it is now thought that they were just the beginning of some larger shift in patterns that could make for a very unpredictable summer. David . . ."

The screen cut back to a two-shot of the correspondent and the news anchor, and Rowlands leaned pointedly toward his colleague.

"Greg, has there been any word at all as to the cause of this extreme weather? We've heard a lot of talk in recent years about the possible effects of global warming. Could this be a result?"

"Possibly, David, though blaming it on that or sunspot activity or any single cause would be premature. The problem is that this recent rash of disturbances doesn't fit any previously known pattern. A lot of theories are being put forth, but frankly, the experts are baffled. One meteorologist remarked, 'It's as if somebody up there doesn't like us.' "

CHAPTER 11

Eye of the Storm

Lois Lane pushed down on the crash bar of a glass door and stepped outside onto the West Terrace of the San Diego Convention Center. She strolled past a series of big potted plants and stood beside a low wall, staring out at the hundreds of boats tied up in the marina below. A gentle breeze wafted over the dockside promenade, and Lois took a long, deep breath.

A pair of high heels clicked across the terrace behind her. "A nice change after the weather back east, isn't it?"

Lois turned to see a familiar face smiling at her. "Tell me about it. It's been so wet in Metropolis that moss is starting to grow on everyone's north side. How've you been, Cat?"

"Fabulous as always, darling." Catherine Jane Grant leaned one hip against the wall and kicked out of her heels. "Fabulous, but weary. The new talk show has had me on the road for months, but it's been worth it in market share." She alternately curled and flexed her toes. "You still slogging around the country for the dear old *Daily Planet?*"

" 'Fraid so. On top of my regular work, I've been filling in on the Washington beat while Sue McMasters is out on maternity leave."

"Get out! Little Susie's having a baby?"

"She's due any day. With twins, in fact." Lois closed her eyes and tilted her head skyward. "I really think Perry sent me on this assignment as a reward. This is heavenly. I couldn't stand being cooped up inside another moment. I had to take a break and catch some sun and fresh air."

"Especially after enduring all the hot air in there, huh?"

"The speeches *were* getting to be a bit tedious. I'm actually a little surprised to find you here, Cat. No offense, but your show doesn't usually cover such high-tech public works."

"Too, too true, darling. But this new desalinization project is attracting a lot of A-list support. And celebrity interviews are my life blood."

"I hear that."

Catherine Grant had started out as a gossip columnist for a major Los Angeles newspaper. She'd gained a reputation for her in-depth interviews with Hollywood celebrities, and had been linked romantically with several famous leading men. As her fame grew, she had been lured to Metropolis, where she'd continued her popular column for the *Daily Planet*'s entertainment section. But the camera loved Cat, and she soon moved on to a series of jobs at GBS, first as a cohost of *Holly-*

wood Tonight, and eventually as the star—and executive producer—of her own highly rated talk show.

Lois sometimes envied Cat's glamorous career. Cat lived in a world of five-star hotels and first-class travel. Lois tended to fly coach.

Cat glanced back at the convention center. "Honestly, Lois, I don't know how you've managed to make sense of all that mumbo-jumbo about distillation and subliminalization."

"Sublimation, Cat."

"Whatever. Seriously, I don't know how you stayed awake. It isn't as if those people in there are going to do anything *but* talk. I usually see you interviewing people who actually accomplish things. You're such a go-getter. You skydive, for heaven's sake. And I'll bet you've never had to wear heels unless you really wanted to. I envy that."

"Oh. Thank you." Lois smiled. *I guess the grass* is *always greener. . . .* "As for the conference, all jargon aside, it *is* a very important project. California can't survive without water, and there isn't nearly enough available for future needs."

"Careful, Lois, you're starting to sound like a candidate, and heaven knows we've had enough of them lately."

"Well, it's about time somebody started thinking about solutions to these problems. Otherwise, our children are going to be stuck with them."

Cat's eyes became watery, and her voice hushed. "Not mine."

"Oh, Cat, I'm sorry. I—"

Cat blinked back a tear. Her son Adam had been killed just a few years before. "I'll be all right. It's just that . . . it still hurts."

"I know." Lois took her hand. "No, that's not right. I *don't* know, but—"

Cat nodded and hugged Lois to her. "You're a good friend. Sometimes, it just hits me out of the blue. I guess that between hearing about Susie's twins and your talking about—" She stopped herself and pulled back to look at her friend. "Lois! Don't tell me that you and Clark are—?"

"Are what?"

"Expecting?"

"No, of course not. I mean, we've talked about it, but—"

Cat arched an eyebrow. "Darling! Married all this time and all you've done about it is *talk?*"

"You know what I mean."

"Just teasing, love. But I am a little surprised that the two of you haven't already spawned."

"Cat, we both have careers that keep us constantly on the go. We're too busy to raise a family right now."

"Well, who isn't? But that's never stopped most people."

"Then I guess we're not 'most people.' "

"No, you're not." Cat nodded approvingly. "So tell me, how is the hunky Mr. Kent these days? Or should I ask, *where* is he?"

"Right behind you."

Catherine caught herself in mid-flinch and whispered to Lois, "How long has he been standing there?"

"Only since 'So tell me . . .' "

"Clark, darling! So wonderful to see you." Cat spun around and stretched up on the tips of her toes to give him a peck on the cheek. "Ooo, that's not easy without heels. Lois didn't tell me you were here on assignment together."

"We're not, Cat. I'm actually chasing down a different story. But I thought that, as long as I was in the area . . ."

Lois took his hand in hers. "Yes, dear?"

Clark raised her fingers to his lips and kissed them lightly. ". . . I'd drop by and see if you were interested in taking a little break. But if I'm interrupting anything important—"

"Hardly! Lois and I were just having a little girl talk." Cat made a show of checking her watch. "And I really do need to get back and see if I can buttonhole the governor. You two have fun now!" She scooped up her shoes and with a wave—and a wink to Lois—dashed back into the convention center.

"So . . ." Lois walked her fingers up her husband's arm. "What did you have in mind, Mr. Kent?"

"I thought an early lunch, maybe a walk along the beach." Clark stooped down and pulled a large wicker picnic hamper out from behind one of the concrete planters. "I came prepared."

"Don't you always? But the beach is so far away."

"Not for us."

Moments later, Clark knelt down beside Lois on a blanket on Coronado Beach. She sat back, feeling the sand shift beneath the soft flannel, and drank in the salty air. Overhead a single gull drifted by. "This was a lovely idea."

"Well, we've missed sharing meals so many times the past few weeks, I decided that I had to do something about that." He reached into the hamper and started pulling out waxed containers. One bore the logo of a famous New Orleans restaurant.

"Clark, you didn't?" Lois grabbed it up and opened the top. "You did! You brought me crayfish jambalaya!"

"I know it's your favorite." He pulled out a brightly colored jar. "I also stopped off in San Antonio and picked up some of that hot salsa you like."

Lois looked closer at the hamper's contents. "Cheese, fruit, bread—you brought us a feast."

"Well, a modest one."

"You sweet, sweet man!" She kissed him quickly across the lips. "You can surprise me like this any time."

Clark returned the kiss and passed her a forkful of jambalaya.

Half an hour later, Lois finally dropped a spoon into an empty container and returned it to the hamper. "That's it. I can't eat another bite." She leaned heavily against Clark's shoulder. "As it is, you'll have to roll me back to San Diego."

"Do you need to be getting back?"

She glanced at her watch. "No, they're breaking for lunch about now. And theirs won't be even half as good as ours was." She reached up and tickled his earlobe. "Besides, you promised me a walk along the beach."

"So I did."

They left their shoes and stockings on the blanket beside the hamper and set out arm in arm along the beach.

"Oh, yes. This is the life. It's a day for pastoral dances!"

"May I quote you on that, Miss Lane?"

"You may, indeed, Mister Kent. This is just about perfect. A beautiful sunny sky, cool ocean breezes, and warm sand between my toes." She kicked a small shower of sand into the air. "We have to grab hold of moments like this and enjoy them while we can. Beautiful days like these don't last forever."

"No, they don't. Not even here." He pointed out to sea. "Just two days ago, water spouts were spotted off the North Island Naval Air Station. They came within fifty feet of the shore before they just . . . disappeared."

"Clark, you can't stop the weather."

"No, but someone is playing with it. And I don't know who."

"You're sure of that?"

"Absolutely sure? No. But I can't shake the feeling that . . ." He let the words trail off.

"What is it, Clark? What's the matter?"

"I flew to the Aegean yesterday, and found Doctor Stratos." He quickly filled her in on his discovery. "So I don't know what to think now. After I got back to the States, I did some more checking and discovered that the CIA had known about Stratos's condition for years. Apparently, it had never occurred to anyone that it might be a good idea to pass the word along to Superman."

"That's bureaucracy for you. The wheels grind slowly, if at all."

Clark frowned. "It makes me wonder what else they've forgotten to tell me over the years."

"At least you finally learned something. Do you think this 'false god' of Stratos's really existed?"

"I don't know. But somebody had stuck needles into his head. And I'd swear that someone or some-*thing* is behind this freakish weather. It all seems targeted. The weather has hit the hardest in areas where members of the Justice League live. We've all been kept hopping, playing catch-up with emergency rescues. This is the first real break I've had since I got back from Europe." He clenched his hands into fists. "If someone is using Stratos's technology against us—!"

"Hey, you! Look at me! There is no way that you are responsible for that. And whatever's going on, you don't have to deal with it alone. If this is affecting the rest of the Justice League, it's their fight, too."

"I've already put out a call for an emergency planning meeting of the JLA's current active membership. That's the other reason why I wanted to be with you today." Clark shifted his feet in the sand. "The meeting is tonight. And depending on how this pans out, we may all become very busy."

"Meaning?"

"Meaning it may be quite a while before we're able to enjoy another meal together." He stared down at the sand. "I'm sorry, hon."

Lois tilted his face toward her and kissed it. "Thank you."

Clark's eyebrows arched high over his glasses. "For what?"

"For being you. I can't begin to tell you how many times my father surprised my mother—and they were never very pleasant surprises—with 'Pack the girls up, Ellie, and be ready to leave in six hours. We're moving halfway around the world.' And Mom would jump and do it without complaining. And Dad never once said he was sorry." She hugged Clark hard. "So thank you for not being a bonehead, like him. And thank you for making me realize that I'm not becoming my mother."

Clark wrapped his arms around Lois, gently lifting her up until they were both eye to eye. "I love you so much. I know it's not easy being married to me."

"Hey, I knew what I was getting into the day I said, 'I do.' " Lois smiled. "And I'd gladly say it all over again. Just remember, I'm always here for you. For that matter, so are Jonathan and Martha."

He nodded. "I know. I've been thinking about the folks a lot lately."

"As well you should. Martha and Jonathan are a couple of gems. Face it, Clark, you hit the jackpot in the parent lottery. And I lucked into the world's best in-laws."

"Believe me, I know it."

"You'd better. Didn't you tell me once that some big storm snowed them in just after they found you?"

"Yeah, it did. Pa mentioned that just last week. They've both lived through a lot of wild weather out on the plains."

"So talk to them about this, too. Get their perspective. It couldn't hurt."

The sun bore down on central Kansas, baking the soil until it cracked.

In rural Lowell County, Jonathan Kent sat on the back porch swing, fanning himself with a copy of the *Smallville Daily Ledger*. His attention was on a tiny portable television, tuned to a cable news station.

"There you are!" Martha pushed the screen door halfway open. "What are you doing, watching TV outside?"

"Too hot to watch it inside."

She pushed back a sweaty lock of hair from her forehead. "Not that much cooler out here."

"I know. But the cable doesn't reach down to the cellar. And sometimes there's the hint of a breeze."

"Maybe this will help." Martha stepped out onto the porch with a pitcher of lemonade and two tall glasses of ice on a tray.

"Looks like a good start." Jonathan pulled up a small table to hold the tray and slid over to make room on the swing. "Thank you, sweetie."

"You old flirt. So I'm still your sweetie after all these years?"

"None other." Jonathan raised his glass and clinked

it gently to hers. "Here's to us. Oh, yeah, that does hit the spot."

"Don't drink it too fast, it'll go to your head. What's on the news?"

"The weather. It's crowding everything else out. Seems there's heavy flooding down in Houston. Looks like they're getting the rain we need." Jonathan ran his glass over his forehead. "It's a dirty shame we can't swap some of this. The corn's never gonna grow if this keeps up."

"Jonathan, look—it's Clark!"

"Huh? Where?"

"On the television!"

Sure enough, the little screen showed Superman hauling the cars of stranded motorists up out of a flooded expressway underpass.

"Quick, Jon, turn it up!"

"—speedy arrival of the Man of Steel, who authorities are now crediting with the rescue of over fifty people over the past half—" The sound cut out as the screen went black.

"What the devil?" Jonathan started to reach for the set.

Through the screen over the open kitchen door, the Kents could hear a short warning beep from the smoke detector and a soft mechanical wheeze as the compressor of their refrigerator shuddered to a stop.

"Don't tell me—" Jonathan pulled open the screen door and reached inside to flip a switch. Nothing happened. "Great. On top of everything else, we've lost power. Probably too many people in town running their air conditioners again."

"Well, there's no good in complaining, Jonathan. It's not the first time, and it probably won't be the last."

"Yeah, you're right, hon." He set down his glass and sighed. "Guess I'd better get out to the barn and see if I can start up that danged—"

From the barn, there came a pop and a chug, followed by the hum of a diesel engine.

"—generator."

Suddenly, both the television and the refrigerator came back to life. Jonathan and Martha looked at each other, then both of them jumped off the porch and dashed for the barn. Inside, they were greeted by the sight of their son, stripped to the waist and holding a five-hundred-pound running generator balanced on his shoulder.

"Clark?"

"Hi, folks. Give me just a minute, will you?" He nudged a row of cinderblocks back into place with the side of one foot, then carefully lowered the running engine down onto the blocks. "That's better. It wasn't until after I fired up the generator that I realized it wasn't seated quite properly. Barn floor must be warping a little."

Clark stepped out from behind the engine and held up his hands. "Don't get too close yet, Ma. My hands are kind of greasy." He rapidly ran his palms together, and a tiny plume of smoke curled up and away from them. "There. Anything else on me?"

"Just a little smudge on your shoulder, dear. Here, let me get it." Martha picked up a clean rag from a nearby workbench and brushed the dirt away. "There, that's the worst of it, but you'll want to come in and clean up. Where's your shirt?"

"Tossed it over on the straw bale." Clark pushed his glasses back up on the bridge of his nose and grinned at her. "I knew if I got it dirty, you'd just want to wash it. Figured I'd save you the effort and the water."

"Oh, you!"

Jonathan's grin was as broad as Clark's. "Good to see you, son. And thanks for getting our power back up. But the TV showed you down in Texas."

"I was. But that was a good ten minutes ago. What you saw must've been on tape. And yes, Ma, I had a very nice lunch with Lois—just a couple of hours before that."

"All right, smarty. You can tell us all about your day after you've had a chance to wash up." She picked up Clark's shirt and took him by the arm. "Come along now, I just made a big batch of fresh lemonade."

"Now, how could I pass on an offer like that?"

Minutes later, Clark pulled up a stool and joined his parents on the porch for lemonade and conversation.

" . . . yeah, son, it's been on the dry side all spring, but this past week has been a killer. Just bone dry all the way to the Rockies. Gonna be a bad year for crops if we don't get some rain soon."

"Do you really think someone could be responsible for all this, dear?"

"Directly responsible? I don't know. But if Stratos's mystery man is causing enough extreme cases in enough places, the weather everywhere might ultimately be affected. Like knocking over dominoes."

Jonathan tapped a finger against his chin. "Yeah, I could see how that would work. Especially on the plains. A wind gets started out here, there's not much to stop it. Lord knows, we've seen a lot of hellacious storms over the years."

Clark looked over at his father. "Like on the day I was born?"

"One of the biggest."

"Tell me the story, Pa. Tell me again."

Martha lay her hand on Jonathan's shoulder and he touched it gently. "Clark, there's not much about that day that I'm ever going to forget.

"It was November. Still fall by the calendar, but it was already starting to feel like winter. The radio had warned of a big storm blowing in from the west, so your mom and I were outside, battening down the last of the shutters. That's how we came to see this bright light shoot across the sky. It passed low over the house and just missed grazing the roof of the barn. About a second later there was a big boom and the ground, the barn, the whole house shook.

"The thing had been so bright and passed over us so fast that I thought it had to be a meteor. Your ma was afraid it was a small plane. Anyway, we hopped in the old truck and headed out across the fields to see if we could find out what it was. And there, in a far corner of the back forty, sitting in a shallow crater—that's where we found your spaceship.

"It was like a big, silvery egg, all scarred and pitted and smoking. At first, we didn't know what to make of it. But the 'egg' was sort of translucent, and Martha swore she could see something moving just under the surface. I was still wearing my work gloves, so I reached out all cautious-like. I expected the egg to be hot, but it wasn't. And as I ran my hand over the surface, darned if the shell of the egg didn't begin to melt away at my touch.

"And inside the shell, I could see a pair of eyes looking back at me. Then a little mouth opened up and began to wail. I just stood there with my jaw down around my collarbone. I remember Martha shouting, "It's a baby!" Then she pushed past me and gathered you up into her arms.

"By the time we got you home, your ma here already had you named. She was bound and determined to keep you."

Clark nodded. "And that's when the storm hit?"

"I'll say it did. Flurries were already swirling as we pulled up beside the house. I had no sooner put the truck away than ol' Mama Nature hit Lowell County—most of Kansas, really—with the worst blizzard in over a hundred years. Dumped a good four to six feet of snow around here. We had some drifts up to the eaves. It's a good thing our larder was full, 'cause we didn't get back into town for going on five months.

"When we finally did, we had ourselves a new son to show off. We'd had a couple of miscarriages and some false alarms, and well, when we told everybody that we'd been keeping a new try a secret, they believed us. Told 'em that I'd delivered you myself—which, now that I think of it, was more or less true." Jonathan leaned back in the porch swing and grinned. "I never get tired of telling that story, and you and Martha are just about the only ones I can tell it to."

"Yes, dear. We know." Martha began refilling their glasses. "Everyone was so happy for us, Clark—they really wanted to believe you were our own. People were always saying how much they thought you took after my great-grandfather Conrad."

"Yeah, or *my* great-uncle Truman. No one ever suspected that we'd found you in a rocket or that you'd come to us from another planet."

"Well, even *we* didn't know about that 'other planet' business then, Clark." Martha sat down on the swing alongside her husband. "And didn't for years. I thought that we'd rescued you from some awful experiment."

"Speak for yourself, Martha. I'd always suspected something, son. I wasn't exactly sure what, but that ship of yours didn't look like anything the Russians had ever made, and it sure as shootin' wasn't American."

"Well, the important thing is that we didn't care where you were from. We just raised you as our own."

"And if you don't mind my saying so, you did a fine job of it, both of you."

"Thank you, Clark." Martha ruffled his hair. "It's sweet of you to say that."

"I'm serious. You've always been here for me. When I had to make the hard decisions about what to do with my life, you helped me create Superman." He thought of all the hours Martha had spent over the years, just sewing his capes. "If we hadn't come up with the Superman identity, and figured out how to make him seem like a different man from Clark Kent, I don't know what I would have done."

"We all do what we can, son. That's all anyone can do." Jonathan clapped Clark on the back. "You're just able to do more than most, is all."

"Still, it's hard enough, just raising a growing boy. You had one who kept getting stronger and developing strange new powers. It couldn't have been easy."

"Well . . ." Martha and Jonathan looked at each other.

Clark had been normal enough at first, thank God. Disciplining a super-toddler would have been just about impossible. His powers hadn't really started manifesting themselves until he was eight.

Jonathan had been the only witness when a neighbor's bull trampled Clark. The elder Kent was afraid that he'd find the boy all bloodied and broken, but his son had survived without so much as a scratch. It wasn't long afterward that Martha had caught Clark lifting up the back of their old truck in search of his softball.

By the time their boy reached puberty, he was seeing through solid objects. And during that last golden summer before his senior year in high school, Clark had taken a backward step over a drainage ditch and discovered that he could defy gravity and fly.

They remembered it all.

". . . it was a challenge at times, dear. But you were such a good boy—I wouldn't have traded you for any other child in the world."

"And what your ma just said goes double for me. What you've accomplished with your life has done us proud."

"I had good role models. I only wish I could make sense of this weather mess."

"You will, son. Just remember, you're not alone in this."

Clark laughed. "Lois used almost those exact words earlier today."

"You found yourself one smart wife, Clark." Jonathan threw an arm around Martha's shoulders. "Of course, so did I. Do we know how to pick 'em or what?"

CHAPTER 12

Revelations

Mark's head bobbed in time with the beat of drums that sounded all around him. There were so many, the rhythm was almost hypnotic. He tried to count all the drummers as they passed him by. *No, that isn't right. They're standing still—I'm passing them by. But how is that possible? I'm sitting down.* Mark slouched back in his seat and stared at the heads of the hooded men who moved along with him. *Oh, right . . . now I remember. They're carrying me in a . . . what's it called? A sedan chair!*

He smiled broadly, proud of himself for recalling the words, and felt a wet stickiness on his upper lip. Mark ran his finger under his nose, wiping away a small trickle of blood. *'Nother nose bleed? Oh, well . . . that's why God invented tissues.* He blinked, trying to remember where they were going. He knew that something was supposed to happen, and he had to be there.

A set of golden doors opened before them, and Mark's

bearers carried him into a vast open chamber draped in silks of purple and gold. Two hundred men, all dressed in green, stood by in silence, heads bowed beneath their hoods. *Man, never even seen this hall before. How many rooms are there in this place?* Mark tried to take it all in. Of all those gathered here, the only ones not wearing hoods were himself and Adam. When Mark spotted his host, he was momentarily tempted to call out, but some inner voice stopped him. *This . . . this is important. Just sit and watch.*

At the far end of the chamber, atop a marble dais, Adam sat in a lotus position on a simple woven mat. He wore only a cotton breechcloth, a light sheen of perspiration glistening over the muscles of his upper body. Behind him knelt a hooded man brandishing a ceremonial dagger. As the drums beat on, the underling first kissed the blade and then began to shave the head of his master.

The hooded man worked quickly and with great precision. In minutes, Adam's scalp was bare. The underling left not a single nick or cut. When he was finished, the only hair that remained on his master's head were the eyebrows and two tufts of beard on the lower jaw, framing a strong, prominent chin.

As Mark looked on, Adam rose and the drumming ceased. The shaved man clapped his hands together, and four other hooded men scurried to his side, bringing with them new vestments. For several moments Adam all but disappeared from view as the underlings surrounded him, dressing him. Then they stepped aside and he strode to the edge of the dais.

He stood before them all, dressed from head to foot in sleek golden metal mesh. A toga of forest green hung from his left shoulder to his knees, held at his waist by a broad golden belt. In his left hand he grasped a long golden staff topped with the carved head of a great hooded serpent. A final underling approached him from behind and fitted an ornate mask and hood into place over his head, concealing all of his face above the mouth.

The golden man raised the staff high above his head, and a cry went up from his assembled followers:

"All hail the Most Holy One! Hail to the Naja-Naja! And to the glory of the Kali Yuga!"

His followers, to a man, bowed low as their lord and master descended the marble steps at the front of the dais. The Naja-Naja approached the sedan chair and raised his right hand in greeting. "Well, Brother Mark, what do you think of us now?"

Mark just gaped at him. He tried to find something profound to say, but all he could manage was: "That's . . . one of the bravest things I've ever seen."

"Brave? What do you mean?"

"There's no way I would ever let anybody dry-shave *me* like that. How'd he do that without drawing blood?"

The Naja-Naja laughed. "The secret is in using a very sharp blade and employing a faithful man with a very steady hand. But the shaving is just part of the ritual. This—" He swung his staff around, gesturing to the chamber around them. "—is all very important

to us, as well as to you. Here we prepare for the greatness that is yet to come."

"Uh-huh." Mark nodded his head. "Gonna be great,
all right. Nobody's ever tried anything this big before.
When we're done, the big nations'll all be lining up to
fill our pockets." A glazed look came over his eyes
and another trickle of blood appeared at the corner of
his nose. "They'll pay anything to have good weather
again. We'll be richer than Croesus. We'll have it
all . . . all the money in the world."

The Naja-Naja gently patted Mark's hand, speaking to him slowly and softly, as one would to a small
child. "Yes, the world will soon learn our intentions.
But we must part company now."

"We must?" Mark seemed confused.

"Yes, Brother Mark. As I have told you, I have many
enemies in this world. I must travel far from here so
that you may remain safe and in control." He gently
squeezed the other man's hand. "But I shall remain in
close communication with you. My words to your
ears. You understand?"

"I gotcha, Sahib!" Mark winked and weakly curled
his left hand, pointing his index finger like the barrel
of a gun. "We'll show 'em. We'll show 'em all!"

"Yes, yes. But it is important that you relax now."
The Naja-Naja waved his hand in a serpentine pattern
before Mark's eyes. "You must save yourself for the
missions yet to come. Sleep, my friend. Sleep . . ."

Mark went limp and slumped back against the
sedan chair, dead to the world.

*   *   *

The Naja-Naja clapped his hands together sharply and the bearers again lifted the corners of the chair. "Take him to Vault Seven and prepare for the Omega Mission."

The lead bearer bowed his head. "Your will be done, Most Holy One."

The Naja-Naja watched as the unconscious man was borne away. Then, he turned and retraced his steps across the chamber. But as he strode to the foot of the marble steps, one hooded man separated from the crowd and ran, bowing and scraping, after him.

"O great Naja!"

"What?" The golden-clad man whirled on his heels and affixed his follower with a withering stare. "Who dares?"

"A thousand, thousand pardons, Sahib." The hooded man crawled forward on his knees, groveling before the master. "I but seek enlightenment. The words Brother Mark spoke leave me confused. They had the sound of extortion!"

"Silence!" He raised the staff high, and all averted their eyes. The groveling man pressed his face to the floor. "You seek enlightenment, fool? Very well. Know you this: In his earlier life, Brother Mark was a gifted man, yet a common criminal. He was led into our service by the suggestion that the weather could be used as a tool to extort tribute from the governments of the world. That was merely the initial ploy used to enthrall him. The truth is something he need not know. Nor would he understand."

"I . . . I see, Most Holy One. Forgive me."

"No."

"But, Sahib, I—!"

"The Naja-Naja never forgives doubters." He struck his staff against the floor twice, and a trap door yawned open just three feet behind the groveling man. The master then picked the man up by the throat and hurled him down through the opening. "All who doubt must be disciplined for their sin."

The doubter picked himself up from the floor of the chamber below. The only illumination came from the shaft of light shining down from the open trap above, and the room bore a strong stench of blood and offal.

A heavy footfall echoed from the darkness, and a huge, hulking shadow fell across the doubter.

"No, Most Holy One! Not the Servitor! Please! Mercy—!"

A gigantic metal hand closed around him, and he began to scream.

The hand did not open again until the doubter was silent and still.

High above the Earth, the Watchtower hung over the Western Hemisphere in geosynchronous orbit. Unless deliberately moved, it would always remain in the same location relative to the surface.

Afternoon was just turning to twilight along the East Coast of the United States far below, when Wonder Woman, the Flash, Manhunter, the Atom, and Green Lantern joined Superman in the Watchtower's innermost chamber.

As the Justice League took their seats, Superman paced impatiently around their big circular meeting table. "Still no word from the Batman?"

The Atom adjusted the headset he wore over his mask, checking with the satellite's communication systems via remote hookup. "None. I've been trying all day, but I haven't been able to raise him."

Wonder Woman looked unconcerned. "Batman must be preoccupied. He often goes incommunicado when he's on a personal mission."

Green Lantern shrugged. "You guys know the Batman a lot better than I do. I can never figure out why he does half the stuff he does."

The Flash drummed his fingers on the tabletop. "Don't let it bug you, Ringo, you're not alone on that score. I mean, *I* think fast, but the Bat is always a page or two ahead of me."

"Much as I respect the Batman's abilities, perhaps we should start without him." The Manhunter turned to Superman. "The situation we face is of pressing importance."

"Yes, you're right, J'onn." Superman moved to his chair, but did not sit down. "As current chairman, I hereby convene this special council of the Justice League of America to discuss the current weather emergencies. You'll recall that I first suspected something unnatural about the storm we encountered in Anchorage. And everything we've seen since just reinforces my feeling that someone has been deliberately manipulating the weather. It's as if we're all being tested, toyed with. And I may have uncovered a lead. . . ."

The Man of Steel briefly outlined what he had learned from questioning Doctor Stratos. "Now, I'm not certain how much credence we should place in his ravings, but if anyone has gotten even a hint of how his satellite system worked, they could conceivably find a way to control the weather."

"Y-e-s, that might be." The Atom swung a keyboard up from under the arm of his chair, and a series of small screens inlaid in the table in front of them lit up. "I've been looking for a cause of all this ever since J'onn and Diana helped me recalibrate our global scanners after the Anchorage storm. I still haven't found out what's responsible, but I have found an intriguing common factor." A map of North America appeared on the screens, showing a series of glowing patterns around the locations of the major weather events. "It's very subtle, but there's definitely an unusual electromagnetic disturbance accompanying each case of extreme weather. Whether it's a side effect of the storms, or part of what is triggering the fronts, I don't yet know."

Superman pored over the screens. "This is a good start, Ray. Keep after it. Have you detected any signs of particle beam transmissions?"

"None so far. Something that radical should stand out like a sore thumb, but I'll expand the spectrum search."

"Wow." Green Lantern looked up from the screens. "This stuff is way out of my field of expertise. But shoveling out the Ivytown blizzard convinced me that something weird is at work here. And we'd better get to the bottom of it fast."

"Agreed." Manhunter swung out a keyboard of his own. "Presuming that there is a deliberate agent behind the weather, who would have the power to do this? Let's consider possible suspects. I see that Mr. Freeze is currently locked away in Arkham Asylum."

"I've already been thinking along those lines, J'onn." The Flash peered over the Martian's shoulder. "If you'll check my database, you'll see that the Weather Wizard escaped from Federal custody—again—a couple of months ago. I've tried to get a line on him, without much luck. But I really don't think the Wiz has anywhere near the power needed to pull off a series of storms this big. There might be a remote chance if he were working with other super-types with complementary powers, but that's a mighty big 'if.' And my list of other possible 'weathermen' is pretty slim."

Wally held up a hand and started ticking them off. "There's Heat Wave, but he served his time and has gone straight. I checked him out personally. Aside from him, there's Captain Cold, the Icicle, and Chillblaine—and I know for a fact that they are all currently behind bars."

Wonder Woman looked up from the database display. "I don't know who Stratos's 'false god' might be, Superman, but I am certain that no Olympian gods are involved. Have any of you considered the possibility of an alien menace? Brainiac, perhaps. Or Kanjar Ro?"

Before Superman could reply, a wall-size display screen lit up behind Wonder Woman, and a voice called out: "You don't have to look off-world to find the hand behind this, Diana."

The members of the League turned as one to see the on-screen image of the Batman looming over them. He sat regally in a command chair, his black cape draped around him. From the eerily lit stalactites in the background of the picture, it was obvious to Superman and the others that their secretive ally was speaking to them via a direct communications link from his Batcave lair.

"Hey, nice of you to finally check in, Bats."

The Batman ignored the Flash's jibe and looked directly to Superman. "Mister Chairman . . . I regret the recent silence I have had to maintain. It was necessary for the purposes of my investigation that our common enemy believe that he was successful in killing me."

The Man of Steel stood and addressed the screen. "By 'common enemy,' you mean you've been able to identify the force responsible for these weather attacks?"

"I have. I've yet to locate him, but I know for certain that it is the work of the Naja-Naja, the cult leader better known as Kobra."

Superman, Flash, and Green lantern reacted in unison: "Kobra?"

"The international terrorist?" The Amazon looked skeptical. "Is he capable of such a thing?"

"He's capable of just about any—" The Batman's image suddenly froze, then began to break up into digitized bars and pixels.

Superman approached the screen. "Batman? Can you hear me? We're losing you."

The big monitor screen filled with electronic snow. The Atom used his keyboard to check the settings. "There's some strange interference. And it's building."

The Manhunter checked his table screen. "Someone is trying to jam the frequency?"

"No, J'onn, it's . . . this can't be right." Atom rapid-clicked through a series of preset functions. "It's on *all* the frequencies—all across the band!"

The big screen flickered and rolled. And then, a golden-clad figure appeared in sharp relief at three times life-size.

The Flash was instantly on his feet. "It's him—Kobra!"

Superman's eyes narrowed. "Speak of the devil."

"Superman?" The Atom looked up from his table monitors in amazement. "We're not the only ones getting this."

On television sets across North America, all regular broadcast and cable programming was suddenly interrupted. A masked, hooded face appeared on all channels.

"I am Kobra—the Naja-Naja—the chosen leader of the Order of Nulla Pambu and of my faith. It is now my sacred duty to deliver the gravest of warnings to all the peoples of the world.

"We stand now at the threshold of a new age—the Kali Yuga, an Age of Chaos. And for those who do not soon awaken to the Truth, it will be an Age of Doom.

"In recent days, the world has felt the wrath of nature. Great cities have been shaken by the wind. Vast stretches of land have been seared by fire or inundated with water. Temperatures have both risen and fallen to great extremes.

"And nowhere has nature's sword been felt as it has in America."

At Yankee Stadium, and a dozen other ballparks across the United States, thousands stood in horrified silence as the ominous image of Kobra addressed them from giant JumboTron screens.

"America has long thought itself blessed. But that blessing is now at an end. America has embraced the unholy. It has become a corrupt state, rotting from within, openly hostile to true faith.

"My own religion has come under attack. The American Central Intelligence Agency has persecuted and even killed some of my followers. And when we have spoken out against this injustice, they have branded us all as terrorists.

"Over the past century, America has plundered the riches of other lands and exploited their peoples. It has dictated the course of the world, insisting upon its terms over all others. Americans have befouled its holiest of places with their presence. They are aggressors who delight in humiliating smaller, weaker nations.

"And, most sadly, as America has spread out across the globe, it has exported its corruption to other nations. It is the destroyer of tradition, polluting the world with its media. Its television, its movies, its very culture seduces people, occupying their thoughts with the trivial and stirring their baser emotions and desires. As a result, corruption grows, even amongst believers.

"America has come to dominate the world. Americans claim to seek peace, but they have brought themselves—and the world—to the brink of destruction."

In Tokyo, pedestrians along the Ginza stared up in horror and amazement at the hooded face that filled the giant display screens on the sides of their buildings. To them, Kobra's voice spoke in Japanese.

"Americans have been victimized by traitorous behavior on the part of their leaders. They have succumbed to greed. They have become both amoral and immoral. They are openly hostile to seekers of true faith.

"But they and their judges shall soon themselves be judged by a higher, more natural law.

"I am not the first to recognize these portents. Thoughtful clerics around the world—some within America itself—have warned the United States of its moral failings and its imminent demise. But even these enlightened few have seen naught but a small glimmering of the truth.

"The other religions of the world can *never* perceive the whole of the truth. They have strayed too far from their core beliefs. The twin curses of secularization and modernization have corrupted what pitiful scraps of the truth their earliest prophets had been able to glean.

"Only the Naja-Naja has been blessed to perceive the truth in all its fullness. And I tell you now, a day of reckoning is at hand—not just for America, but for our entire planet."

At La Bombonera soccer stadium in Buenos Aires, attendees at a rock concert were frightened and confused by the image that appeared on the screens surrounding the band. They all heard Kobra address them in Spanish.

Around the globe, wherever there was an active television, radio, or telephone, the voice of Kobra was heard. His image was seen via streaming video on computers worldwide. And in each nation, his voice came across in a language understandable to the majority of the people. In Russian, French, and German—in Farsi, Urdu, and Chinese.

"The Kali Yuga—the Age of Chaos—is upon us. It will bring about the destruction of all corrupt nations. It shall bring death from the heavens—both by fire and by ice. It shall come in the form of the hurricane, the tornado, and the flood. And there shall be no room in the Ark for those who do not believe.

"All this I know. I have foreseen the Kali Yuga, and I welcome it. By the power of my faith have the forces of nature been unleashed to cleanse the Earth of corruption.

"But I come before you with this message not out of hatred. Heed my words, not as a threat, but a warning—and a prayer for redemption.

"There is yet hope for an enlightened humanity. Throughout the chaos, the truly righteous—and *only* the truly righteous—shall prevail. The land shall be purified of the corrupt and the believer shall triumph over the ungodly.

"To that end, I now call upon all people of true faith—reject the ways of the unholy and be spared. Shun the corrupt ways of aggression and exploitation, and we shall all walk together in the sun.

"Damnation or salvation—the choice is yours."

In the Watchtower, Kobra's image froze for an instant and then flickered out. The screen stayed dark for several seconds as the six members of the Justice League stood in silence.

And then the Batman reappeared on screen. "He's never tipped his hand like this before. This is very, very bad. This is even worse than I'd feared."

"Kobra!" Superman smacked a fist against his palm. "Doctor Stratos called his abductor 'the snake,' but I thought he was speaking metaphorically."

"Stratos?"

Superman quickly brought the Batman up to date on what he'd deduced from Stratos's ravings. "He said that the 'false god' claimed to serve the forces of chaos."

"The Kali Yuga."

"Yes. If Kobra has all of Stratos's secrets—!"

The Batman stiffly inclined his head. "I don't think that is the source of Kobra's weather control, at least not solely. If the Naja-Naja had learned all of Stratos's secrets during the abduction, he would have used them long before now. No, I believe that Kobra is controlling the weather through a pawn—he's using Mark Mardon, a.k.a. the Weather Wizard."

"What? You've gotta be kidding." The Flash was

instantly in front of the screen. "That's impossible. The Weather Wizard is too small-time for this."

"*Was* too small-time."

"I don't buy it, Bats. Like I was just telling everybody earlier, the Weather Wizard has never shown any ability for controlling weather outside of a small area. And a lot of these weather attacks have happened simultaneously. Mardon was never able to do so much over such a wide area before."

"He never had the backing of someone like Kobra before. Let me show you something." The Dark Knight's hand reached offscreen to touch the keypad of his own master computer. A series of still photos immediately appeared along the bottom of the League's big monitor. "These are security scans taken at Chicago's O'Hare Airport a little over a month ago. Thanks to some bureaucratic heel-dragging, their face-recognition system still has a few bugs in it—but mine doesn't. Watch as I enhance the center photo. . . ." The picture enlarged to twice its size, and the image sharpened to show two men, one wearing a tweed cap pulled low.

"Sonuva—! The guy in the cap is Mardon, all right. I'd know him anywhere." The Flash got closer to the screen. "What's that on his chin?"

"A small bit of blood-soaked tissue. He appears to have shaved en route to the airport, as evidenced by some residue of shaving cream on his collar."

"Where? I don't see . . ."

With a keystroke, the Batman highlighted Mardon's collar.

"Oh, yeah. There it is."

Wonder Woman looked over all the images Batman had called up. "In all of these pictures, Mardon seems to be in the company of this bearded man."

"Exactly, Diana. He matches the description of a man who had met Mardon earlier in a South Side tavern. His hair and beard obscure his face in most of the shots—except this one." The Batman enlarged and enhanced a section of a photo that had captured the bearded man head on. "This was a bit of good fortune. As you can see, his eyes, nose, mouth, and most of the right ear are exposed in this image. Analysis shows that they are a perfect match for *this* man's." A second, similar-sized image appeared alongside that of the bearded man. The man in the new image was completely hairless save for his eyebrows and two exotic tufts of beard.

Superman recognized the second man's chin immediately. "That's Kobra."

"Correct." The Batman punched in a command, and the mask and hood of Kobra were digitally added to the image of the second man. "This is one of a rare handful of pictures that have been taken of Kobra unmasked. I have copies of them all."

"Of course you do." The Flash rubbed the bridge of his nose, trying to ward off the headache he could feel building there. "Okay, Bats, you've proved your point. What sort of fake IDs were they using to get through airport screening?"

"Ones that needn't pass commercial check-in. They left O'Hare aboard a private jet owned by one of Kobra's dummy corporations. They flew from Chicago to San Francisco, refueled, and filed a flight plan listing Kuala Lumpur as their final destination. The plane never arrived there. Manila's air traffic control lost contact with them over the South China Sea. Given Kobra's speech this evening, we can assume that they didn't crash. They could be anywhere on Earth. I have been trying to trace the source of his signal without any success. Doctor Palmer?"

The Atom looked up from his keyboard, suddenly aware that all eyes were on him. "Nothing yet from my end, Batman. But I am able to confirm that the Weather Wizard is mixed up in this. I ran a check of our databanks and found a 'scope reading of energy emissions from the Wizard in action, recorded almost ten years ago by Barry Allen. One of the harmonics matches up with the electromagnetic disturbance I'd detected in the more extreme storms."

The Flash threw up his hands. "That cinches it, all right. It was Mardon all along. I'm officially an idiot." He looked back at the on-screen detective. "Not that I doubt this anymore, Batman—you sold me with the photo evidence—but the thing I can't understand is, why? Robbery and revenge are Mardon's chief stock-in-trade, with maybe a little extortion on the side. I can see him becoming someone's stooge, but why would he throw in with Kobra and his terror cell?"

"I have no idea how Kobra won him over, but the Naja can be very persuasive."

Wonder Woman pondered Kobra's image. "I don't

suppose there's much point in trying to reason with him, is there?"

"Nope. And even less with his followers, Princess." Kyle leaned back against the edge of the table. "I once had to stop a dozen or so of his goons, and it wasn't easy. They were trying to set up a command post at the Statue of Liberty, if you can believe that, and they were absolutely crazed."

"That's been my experience as well, Lantern." Superman again began to pace. "Batman, you're the one who's had the most dealings with Kobra. What can you tell us about him? What can we expect to face?"

"Unbridled ambition combined with total fanaticism." The Dark Knight wiped the security photos from the screen, replacing them with images of a windswept mountain peak. "I first encountered Kobra here, in the Swiss Alps. He had taken over a series of underground bunkers once used by my old enemy, Rā's al Ghūl. I slipped into Kobra's stronghold, attempting to stop him from killing his own brother. I failed. He killed his brother and got away."

Green Lantern and the Flash looked at each other. They had never before heard the Batman admit to failure.

A new image came up on-screen, of a squad of hooded men wearing gas masks and firing wildly in the direction of the camera. "The next time we crossed paths, Kobra was launching a plan to slay the entire population of Portugal. Aquaman and I managed to stop him, but he got away again. And then, there was Kobra's multi-city raid. Some of you were caught up in that."

"I can fill in the back story on that, Bats. I was smack at the heart of it, remember?" The Flash's usually light tone turned earnest. "The attacks were all directed from Keystone City. Kobra had set up a base there, and he had a whole broadcast-power thing going. See, due to its location, Keystone is sort of a nexus of energy production and distribution—hydroelectric, solar, wind, and geothermal. Kobra had tapped into that power grid so he could beam energy to his goon squads around the country—right, Batman?"

"Yes. Kobra channeled the energy via satellite to his sleeper agents, who then launched a series of simultaneous raids on Washington, Chicago, New York, Metropolis, and Gotham, which is when Green Lantern, Superman, and I became involved. And while we had our hands full with those attacks—"

Wally broke in: "Kobra used all that power at his disposal to seal Keystone City off from the outside world with a big force field. But I managed to get inside and disrupt his grid. In the process, I overloaded his system and blew his satellite out of the sky."

"Satellites again." Superman had a faraway look in his eyes. "I wonder if Doctor Stratos's design work figured into that at all?"

Batman considered that. "It is possible. Kobra is the supreme opportunist, often stealing the technology of others and using it to advance his own causes. He is known to possess high-tech weapons systems that were reverse-engineered from alien sources."

The Manhunter shifted forward in his chair. "Extraterrestrial science in the hands of such a fanatic?"

"I am afraid so, J'onn. Kobra possesses no truly superhuman powers, but that doesn't make him any less of a threat. Even without the alien tech, he is one of the deadliest men alive. Kobra has been schooled in nearly every martial discipline. He maintains himself in superb physical condition and is a dangerous hand-to-hand combatant. He has bested me in the past." The Batman paused, as if humbled by that admission. "Kobra is charismatic and utterly ruthless. He has seemingly limitless resources, immense wealth. And he will do anything to meet his goals: To sow chaos and disorder. To destroy. And, ultimately, to kill everyone who is not a part of his cult."

"This . . ." Green Lantern groped for the right words. "This is . . . definitely bad news. If a guy like that is in control of the climate—! What can we do? We can't fight bad weather."

"No. Even if that were possible, it would just be treating the symptoms." Superman looked around at the others. "We have to hunt down Kobra and Mardon and stop them."

"Yes, stopping Kobra is the highest priority. But that will not be easy." The Batman steepled his fingers. "Over the years Kobra has transformed the Order of Nulla Pambu from little more than a fringe cult into a truly international terror network. He has thousands of agents and assassins. They are mainly young men, but there are women among them as well. Kobra has gathered and indoctrinated angry, disaffected youth from all races and nations into his network. They are fanatics—all utterly devoted to the Naja-Naja, and all ready to die for him."

"Hey, when have we ever taken on a job that was easy, Bats? We're the Justice League—united, we can take on all comers."

"It appears that most of the world is uniting as well, Flash." The Manhunter leaned over one of the tabletop screens. "In the wake of Kobra's address, we are receiving offers to share information from the United Nations and several of the world's major intelligence agencies . . . as well as requests from several governments for aid in quelling panic."

"Cooperation at the highest levels? That's a nice change. Yes, of course, we'll help. Ask them to stand by." Superman gathered the League around the table. "This is going to be one of our most difficult challenges. We will need to draw on all the resources we can. J'onn, I want you to be our liaison to the intelligence agencies—gather all the data on Kobra that they can provide."

"I shall."

"Likewise, Diana, we need you to draw on your U.N. contacts. And I want both of you to compile any usable information and share it with Batman—he's our profiler."

"Of course."

The on-screen detective held up a hand. "One caveat . . . my role in this must remain secret. Kobra believes I am dead. It is to our advantage that he continue to believe that."

"Fine. No one mentions Batman to anyone outside this chamber. Flash, Green Lantern . . ."

Wally snapped off a salute. "Yes, boss?"

"You two call up the League's reserve members—Aquaman, Black Canary, Firestorm, Zatanna, Captain Marvel, the Blue Beetle—divvy up the list and contact anyone and everyone who's available. We'll need them to back us up, especially on emergency rescue work while we're looking for Kobra. And if any of them can provide added intelligence, we want that, too. Plastic Man is currently on a special assignment to the FBI—he may be able to help there. All communication is to be routed through the Watchtower . . ."

Superman turned to the Atom. ". . . which is going to put a bit of an extra burden on your shoulders, Ray. You've been all but living in orbit, while the rest of us have been preoccupied."

The blue-masked man waved off his chairman's concern. "No problem. I've been enjoying my sabbatical from teaching. I've actually managed to write a new research paper up here—in between playing switchboard and trying to figure out the source of the foul weather."

"And we need you to keep looking. If we're going to stop Kobra and the Weather Wizard, first we have to find them. Is there a chance that your scanning system can help track them down?"

"Possibly. The trick will be in finding a carrier signal and tracing it back to the point of origin. I can't make any guarantees, Superman, but I'll do my best."

"I'm sure you will. But you'll need help—with that and with monitor duty. We'll get some of the reserves to back *you* up, too."

Superman looked around the room. Before him were assembled five of the world's most powerful individuals. On-screen was the World's Greatest Detective.

"We're all going to have to pull double duty until this crisis is over. Billions of people are depending on us. We have to do all we can to protect them, while we hunt down the man who's threatening them."

"We're with you, big guy." The Flash looked to his teammates. "Let's go catch us a Kobra."

CHAPTER 13

Breaking News

From a Sunday extra edition of the Metropolis *Daily Planet* . . .

JLA: KOBRA WEATHER CLAIMS TRUE
Nations of the World Respond to Terrorist Threat

By LOIS LANE and RONALD TROUPE
Special to the *Daily Planet*

METROPOLIS, June 27—In a statement late Saturday night, spokespersons for the Justice League of America confirmed their belief that as many as a dozen extreme weather events across North America have, in fact, been the work of a secretive international terrorist organization headed by the man who calls himself Kobra.

Kobra, the masked leader of an extremist cult known as the Order of Nulla Pambu, broke in over

communications systems worldwide last night to
claim responsibility for a series of recent weather
attacks in the United States and to threaten "the
destruction of all corrupt nations."

Officials at the Federal Communications Com-
mission have been unable to explain how Kobra
was able to commandeer not only all broadcast
and cable channels, but telephone and Web communications as well. International communications
agencies have pledged their full support to the
FCC in an investigation of the incident.

Sources within the Central Intelligence Agency
described Kobra as a "profoundly dangerous fanatic" who has used his religious cult as a guise
for fomenting terrorist activity throughout the
world. "He is a total wild card," said one high-
ranking official. "The Order of Nulla Pambu originally worshipped a cobra god, but Kobra has
pretty much transformed it into a fanatical personality cult under his command."

International reaction was swift, as the world's
governments closed ranks with the United States.
Meeting overnight, foreign ministers of the Euro-
pean Union issued a joint statement, condemning
Kobra's address as "a usurpation of the airwaves
for the purposes of terror." In London, the British
Foreign Secretary's office called the address "nothing less than a declaration of war against all of
civilization." In New Delhi, Indian officials announced the arrest of five men linked to a Kobra
cell. And in Moscow, sources at the Kremlin of-

fered to share "any and all intelligence on the Order of Nulla Pambu gathered by the SVR," Russia's Foreign Intelligence Service, with the U.S. Central Intelligence Agency.

The Secretary General of the United Nations will convene a special session of the General Assembly this morning to discuss what measures can be taken to counter Kobra's threat. Ambassadors to NATO and SEATO plan separate meetings on that subject today.

The Order of Nulla Pambu also came in for massive criticism from the world religious community. In Calcutta, a man speaking on behalf of a group calling itself "The Seekers of the True Naja," denounced Kobra as a "terrorist and heretic who casts an evil light on all legitimate cobra cults." He joined with Christian, Jewish, Islamic, Hindu, and Buddhist leaders in a near-unanimous worldwide condemnation of Kobra and his followers. In Riyadh, one imam called the Order "terror wearing the mask of faith."

Meanwhile, in Washington, the U.S. Army Corps of Engineers worked overnight, placing sandbags along the shores of the Potomac River in preparation for possible flooding.

Continued on Page A7

In a suburban cable television studio, a choir finished singing a beloved old devotional, and the cameras swung around to focus on a big, fleshy man with a silver gray pompadour. In the studio control booth, an engineer carefully raised the levels of the man's microphone.

"Good morning, friends, I'm the Reverend Joe Cuthbert of the Holy Light Fellowship—and those were our own Holy Light Singers. Thank you so much, dear hearts. Weren't they wonderful, friends? Such spirited sounds cannot help but *lift* the spirit, and surely we all could use a lift in these trying times.

"You know what I'm talking about, friends. Once again, we have been threatened by forces from beyond our borders. Once again, our great nation is under attack by a false prophet of a gutter religion. And we must rise up—we must gather together and draw strength from our faith in the Almighty—to thwart these cowardly attacks. We must not give in to the unholy."

The camera dollied in on Cuthbert, picking up the glint of a tear in one eye.

"But, my friends, I must confess . . . I do fear for this land of ours. For many of the unholy dwell amongst us. This self-proclaimed 'leader' of his so-called 'faith,' this Kobra—a man who cannot even spell his name properly—accuses our fellow Americans of greed and corruption, of rampant immoral secularism. And though it pains me deeply to say this, my friends, he is not completely wrong.

"Too many of our neighbors have turned away from our Lord. Too many have refused to accept Him. Instead, they have been taken in, seduced by the purveyors of an atheistic, socialist movement that is both anti-family and pro-perversion.

"It's a sad, sad day when a snake-worshipping heathen can point directly to the sins that have brought us to such a pass. But just as a broken watch can show the correct time twice a day, so can the non-believer recognize sin.

"Now, this Naja-Naja thinks to put the fear of the snake into all of God's children. He says that he has sent the storm to cleanse the world of sin, but I say that only the Lord can perform such miracles. And, what's more, the Lord can hear His flock through the power of prayer.

"You may remember the time, just a few short years ago, when our beautiful local countryside was threatened by a hurricane. We did not shirk our duty then—oh, no, my friends! We prayed to the Almighty to protect us. We prayed for that hurricane to turn away. And, sure enough, turn away it did!"

In the booth, the sound engineer muttered under his breath. "Oh, yeah. It 'turned away' all right. It veered off and leveled a town in the next county. Guess those folks weren't in your prayers."

"But I cannot take all of the credit for that, my friends. Reverend Joe did not do it alone—oh, no. You and I did it together. And He listened!

"Well, if we did it before, then we can do it again. Together, we can find our miracles through prayer!

"But to do so, we must ensure that we can make our voices heard not just across this nation, but around the world. Just as that devil snake charmer broadcast his threats, we must broadcast our prayers and bring the word of the Holy Light Fellowship to those in need.

"Now, I can hear you asking, friends—'Reverend Joe, what can I do?'

"You can help us spread the word through your donations. The more we raise, the more satellite time we can buy, the more repeater stations we can establish, and the more souls we can reach. So dig down deep into your pockets, friends! Show the snake that he has no monopoly on the airwaves! Show him that—!"

Suddenly, all of the lights went out in the studio. "What the devil—?" A second later, a peal of thunder rattled the overhead fixtures.

Stagehands stumbled about in the dark, finding flashlights as the floor manager tried to get through to the director over his phones.

In the dark, the Reverend Joe hit his shin on a table and stifled a curse that would have shocked his on-air congregation. He yanked a flashlight away from his makeup man and hobbled over to the floor manager. "What in Sam Hill is going on?"

The manager looked a little spooked. "A lightning strike just killed the power and fried our satellite uplink. We've been knocked off the air."

In the Middle Eastern nation of Qurac, the archfundamentalist Mullah Hamdun rose from his seat and shook his fist as he addressed the cameras of al-Talib Television.

"The godless Kobra now seeks to take credit for the

havoc being wreaked on the Great Satan America. This is nonsense! Does he expect us to seriously believe the word of a pagan, a worshipper of snakes?

"No! The winds blow, and the storm rages, only at the will of Allah. It is Allah who now punishes the Great Satan, not the infidel Naja-Naja.

"May Allah bring His winds down upon the Kobra and all his followers. I call for a jihad against the heathen Order of—!"

But although his viewers assumed that he meant to invoke jihad against the Order of Nulla Pambu, no one ever saw the rest of Hamdun's address. A bolt of lightning struck without warning, vaporizing the transmitters of al-Talib Television.

In a midtown Metropolis studio, a lean dark-haired man took a quick swig of coffee as a jazzy rendition of John Sebastian's "Rain on the Roof" echoed in his headphones. *Oh, very funny.* He grinned at his engineer. *The way things have been going lately, today's summer shower could last for* days, *instead of hours.* He cleared his throat and leaned toward the microphone that hung suspended before him.

"Welcome back to Jack Ryder's Hot Seat. That's right, citizens, the man who's too hot for television is back on the radio, coming to you live across the nation on the Fairbrook Radio Network. If you've got a beef, let's hear it. 1-555-555-5225 . . . that's one, triple-five, triple-five, Jack!

"For those of you just joining us, this is our first new show for the media barons at dear old Fairbrook.

It's Monday the twenty-eighth, and we're coming to you live all this week from the luxurious studios of WMET-FM in Metropolis, currently the monsoon capital of America. And by 'luxurious,' I mean one step up from a Gotham City men's room. I really want to thank you guys for redecorating for me."

A wheezing laugh echoed through the studio.

"Oh, you laugh! That's my engineer, Rudy Brelesford, who's shooting coffee out his nose. Say hello to the folks, Rudy."

"Hi, folks."

"That's why he's behind the board, and I'm behind the microphone. The man has a face for radio and a voice for mime. That number again, 1-555-555-5225. Give me a call and we'll air your beef.

"Me, I've already got a beef, and you can probably guess what it is. That's right, this Kobra sleaze. I mean, it's bad enough we have to put up with the lousy weather, without having some lunatic snake charmer trying to take credit for it. How crazy is he? None of the other snake charmers want anything to do with him. That's a major clue right there. But what do you think? Let's go to the phones. We have Barney from Pittsdale, Iowa, on the line. Talk to us, Barney."

"Hiya, Jack! It's great to have you back on the air."

"My creditors agree with you wholeheartedly."

"Yeah, well, I just wanted to say that I'm with you about this Kobra bum. I've had it with all those lowlifes out there putting down the USA. I think we should track that slimeball down and wipe him and all of his camp followers off the face of the Earth."

"Well, that's a natural enough reaction."

"Yeah, and once we're through with him, there's a lot of others that nobody'd miss."

"You've got a little list, eh?"

"That's right. And we can start with the Middle East! We oughtta just pave over that whole sandbox and string up every last one of those no-good—!"

"Okay, that's enough." Ryder hit a switch, cutting the connection. "Let's leave the death lists to the Mikado, okay? I always say, there's nothing like an intelligent audience, and some people do their best to prove that there's nothing like an intelligent audience *at all!* But let's see if we can correct that. Say hello to Donald in Elmond, Virginia."

"Hello, Mr. Ryder."

"Please! Mr. Ryder was my father. It's just 'Jack,' assuming that you want to be nice."

"Heh-heh. Okay, Jack. I just wanted to say that I'm as upset by this Kobra business as you are. But we have to be careful about this."

"What do you mean?"

"Kobra has made a lot of wild claims about controlling the weather, but how do we know he can really do it? I know the government and supposedly even the Justice League believe that he's responsible. But we shouldn't go rushing into things until we're absolutely sure."

"Well, what do you think we should do, Don?"

"I wouldn't do anything. We don't know that he's really done anything wrong."

"That's where *you're* wrong, pal!" Ryder hit another switch, muting the caller. "First, there's one thing we know Kobra did that's obviously *very* wrong—he broke in on every radio and television transmission in the world, not to mention interrupting telephone calls, crashing computers and the like. If he can do that, then—hey—maybe he *can* control the weather. I don't know. But speaking as someone who tries to make a living as a broadcaster, I'd say taking over the airwaves is reason enough to make me want to see Kobra tracked down. And that's just for starters. Our number, once again, is 1-555-555-5225. That's one, triple-five, triple-five, Jack! What's this? We're actually getting a local call? That's great—hello to Stephen in Metropolis."

"Hello, Jack. I was just listening to your other callers, and I think they're both wrong."

"I couldn't agree more."

"The thing of it is, I think you're overlooking something, too."

"Anything's possible, Stephen. It's a Monday, after all, and I haven't had nearly enough coffee yet."

"Kobra is just the latest in a long line of unfairly maligned religious leaders."

"Excuse me?"

"That's right. Kobra is trying to enlighten the world. If we oppose him, we'll just get what's coming to us."

"Easy, now, Stephen." Ryder rolled his eyes for the benefit of his engineer. "I think you need to check your medication."

"Very funny, Ryder. But you won't be laughing when Kobra manifests in all his greatness."

" 'Manifests,' now there's a word I don't hear every day." Ryder kept his tone light, but he recognized something unsettling in the caller's voice, and he signaled his engineer to trace the call. "If I didn't know better, I'd say you're a fan of that two-bit would-be Hitler."

"You don't know what you're talking about now, Mr. 'Hot Seat.' The Naja-Naja is the one true avatar of the eternal."

That did it for Ryder. "Real wrong, fella! Your 'avatar' is nothing but pure scum. Even other terror groups have admitted that Kobra is responsible for a list of atrocities as long as my arm. He's killed, he's tortured—"

A low, cackling laugh came over the talk jock's headphones. "And you have sealed your doom, Ryder. You will fare no better than the others. The wrath of Kobra shall strike you down!"

"Buddy, you give me the creeps." Ryder jammed down hard on the mute button. But as he pulled his hand back, a spark jumped from the button to his finger. Lights flickered in the studio and the phone lines went dead. Through the walls, Jack and Rudy could hear a muffled clap of thunder.

"Are we still on the air?" Ryder looked around the studio and Rudy gave him a quick thumbs-up. "Looks like we are. Well, 'Stephen'—if that's your real name—I guess your Kobra god isn't as tough as you thought." He grinned. "But our sponsors are. It's time once again to reaffirm our capitalist tendencies. We'll be back after this word from Gotcher Coffee."

A catchy jingle started playing, and Ryder yanked off his headphones. "What gives, Rudy? I got a shock from the phone when the lines went dead. Is it the storm, or did somebody screw up?"

"You got me, Jack. Everything on the board flickered, too."

"You guys!" A station intern, all out of breath, pushed open the studio door. "You won't . . . believe this."

Ryder cocked an eyebrow at the newcomer. "Try me."

"A lightning bolt . . . nearly took out . . . one of the dishes . . . on the roof . . . but he . . . he stopped it."

"He? He who?"

"Superman."

"Superman?! Is he still up there?"

Another clap of thunder, closer this time, rattled the studio windows.

"I guess so."

Ryder was up out of his seat as he turned to his engineer. "Rudy, can you get me a live mike up there?"

"Sure, but—"

"Let's go!"

Moments later, Ryder emerged on the roof of the building to find Superman standing in midair just twelve feet above an array of microwave relay dishes.

"Hey, Superman! Over here! It's Jack Ryder!"

"Get under cover, Ryder!" No sooner had Superman shouted the warning, than another bolt of lightning arced down from the sky, catching the caped man full in the chest, driving him several feet back through the air. But the lightning was diverted to the building's grounding system and safely away, both from the relay dishes and from Ryder and his engineer.

Superman landed roughly on the roof in a half crouch and held that position for a moment, taking a long, slow, deep breath.

"Superman?" Ryder cautiously approached him. "Hey, are you okay?"

The Man of Tomorrow slowly straightened up, waving the talk jockey off. "Don't get too close. I'm still a little hot."

"No kidding." There was a light drizzle in the air, and Jack could see steam rising from Superman's chest. "I want to thank you. For helping to keep me on the air, I mean."

"You're lucky I was in town. You made your new show a tempting target to Kobra's followers."

"You think?" Ryder regained his grin. "I didn't know you were a listener. So you really believe that Kobra's responsible for this?"

"Trust me. That wasn't ordinary lightning."

"What are you saying? You don't expect me to lay off the creep, do you? Listen, I'm used to getting death threats. I've never walked away from a fight in my life."

"Neither have I." The Man of Steel stared hard up into the sky. "For what it's worth, the thunderheads seem to be letting up . . . for now. But if it comes back, I can't guarantee that I'll be fast enough to keep you on the air. I can't be everywhere. And neither can the Justice League."

The engineer flashed a hand signal to Ryder, telling him that they would be going live in thirty seconds.

"I appreciate your honesty. Could you say a few words to my listeners? A lot of them are worried about . . . Superman?"

But the caped man was again standing several feet in the air, looking off to the south, listening to much more than just the voice of the man next to him. "Sorry, Jack. Duty calls."

Superman shot away from the rooftop, leaving Ryder and Brelesford standing in the drizzle.

Jack cleared his throat as the engineer poked him in the arm and gave him a five count.

"Welcome back to Jack Ryder's Hot Seat, citizens. This morning, we're coming to you live from Metropolis, where—you can take it from me—it's a rainy, rainy day."

Superman sliced through the stormy skies, flying south out of Metropolis's central business district. Passing over the West River, he dove down into the residential neighborhoods of the borough of Queensland Park. Not more than a hundred feet below him sat a modest apartment building whose most distinguishing feature this morning was a six-foot hole blasted into the brickwork on the fifth floor.

The Man of Steel flew in through the still-smoldering opening to find a charred spot on the floor, a shrouded body, two crime scene investigators from the Metropolis Police Department, and Inspector Daniel Turpin.

"Superman! What are you doin' here?"

"I overheard a radio report of an unusual lightning strike here, Inspector. I'm a little surprised to find you already on the scene."

"Hey, you ain't the only guy who gets around. Seriously, the vic had just called the Jack Ryder show to put in a good word for Kobra, if you can believe that. The station traced the call and tipped us off. I actually saw the strike, from a few blocks away." Turpin doffed his hat and fanned himself with it. "This place would still be burnin' if not for the building superintendent. He broke down the door and used an extinguisher to put out the fire. Come get a load of what he saved for us."

The inspector led Superman to a closet at the back of the room. Inside were a small arsenal of weapons and a hooded coverall of green metallic mesh.

"Kobra cult gear."

"Yeah, we're lucky the fire didn't reach that weapons cache. We coulda lost the whole block. This guy had enough ordnance in here to give the Special Crimes Unit a run for the money."

"And you're certain that the victim is the apartment's resident?"

"Got a tentative, pending a DNA check, but it's pretty solid. His face was mostly untouched. Superintendent ID'ed him, and he looks like the face on his driver's license. But check this out." Turpin pulled back a corner of the shroud, and there, visible on the dead man's shoulder, was the ritual cobra tattoo of the Order of Nulla Pambu.

"Crazy, ain't it? His boss is supposed to be controllin' the weather, and here a lightnin' bolt goes and takes him out by accident."

"Accident, Inspector? I doubt it."

On the outskirts of Gotham City, hidden far beneath the sprawling grounds and stately edifice of Wayne Manor, stretched a cavern that housed the secret subterranean headquarters of the Batman. He seldom spoke of this Batcave, and few—very, very few—even knew of its existence. Access was tightly restricted.

To know the location of the Batcave was to know that Bruce Wayne, heir to a multibillion-dollar family fortune, CEO of Wayne Enterprises, and trustee of the nonprofit Wayne Foundation, was also the Batman.

Late Monday afternoon found the Dark Knight seated before the supercomputer that housed his vast databases. The detective's eyes flashed from window to window on the huge monitor before him. His mind analyzed the new incoming data—relayed from the Justice League—nearly as fast as his microprocessors. When a figure approached him from behind, he didn't even bother to glance back.

"What is it, Alfred?"

"Because you ingested nothing more than one of those abominable 'protein shakes' for lunch, I thought I would prepare something more substantial for dinner. You do recall dinner, don't you, sir? Chief meal of the day? Often eaten in the company of others?"

"I'll have mine down here."

"Of course, you will. Beef or fish?"

"It doesn't matter."

"No, I suppose it does not." As Alfred turned to go, a gust of wind shot by him and he shivered involuntarily. "Extraordinarily drafty down here today. I don't know how you stand—" The butler halted in both mid-sentence and mid-stride, then drew himself up and cleared his throat. "Sir? You have a visitor."

The Batman swiveled his chair around. A familiar red-and-blue-clad figure stood next to the family retainer. "I see that I need to improve my security systems."

"Don't bother getting up on my account, Bruce. You should be taking it easy until those ribs have a chance to heal completely."

"Nice of you to be concerned about my health, but at the moment, I don't have time to take it easy. See anything else on my X-ray?"

"I don't need X-ray vision to diagnose your problem. I could tell just from watching you on the League's monitor that you'd been injured. It was clear from the way you moved—or didn't."

One corner of the Batman's mouth rose in an approximation of a smile. "We'll make a detective out of you yet."

"I do my best."

"I beg your pardon, sir. Will you be joining us for dinner? I could offer you a lovely filet of salmon—or, perhaps, beef bourguignon?"

The Man of Steel smiled. "Thanks for the invitation, Alfred, but I'm afraid that I can't stay long."

"Ah, well. Perhaps another time then." The butler gave a half bow and strode away. As he disappeared into a nearby elevator, Superman turned back to the Batman.

"Any new word on Kobra?"

"Not yet, but I'm chasing down several leads."

"We have to put an end to this, Bruce."

"We will. Kobra's ego will trip him up. His global address was proof of that. It all fit in with his desire to sow terror around the world, but he could have kept his mouth shut and still achieved that goal. No, he wanted people to know who was responsible for their misery."

"Stratos made the same mistake." Superman leaned back against a stalagmite. "I need your help in trying to understand Kobra. You've fought him before. Something happened in Metropolis earlier today . . ." Superman quickly related the story of the cultist's death. "I suppose that the lightning strike could have been a coincidence, a freak accident, but I don't think so."

"Neither do I. It is much more likely that Kobra eliminated an agent who had acted out of turn."

"Out of turn? the man was publicly supporting Kobra, and he gets eliminated, just like that?" Superman shook his head. "Why? Why is Kobra doing this?"

"For much the same reason that you do what you do, Clark. It's how he was raised. Like you, he never knew his biological parents. But unlike you, he never knew a normal childhood. You were brought up by the Kents on a working farm, learning responsibility every step along the way. He was abducted by an already fanatical cult and raised to believe that he was essentially the Second Coming.

"Kobra's father was an American industrialist, very ambitious, very much the corporate empire-builder, but he tended to play fair. He wasn't one of the bad ones."

"More a Steve Jobs or Lee Iacocca than a Lex Luthor?"

"Exactly. And Kobra's mother was a biologist from India. I have no doubt that they would have provided a good home for both their sons, if only they'd had the chance. Their twins—conjoined twins, Kobra and his brother—were born during a visit the couple made back to the subcontinent.

"The boys were separated after a day-long operation, and his parents were told that one of the children had died. They were heartbroken, and returned to the United States with their surviving son. They went to their graves never knowing that their other child was alive. He had actually been abducted by one of the hospital's doctors, an intense fellow who secretly belonged to the Order of Nulla Pambu. The doctor saw the infant as the reincarnated avatar of his cobra god.

"The boy was raised by the cult to be their new leader. And on his twenty-first birthday, he underwent a bizarre ritual and was anointed as the Naja-Naja. Once the order recognized him as the avatar of their god, he seized control of the cult and made it what it is today. Game, set, and match."

"High tragedy, you mean. But what you've given me I already know from the files. I need to find out what makes Kobra tick. Does he truly believe that he's the avatar of a god?"

The Batman paused, taking a moment to reflect. "I think he believes that he might as well be. He did rebel against the cult elders when he was in his late teens, even left the order for a while. But he wasn't equipped to deal with the real world. The world treated him badly as well; there are reports of a romance that didn't work out at all.

"So he returned to the cult, convinced that his mentors were correct, that the world needed to be totally remade. And he began by remaking the Order into a personality cult. He co-opted Nulla Pambu, cutting it off from other cobra cults. For years now, religion has been just another tool to him.

"But on some level, I think he truly does believe in his image for the world. He's convinced that the planet would better off with a population in the thousands, rather than in the billions. And all of them believers in the Naja, of course."

"We have to stop him, Bruce. We *must!*"

"No argument. We'll need all our resources." The Batman looked at his visitor. "How much sleep have you had in the past week?"

"Sleep?" Superman shrugged. "Four or five hours. The weather attacks kept me busy—even before we knew of Kobra's involvement."

"And some people tell *me* to take it easy."

The Man of Steel frowned. "My physical requirements are different from yours, Bruce. Let's get back to Kobra. You were saying that the boy endured a bizarre ritual. What did you mean by 'bizarre'? Bizarre by whose standards?"

"By any standards. After Kobra had beaten over a dozen men in hand-to-hand combat, he had to drink a goblet full of cobra venom."

"Venom?"

"That's not necessarily as dangerous as it sounds. The venom is considerably less toxic when taken orally."

"Yes, but if he'd had any lesions in his mouth or GI tract, if it got into his bloodstream, he'd have been a dead man."

"Then, perhaps. Over the years, Kobra has developed immunity to virtually every kind of toxin. He's an accomplished scientist. He synthesizes new analogs of the venoms himself. And though it galls me to admit it, he's always managed to stay ahead of my efforts to synthesize antidotes."

"And you're one of the best chemists I know. This is truly tragic, Bruce. Kobra clearly inherited his mother's talent for science along with his father's ambition and drive. With a different upbringing, he could have become a hero, a pioneering doctor or scientist."

"Perhaps. If he'd become a doctor, he'd be the sort who works his interns and residents half to death. But only half. And his patients would live."

"But as it is, his people die."

"Yes. All of his field agents carry suicide pills. He

sometimes uses venom to discipline those followers who offend him."

"And yet he still *has* followers."

The Batman sighed. Sometimes, he envied Superman's faith in human nature. Other times, he despaired of it. "Never underestimate the draw of fanaticism, Clark. There are, unfortunately, many, many people who will swear absolute loyalty to anyone who can give them absolute answers."

"I know, I know. It's the one thing I wish I could change about human beings, this terrible yearning for extreme certainty. But . . . venom?"

"Neurotoxins are a favorite of his. Remember, he once tried to wipe out an entire nation. He intended to smother Portugal under a toxic cloud. He'd probably try stunts like that more often if the compounds were more controllable."

Superman looked at the Batman. "That's right, they're not . . . normally. It's difficult to make a gas go where you want it. Gases are too easily dispersed by the wind. But—!"

The Batman simultaneously had the same thought: "But if you can control the wind—! Of course! It was staring me in the face the whole time." He began entering numbers into his keypad. "Kobra and his people set up a death trap for me aboard a freighter. I had come to think that the component toxins being shipped were just bait to lure me in. But maybe there was more to it than that. Look at this."

A series of digital photos appeared on screen. "I snapped these in the hold of that freighter. At the time,

I couldn't figure out why these plastic ovoids were part of the cargo. But now it occurs to me that they could be part of a delivery system for Kobra's nerve gas. Look at their construction—the containers could be filled with the gas and then dropped from planes or missiles over major population centers. They would burst open on impact, releasing the toxic gas."

Superman's hands clenched into fists. "And after the release, a controlled heat inversion would hold the gas in place . . . until everyone in the targeted area was dead."

"Exactly."

"He could leave our cities intact, while killing everyone in them."

"And he would do it without a moment's hesitation."

"This just keeps getting more and more horrific. We have to find him, Bruce."

"And you have to be careful, Clark."

"Me? Why?"

"I think Kobra has been targeting the members of the Justice League, trying to wear them down. And Superman is target number one." Batman pointed a finger at the Man of Steel. "You're the strongest of all of us, but even your power isn't without limits. You're being run ragged by this emergency. Don't deny it, 'Mister Chairman,' I can see the signs. You're trying to carry the whole load on your shoulders."

"You know me too well."

"I know Kobra, too. There are few things he would rather do than humble Superman."

"Don't worry. I won't let that happen." The Man of

Steel rubbed a hand across his chest. "I've already been in Kobra's crosshairs once today. But I won't be a sitting duck for him."

"Good. We need you—now more than ever."

"You really think I'm his number one target?"

"Who else? Kobra thinks that he has already killed the Batman."

A rainy haze obscured the setting sun as Superman descended over the far west side of Metropolis. He touched down on a rooftop helipad and entered the suburban complex of the Scientific and Technological Advanced Research Laboratories.

Over the past quarter century, S.T.A.R. Labs had become the world's largest dedicated research and development corporation, with over a dozen laboratory facilities in the United States and Canada alone. Ordinarily, the Metropolis center would be conducting experiments in dozens of different fields, but now all personnel seemed to be working toward one goal—finding and stopping Kobra.

The entire complex was on a war footing. Two armed guards escorted the Man of Tomorrow down an underground corridor and through a series of heavily fortified checkpoints to a secure laboratory where Doctor Karen Lou Faulkner was in the midst of a teleconference with the Atom.

"Superman!" Doctor Faulkner brightened considerably as the caped man was admitted to the chamber.

"Hello, Kitty. How have you been?"

"A lot busier these past few days." She nodded to

the monitor screen. "Doctor Palmer and I were just comparing our readings from the various weather patterns while we waited for you and our . . . special courier."

"You mean me?" The Flash skidded to a halt alongside Superman and Doctor Faulkner.

Startled by the red-suited runner's sudden appearance, the guards instinctively drew their sidearms.

The Flash held up his hands. "Whoa! I'm one of the good guys, fellas! Great reflexes, though. I'm impressed!"

Kitty Faulkner stepped to his side. "Yes, we were expecting him, remember? Everything's under control here. You can go now."

The guards holstered their pistols and departed, sealing the door behind them.

Superman looked at the speedster. "Did you even bother to go through the security check?"

Wally shrugged. "I was told this was a rush job." He reached down and pulled a small silvery disc from the cuff of his glove. "Here you go, Doc. All the data that my predecessor had compiled on the Weather Wizard—direct from the secret vaults of Central City's Flash Museum via Fleet Foot Express. Sorry I'm late, but there were some emergencies along the way."

"Thank you, Flash." Kitty inserted the disc into a slot in her computer console. "You know, there *is* a branch of S.T.A.R. in Central City. You could have just transmitted this to us."

"I know, but the data was more secure with me. And besides, I'm faster."

A series of mug shots came up on screen, showing full-face and profile shots of a dark-haired man, both barefaced and masked. The Flash pointed to the face. "That's our man—Mark Mardon, also known as the Weather Wizard. Better known, actually."

As Doctor Faulkner scanned through the data, Superman turned to the Flash. "This is all very helpful, but I'm just as interested in what you can tell us about him."

"Are you sure, big guy? I was the one who originally dismissed him as a suspect in this."

"Even so, you've had more first-hand experience with him. Any insights you could pass along might be valuable."

"Okay." Wally leaned one shoulder against the wall and crossed his ankles. "Let's see . . . before he became the Weather Wizard, Mardon was just a run-of-the-mill burglar who had gradually worked his way up from petty to grand larceny. I suppose you could say that he was moderately successful at the breaking and entering part of his 'craft,' but he had a bad habit of getting caught. Mark's real talent was in escaping from police custody. He was pretty canny in that respect, but he never showed much in the way of common sense. His brother Clyde apparently had most of the brains in the family.

"From all I've ever read, Clyde Mardon was a true genius—a real whiz at software design—but the ultimate shut-in. He made a fortune early on and bought an island where he could be by himself and indulge in pure gonzo research, just for the hell of it."

Superman's brow furrowed. "He sounds like Doctor Stratos in that regard."

"Yeah, I guess he does at that. Clyde also spent several years and a good bit of his fortune studying the weather and trying to find a way to control it. And somehow, he managed to do it, just before he dropped dead. Depending on whom you talk to, Mark either found his brother slumped over a keyboard, dead of a heart attack, or he killed him. Whatever happened, Mark discovered his brother's work and understood it well enough to set himself up as the Weather Wizard.

"But even though he could make it rain—or snow—on your parade, Mark still *thought* small-time. He was able to control the weather, and what did he do? He tried to get revenge on the people who had locked him away. Or he'd set out on a series of high-profile but still largely petty crimes. Barry always stopped him. *I've* stopped him many times. But like I said, his most natural talent was for escape." The Flash grew silent as a streaming video capture of the Weather Wizard in action came up on-screen.

Superman pointed to a freeze-frame image of the Wizard. "The source of his power, I take it, is that metal rod?"

"Sort of." The Flash scratched his chin. "But it seems to be more of a focus. Mark destroyed his brother's notes, so we don't have much to go by. Once, while the Wiz was a guest of the state, Barry turned Mardon's magic wand over to the big brains at S.T.A.R. Labs in Central City. They took the thing apart, but even they couldn't figure out how it was supposed to work."

Kitty looked up from her work station. "Yes, their reports are included here. Analysis of the rod revealed nothing but a maze of integrated circuits, and ICs don't power anything."

"Right. Barry had a hypothesis that Mark might have used some other gizmo of Clyde's to energize the rod—or himself. And for a while, the Feds thought that he might be some sort of metahuman, but they put him through a whole series of exams and couldn't find anything out of the ordinary about him or his DNA. However Mark makes that rod work, it seems to work only for him . . . which suggests that there *is* something unique about him. It's just that no one has figured it out yet. The most Mardon ever told anyone was that he used 'aeolic energy'—whatever that's supposed to be—to alter weather patterns."

"He was probably being facetious. Aeolus was the Greek god of the winds." Superman turned to Faulkner. "Any operating hypotheses from the old S.T.A.R. reports?"

Kitty scrolled through the data. "A few. One possibility is that Mardon is able to create a tiny space warp that draws the weather he wants from elsewhere on the planet. But that still doesn't fully account for all the unnatural phenomena that he's generated over the years—the solid rainbows, the 'flying carpet' clouds. One quantum physicist believed that the Weather Wizard's power could be a phenomenon best described by chaos theory. That part of his report went on for one hundred and fifty pages of very difficult reading, but he was ultimately unable to explain how it all worked or, more important, how to counteract it."

The Flash shook his head. "What I can't figure out is how the Wiz is using his power on such a large scale all of a sudden. Or how he's directing it! In my experience, whenever Mardon worked his weather magic, he always had to be somewhere in the vicinity. But there's been no sign of him—anywhere—since he dropped out of sight in Chicago over a month ago."

"I think we may have an answer to your second question." Kitty brought an eccentric wave pattern up on the screen. "Doctor Palmer and I have managed to isolate the Weather Wizard's harmonic signal, his electromagnetic signature, as it were, in transmissions from sources in Earth orbit."

"From orbit? Hah!" Superman inspected the pattern. "I *knew* Stratos's technology was involved in this! Which satellite is transmitting the signal?"

"That's the problem. It's not coming from any one satellite. It's coming from *all* of them."

"What?"

"That's correct, Superman." The Atom's on-screen image broke in. "As you know, I'd set up the Watchtower's long-range scanners to try to home in on Kobra's weather control system. I was looking for a satellite or series of satellites, but wasn't finding anything traceable. The energy telltales connected to the weird weather patterns didn't seem to come from any fixed location—nor did the transmission carrier of

Kobra's address. So I linked up with S.T.A.R.'s tracking systems to both widen and concentrate the search."

Faulkner chimed in. "And working together, we eventually found the signal, or rather the signals, that we were looking for. Kobra appears to be channeling the Weather Wizard's power and transmitting it through a shifting series of satellites, altering the Earth's weather patterns via remote control."

"Yes, and I believe that Kobra is amplifying the Weather Wizard's power—either via Stratos's gear or through the use of some alien technology. Then he splits the energy into different wavelengths and piggybacks them onto signals transmitted over existing communications satellites. His address was sent out in a similar fashion." The Atom paused to let that sink in. "We can't shut him down without shutting down all worldwide communication as well."

Superman silently fumed for a moment. "And there's no way to trace the energy?"

"I didn't say that. There's no *easy* way—yet. Kobra is employing a system that enables him to bounce the energy from several satellites simultaneously. That's why the signal seems to come from everywhere at once. But I'm confident we'll find a way to zero in on the main source. There's only one Weather Wizard, right, Flash?"

"Yes, thank God."

"Then we'll find him. It's just going to take some time."

Superman's keen hearing picked up the sound of a

sudden wind gusting outside the laboratory complex. "As fast as you can, people. The weather's getting stranger with each passing hour."

The rain was beating down on Bakerline as Jimmy Olsen arrived at the northern borough's Salvation Army shelter. The young photographer checked in with the mission's captain and presented his press pass. Minutes later, Olsen stepped into the shelter's big dining hall. Hundreds of people were gathered there, refugees from area flooding, most of them. Jimmy passed through the crowd, snapping pictures and stopping every few minutes to take down a name or listen to a story. He was snapping a new memory card into his camera when a loud voice boomed out from across the room.

"Hey, Red! Long time no see! How ya doin'?"

Jimmy turned to see Bibbo Bibbowski shoulder his way through a set of double doors at the rear of the dining hall. As always, Bibbo was wearing his battered old leather cap, but today he had a spattered apron on over his T-shirt and jeans, and he pushed a cart holding two huge kettles of soup.

"Bibbo? I never expected to find you working at the Salvation Army."

"Heh. Yeah, I prob'ly wouldn't do much good ringin' a bell or slappin' a tambourine, not with this mug. But I can rustle up grub with the best of 'em. Lamarr an' Highpockets are holdin' the fort at the Ace o' Clubs, runnin' it better'n I do, most likely.

"I already dished lunch up at the Catholic Charities. Tomorrow, I go to the soup kitchen that them Unitarians run. Day after that, I'm headin' over to the UJA and that big mosque over on Fifty-third."

"Wow. That's . . . very ecumenical, Bibbo."

"Yer damn straight, Red. I ain't been much of a churchgoer in a long time, but I still got me a lot of respect for the Big Man Upstairs. He's always done pretty good by me, and I figure it's up to us who got, to help them that don't got. 'Scuse me."

Bibbo hustled the kettles over to the serving line and began ladling out big steaming bowls of soup. "Here ya go! Bibbo's special potato-leek chili, guaranteed to fill ya up and keep ya happy. No shovin' now, there's plenty for everybody!"

Jimmy snapped off a few more pictures as people began filing by.

"Hey, Olsen! Why don'tcha make yerself useful and gimme a hand here?"

Jimmy looked up from his camera and his cheeks flushed. "Sure, Bibbo." He stashed his gear under the table, rolled up his sleeves, and joined the old roughneck and the rest of the volunteers in dishing out dinner.

When everyone was finally fed, Jimmy plopped down at the far end of a table with his camera gear and a big mug of coffee. He'd just stirred in a creamer and two sugars when Bibbo slid in beside him, carrying two bowls. "Nice job, Red. Here, I saved ya some."

"Thanks, Bibbo." Jimmy scooped up a spoonful of the thick soup, blew on it, and took a cautious taste. "Hey, this is really good chili!"

" 'Course it is. The secret is in adding plenty of mushrooms and ground turkey kielbasa to the stock. That, plus just the right amount of cayenne and chopped jalapeños."

"Oh, yeah." Jimmy could feel himself start to sweat. "This'll keep me warm all night."

"That's the idea. A lotta these folks're cold and damp."

"No kidding. It's like the deluge out there. I'm just glad my mom lives on higher ground. What's your take on all of these storms, Bibbo?"

"Aw, there's a lot of crazy stuff going on, but we'll get through it somehow. We always do. It's like with Sooperman! Sure, he's taken it on the chin a few times from crumb-bums like Doomsday or that Brainiac guy, but he always sucks it up an' comes back stronger'n ever. And he'll take care of this Kobra guy, too. You'll see!"

"Then you buy Kobra's claims that he's responsible for this weather mess?"

"Oh, yeah, it's Kobra all right. If Sooperman and his buddies say that snake in the grass is behind this mess, that's good enough for me. I sure as heck don't believe that the Holy Ghost is doing this." Bibbo glowered over the steam that rose from his bowl. "I just wish I could get a chance to get in the ring with that Kobra creep."

"You? You want to fight Kobra?"

"Yeah, why not? Anybody who'd send floods and blizzards against innocent folks needs to have his butt kicked! I'd love a chance to hand him his head. Yeah,

print that in yer paper, Red! I challenge Kobra to fifteen rounds, and I bet he don't last half that. He can
even fight dirty, and I'll *still* take 'im!"

"I don't know, Bibbo. This guy is supposed to have
a whole army of killers."

"Then I'll take 'em *all* on, one at a time! C'mon,
Red, get out your camera and let's show 'im what he's
up against." Bibbo stood up, pulled off his cap and
ran a hand back through his graying hair. "Let Kobra
see my face!"

Jimmy started clicking off shots as Bibbo brought
his fists up.

"That's right, Kobra! I'm callin' you out! Me, Bibbo
Bibbowski! This is my face, lowlife! An' these are my
fists! Get a good look at 'em, ya lousy crumb-bum,
'cause they'll be the last thing you see before you hit
the ground!"

Early the next morning, Kobra strode down a long
corridor and into the heart of a hidden command center. As their avatar entered the chamber, hooded men
rose from their monitor stations and bowed low.

"All hail the Naja-Naja!"

Kobra stood silently for several seconds, absorbing
the adulation. Then he rapped his staff twice on the
floor. "Return to your stations. There is much work
yet to be done."

He moved toward the center of the chamber, where
a large command chair sat atop a raised circular platform. Surrounding the platform was a ring of monitor
screens, each manned by a loyal hooded follower.

When Kobra approached the platform, three hooded men threw themselves down face-first on the floor, and he walked across their backs to his chair. The Naja turned and settled back into the chair, like a king on his throne.

"How goes Operation New Dawn? Report!"

A hooded man on his left rose from his monitor station. "All goes as planned, Most Holy One. The jet stream is shifting steadily. Inversion pockets should all be in place within the next twenty-four hours."

Kobra swiveled his chair thirty degrees to the right, and the next subordinate arose. "All launch sites are green for go, Sahib."

"Good. Initiate fail-safe Program Omega."

"Your will be done, great Kobra."

"It shall indeed. Number Nine!"

A subordinate arose to the right of the platform, his palms pressed together before his face. "Yes, Most Holy One?"

"What are the latest reactions of the infidels?"

"The American news media reports continued defiance at all levels of governance, but growing fear and uncertainty amongst the population."

"Good. I would see this for myself. . . ."

A large display screen descended from the ceiling and hung suspended before the cult leader. Kobra zapped through the cable news channels, smiling once at coverage of the Black Canary and Green Arrow struggling to calm a panicking mob on the West Coast. He next scrolled through the websites of a dozen major newspapers, from the *Star City Examiner* to the *Boston Globe-Leader*, nodding with satisfaction at the rising estimates of weather-related deaths, injuries, and property damage. It was not until the *Daily Planet* web page filled his screen that a story made the Naja pause for more than a moment.

There, near the top of the *Planet*'s Metro Section, was one of James Olsen's photographs of Bibbo Bibbowski scowling defiantly. And beneath the image was a bold headline:

Local Tavern Owner Challenges Terrorist

Kobra scrolled down through the copy, digesting every word. He lingered for a moment over the final quote: " ' . . . the last thing you see before you hit the ground.' " Then, he began to laugh.

"Most Holy . . . ?" The subordinate looked surprised by the Naja-Naja's reaction.

"I find this man amusing." Kobra gestured to the screen. "I believe he is what the Americans call a 'local character.' "

Number Nine accessed the web page from his workstation and his jaw tightened. "Such impertinence! He must be punished!"

"And so he shall be. But at this point, he is just a petty annoyance. I doubt that he will survive the destruction of his beloved nation." Kobra slouched back into his throne. "I almost wish that he would."

"Sahib?"

"I would happily face this aging fool. It would be

most satisfying to best him in unarmed combat—to break him in body, to crush him in spirit, and then to choke the last, dying breath from him amid the ruins of his city." Kobra's teeth flashed from behind curled lips. "Yes . . . most satisfying."

CHAPTER 14

Battle Lines

The sun broke through the clouds over southeastern Iceland, lighting the broad surface of the Vatnajökull glacier in blinding white. Four hundred meters beneath the icecap, a vast system of tunnels was suddenly illuminated by a series of dazzling emerald beams from the power ring of the Green Lantern.

As he flew through the subglacial corridors, the Lantern's beams glanced across the silver-gray body armor of a score of Kobra troopers, who immediately responded with a blue-white fire from their pulse-rifles.

"Whoa-ho!" Green Lantern ducked and weaved between the first wave of pulse-fire, quickly erecting a green energy shield to ward off the troopers' continuing assault. *Looks like Interpol was right about this hidden base.* Kyle's shield deflected his enemy's beams up into the glacier overhead, bringing hundred-pound chunks of ice raining down between them. "You want to play this the hard way? Okay, how about if I meet you *half*way?"

The energy of the ring swept over Green Lantern, covering him from head to toe in thick, emerald armor. A long, medieval shield took form over his left arm, and the handle of a huge mace filled his ring hand.

"Now, let's see just how good your armor fares against Sir Smites-a-lot!"

The armored Lantern smashed his way through the first line of troopers, sending them flying. The pulse-fire of the second line failed to even slow him down. He batted their rifles from their hands with his mace, even as his ring fired a verdant energy net over them. In seconds, they were hopelessly ensnared.

A giant green bottle-opener flew over the captive troopers, gently popping off their helmets. As the troopers' jaws widened in amazement, they each found their mouths held open by oversized green tongue depressors.

"That's it. Everyone open up and say 'Ah'!" Green Lantern lifted his visor and strolled toward his captives. "No one is going to be chomping down on any poison pills today."

"Lantern—NO! Don't let them move a muscle!"

Kyle whirled about to see Superman rocketing down the tunnel toward him. "Huh? Why—?"

"Just do it!" But as Superman reached for the first of the captive troopers, the man's armor blew apart with enough power to knock the Man of Steel back several yards.

"Son of a—!" Before Green Lantern could tighten his net around the others, their armor began exploding as well. The concussive force of the explosions knocked Kyle off his feet and brought more ice down around him. The entire cavern shook with deafening, echoing booms.

"The armor . . ." Breathing heavily, Superman helped Green Lantern to his feet. ". . . all loaded with self-destruct charges. They sacrificed themselves for Kobra . . . rather than let themselves be taken captive."

"Damn." Green Lantern let his armor melt away. "I thought I had everything here under control. I was cracking jokes, making fun of them. And now they're dead . . . they're all dead."

"You didn't know."

"Maybe I should have. We were warned about the hollow teeth with the suicide pills." Kyle plopped down on a big chunk of ice. "I should have guessed that there'd be a backup. Kobra doesn't leave anything to chance." He leaned his elbows against his knees and held his head in his hands. "How long does it take to get good at this?"

"When I find out, I'll let you know."

"Huh?" Kyle tilted his head toward the Man of Steel.

"I ran up against the same thing at the Kobra base that I found in Sardinia, just a few minutes ago." Superman sat down on the ice next to the young Green Lantern. "And I didn't do any better. They all blew up on me, too. I tried to get word to you via the Watchtower, but there was too much interference. Try not to be too hard on yourself, okay?"

"O-Okay." *Never thought of him screwing up. He always seemed to know what he was doing.* Kyle looked closer at his teammate. *Are those bags under his eyes?* "Hey, Superman . . . are you all right?"

"Just a little weary. I've been on the go a lot this past week." He broke off a fist-sized chunk of ice. Cupping his hands around it, he melted the ice with his heat vision, and gulped the water down. "Batman was right. I need to recharge."

"I can hear that." Kyle looked at the shattered bodies of Kobra's troopers, and ringed body bags over them. "You must get pretty tired of stuff like this. Sometimes, I'm surprised you haven't just taken over by now."

"Taken over what?"

"The world. Everything. Haven't you ever considered running things yourself?"

"No. That's not the way I was brought up."

"Yeah? Me neither. But let me play devil's advocate for a moment. Seriously, it's not like the world's leaders have been doing all that great a job. Do you mean to sit there and tell me that, with all the power you have, you've never given it any thought?"

"All right, I won't say that I *never* gave it any thought. But not for any great length of time, and never very seriously. Even if I wanted that kind of authority—and I don't—it wouldn't work. There would still be despots like Kobra. And besides, I'm not immortal. Let's say that I set myself up as world dictator.

It wouldn't last. Whatever I accomplished would come apart once I died."

"You think so?"

"It's the history of the world. Warlords die and empires crumble." Superman got to his feet. "I've always thought that George Washington set the best example for how to run things. He could probably have become a king, you know."

"I'll have to take your word for it. Junior-year history class was a long time ago, and all I remember about Washington is the 'Father of Our Country' stuff."

"From all that I've read, he was a fascinating man. He had two opportunities to establish an American dynasty, and passed on both of them. Remember, Kyle, Washington was the great general, the hero of the revolution. At the end of that war, a lot of colonists would have accepted him as king—they were used to answering to a monarch, after all. But all he wanted to do was go home to Mount Vernon. Even George III was impressed."

"The King of England? Really?"

"Absolutely. When George III heard that Washington planned to retire to Mount Vernon, the old king said, 'If he does that, he will be the greatest man in the world.' But that's exactly what Washington did. *Twice.* After the constitution was adopted, he accepted the country's call to come back and become its first president. But then he stepped down after just two terms in office, ensuring a peaceful transition to a newly elected leader. He willingly walked away from the office, establishing one of the first great precedents of the republic." There was a fire in Superman's eyes, an urgency to his voice. "He *believed*, Kyle. He believed in the idea that power belongs to the people, not to their leaders. And that is true greatness."

"Yeah. Yeah, you're right. And so was Washington." Kyle stood up, dusting ice from the seat of his pants. "Thanks, Superman. I read stuff like that in school, but the books always made it seem so dead and dry."

"I was lucky. I had good teachers. Ever heard of Blaise Pascal?"

"Pascal . . . didn't he have something to do with triangles?"

"Among other things. He was a seventeenth-century scientist and mathematician, but he was also something of a philosopher. There was a passage from Pascal's papers that's always stayed with me. He wrote that 'justice without strength is helpless, strength without justice is tyrannical.' "

Green Lantern's ring glowed brighter. "Then it's up to us to help keep justice strong."

"That it is, Lantern. That it is."

Fifty feet above the South Atlantic, Wonder Woman's robot plane hovered silently several miles off the north coast of a tiny island in the Tristan da Cunha group. The little cluster of volcanic islands—midway between South America and South Africa—were administered by the British Colonial Office, and Her Majesty's government had received reports of suspicious activity in the area.

The Amazon warrior dropped from her invisible plane and flew low over the ocean toward the island. As she drew near the rocky coastline, Diana took a deep breath and dove beneath the waves. With long, powerful strokes, she circled the island until she came to the mouth of an underwater cave. The entrance showed signs of having been enlarged and reinforced. *Yes. Suspicious, indeed.*

Wonder Woman rapidly swam the length of the passage to a spot where light shined softly from an interior source. There, she kicked off from the cave floor and ascended alongside a docked submarine. The sub bore no national ensign; its only markings were the serpentine insignia of the Order of Nulla Pambu. Diana paused for a moment at the stern of the vessel and grabbed hold of the craft's propulsion screws, yanking them off their drive shafts and letting them sink to the bottom. Only then did she surface amid the shadows of the secret submarine pen.

Emerging from the water, she caught a lone guard by surprise. The Amazon quickly threw a hand over the hooded man's mouth and sank her fingers into certain pressure points on his neck, rendering him unconscious before he could draw breath to raise an alarm. She then bound and gagged the guard with strips torn from his clothing and hid him behind a stack of crates.

Wonder Woman leaped up above a row of electrical lights suspended by cables from the high cave ceiling and flew deeper into the complex. Thirty feet on, she stopped and clung to a thick stalactite as one hooded cultist passed by below. She trailed after him until he encountered another masked man and handed a parcel over to him. Their voices carried easily in the silence of the tunnel.

"Hasin, make haste! You must deliver these maps to the Naja-Naja at once!"

Two corridors away, in a tightly guarded inner chamber, a regal, golden-clad figure addressed a corps of elite assassins.

"You will soon embark on a most important mission to the coastal cities of Brazil. When North America falls, you must be prepared to seize control of the South—all for the greater glory of the Kali Yuga!"

"The Kali Yuga!" The assassins raised their fists high into the air. "We live but to serve the Naja-Naja. We pledge our lives to the Kali Yuga!"

The chants of the faithful drowned out the sound of the chamber door opening, but the golden figure looked up expectantly as a hooded underling entered with a parcel.

"Ah, Hasin. Bring the maps here."

But as Hasin crossed the chamber, the sounds of combat could be heard through the wall. And then, Wonder Woman came smashing through the door.

The Amazon swept through the assembled assassins, rendering them all unconscious in a matter of seconds. Hasin fell to a passing blow, as she notched her lasso and cast it over the man in gold.

"You cannot resist my Lasso of Truth, Kobra. Those bound within its coils are compelled to speak honestly."

He stared blankly at her. "I . . . am not Kobra. I am

but one of the Sahib's many lookalikes . . . sent here to the rally the corps and deliver the Most Holy One's orders."

"What can you tell me?"

"I can tell . . . the orders for these assassins."

"What else do you know?"

"Only that I am to remain here until summoned elsewhere by the Naja-Naja."

"You know nothing else? Explain! Where is the Weather Wizard?"

"I do not know. The Naja's doubles are of the Order's lower levels. We are informed of plans only on a need-to-know basis. All I know is the orders that I am to deliver. They are for the mission that is to follow the successful completion of Operation New Dawn."

On an island in the South Pacific, the Martian Manhunter skimmed low—invisible—over the rim of an inactive volcano. Information relayed to the Justice League by Australian intelligence indicated that this might be another Nulla Pambu stronghold. And so, J'onn had flown there to check it out.

Peering down into the cone with his Martian vision, he could see hooded men moving about in an underground base. The invisible Manhunter immediately lowered his density and passed down through rock and steel into the heart of the facility. Maintaining his invisibility, J'onn returned to solid form.

Alarms instantly started wailing—to the surprise of the Manhunter and the cultists around him. The

Martian reached telepathically into the mind of the nearest man, grasping surface information about base security.

In seconds a heavily armed squad of men burst into the chamber, weapons drawn, ready to capture or kill any intruder. What they found was a tall dark figure facing a cluster of their fellow cultists, the hooded men bowing low before the mysterious form.

The squad leader warily approached the strange figure from behind. "In the name of the Most Holy One, I demand your surrender. Turn around slowly, with your hands elevated."

"Hands?" The head that turned to face the squad leader was huge and serpentine, staring at him with unblinking eyes.

The entire squad jumped back as a massive, twenty-foot long cobra reared up before them.

"How many hands do you want?" Three pairs of arms grew out of the giant snake's body, six fingers pointing in accusation at the hooded men. The cobra hissed its displeasure with them. "You follow a pretender who leads you on a false path. I am the *true* Naja-Naja!"

Some of the squad members fell to the floor, screaming and tearing at their clothing. Others pushed them out of the way and opened fire on the "Snake God" with their energy rifles.

"You dare defy your god?" The snake angrily whipped his way through the weapons fire and lashed out with his tail, knocking the disbelievers unconscious.

The more pliant cultists lay on the ground, sobbing and twitching. The Snake God flowed among them, touching each one in turn. *"Do not fear. Sleep . . . sleep . . ."* And they did.

Surrounded by unconscious men, the Snake God morphed back into the form of the Manhunter. Looking over the prone forms around him, he reached out with his mind to the other cultists elsewhere in the base.

From the Watchtower, the Atom transmitted the latest reports to the Batman over his secured communications link.

". . . And that's all Diana and J'onn were able to uncover. The bases they found were staffed with cultists of the lowest levels. They didn't know where other strongholds might be found—a lot of them didn't even know where in the world they were."

"And yet, the Pacific location boasted a more sophisticated security net. Why?"

"Good question. Of all the League regulars, J'onn has been the most active in the Pacific Rim. Could Kobra have taken special precautions in anticipation that he'd be the one to show up there?"

"All things are possible where Kobra's concerned, Atom." The Batman frowned. "This is getting us nowhere. The world's intelligence agencies have not found much more than I had already." He gazed over his screens. The main monitor showed weather patterns worldwide, none of them particularly good. "We're running out of time. The jet stream is undergo-

ing a radical shift, and conditions conducive to heat
inversions are building around our major cities.
Kobra will be striking soon, and we still don't know
from where."

The Dark Knight tapped in a code, calling up a
search for airfields or possible launch facilities. Thousands of locations suddenly lit up on a digital image
of the continent. "There are simply too many places to
search, in North America alone. Even for the Flash."
The Batman closed his eyes and rubbed the bridge of
his nose. It was the weariest gesture the Atom had
ever seen from him. "Have you had any luck in tracking those signals to their source?"

"Some, but not enough." In the Watchtower, the
Atom checked a new series of wave patterns on a
planetary grid. "The Blue Beetle is here, helping fine-
tune the scanners, but there's still so much electromagnetic noise in the way. None of the algorithms
I've tried has made much headway. . . ."

Doctor Palmer slumped back in his chair, letting
his own exhaustion show. He closed his eyes and visualized his favorite trails along the glens and gorges
in and around Ivytown. He had to believe that he
would somehow solve this problem, so he could see
those waterfalls again. Potter's Falls were his favorite,
a taller drop than Niagara. They were beautiful even
in bad weather. On a sunny day in springtime, with a
fresh snowmelt thundering over the brink, they were
breathtaking.

He visualized himself standing at the overlook,
watching the sunlight glitter on the falls. Tall oaks and

maples grew right up to the edge of the gorge, and he pictured the ever-changing interplay of light and shadows among the leaves.

Midway through the daydream imagery of light and falling water, an idea suddenly popped into his head. Just like that. The subconscious doing its job, making connections.

The Atom sat up as if the idea had released a giant spring behind his back. *This must be how Kekule felt, when he woke up with the structural formula for benzene.* "Here's a thought. What if we map the signal patterns against the weather patterns? If the signals correspond to any places with halfway decent weather . . . ?"

"Interesting. It's worth a try." The Batman called up the two sets of readings in adjacent windows. "We'll adjust the weather patterns to blue and your signal traces to amber, and then . . ." A keystroke merged the windows, superimposing one map over the other.

A small series of green dots appeared on the merged maps.

"Hello! I think we've got something here." The Atom punched in a code, directing his scanners to concentrate on those areas. Two of the dots glowed much more brightly than the others. "There are definitely two major loci here. And I'm reading strong transmission patterns between the two sites—one in the Indian Ocean and one in North America, almost in the middle of the continent! Do you have any idea of what's in that spot?"

The Batman's fingers were already flying across his keypad, checking the North American location. The information came up almost immediately. "Yes, Atom. Yes, I do."

A weary Man of Steel floated in orbit, high above the Northern Hemisphere, a compact oxygen mask over his nose and mouth. He breathed deeply, slowly, as he soaked up the rays of the sun. Miles below, a few clouds were beginning to part, revealing sections of North America. Normally that sight would have cheered him. But now, he feared that it meant Kobra was ready to strike. The weather looked most turbulent over areas that were home, Superman knew, to major military bases. That seemed horribly ominous.

Where is he? Where?!

"Superman." The Batman's voice rang in his right ear.

The caped man tapped a transceiver on the side of his breathing mask. "Yes?"

"We've found him."

"Kobra or the Weather Wizard?"

"Both, I think. The Atom and I have narrowed the search to two sites, and knowing Kobra, I'm sure which one is his. He's hiding right in the United States, hundreds of feet underground."

"What? Where?"

"It's a decommissioned missile silo in South Dakota. I've run a check, and it turns out that this particular facility is one of several across the country that were purchased over the past two years by a chain of dummy companies. The weather is starting to clear over each of those locations. This must be how he plans to launch his attack, by missiles fired from within our own borders."

"Have you alerted the Pentagon?"

"Affirmative. But wind conditions have the air fleet all but grounded, and ground troops will never arrive in time."

"Understood. Give me the coordinates of the Dakota base and dispatch the others to the launch sites."

"Will do. Just remember—Kobra takes special precautions, wherever he goes. An incursion into his private lair is likely to trigger the launch sequences."

"I'm sure it will. But do we dare wait any longer?"

"No."

"Then we all must act—and act fast. The coordinates?"

The Batman read them off. "Remember, Kobra will want to—"

"Make an example of me? Don't worry, I've taken precautions, too." The Man of Tomorrow peered down at the Earth, his eyes focused on a South Dakota plain. "I see the footprint of the silo now. Are the other sites covered?"

"Affirmative. The Justice League is en route and closing on their targets now. Green Lantern will provide emergency backup as needed."

"Then I'm going in."

Superman dove toward Earth like a living missile. His breathing mask melted away from the friction.

The edges of his cape began to smoke and char. A half-mile above the ground, he tucked himself up into a ball and dropped straight for his target.

The Man of Steel cannonballed through protective blast shields and kept going. He crashed through level after level of new construction, as alarms sounded and hooded cultists reflexively jumped back out of his way.

As the caped man smashed deep into the hidden lair, an automated signal went out. At half a dozen decommissioned military sites across the United States—in Colorado, Kansas, and Nebraska; in Iowa, Ohio, and New York—blast doors yawned open, and missiles were readied for launch.

One hundred feet down, Superman finally braked to a stop and looked around him. Much of the underground lair was hidden from his view by lead shielding, but he could see enough to know where he had to go.

Superman sped down a corridor to a massive, foot-thick steel door and ripped it off its hinges. At the opposite end of the room, a golden-clad man sat upon a throne.

"Superman. Do come in."

As the Man of Steel advanced on his foe, sections of the floor opened up and three huge robots emerged—one directly in front of Superman and two on either side of him. The massive fifteen-foot-tall automatons closed in.

Superman stared hard at the robot ahead of him, sending twin beams of heat melting into its core. Its systems fused—and the front third of the robot suddenly exploded away, slamming hard into the Kryptonian and knocking him to the floor. The flanking robots closed in and started pounding on Superman. He momentarily disappeared beneath their flailing metal fists.

Then a hand shot out and grabbed one of those fists just behind the wrist. Fingers dug into metal and tore off a robotic forearm. Superman kicked the disarmed robot away and dove against the third, smashing it to the floor. He stood up from the wreckage of the third robot as the second advanced on him once again. Superman picked up the discarded arm and swung it around like a club, decapitating the second robot. It sank to its knees and collapsed.

Superman then turned again toward Kobra.

The Naja-Naja grasped his staff and leaned forward. "I *am* impressed, Superman. No one has ever stood up to one of my Servitors before, much less three." He smiled. "A pity there is still a fourth."

A powerful energy beam blasted into Superman from behind. Stunned, he fell to the floor. Then two more metal fists began pounding him mercilessly.

They did not stop until he was unconscious.

CHAPTER 15

Enemy Action

Halfway around the world, the Flash raced across the Indian Ocean toward a tiny atoll in the Maldives Islands. There were no signs of any human habitation on the atoll, just a small, automated satellite relay station, barely bigger than a one-car garage. As he zipped around the tiny building, he could see the logo of S.T.A.R. Labs stenciled on its side.

"No security cameras out here. Are you sure this is the right place, Atom?"

Ray Palmer's voice was a whisper in his right ear. "It must be. S.T.A.R. Labs has never maintained a station on this atoll."

"Uh-huh. This door looks locked, and breaking in would be bad form. We don't want to announce ourselves."

"Right. This requires more of a stealth approach." The Atom—his height reduced to just half an inch—emerged from the Flash's right earcup and leaped onto his teammate's outstretched palm. Once he landed, he grew another three inches in height and increased his weight to two pounds. "Throw me at the door, Wally, but not too fast. A normal toss will do."

"Okay, but you don't know how hard it is for me to hold back." The Flash cocked his arm and let fly.

The Atom shrank again as he flew, dwindling to subatomic size and passing through the door.

In moments the metal door slid open, and a human-sized Atom motioned the Flash inside. "Come on. I've wired around the security circuits in the entryway, so no one downstairs should know we're here. But just the same, keep your voice down."

The Flash nodded, and the Atom shrank back down to a six-inch height, taking up position on the speedster's shoulder.

Under the illumination of a single safety lamp, they could see that the inside of the building was lined with cables. A huge freight elevator dominated the center of the room. A ladder stretched down a utility shaft alongside the lift.

Wally peered down the shaft. It appeared to drop straight down for several hundred feet. "I think you'd better take your seat and strap in, Ray. I'm going to need to move really fast."

"Check." The Atom shrank back into the Flash's earcup.

"Ready? Then hang on tight." The Flash jumped feet first down the shaft. As he fell, he pumped his legs faster and faster, generating a cushion of compressed air beneath him to slow his fall.

At the bottom of the shaft, a corridor led off in just
one direction. The Flash raced down the passage, dropping each cultist he met. So fast did he run that not
one of them ever saw him. No one had a chance to
register more than a sudden rush of wind before they
were knocked unconscious.

"Okay, Atom, you can come out now."

The Atom emerged to find two hundred unconscious men, all blindfolded, with their hands and feet
securely tied up. "That was forty-five seconds. What
took you so long?"

"I had to make sure we had someone to question
later." Wally added another handful of teeth to a big
bag he'd appropriated. "Just following the Batman's
advice. Every one of 'em had an artificial molar filled
with poison."

"Good work. What are we looking at down here?"

"Some pretty lavish digs, considering how far underground we are. Parts of it are like Hef's place, only
without the Playmates. But I've found something
you'll really want to see."

The Flash led the Atom past a thick steel door labeled "Vault Seven." Inside was a wall lined with
video screens showing weather patterns over major
American cities.

The Atom quickly checked out the control console.
"That strange energy is being channeled through this
equipment. But where is it coming from?" He hit one
of the switches on the console, and one wall of the
chamber slid open, revealing an eight-foot cylindrical
capsule.

The Flash rushed over. "I didn't know this was here. Is this what we're looking for?"

"Wait a sec, I have to route around the locking mechanisms. Here, this should do the trick."

The top third of the capsule swung open, and the Flash's eyes widened. Inside, Mark Mardon reclined limply on foam padding, an intravenous drip line in one arm. His eyes were glazed, and a thin stream of blood trickled from his nose.

Superman came to, aching all over. He could neither move nor see. His arms and legs were bound up in super-thick manacles. Steel goggles, lined with lead, blocked his vision. Superman concentrated, his eyes glowing red, and the goggles began to melt away. But as the molten metal dripped from his battered face, the glow of his heat vision faded out. He jerked his head from side to side, dislodging the last of the goggles.

"Running out of steam?" Kobra stood just six feet before him, smiling triumphantly. "It appears that my calculations were correct."

Superman looked around. He could see that he'd been moved, but to where he could not tell. The chamber around him was fifteen feet in each dimension. The walls, floors, and ceiling were composed of five-foot-square slabs—those in the ceiling glowing with a faint light—all backed with lead. There were no visible doors. He and Kobra appeared to be sealed in.

"That's a nasty bruise." Kobra turned the Man of

Steel's swollen cheek with his staff. "You are at my mercy, Superman. I know that your power is derived from the sun, as much as from your alien genes." He waved the staff around him. "These walls are very thick and very dense. You will find no sunlight here."

"What now, Kobra? Will you try to kill me?"

"Only if you are fool enough to try to escape. Killing you would be a terrible waste. After all, we have so very much in common, you and I."

"Hardly."

"On the contrary, you are more like me than you realize. Neither of us knew his natural parents. We are both men of great power. At times, there have been those who have worshipped you as a living god. Even more, perhaps, than who now worship me."

"I never sought that."

"Neither did I, at first. Godhood was something expected of me by my followers. In my youth, I once rashly rejected the Order of Nulla Pambu and went out into the world on my own. What I saw there disgusted me."

"I've seen a lot of the world myself, Kobra. It's far from perfect, but what you're doing to it is madness."

"There is no madness in true change. But that will occur only when it is forced upon humanity. And that is where we do differ, you and I. You seek to bring order to a world that is anything but orderly. Chaos is the natural state of the world, Superman. You squander your power in defense of a people who waste their resources. You foolishly seek to change people by the example of your 'good works.' "

"You're wrong, Kobra. I don't try to change people. I just try to help. Changing is up to them."

"The aid you render only enables the people you prize so highly to muddle along on the path to oblivion. They continue to cheat and steal and kill."

"Some of them, yes. But I try to help anyway."

Kobra drew back. "History has proven that the 'good' you do one day is wiped out the next."

"Sometimes. But I believe in 'doing good' anyway."

"That is truly madness."

"No. Paradoxical, maybe. But not madness."

"Eh? Ah, now I understand. The 'Paradoxical Commandments.' I have read of them, of course. If they constitute your creed, then you were right—we *do* have very little in common. You are a fool, Superman. You and your band of 'super heroes' are doomed to fail."

"Are we? The League has never had to trick people into buying into our ideals. Tell me, how did you convince the Weather Wizard to join your cult? I assume it was a different sort of lie than the one you tried on Doctor Stratos."

"So, you learned of the Stratos connection, eh?" Kobra raised his staff in salute. "Very good, Superman. Stratos was a stubborn case; he resisted me mightily, but I *was* able to extract some interesting technology from his muddled mind. Whereas Mardon, that poor fool, believed that I would be content to extort the wealth of nations. He has no idea just how much I intend to remake the world."

"You can't win, Kobra. Humanity is too resilient. You'll never be able to overwhelm us all."

"Such optimism from one who is a helpless captive." Kobra loomed closer, jabbing his staff up under the Man of Steel's chin. "But you are the one who is wrong. You and your pitiful Pardoxical Commandments. How on earth can you have faith in such drivel?"

"It's hard, sometimes. But then again . . ." Superman gave a sudden, mighty heave. His right arm broke free of its bonds and his hand shot out, grabbing Kobra by the shoulder.

"How—?" The word caught in Kobra's throat as the Man of Steel wrenched his other arm free

". . . I'm stronger than you are." Superman kicked his left foot free of its manacles.

Kobra's eyes rolled up and he dropped his staff. He went limp—and abruptly slipped out of his tunic. Bare-chested, he back-flipped away from the startled Man of Tomorrow.

Simultaneously, a wall panel swiveled around, deploying a cannon that fired a punishing particle-beam blast against Superman.

"I have my own reserves, fool!" A trap door fell open at Kobra's feet and he dropped from sight. It sealed tight after him.

Caught in the energy stream, Superman fought to kick his right foot free. As he struggled, a voice echoed from speakers concealed overhead.

"Hello, Superman. If you can still hear this, you are in the final moments of your life. That particle beam is locked on to your heat signature and will follow your every turn. It's more powerful than the one that fool

Stratos designed, and it will burn you worse than kryptonite. The walls of this chamber are eight feet thick. Enough to slow you down, should you attempt to break out. But there will be no time for that—the air is being drawn from the chamber as well. This will be your tomb, Superman. Farewell."

A hundred miles east of Colorado Springs, a sequence of launch codes cleared, and three guided missiles erupted from their underground silos and shot into the heavens. Each carried multiple warheads bearing thousands of toxic gas capsules, all earmarked for major cities in the west and the Pacific Coast.

Hot on their tails was the Martian Manhunter.

The Manhunter accelerated after the first missile, lowering his density and reaching into the guts of its guidance system. There was a sharp electrical pop deep inside the missile and it began gyrating. J'onn swooped under the wobbling missile and gave it a hard shove upward.

The missile obediently followed a new path straight up—out of the atmosphere and off into the depths of space.

The Manhunter spun around and shot after the next missile, already several miles downrange.

Deep inside Vault Seven, the Flash pulled the Weather Wizard's control rod out of the cylindrical capsule. "Does that help any?"

The Atom checked the readings on the console.

"No, nothing's changed. What the Wizard set in motion is still going on."

"Help me prop him up." The Flash broke an ammonia ampoule under Mardon's nose and slapped his cheeks. They pulled the groggy man up into a seated position and the Flash dashed away, returning an instant later with hot coffee. He held a cup to Mardon's lips. "Here, take a good, long swallow. Attaboy."

"Whaa—?" The Weather Wizard looked around in confusion. "You? Why're you bein' nice t' me?"

"Because we need you awake and alert, jerk. Kobra's been playing you for a fool. He's using you to destroy the world, piece by piece. And, God help us, we need you to save it."

"I don' b'lieve you."

"You'd better believe, or we're all dead." The Flash wheeled him around toward the wall of monitors, and the Atom switched the screens to satellite news feeds. Disaster after disaster filled the monitors, while the center screen replayed Kobra's world address.

After several minutes Mark slumped down, cradling his head in his hands. "No, no, no . . . that's not the way it was supposed to be. Kobra said—"

"Guess what? Kobra lied. And the only way you can get back at him is to return the weather to the way it was."

"I . . . I . . . don't know if I can." Mardon stared wide-eyed at a display of world weather patterns. "It's all so big . . . so out of control!"

"Don't give me that!" The Flash thrust the wand

back into his hand. "You shuffled the deck, you can sort it out again."

The Atom leaned in close to him. "That's right. The wand is just a focus. You're the trigger—and the power provided by Kobra is still online. I have the transmission systems ready to go. You have to do this now!"

The Weather Wizard looked from the Atom and the Flash to the screens, then back to the wand. He took a deep breath.

Fifty feet below Superman's death chamber, Kobra jumped into a small rail car and shot across an emergency escape tunnel. In minutes he emerged into an immense underground hangar, many miles away.

In the center of the hangar a tall metal rocket— seventy-five feet tall and fifty feet across at the base— sat perched atop a massive tripod. This was the Ark, his aerial flagship.

Warning lights flashed and Klaxons sounded as Kobra strode toward the rocket. Underlings immediately ran to him with a fresh tunic.

"Status report?"

"Operation New Dawn is under way, Sahib. The moment your lair was breached, the fail-safes automatically transmitted the launch protocols. By now, all missiles are away."

"We are pleased. But one major target remains. Prepare to depart at once."

High over Lake Michigan, Green Lantern dropped from the ionosphere and chased after a missile. *Think,*

Kyle! What would Jordan have done? Kyle Rayner's mind raced. His predecessor, Hal Jordan, had been a test pilot before he'd become a Green Lantern. *Test Pilot . . . real* Right Stuff *kinda guy, always flying faster. Faster . . . maybe that's the answer? Yeah!*

Green Lantern channeled his will through the power ring, creating two huge booster engines on either side of the missile. The added thrust threw off the rocket's trajectory and increased its speed, causing it to burn up harmlessly in the upper atmosphere.

Okay, that saves Chicago. But now I have to step on it or I'll lose St. Louis, Memphis, and New Orleans.

Superman fought on, slowly making his way—step by painful step—across the room. True to Kobra's words, the cannon tracked his every move. His cape was nearly torn away, his hair plastered back against his scalp, by the ferocious energy stream.

He couldn't evade the beam, couldn't destroy it. *Energy can't be destroyed. But it* can *be transformed.*

He dropped to the floor, and his fingers found purchase along a seam of one of the stone slabs. He could feel the seam crack and widen under the ceaseless particle beam. As it loosened, the Man of Steel thrust his hands down into the crevice and wrenched up an eighteen-inch thick section of one entire slab. Then with a mighty heave, he hoisted it before him, holding it like a shield.

Its target hidden, the cannon swung back and forth, the particle beam sweeping across the slab, across the entire chamber.

Catching his breath, Superman put his shoulders to the back of the stone barrier and shoved it forward. His head swimming, he gritted his teeth and jammed the slab full against the wide bore of the cannon. The metal barrel instantly grew white hot. His stone shield glowed red, then orange and yellow. And then it, too, glowed white hot—as radiant as a small sun. Raw energy rippled over Superman, and he smiled grimly. *'That which does not kill me, makes me stronger.'* Literally, in this case.

And then, the cannon blew apart, sending fist-sized shards of searing metal flying with terrible force.

Beyond the chamber, the entire underground complex shuddered. Hooded men were thrown to their feet.

"What was that?"

"An explosion?"

"Are we under further attack?"

Cracks appeared along one wall, and the floor shook again. A dozen men dove for cover as an eight-foot-thick section of granite, lead, and reinforced concrete erupted into the hall.

And a Man of Steel stalked out through a cloud of dust and debris, and seized the nearest man by the jaw. "Where is he? Where's Kobra?"

Thundering across the skies of eastern Massachusetts, Wonder Woman threw her translucent robot plane into a steep power dive. She had already dispatched a score of Kobra's missiles, but as the Amazon closed on the last one, the plane suddenly began to pitch and roll. *What—? Never encountered anything like this before. Even worse than a wind shear. I'd almost swear that the jet stream was trying to reverse itself.*

Thrown about by wildly fluctuating gusts, the plane slammed hard into the missile. Both fell earthward.

Diana gripped the control yoke, struggling to steady her craft, as the missile split apart, releasing its payload.

After several precious seconds, Wonder Woman finally fought the nose of her plane up, leveling off at ten thousand feet.

But now thousands of gas pods were raining down over the Boston metroplex.

The Amazon sent the plane screaming after them. At her command, the lower fuselage began morphing into a huge web-like snare.

I mustn't let any hit . . . not a single one!

In South Dakota, Superman rocketed up from the underground hangar. Focusing his Kryptonian eyes beyond the visible spectrum, he soared after the heat trail left by the Ark. And as he rose, the rays of the sun once again washed over him, further replenishing his energy reserves.

Pushing himself, he accelerated to four and then five times the speed of sound.

The trail led Superman high into the upper atmosphere. There seemed to be nothing but empty air in front of him. A light-distortion field had rendered Kobra's flagship invisible to normal detection.

But not to the Man of Tomorrow. He clearly saw the infrared outline of the Ark dead ahead.

Superman reached the aft section of the supersonic craft and grabbed on, clawing a handhold into the metal of the Ark's hull near a rear hatch. He peeled it open and air roared out at him from the inner compartment.

The caped man dove through the open hatch and found himself facing a dozen Kobra troopers outfitted in heavy armor. Magnetic boots held them upright against the rush of decompression. Ray blasts from their rifles pounded Superman's body—but nothing would stop him now.

The Man of Steel picked up the nearest armored form and swung him around like a bat, knocking the others aside as if they were cardboard cutouts.

Alone in the command cabin, Kobra grimly watched on a view screen as his elite forces were routed. The image began breaking up, and his thumb jabbed down on a control surface marked "Jettison."

The Ark lurched ahead as its aft section dropped away, fell for fifty feet, then exploded.

Kobra closed his right hand over a metal handle and thumbed a microphone switch with his left. "Divert all shield power to the engines, and proceed to the primary target area. You fly to inaugurate the Kali Yuga!"

The Ark lurched again, but this time the door to the

command cabin was kicked in. Superman filled the portal.

"This is the end."

"It is indeed." Kobra thrust out his left hand in warning. "Make no sudden moves. This ship carries a cargo of my neurotoxic gas for your beloved Metropolis."

"And what? You'll spare the city if I let you go? No deals, Kobra."

"You have little choice, Superman. Do you see what I hold in my right hand? My grip on this handle is all that prevents the release of the gas bombs. It's called a dead-man switch. You do understand what that means, don't you?"

"Yes." The Man of Steel drew back half a step. "It's a switch held by a dead man."

Then he leaped across the cabin in a single bound.

Superman's hand clamped down on the handle, even as he flung Kobra away from the controls. The terrorist leader hit hard against the bulkhead, slid to the deck, and did not move.

Lights flashed on the control panel. The Man of Steel knew instantly that, despite his speed, the bomb release had been tripped.

Superman smashed down through the deck into the bomb bay of the Ark. Gas pods were already starting to spill from the open bay. Dying cultists had smashed some of the pods against the side of the bulkhead. At the sight of the Man of Tomorrow, one hooded man raised his arms in shaking, twitching agony and screamed: "The Kali Yuga is upon us. All yield to Chaos in the end!"

As the man fell dying at his feet, Superman took a faceful of the deadly gas.

Spinning like a top, the Man of Steel dove through the open bay doors. As he left the Ark, he gave the ship one parting kick, sending it spiraling toward the Atlantic far below.

Faster and faster he spun, creating a mini-tornado, drawing the pods and the escaping gas up and around him. Superman streaked heavenward, dragging his deadly burden high into the outer reaches of the atmosphere. Not until he was on the very edge of space did he stop spinning. There, the pods ruptured, their gases dispersing harmlessly. The Man of Steel expelled the gas he had inhaled on the Ark, watching its toxins crystallize and disperse in the frigid vacuum.

Weakened by his ordeal, and unable to take a breath, Superman threw himself earthward. Colors swirled before his eyes, then started to fade. He was still far from the surface when he blacked out.

As he dropped, the last tattered remnants of his cape tore away and burned up. The very air around him glowed brightly from the heat of reentry. He fell for over a hundred miles before slamming into the North Atlantic and disappearing beneath the waves.

On the roof of the Daily Planet Building, Lois Lane stood just outside the shadow of the big golden globe. After days of rain, the sky was finally clearing and the newspaper's star reporter had ascended to the rooftop. She often came up here with her husband. It was one of their favorite "secret places."

But despite the clearing skies, there was an unpleasantness this afternoon. The very air felt heavy, oppressive.

It had been days since she'd last seen Clark—or even heard from him—and now she paced nervously around the globe. *What were you expecting, a note in a bottle? Maybe a message written across the sky?*

Lois looked up at the thought—and glimpsed what appeared to be a shooting star streak down from the heavens.

It quickly burned out.

The weird timing made her jump, and Lois felt a sudden, almost painful shiver of foreboding. She closed her eyes tight and made a wish. "Come home, Clark. Come home safe."

The sun shone brightly on Superman's bruised and swollen face. His eyes fluttered, and he slowly raised a hand to shield them.

"You look as though you've been through a war."

The Man of Steel blinked and lifted his head to the right. He found himself lying across a wing of Wonder Woman's robot plane, just a few feet above the Atlantic Ocean.

"Then I must look as bad as I feel. Sun feels good, though."

The Amazon knelt down beside the Man of Steel,

helping him sit up. "Easy now. You hit the ocean pretty hard."

"I did? I don't remember." He ran a hand through his hair. It was still damp with salt water. "It's a big ocean. How did you find me?"

She smiled past Superman. "Oh, I had a little help."

Superman turned to find Aquaman crouching to his left. The Sea King grinned at him.

"First Batman, and now you. I'm becoming the Justice League's designated rescuer. Actually, *I* had a little help, too. I'd alerted marine mammals worldwide, just in case. And when the Watchtower radioed your trajectory, I sent a second telepathic alert to the whales and dolphins in the area. A couple killer whales kept you afloat until I arrived.

"They were happy to help, by the way. Their pod still sings of how you handled that careless chemical tanker captain last year."

At the mention of chemicals, Superman's eyebrows shot up, and he leaped to his feet. "The nerve gas—!"

"It's all right," Diana assured him. "The missile payloads were all intercepted and neutralized. Green Lantern reported that you took out the last of them." He's off plasma-torching any poisons that were released into space."

"And Kobra?"

The wreck of the Ark sat half in and half out of the water along the coast of northern Maine.

The Batman picked his way through the wreckage.

Every few feet he knelt slowly, collected a sample, and tucked it carefully into a labeled vial.

When he finally emerged from the Ark, the rest of the Justice League had gathered on the nearby shore.

"Batman?" Green Lantern swooped down from the skies, looking genuinely surprised. "I'm not used to seeing you out in the daytime."

"It is late afternoon. Twilight is falling. And these are special circumstances." The Batman handed his vials over to the Manhunter, who inserted them into a portable analyzer brought down from the Watchtower.

"Nicest day I've seen in a long time—and all thanks to the Weather Wizard, believe it or not." The Flash turned to Superman. "The Atom and I finally got through to the guy. It took a major effort, but the Wiz managed to restore things to normal—or at least as normal as the weather ever gets. I think he burned out about fifty million brain cells in the process."

The Atom cleared his throat. "That's a bit of an exaggeration. But between the strain he underwent, putting the jet stream back in place, and the realization of how he'd been used, Mardon has suffered a serious breakdown. S.T.A.R. Labs currently has him under sedation, and they're keeping him under a suicide watch. He shouldn't cause any more trouble, but they're not taking any chances."

Superman shook his head. "Any estimates on the day's final toll?"

"Let's see . . ." Green Lantern looked over a ring-generated PDA. "Six missile sites shut down. Five other bases raided. Over eight thousand cultists were taken alive. And another seven hundred forty-three died, most by their own hand . . . not counting the dozen or so from the crash of the Ark. All in all, the sun has pretty much set on Operation New Dawn."

Superman looked back at the crash site. "And yet, there was no sign of Kobra in the wreckage?"

"None, regrettably." The Batman and the Manhunter joined the others.

J'onn confirmed the Batman's assessment. "We will do a more thorough analysis of the DNA we gathered. But, for now, the evidence is inconclusive."

"Well, that's just great!" Flash kicked a rock in disgust, sending it skimming out across the ocean. "If that creep has gotten away again—!"

Green Lantern patted his buddy on the back. "Hey, Flash, we didn't take this gig because it was easy. Otherwise, anybody could do it. At least, that's what you keep telling me."

Wonder Woman turned to the Flash. "Never forget, the League was founded to uphold justice against all threats. In that, we've succeeded."

"Yeah, you're right. I just hate it when the real monsters get away."

"We all do, Flash." Superman put a hand on his shoulder. "But we don't *know* that Kobra got away, and even if he did, he isn't immortal. If he's still alive, we'll find him—if not today, then tomorrow. And when we do, we'll stop him. Him, and those like him."

"Yes," agreed Wonder Woman. "Our work is not over until all such as Kobra are defeated."

"All?" Light rippled over Green Lantern's ring. "You realize that means we'll have to be on guard forever?"

The Manhunter shrugged. "We, or our successors."

The Batman stared off into the twilight. "I believe it was Jefferson who said, 'Eternal vigilance is the price of liberty.' "

"Yes." Superman nodded. "It is a never-ending battle."

EPILOGUE

Promises to Keep

Ray Palmer looked up from his screens as the Manhunter entered the Watchtower's monitor bay. "Good morning, J'onn. What brings you up here so bright and early?"

"I am here for the official changing of the guard, Atom."

Palmer laughed. "What, is it July already?"

"It is, indeed. You have been very good about this. You have been on duty up here since before the weather crisis."

"Oh, I didn't mind." Palmer stood and stretched. "Though it *was* nice when the Blue Beetle filled in for a few hours."

"That hardly constituted a break. You were on a mission with the Flash."

"I knew what the job entailed when I took it, J'onn."

"Be that as it may, I am here to stand a shift at the monitors. Go home, Ray."

The Atom grinned. "Okay, you talked me into it. Just as well. I'm scheduled to deliver a paper before a symposium next week, and I could use the prep time." He handed his headset to the big Martian. "It's all yours. Oh, by the way, there's a message waiting for you—two, in fact."

"Messages?"

"E-mails over our public-access link, directed to you. And neither one looked like spam."

As the Atom took his leave, J'onn settled into the monitor bay. *Who would be sending me e-mail?* Two clicks brought up the link. The first message was from the Rocky Mountain Smokejumpers, thanking him once more for all his help and inviting him to their next chicken barbecue. He replied immediately, accepting the invitation. *Ice cream might go well at a barbecue . . . I should check with Arnie.* He read and re-read the message several times, enjoying it more with each reading, before saving it to a text file.

When J'onn finally clicked on the other message, he was thinking that—whatever it was—it couldn't top a chicken barbecue.

He was wrong.

The second message was from Elmendorf Air Force Base—an electronic letter of commendation and thanks from Colonel Hollister.

Attached to the e-mail were two photos. The first was of the aircrew he had rescued. The three airmen and the female staff sergeant all stood in three-quarter profile, each with identical grins, their sleeves rolled up to reveal new tattoos—also identical—of J'onn's own likeness encircled by the astronomical symbol for Mars.

The Martian drew an audible breath. Over the years he had seen a few Manhunter tattoos (roughly one for every thousand or so tattoos of Superman's S-shield), but he had never before seen a group of people bearing his likeness. He could hear his heart pounding as he clicked open the second photo.

The image of Chief Master Sergeant Lopez filled the screen . . . Lopez, the man who had drawn a gun on him. The master sergeant solemnly faced the camera, his right hand raised in salute. His left hand had pulled open his uniform shirt to show *his* Manhunter tattoo. Lopez's tattoo was bigger, on his chest and just over the heart.

J'onn sat staring at the photos, tears running freely down his face.

"Case 1066, the State of Nevada versus Orrin Skinner."

The judge looked down from the bench and sighed. "Hello, Orrin. Can't say that I'm surprised to see you again." He adjusted his glasses and read through the charges. "How do you plead?"

"Guilty, Your Honor."

"Guilty? Really?" Unaccustomed to hearing such an admission from Skinner, the judge glanced over at the public defender. "Counselor, have you advised your client of the seriousness of these charges?"

"I have, Your Honor. This is my client's decision."

"Let the defendant approach the bench." The judge

leaned over and addressed Skinner directly. "You realize, Orrin, that you're going to do time for this one?"

"Yes, Your Honor. I . . . I think I need to." He trembled slightly as he stood before the judge. "I've been denyin' a lot of things for a long time. I went through detox in the lockup, and I think I need rehab . . . anger management . . . whatever help I can get. If servin' time is what it takes, well, I guess I want that, too."

The judge considered the man before him. "I never thought I'd say this, but I believe you are sincere."

"I am, Your Honor. I got a scare that . . . well, what I saw convinced me that I need to change the way I live. An' that's all I care to say about that. But I'll do whatever it takes to make restitution and turn my life around. So help me God."

"If you'll forgive my saying so, you look as though you could use some serious R-and-R."

Bruce Wayne looked up from the desk in his study to find Clark Kent strolling over to him. "Don't you ever knock?"

"Alfred was busy, so I let myself in."

"I don't know why I bother with alarm systems. You look disgustingly healthy, Kent." He studied the reporter's face with professional detachment. There were no signs of the punishment Superman had taken from Kobra's robots. "Not so much as a single lingering bruise."

"I've always healed fast. How are *you* doing?"

"I'm healing, too. . . ." Bruce shifted in his chair, wincing slightly. "Just a bit slower."

"What do you expect, after crawling around the wreckage of that Ark the way you did? Really, Bruce, J'onn could have handled that."

"I like to be thorough where Kobra is concerned. As do you, it appears."

Clark spread his fingers across his chest. "*Moi?*"

"The various national security agencies have been scouring the Kobra bases that the League uncovered, and apparently not one scrap of Kobra's tech survived intact. Zip. *Nada.*"

"Is that a fact? Everything was destroyed?"

"Not a single schematic remained."

"Imagine that." Clark removed his glasses and began to polish them with the end of his tie.

"Various countries, as well as several . . . shall we say . . . 'stateless' organizations who had shared intelligence resources with the League, expected some sort of spoils from this little war. Many of them are bitterly disappointed."

"No doubt, but we can't always get what we want."

"There are even certain highly placed individuals within our own administration who are upset by this. They feel that national security would be greatly enhanced if they had access to control over the weather."

"Do they?" Kent slipped his glasses back into place. "Well, it's a free country. They're entitled to their opinions."

"You know, Clark, sometimes you surprise me. Just when I think I have you all figured out, I realize how wrong I can be."

"Well, thank you, Bruce. I'd hate to be predictable.

If I can surprise even *you*, I must be doing something right."

"Oh, I can be surprised, all right. I owe you. If you hadn't paid me that visit the other week, we might never have realized the full scope of Kobra's plans."

"You'd have figured it out. Either working with me, or working with someone else from the team."

"Perhaps." Bruce frowned. "But in time?"

"We'll never know. Fortunately, we don't need to. It's a hypothesis contrary to fact. Let it rest." Clark stepped back, folding his arms. "And let yourself rest, will you? You've been getting by on as little sleep as I was."

"You really *are* becoming a detective. How the hell did you know?"

"I have eyes, Bruce. We're about the same age, but right now you could pass for ten years older. And I can hear the exhaustion in your voice." He held up a hand. "Don't get paranoid—you could probably still fool anyone else. Except Alfred. But if you keep running yourself into the ground, you won't be able to fool anyone."

"Fanaticism never rests." Wayne's voice dropped most of the way to the ominous bass he employed as the Batman. "I can't either. Kobra wasn't the first, and he won't be the last. I have to be better prepared for the next one."

"And total exhaustion will help you accomplish that, how? Look, you don't have to book a cruise, but it wouldn't kill you to take a day off. Two days . . . ?" Clark shrugged. "That might be too much of a shock to your system, so be careful. Maybe I *am* becoming a pretty good detective, but I wouldn't want to do the job by myself."

Bruce almost smiled. "I'll think about it."

Clark's right eyebrow rose above the rim of his glasses, but he said nothing.

"Seriously, I'll think about it."

Clark settled into an adjacent armchair and pulled a small notebook from his pocket. "In that case, Mr. Wayne, do you mind if I ask a few questions?"

"Clark . . . what are you doing?"

"Just think of this as an informational interview. I should learn about the 'special projects' you're currently working on, Bruce. Just in case I need to take over on short notice."

"All right, I get the point. You . . . you're right. I'll take care of it."

"Oh?"

"Word of honor." Bruce Wayne extended his right hand.

"Good enough." Clark shook the offered hand. "The world would be a scarier place without the Batman around." He walked to the window, then paused and turned. "Take care of yourself, Bruce."

And with that, Kent was gone, the curtains swaying where he had stood. Bruce Wayne stared at the curtains until they stopped moving, and then rang for his butler.

"Yes, sir? Have you finished your list of things you needed to accomplish by yesterday?"

"No, Alfred. I think that can wait until tomorrow."

The butler looked at him with some concern. "Are you ill, sir?"

"Not yet, but if I continue at this pace, I soon will be. It's a beautiful day, and I think that I'll spend it lounging by the pool. Maybe catch up on my reading. Why don't you take the rest of the day off as well?"

For once, Alfred Pennyworth was absolutely speechless.

Inspector Turpin paused to admire his reflection in the glass window of a storefront. He straightened his tie and adjusted the collar of his uniform jacket. *Good to see that the ol' dress blues still fit me after all these years.* He turned to the young patrolman at his side.

"Beautiful day, ain't it, Harris?"

"Nicer than I've seen in a month, Inspector."

"Yeah, it's the kind a day that makes ya glad to be alive an' outside in the open air. I've missed this."

"You've missed walking a beat?" Patrolman Harris scratched the back of his neck.

"Darned right. Ridin' 'round in a patrol car just gives ya a fat keister. There's nothing like walkin' a neighborhood beat for stayin' in shape. I've been tryin' to stop smokin', and a good walk cuts down on the cravings. Works better for me than those darn patches."

"Yeah? You ever try using the treadmills at the gym? I see you there using the free weights all the time."

"Oh, sure. Those free weights are great. Gotta protect the ol' muscle mass, after all. But treadmills an' me weren't made for each other. I hate walkin' and gettin' nowhere. Besides, on a beat, I get to stay in touch with the community. I've put in to do this every Saturday."

"Kind of a busman's holiday, isn't it?"

"So what if it is? For a lot of us, bein' a cop's not just a job. It's more of a calling."

"You don't have to sell me on that, Inspector. I'm third generation. My dad and my granddad both were cops."

"No kiddin'?" Turpin's grin went from ear to ear. "Harris, lunch is on me!"

"Wonder Woman! There are more of them over here!"

The Amazon ambassador flew down the corridor of an underground installation. She had accompanied a United Nations team to the Mediterranean to assist in a final inspection of the Kobra base that Superman had shut down in Sardinia. But the U.N. inspectors had found something they hadn't anticipated.

Dozens of Indian cobras had been housed in the secret lair, and now they roamed free.

"It's all right. I'm here right behind you. Don't make any sudden movements."

"Whatever you say, ma'am."

Diana eased past two blue-helmeted soldiers who stood stock-still and perspiring. Just a few yards ahead of the men, two eight-foot cobras coiled, wary and ready to strike, their hoods spread wide.

"Do not be alarmed." She slowly knelt before the snakes. "No one will harm you."

The cobras settled down almost immediately. And when Wonder Woman produced a large cloth bag, they calmly flowed across the floor and took up residence inside.

Not until she tied the bag shut did the helmeted men dare to move.

"I do not understand how you can do that, Ambassador. It was as though they understood your every word."

"Actually, Private, snakes are deaf. But I've found that it helps me focus if I speak to them. And yes, there is . . . understanding. The goddess Artemis granted me unity with all living creatures."

The other soldier lifted his helmet to mop his brow. "I don't care how you do it, ma'am, just as long as it works."

Wonder Woman smiled, and gently lifted the bag. "Happy to do my part, gentlemen. And happier still to prevent these beautiful ladies from harming or being harmed. They belong back on the subcontinent, and that's exactly where I'll be returning them."

But as Wonder Woman neared the entrance to the base, she found a young soldier with his back against a wall, his face rigid with fear. He had his pistol out and was drawing a bead on another serpent. The snake, too, was rigid with alarm.

"No!"

As he pulled the trigger, Diana's arm flashed out, intercepting the bullet with her bracelet and deflecting it safely away.

The soldier's face went from bone-white to deep crimson. He looked mortally embarrassed. "Sorry,

Ambassador. I tried to call out, but my throat went dry . . . couldn't speak."

"You *do* have a serious snake phobia, don't you?"

The soldier stared down at the floor. "Yeah."

"Well, you had nothing to fear from this youngster. He's not a cobra. He's not any kind of venomous snake." She held out her hand, and the olive-brown creature slithered up her arm.

"This is an *Elaphe longissima*, an Aesculapian rat snake. They're native to the region." She tilted her head and smiled at the serpent. "And this one is a very gentle little boy, aren't you?"

The snake tilted its own head, mirroring her, and began flicking its tongue. Its breathing slowly returned to normal. So did the soldier's. He began to look interested, so Diana continued.

"The species was named for Aesculapius, the god of healing. That was his Roman name, of course. I know him as Asklepios."

The soldier looked at her with amazement as she let the snake twine around her arm. "You . . . *know* this . . . Asklepios?"

"Not personally, no. But I know those who do. And I am sure he would not appreciate so benign a creature being destroyed. Come, little one, let's find you a nice warm rock to bask on."

Bibbo lumbered across the floor of the Ace o' Clubs and set steaming bowls and mugs down in front of the two newcomers at the corner table. "Here's yer chili and yer coffee, gents. Sorry I didn't have any o' that fancy mocha whatsit."

"Fine by me." The fairer of the two customers shoved one of the mugs toward his buddy. "It's about time that Rembrant here discovered *real* coffee."

His dark-haired friend looked up from his sketch pad and gave the mug a tentative sniff. "Well, it smells good." He blew across the surface of the liquid and took a sip. "Whoa! That's . . . strong stuff." He coughed as tears came to his eyes. "Got any creamer?"

"Haw-haw! Sure, kid." Bibbo slid a small metal pitcher across the table. "You boys don't sound like yer from around here."

"We're not." The fair-haired one swallowed a big spoonful of chili and smiled. "I was raised in Nebraska, but now I live in Kansas. Whereas Kyle here," he punched his buddy's shoulder, "is from all over. He's bounced around from California to New York, and probably several places in between. But he spends a lot of time off in outer space."

Kyle shook his head. "Thanks, Wally."

"We don't get many astronauts in here." Bibbo gave them both a crooked grin. "But I see we get us plenty o' wise guys! What brings you jokers to Metropolis?"

"A buddy of mine, a friend I go running with, said that the chili around here was first-rate, and I just had to check it out."

"You must like it, the way yer shovelin' in."

"Oh, yeah. This is some of the best I've ever tasted."

"Well, there's plenty more where that came from. Seconds are on the house."

"Hey, thanks, Bibbo!" Wally began scraping his spoon across the bottom of the bowl. "You're a gentleman and a scholar."

Kyle nodded. "We saw your picture on the *Daily Planet* website. But photos don't really do you justice. I see you more like this. . . ." He handed the big man a page from his sketch pad.

"Hey, that's me! Lookit that! You drew me bendin' steel, jus' like Sooperman!"

"And why not? Anyone tough enough to challenge Kobra is a Superman in his own right."

"An' up in the corner, it sez 'To Bibbo!' This is for me?"

"Sure, Bibbo."

"You kids . . ." The old roughneck looked away for a moment, blinking back a tear. Then he reached back across the table and tore up the check. "Yer money's no good here. It's *all* on the house." Bibbo held the drawing back up to the light. "This's nice. I'm gonna get me this framed."

Sunday, July fourth, Clark Kent and Lois Lane sat huddled on a bench in the back of a twin-engine plane as it climbed to thirteen thousand feet.

Clark gazed into his wife's eyes. "Nervous?"

"No." Lois shook her head. "Okay, a little."

"That's only natural, but there's nothing to worry about. I'll be with you all the way."

"I know. I feel so silly, Clark, getting butterflies like this. I've been on hundreds of jumps, but this feels

so . . . so different." She ran a hand over the ballistic
nylon that puckered beneath her arms. "So does this
gear. These 'BirdMan' suits. The mind boggles. . . ."

A big, broad-shouldered man entered the compartment and the couple got to their feet.

"All right, you two, we're almost to the drop zone.
Just remember that you want to keep your arms symmetrical to your body. And you'll need to pull the arm
and leg releases when you open your main chute." He
patted a handle at the hips of their jumpsuits. "If you
get into any trouble, just yank on that emergency cut-
away. All clear?"

"Clear."

"Very clear."

The jumpmaster smiled. "You'll do fine." Overhead
a buzzer sounded. "Okay, that's thirteen thousand
five hundred feet—we're here." He threw a switch,
and the floor at the back of the plane began to swing
open. "Go! Go!"

Lois and Clark leaped out into space, arms and legs
spread wide.

As they fell, air rushed through special mesh vents
in their jumpsuits, filling the double layer of parachute fabric that stretched between their arms and
torsos, and their legs.

The fabric wings become rigid as they filled, creating an airfoil profile and lift. Downward velocity
dropped, and Clark and Lois both shot forward through
the air.

"This is incredible! This is *incredible!*" Behind her goggles, Lois blinked back tears. "I'm flying! I'm *flying!*"

Clark swooped in close alongside her, his voice crackling in her helmet's headset. "And very well."

"This is awesome. *Awesome!* So this is how it feels?"

"No." He looked all around him. "Actually, this is better."

"Get out!"

"Really. It's so . . . effortless."

"How fast are we going?"

"Forward, about eighty. But we're still falling at thirty-five miles an hour."

"Don't remind me. I want to enjoy this for as long as I can."

On they flew, skimming the edges of low clouds. Swooping down from the skies, they traveled over four miles before their wrist altimeters buzzed.

"It's time, Lois."

"Do we have to?"

"Lois!"

"Kidding . . ." She pulled the first releases, freeing her arms from the wings. A sharp tug on the ripcord, and her parachute deployed. Her fall slowed, she looked over and saw Clark in a similar position. Simultaneously, they pulled the second releases, cutting the wings free from their legs.

Moments later they drifted down to a soft landing, less than a hundred yards from the little airfield where they'd taken off.

Lois quickly unhitched her silks, then took off her helmet and ran to join her husband. "Thank you, Clark! Thank you, thank you, *thank you!*" They hugged for longer than they'd been airborne. "How did you learn about this?"

"The BirdMan suits? I interviewed their creators the other day for an upcoming piece in the *Planet*'s feature section. Fascinating fellows."

"Mmm, I'm glad that I know a fascinating fellow of my own."

He smiled. "So tell me, Lois. What's it like . . . flying?"

"It's amazing! Just incredible! I . . . I . . ." she felt her face flushing. "I know I'm babbling. But I can't help it. I have to say that it's just about the best present anyone ever gave me."

"Happy belated anniversary, Ms. Lane."

"Happy belated anniversary, Mr. Kent." She kissed him full on the lips, then pulled back to arm's length. "You're sure you don't have a Justice League meeting to run?"

"Not today. Not for many days. It's not my job anymore."

"Really? Since when?"

"Since yesterday. My term as chairman was up, and I chose to exercise the Washington prerogative. I turned the gavel over to the Manhunter. Running the show is his headache for the next year."

"Well, in that case . . ." She looked him deep in the eyes. "When can we fly again?"

Clark scooped Lois up in his arms and carried her to a waiting plane.

About the Author

ROGER STERN is the author of the *New York Times* bestseller *The Death and Life of Superman*. He has written for radio, television, the stage, and even the computer screen, creating scripts for everything from commercials and sketch comedy to trading cards and flash-animation. With more than a quarter century of experience in the comic book industry, he has written hundreds of stories about such diverse characters as Green Lantern, Supergirl, and Starman for DC Comics; and Spider-Man, Captain America, and the Incredible Hulk for Marvel. For ten years he was the senior writer of the Superman series of comics for DC, contributing to *Action Comics, Superman, The Adventures of Superman, Superman: The Man of Steel,* and *Superman: The Man of Tomorrow*. He has written several graphic novels, including *Doctor Strange & Doctor Doom: Triumph and Torment, Superman: A Nation Divided, The Incredible Hulk vs. Superman,* and the rare, long-out-of-print *Superman for Earth*. His second prose novel, *Smallville: Strange Visitors*—an original story based on the characters from the hit WB television series—was published by Warner Books in 2002. Mr. Stern lives and works in Upstate New York with his wife, Carmela Merlo.